ABOUT THE AUTHOR

From an early age, Martin was enchanted with old movies from Hollywood's golden era — from the dawn of the talkies in the late 1920s to the close of the studio system in the late 1950s — and has spent many a happy hour watching the likes of Garland, Gable, Crawford, Garbo, Grant, Miller, Kelly, Astaire, Rogers, Turner, and Welles go through their paces.

It felt inevitable that he would someday end up writing about them.

Originally from Melbourne, Australia, Martin moved to Los Angeles in the mid-90s where he now works as a writer, blogger, webmaster, and tour guide.

www.MartinTurnbull.com

This book is dedicated to

Terese Scalise

because so much can come from a simple "Hello."

ISBN-13: 978-1523288458

ISBN-10: 1523288450

Copyright © Martin Turnbull 2016

DISCLAIMER

This is a work of fiction. Names, characters, places and incidents are either the product of the author's imagination or are used fictitiously. Any resemblance to actual persons, places and incidents, events or locales is purely coincidental.

REDS IN THE BEDS

a novel

by

MARTIN TURNBULL

Book Five in the Hollywood's Garden of Allah novels

CHAPTER 1

Kathryn Massey unclenched her fists and wiped the
clamminess from her palms as best she could with a pitifully
inadequate lace handkerchief. She hadn't expected to be this
nervous — it was hardly the first time she'd appeared on the
radio — but she'd never shouldered the duties of host by
herself. With only a few minutes before showtime, she could
feel sweat prickling her scalp, so she cast about the
Hollywood Canteen for a distraction.

She found it in the indomitable form of Bette Davis
shouldering through the crowd like General MacArthur
storming the Pacific. First to the sandwich table, then to the
coffee station, where she stopped by a cluster of tuxedoed
Warner Bros. executives before she pressed through a jungle
of servicemen toward Kathryn, shaking hands as she went.

Bette's famously large eyes bulged when she broke free
of the throng. "Heavens!" she exclaimed, accepting
Kathryn's hand to help her climb onto the edge of the stage.
"What I wouldn't give for a bourbon!"

"What else did you expect on closing night?" Kathryn
glanced at Harry James and his orchestra, who'd launched
into "Waitin' for the Train to Come In." It was her cue that
she'd be up next. She wiped her hands again on the limp
handkerchief.

Bette shrugged. "I can scarcely believe it's all coming to
an end." She examined Kathryn's face. "Are you as nervous
as you look?"

For over two years now, Kathryn had appeared on the *Kraft Music Hall* radio show as the resident Hollywood gossip columnist, and had proved that she could match Bing Crosby's impromptu banter quip for quip. A couple of weeks ago, NBC approached her with an idea for a special broadcast from the Hollywood Canteen on its closing night. "Bing's going to be back East promoting *Duffy's Tavern*," they said, "so we want you to host it."

Kathryn figured if she could pull this off, who knows what it might lead to? Her own show? She'd barely been able to contain her excitement, but now the dread that she might screw it up was pressing on her shoulders.

As the Harry James Orchestra plowed into its final sixteen bars, Bette and Kathryn positioned themselves in front of the chrome microphone with "NBC" painted in red along the base. A technician at his console held up his right hand. He folded his fingers one by one until he was down to his thumb. Kathryn took a deep breath.

"A big hello to all our radio listeners across these United States. My name is Kathryn Massey, and I am thrilled to welcome you to a very special edition of *Kraft Music Hall*." While Harry James played the show's jaunty theme song, the navy blue and army green uniforms erupted into a roar. "We are broadcasting to you live from the world-famous Hollywood Canteen, which closes its doors tonight.

"We have a number of special guests, and I'll be welcoming them to the stage very soon. But first, I want to thank and congratulate the woman without whom the Hollywood Canteen would never have become such a vital epicenter of the war effort here." Kathryn raised her arms. "Come on, fellas, help me give the loudest cheer you can muster to the tireless Miss Bette Davis!"

This time, the crowd — not just the servicemen, but the dance hostesses, kitchen staff, and all the volunteers — let loose with a foot-stomping ovation so thunderous that the wagon-wheel chandeliers started to sway.

"Thank you, everybody!" Bette shouted into the mike. "Really, and I mean this from the bottom of my heart, it's been my greatest pleasure and deepest honor to serve our brave boys." She wrapped her arm around Kathryn's waist. "It's the least we could do."

Kathryn showed the crowd a piece of cardboard. "Bette, I want you to read the statistics printed on this card to show the people at home what an undertaking this has been."

Bette took the card and scanned the figures. "The Hollywood Canteen has been open three years, one month, and twenty-eight days, during which time we have fed nearly four million servicemen, poured nine million cups of coffee . . ."

As Bette made her way down the list, Kathryn looked out across the hundreds of faces, every last one of them thrilled to make it into what had become a Los Angeles institution during the war. But then the one brooding face among a thousand buoyant ones caught her eye. She swallowed hard.

Halfway through the war, Kathryn had been recruited by the FBI. It was more like conscription than recruitment, really, leaving her little option but to spy on her neighbors, friends, and coworkers. For Kathryn Massey, the face of the Bureau was Nelson Hoyt, who stood in the crowd smiling that unctuous smile of his. She hadn't seen it since a particularly nasty clash outside the NBC studios on the day Japan surrendered. But here he was, popping up again like a groundhog with distemper.

Kathryn felt Bette's fingernails jab into her waist. Bette's eyes flared. *For God's sake, say something!*

"Thank you, Bette," Kathryn burst out. "Four million thank-yous, one for each of the servicemen who have passed through these doors." Her first guest joined them onstage. "Next up, I am excited to welcome one of America's favorite vocalists, here to treat us with a slice of 'Shoo-Fly Pie and Apple Pan Dowdy.' Ladies and gentlemen, I give you Miss Dinah Shore!"

* * *

A dry Santa Ana wind blew along Cahuenga Boulevard as Kathryn lit up a Chesterfield and rested against the Canteen's northern wall. Apart from that one little glitch near the top of the show, everything had gone exceptionally well, but she hadn't approached the NBC brass yet. She needed a cigarette first.

"I believe congratulations are in order."

Ugh. Him. Kathryn fired off her best stink eye. "I think the show went very well."

"I'm talking about your recent nuptials."

"I hoped I'd seen the last of you."

"I take it your mother was happy to learn you'd finally settled down?"

My mother? The streetlamp behind Hoyt's left shoulder threw his face into shadow, obscuring his smile. But Kathryn could tell from his tone that it was more of a smirk. "Of course," she lied.

"Married life is treating you well?"

"It is." At least that much was true. Kathryn and her husband had found a way to make their marriage work—a plan that chiefly entailed separate villas at the Garden of Allah. She started for the Canteen's entrance, but Hoyt stopped her with a simple statement.

"I have something I need to ask you."

When the FBI says it has a question, a girl had better stop.

"Ring Lardner Junior. How well do you know him?"

The non sequitur propelled Kathryn to face him more squarely. "The screenwriter?" When he nodded and crossed his arms, she knew she had to give him some sort of answer. "He and Garson Kanin holed up with Katharine Hepburn in the villa next to mine to bash out the screenplay for *Woman of the Year*. Outside of that, I've seen him at parties here and there."

"What about Lewis Milestone?"

—
8

The sudden switch raised Kathryn's eyebrow. "He directed *The North Star*, which Lillian Hellman wrote. She's one of my neighbors, too. I went to the premiere at the Carthay Circle, and Lillian introduced us. He and I had such a long chat that I turned it into an interview, mostly about the war movies they—"

"I saw the interview."

She threw her hands up, wishing now she'd made her getaway. "Then why even ask?"

"One more, and I'll let you go back inside." Passing headlights caught him full in the face. He smiled again, this time not nearly so smugly, and it reminded her that he was halfway decently attractive. For an FBI fink. She made a go-ahead-ask-your-damned-question gesture.

"Leilah O'Roarke."

Kathryn tried to cover her surprise with a cough, but knew the guy was too shrewd to be fooled. He would be aware that Leilah's husband headed up security at Warners, but did he also know she ran a trio of high-class brothels? Or that her best friend, Gwendolyn Brick, had sold Leilah black-market nylon stockings during the war?

"She shops regularly at Bullocks Wilshire, where my ex-roommate works. Gwendolyn's mentioned her a few times."

Hoyt nodded slowly.

"What do these people have in common?" Kathryn ventured.

"Who said they had anything in common?"

Kathryn stubbed out her cigarette into the gravel. "Suit yourself, Mr. Mysterious." She headed for the Canteen's front door and didn't even break her stride when he called out,

"See you around . . . Mrs. Adler."

* * *

For a couple of hours, Kathryn worked the donut table with Martha Raye and Billie Burke until there was nothing left to hand out, and then accepted a series of invitations to dance. Even though she wasn't officially a hostess, she figured it was the final night, so she said yes to every soldier, sailor, marine, and pilot who asked her.

It was one o'clock in the morning when she looked around for Bette to say goodbye. The kitchen supervisor guessed that Bette was hiding in the office. "But knock gently, she's probably asleep."

Kathryn pushed open the office door and peeked inside. Bette was sitting on the ratty sofa with her shoes kicked off, resting her feet on a stack of city directories. One hand held a half-filled tumbler of something Kathryn guessed was stronger than grape Kool-Aid.

"Come in if you've got a light," Bette told her.

"Since when is Miss Davis without means to light a cigarette?" Kathryn asked.

"Ordinarily, I wouldn't be caught dead without matches, but this ain't no ordinary night." Bette held out her cigarette while Kathryn pulled a book of Mocambo matches from her purse.

Kathryn lit Bette's, then one for herself, and joined Bette on the sofa. "You going to miss all this?"

"It's been a hell of a lot of work," Bette admitted, "but so damned fulfilling in ways I never imagined when we first started."

"You should be very proud. Tonight went off without a hitch."

"Except for that moment at the top of the broadcast. Rule number one: *No dead air.*"

"Don't remind me!" Kathryn helped herself to a slug of Bette's tumbler. Whiskey. Expensive.

"So who was he? The handsome puss with the chin and the smirk. Don't tell me you've taken a lover already. You've only been married three months. That's the last thing I need to hear — I'm getting hitched soon."

Kathryn had shared her secret with only a very small handful of people. She'd told Humphrey Bogart, but that had backfired and gotten her mired even more deeply with the Bureau. Still, she knew she needed to do something, and Bette knew a thing or two about survival.

"Remember that night you sang on *Kraft Music Hall*? We were in my dressing room when the *New York Times* arrived for an interview."

"Sure I do."

Kathryn gulped another belt of Bette's whiskey. "The *Times* thing was just a cover. He's actually with the FBI."

"NO! What did he want?"

Kathryn had never suspected Bette Davis was so shockable. "To recruit me as an informer. The Bureau harbored strong suspicions that Bogie was a Commie."

Bette got up from the sofa and headed for one of the filing cabinets, where she pulled out a half-empty bottle. "Don't stop now."

"Long story short: Bogie was one of my neighbors so I told him, and we hatched a plan. We nearly got away with it, but not quite. All I managed to do was piss off the Bureau, who then threatened to short-circuit my career by spreading a rumor that I'm a lesbian unless I did what they wanted."

"Bastards! Wait—is that why you got married so suddenly? And your husband, the screenwriter, is he your *actual* husband, if you catch my meaning?"

This was the first time Kathryn had alluded to her sham marriage to someone outside the Garden of Allah. It made her feel naked.

Bette dropped back onto the sofa and held her refilled tumbler out for Kathryn. "My dear, that makes you far more interesting than I ever gave you credit for." She let out a belch, then paused for a moment. "You know how all my Canteen volunteers were ID'd and fingerprinted by the FBI?"

"You said it was just a formality."

"So I thought! About a year ago I found out that they had this place under surveillance."

"Why?"

"In their eyes, my policy of allowing anyone of any race to dance with whomever they wished was a breeding ground for Communism. They convinced themselves that the Commies sent party members in here to stir up trouble. They expected a race riot every night!"

Kathryn could feel Bette's high-priced booze beginning to calm her Nelson-Hoyt jitters. "That's absurd."

"Try and tell them that. They now suspect *me* of being a Communist. Or at least a sympathizer. Does that make me a Pinko? I can never keep that baloney straight. It's *such* a relief that we've made it to the end without so much as a flicker of a race riot."

Kathryn got to her feet. It was getting close to two A.M. and she was beat. "I'm glad your tango with the FBI has come to an end. I fear mine is only halfway through."

Bette alighted from the sofa and took Kathryn's hands in hers. "You can't let them do this. Didn't we just fight a world war to ensure we keep our First Amendment rights? Otherwise, what the hell were the last three and a half years for? We need to come up with a way to get them off your back."

Kathryn felt tears sheen her eyes. Bette had a lot to lose if the FBI decided to take her down. "But what can we do?"

"I haven't the foggiest idea," Bette said, squeezing Kathryn's hands. "Tell you what. Bill and I are getting married at the end of the month. Once we're back from the honeymoon, let's get together. I'll make sure the maître d' at Chasen's gives us a quiet corner booth. Surely we can come up with something, because if a couple of smart broads like us can't do it, then this whole damn country is in far worse trouble than either of us realize."

CHAPTER 2

Marcus Adler had been head of the MGM writers' department for nearly four months, and so far everything had gone swimmingly. The first picture he okayed was shaping up to be an all-star knockout: a biopic of Broadway composer Jerome Kern called *As the Clouds Roll By.* It was a little on the cotton-candy side, but that's what postwar moviegoers wanted. After enduring years of drudgery, rationing, and not knowing what bleak news would greet them in the morning paper, they needed Technicolor smiles and catchy tunes.

As department head, Marcus wielded an influence that few people possessed. He had the power to put on-screen the motion pictures that could help Americans rebuild their lives toward a cheerier horizon.

He took the job with an agenda of three pet projects. The Kern biopic was one, and that was now on its way. The second was a love story set in London during the blitz. It reminded war-weary audiences that love can bloom even in the grimmest circumstances.

Marcus assigned it to one of MGM's best writers, Dalton Trumbo. The guy had turned in such a wonderful script for *Love in an Air Raid Shelter* that Marcus knew Mayer's rubber-stamping was just a matter of course.

And then there was *Hannah from Havana.*

Marcus stared at the *Hannah* script lying on his desk in front of him and strummed his fingers while he wondered if three o'clock was too early for a gulp of Dutch courage.

He walked around to the large window that overlooked the studio's soundstages. They were each the size of a high school football field and were painted a shade of brown soft enough to prevent studio workers from being blinded by the California sun.

He watched a girl push a rack of nineteenth-century waitress uniforms needed for a reshoot of the new Garland picture, *The Harvey Girls*. The movie had had a long and troubled shoot, due in part to Judy's unreliability. Marcus hoped her recent marriage to Vincente Minnelli would help settle her down.

Marcus had been working on *Hannah from Havana* since before the war, when it was first called *The Making of Merry*, then *Pearl from Pearl Harbor*. He'd had Judy in mind all along and hated the thought of someone else in the lead. Casting was out of his hands, but at least he was in a position to get the story approved now. Still, the script needed to be rewritten for moviegoers who'd survived a world war.

It was time to bite the proverbial bullet. He pressed the button on his intercom and told the receptionist to send in Yip Wainright.

"Sure," Dierdre replied. "By the way, a package just arrived by special messenger."

Marcus was out of his office before Dierdre even hung up. Last Friday night, Marcus had found a diamond-shaped gold tiepin at his favorite department store, Desmond's on Wilshire.

It was half an inch across and unadorned, and he'd asked the store's jeweler to set three rubies into the front and etch an inscription into the back. It was supposed to take a week, but here it was, only four days later.

Marcus picked up the Desmond's package and returned to his office, slipping the contents out of its signature wrapping before he reached his seat.

The three rubies sparkled in the light of the desk lamp. The jeweler had set them in a perfect equilateral triangle, just as instructed. Marcus turned it over and read the inscription—"Happy birthday, Oliver, one two three."

He put the tiepin back into the maroon velvet box and tapped it three times on his desk: their secret code. Three little taps, or three soft knocks, or three quiet finger snaps equaled three little words.

Yip Wainwright steamed into Marcus' office without knocking. Like so many greenhorns his age, Wainwright carried around the insufferable assumption of entitlement. *They get hired by the best studio in Hollywood and immediately start wondering why they're not getting two grand a week.*

In his years at MGM, Marcus had seen it all, but now he had to deal with it head on. He slipped the velvet box into his drawer.

Wainwright spotted his script. "You've read it?" He sat down, uninvited, on one of Marcus' two visitor chairs and slung a leg over its arm.

Marcus pointed to the guy's foot. "How about you sit in a chair like a professional? This is MGM, not the YMCA."

Dressing down employees had come easily to his predecessor, Jim Taggert. Marcus hoped it'd eventually be the same for him, but meanwhile, he'd have to fake it. He was relieved to see Wainwright put his foot on the floor.

"My mistake," Wainwright said, with just enough insouciance to get his point across.

Marcus adopted one of Taggert's trademark postures — leaning forward, shoulders hunched, red editing pencil in hand. "Your script is a mess."

"What?!"

"I know a slapdash effort when I see one."

"Slapd — ?"

"You made Hannah's love interest so damn cocky that the audience is going to start booing him halfway through the picture. Not to mention your jokes — I can see them coming a mile away." Whatever Wainwright was about to say, Marcus cut him off by swiping his red pencil through the air.

"You were hired by this studio because we thought you were capable of a screenplay far better than this." He jabbed at the script. "If you want to get away with putting as little effort into your work as possible, I suggest you try Republic or Monogram." He used the pencil to push the script toward Wainwright, as though it stank like last week's garbage. "You'll find notes on nearly every page. Go back to your office and show me our faith in your abilities wasn't misplaced."

Marcus didn't let out his breath until Wainwright closed the door behind him, and then he slumped into his chair, telling himself that wasn't half as grueling as he'd imagined, and that he might not have to fake this tough-ass attitude for too long. There was a knock on the door.

Thinking it was Wainwright back for a rebuttal, he shouted, "WHAT?"

Dierdre cracked open the door holding a brown paper package in her right hand. "This came for you in the mail. It's marked 'Personal' so I didn't open it." She placed it on his desk and retreated, leaving Marcus to ponder whether his scolding had carried through the office walls.

The sharp corners of the package were already poking through the wrapping. Marcus tore away the paper. It was a hardback novel, and fresh off the press, by the look of its pristine cover.

Reds in the Beds by Julian Caesar.

Clearly a pseudonym, and an artless one at that.

The dust jacket featured a double bed, the sort of thing usually found in a cheap motel, draped with a crumpled red chenille bedspread. An anonymous hand, scratched and bloody, was lifting a corner of the bedspread off the floor to reveal a face silhouetted in shadow. Behind the bed, a window framed by raggedy pink lace curtains looked onto the deteriorating Hollywoodland sign in the distance.

Publishing houses often sent Marcus books they hoped to sell as movies. Generally, he handed them to staff members who would summarize them if they had potential. But there was something about the title — *Reds in the Beds* — and the striking cover that made him open the novel and read the first line.

Hollywood was the sort of place where deadbeats become kings, kings become paupers, paupers become whores, and whores become stars who marry deadbeats.

It was catchy, memorable, provocative.

The clatter of the office typewriters receded as he read the second line, and then the third. By the time he reached the end of the page, he couldn't stop. By the end of the chapter, he found himself short of breath and wished he'd never started.

CHAPTER 3

Gwendolyn Brick had never lived by herself. Eighteen years ago, she went straight from her mother's funeral to the bus that took her to the train that brought her to Hollywood, where she shared a villa at the Garden of Allah with Kathryn Massey. But after Kathryn and Marcus got married, it didn't seem right for the women to keep living together — not even at the Garden of Allah Hotel, where nothing ever seemed inappropriate.

But the wartime housing crunch didn't evaporate when the war ended; the Garden was still operating at full capacity for months after Japan surrendered. Gwendolyn couldn't conceive of living anywhere else, and Kathryn was in no hurry to push her out the door. But finally, in late November, a villa opened up, and at the age of thirty-five, Gwendolyn finally had a place she could call her own.

It sat at the far end of the Garden, which meant it was quiet, but dark, too. The only significant window was in the kitchen, and it faced the high fence along Havenhurst Drive, which blocked out most of the sunlight. But it had a five-sided nook that squeezed out of the living room like an extra limb, and that's where she set up her sewing machine and mannequin. She was standing in her sewing nook admiring how much space she had when she heard a knock at the door. Her first visitors!

"We come bearing gifts!" Marcus presented her with an enormous bouquet of baby-pink azaleas. He held up his left hand. "Champagne!"

"And paint!" Oliver added, lifting a can. "They call this shade Pale Butterscotch." He cast his gaze around Gwendolyn's new home and grimaced. "You weren't kidding. It *is* a little on the murky side. I can see why you requested a jollier color."

"Light or dark, it's all mine and I love it." She ran her finger over the three rubies on Oliver's tiepin. "This is lovely. You have a thing for the number three."

"I do?" Oliver asked.

"You've got a pair of cufflinks with three little emeralds, too."

"Those are mine." Marcus wore a grin Gwendolyn couldn't quite interpret. He deposited the flowers and champagne on Gwendolyn's drain board. "We shouldn't let this champagne get any warmer."

"I don't suppose you bought glasses?"

Marcus laughed. "Was *everything* Kathryn's?"

"Pretty much."

He shot Gwendolyn a sympathetic look. He was one of the few people who knew she'd spent the whole war socking away nearly three grand by selling nylon stockings on the black market, only to have her boyfriend disappear with every last dime. That money was supposed to bankroll her store—Chez Gwendolyn—but Linc Tattler's disappearance put the kibosh on that.

"Not to worry," Marcus said. "We'll just pop the bottle and take turns."

They were four or five swigs down when Oliver pointed to the empty wall. Six feet across and eight feet high, it was the largest wall in the place, and bare as a newborn. "What do you plan on hanging there?"

Gwendolyn shrugged. She'd never had a wall of her own to fill, and wasn't even sure what her taste in art was.

They gazed at the blank space for a few moments before Marcus ventured, "What about your portrait? It'd fit, wouldn't it?"

Gwendolyn lit a cigarette and tried to picture her portrait hanging on the wall. It'd been so long, she wasn't even sure she remembered it accurately.

"Someone painted your picture?" Oliver's words came out a touch slurred. It was one of the things she liked about Marcus' boyfriend: booze affected him about as fast as it affected her.

Marcus nudged Oliver. "Remember back in the thirties how we were all obsessed with the casting of Scarlett O'Hara? Well, our enterprising young Gwendolyn here concocted this plan to get her portrait painted as Scarlett and have it hung in Selznick's living room."

"How did that work out?" Oliver asked.

"I don't know if you noticed, but I didn't play Scarlett O'Hara." Gwendolyn pursed her lips. "You don't think it's too overpowering for my little abode?"

"*Au contraire*," Marcus said, "I think it'd give the room a focal point. Where is it?"

"I can only assume it's where I left it in the basement of the main house."

Oliver took another swig of champagne. "Whatarewewaitingfor?"

* * *

The painting was bigger than Gwendolyn remembered, and heavier than the boys bargained for. They had to rest a couple of times en route, as well as negotiate the stairs from the basement. Inside Gwendolyn's place, they propped it against the bare wall and stood back.

"I can't believe you hid something so gorgeous in a basement," Oliver panted.

Gwendolyn was surprised at how much she liked it. *It's like bumping into a younger version of yourself.*

David Selznick's wife, Irene, was the one who originally put Gwendolyn in the room with Alistair Dunne, who was supposed to paint her portrait for the Carmichael Prize. Gwendolyn thought the plan to catch Selznick's attention with it was farfetched, but she was desperate to screen-test for Scarlett. What Gwendolyn hadn't counted on was someone who threw such gusto into everything he did, from painting her portrait to making sweaty, animalistic love to her. Their affair burned out in a smoldering heap, but not before he painted this goodbye gift.

He'd arranged her on a faded brown velvet chaise lounge in a huge dress with gold, crimson, and peacock blue brocade, resting on one elbow with her mouth slightly open, as though half shocked and half thrilled.

Marcus nodded approvingly. "In Kathryn's villa there'd have been too much distraction, but this wall gives it the right amount of space, without getting lost in the corner." He wrapped his arm around her shoulder. "It's almost like the you in this painting has been quietly waiting for just the right spot. Welcome home, Gwennie O'Hara."

* * *

The boys left once the champagne was gone. Now that Marcus was respectably married to Kathryn, their mutual social life had opened up, filling their evenings with dinner parties and bridge games at all the right homes around Hollywood. Gwendolyn wondered how Oliver felt, but if there was any resentment, it didn't show. "I get a lot more reading done," he told her once without rancor.

She was still standing in front of Gwennie O'Hara's portrait, marveling at how agreeably it fitted, when someone knocked on her door again. She opened it to find Horton Tattler on her landing.

Horton was the father of her wartime boyfriend who dashed off with all her savings. It was hard enough to tell him his son was a thief, but then she'd had to suggest he look into his own finances, as it seemed his most trusted friend had been laundering money through Horton's company. Gwendolyn had been relieved to put all that sordid business behind her, even though it meant kissing four thousand smackers goodbye.

The last few months had aged the man considerably. His Victorian handlebar moustache that had bristled with pride and confidence now drooped with neglect, and the gray in his sideburns now spread across the top of his head.

He smiled weakly. "May I?"

Gwendolyn widened the door. "I've only just moved in, so I'm still in disarray."

Tattler stopped in front of the portrait and muttered, "Magnificent!" before settling onto Gwendolyn's sofa.

She sat down beside him. "How have you been?" she asked mildly, and received a pinched smile in return.

"My wife left me."

"I'm sorry to hear that," Gwendolyn said, but she was far from surprised. Most of Mr. Horton's purchases at her perfume and lingerie counter at Bullocks Wilshire were for his mistress.

"She went back to Atlanta. I've sold both homes and all the household effects." He cast his eyes around the dim room. "If I'd known, I'd have saved you one of my lamps." He tried for a warmer smile, but fell short of the mark. "I'm living at the Hershey Arms now."

"It's only temporary, I'm sure," Gwendolyn said. The Hershey Arms was prosperous in its day, but that day was a long time ago, and both of them knew it.

Tattler's Tuxedos had been one of LA's classiest menswear stores, but the government had appropriated Mr. Tattler's factories, obliging him to make uniforms at cost for the war effort. He could have survived, but his closest friend, Clem O'Roarke, had been using Tattler's Tuxedos' bank account to launder his wife's brothel money. Gwendolyn was pondering whether Horton's sudden appearance had something to do with Nelson Hoyt bringing up Leilah O'Roarke to Kathryn at the Hollywood Canteen when Horton pulled a postcard from his jacket pocket and handed it to her. It was a black and white photograph of a lighthouse on a tiny smudge of an island.

"What's this?"

"I thought *you* might know."

Gwendolyn shook her head. "Where did you find it?"

"I was packing up Linc's house. That's his handwriting on the back."

Gwendolyn flipped the card over. "El Faro. That's Spanish, isn't it?" Horton shrugged. She read out loud the two other words written there. "Emilio Barragán. Do you know who that is?"

"No idea," Horton responded. "But I figured it might point to his whereabouts."

Gwendolyn could feel her hopes rising. Perhaps her three grand wasn't quite as lost as she'd thought. She studied the picture again. "Maybe this lighthouse is somewhere in Mexico?"

"Or Guatemala. Or Argentina. Or Chile. Or Spain."

"It's the only clue you have to track down your son." *And my money.*

"No," Horton said firmly. "It's the only clue *you* have. I'm not looking for him." He grew instantly red in the face. "My son sold illegal goods on the black market while the rest of the world was fighting for freedom. And then he disappeared without a word after stealing a considerable amount of money from a decent, lovely lass who deserved no such treatment from anyone, least of all my own blood."

Gwendolyn decided against making the point that the money Linc took from her was earned from the black market too. "Mr. Tattler," she said, "Linc isn't a criminal."

"He stole your money!"

"I want to think it was for a very good reason, and we won't know that until we track him down."

Horton Tattler brushed invisible lint from his shabby tweed jacket. "I've washed my hands of him."

"Then why did you bring me this postcard?"

"In some small way, I feel responsible for my son's actions, and while I can't repay the money he took from you, the least I could do was bring you this clue." He glanced down at the picture postcard in Gwendolyn's hand. "That lighthouse could be anywhere, but that name — Emilio Barragán — perhaps could get you somewhere."

He went to stand, but Gwendolyn caught him by the elbow. The tweed felt cheap and scratchy — a sad step down for one of the best haberdashers in California.

"What if I do? What should I say to him?"

"If I were you, Miss Brick, I'd say, 'I want my money back.'"

"I meant what should I say about you?"

He thought for a moment, disappointment seeping from his eyes. "In that unlikely event, I'm sure you'll find something kind to say."

CHAPTER 4

Kathryn set a plate of fileted salmon on rainbow rye next to
Bertie Kreuger's mock pâté de foie gras. Even though
everybody had agreed to make something from scratch for
Robert Benchley's wake, Kathryn suspected Bertie's
contribution came from Schwab's, and she'd just mushed it
up to make it look homemade. Bertie lived in Alla
Nazimova's old bedroom suite up in the main building.
Unlike the villas, it lacked a kitchen, which was fine because
Bertie had never cooked a thing in her life.

Dorothy Parker appeared at Kathryn's side holding a
platter of celery sticks stuffed with crabmeat. Her drawn
face looked as though all the life had been sucked out of it.
Dottie wasn't the hugging type, so Kathryn just kissed her
lightly on the temple. Her hair smelled of cigarette ash and
dog food. "How you doing?"

Dottie's eyes were rimmed in red. "I'm annoyed because
he got there before I did."

It was one of her typical barbed lines, snapped off with
practiced indifference, but Kathryn saw through it. Her
closest friend in the world had died, and there was no
replacing him. Kathryn imagined losing Marcus and she
knew how Dorothy felt.

Dottie grunted. "I hope every last pigeon on Nantucket
is shitting all over his family plot." Benchley was famous for
his hatred of pigeons. "Oh well," she said bitterly. "You
know what rhymes with Nantucket." She slid her platter
next to Bertie's pâté. "Have you seen Lillian? She said she
was bringing Edna."

"Ferber?" Kathryn asked. "She's in town?"

"For the premiere of *Saratoga Trunk*. I haven't seen her since Medusa was in pigtails. She'll be a sight for these bleary old eyes. Point those harpies in my direction when you see them." She headed for the booze table Kay Thompson and her husband had set up. "Martini!" she barked at Bill. "Double! Three olives!"

"She's going to miss Bench more than any of us." Marcus was by her side with the cake he perfected during the war. Although the one-egg-a-week ration was a thing of the past, Gardenites had come to expect him to bring his dense, moist, no-butter-no-eggs-no-milk Marcus Cake. He deposited it onto the table along with a bowl of popcorn.

"Weren't you doing deviled eggs, too?" Kathryn asked.

Marcus pouted. "You remember that special plate I had? The light blue one with the individual scoops to place the eggs in? I can't find it. So I thought, Screw it, and made popcorn instead." He ran a fingertip down her arm. "Who'd have guessed we'd lose him at fifty-six?"

Harpo Marx arrived with Humphrey Bogart—an odd pairing by Hollywood's standards, but not at the Garden of Allah. They'd both been residents at one point or another, as well as recipients of Benchley's boundless hospitality.

Robert Benchley had been the Garden's social hub. His door was always open and his bar perpetually stocked with every conceivable variety of hooch. A man of infinite kindness and genuine warmth, he'd had few equals in Hollywood.

Kathryn gazed across the crowd clustered around the pool. Its haze of cheerlessness reminded Kathryn of the day everyone assembled at the radio to listen to Roosevelt's funeral procession.

Don Stewart, a screenwriter Marcus worked with at MGM who was an usher at Benchley's wedding, sat on the diving board chatting somberly with Bertie on one side of him and Oliver on the other. Kay Thompson and her husband, Bill Spier, were huddled with Bogie.

Kathryn hoped Bill wasn't trying to interest Bogie in his new radio show, *The Adventures of Sam Spade*. This was a gathering to remember their dear friend, not a chance to talk shop.

Marcus pressed his head against Kathryn's. "After a few drinks, I bet the stories will come tumbling out."

"It's like you can read my mind," she told him.

"I *am* your husband."

They looked at each other for a long moment, then started to giggle. "It's still so strange to hear," she said.

"That you have a husband, or that your husband is me?"

"Both! I never thought I'd get married."

He frowned at her in genuine surprise. "Never?"

"My romantic track record is hardly inspiration for the next Hollywood happy ending. Still, the marriage has done wonders for our social life. All those dinners and bridge parties we get invited to now. I feel so damned respectable."

Marcus took off his glasses and polished them on his tie. "I don't know how much longer it'll last. Have you finished reading that book?"

Reds in the Beds had consumed Hollywood like a Santa Ana forest fire. The inside flap proclaimed that it "told the story of an imaginary Hollywood infiltrated with treacherous Communists and their Pinko sympathizers." Anyone who read it — which now seemed like everyone Kathryn knew from the Pacific shore to the Nevada border — could see the hateful book was a roman à clef veiled in the sheerest possible gauze of fiction. The only game played around Hollywood now was guessing who was really who in *Reds in the Beds*.

This was especially true at the Garden of Allah.

Much of the book's action took place in the Divine Oasis, a residential hotel just off the Sunset Strip filled with fellow travelers who worked to sneak the Communist creed into every movie they wrote, directed, produced, or acted in.

The Garden's residents had taken to referring to their home as "the simply divine oasis" in an attempt to deflect the poisoned arrows. However, Kathryn sensed a hardened shell of "Don't look at me!" defensiveness every time it came up. And it was starting to come up a lot.

Instead of Twentieth Century-Fox there was New Century-Wolf, instead of Paramount Pictures there was Tantamount Films, and instead of MGM, there was NJN. The head of NJN's writing department was an especially devious conniver married to a gossip columnist for the *Hollywood Correspondent* newspaper. The hateful novel devoted many pages to describing the marriage between Eugene Markham and Beatrice Kahn as a loveless union of convenience arranged to help ingratiate the pair into Hollywood's social merry-go-round.

"I have finished it, and—" Kathryn blew a wet raspberry. "Whoever this Julian Caesar cretin is, I hope there's a special circle of hell reserved just for him."

"You know that couple is supposed to be us, don't you?" Marcus asked.

The wave of nausea that kicked Kathryn in the stomach when she read that chapter rolled forth again. "Helen Keller could tell it's us. Has Mayer read it yet?"

"Nobody's mentioned anything. What about Wilkerson?"

Kathryn let fly an apprehensive laugh. "I never thought I'd be thankful for his obsession with that grand folly of his."

Kathryn's disapproval of her boss' plan to build a luxury casino in the middle of the Nevada desert had been a source of considerable friction around the office. Like so many of Hollywood's high rollers, Wilkerson was reckless with his money, often gambling more in one afternoon at Santa Anita than most people earned in a year. Kathryn felt that putting a chronic gambler in charge of a casino was like locking a ten-year-old inside a chocolate store.

"He's going ahead with it?"

"I've given up asking."

Bogart's voice fired across the crowd. "Well, if it ain't the fifth Warner brother!"

Bette Davis strode out of the main building swathed in a silver-tipped fox fur to ward off the November chill. "Hello, everyone!" She approached the subdued crowd with all the confidence of the characters she played on the screen. As far as Kathryn knew, Bette had never been to the Garden before, and she certainly wasn't part of the Algonquin Round Table contingent, like Edna Ferber and Lillian Hellman.

"Goodness gracious!" she exclaimed. "When I heard there was a wake going on for Robert Benchley at the Garden of Allah, I thought to myself, Now *that's* a wake I want to be a part of. I'm sure there are a number of people here who knew Bench better than I, but I have no doubt he'd want his sendoff to be a much gayer affair than this!"

"Bette!" Kathryn greeted the star with a kiss to the cheek. "You knew Benchley?"

"He volunteered at the Canteen at least once a week. He'd often help me close up for the night. We spent a number of evenings afterhours chatting on that office sofa about life, work, Hollywood — and especially death."

Dottie Parker appeared. "Whose?"

"He seemed haunted by the possibility that he'd somehow failed to live up to his potential."

A glimmer of knowing flickered in Dottie's eyes. "I'm familiar with that conversation." She smiled halfheartedly, then lifted her martini glass as though in toast, failing to notice it was empty. "Welcome to the wake of our dearest lost comrade."

Bette accepted a highball from Harpo, and barked out a laugh. "Comrade? I'm surprised anybody would dare use a word like that here at the — what does that dreadful book call this place? The Divine . . . Sanctuary?"

Bette's comment flipped a switch, rallying the mourners into a madly chattering congress, eager to chirp their own pet theories over who had written *Reds in the Beds*, who he'd based his characters on, and his motives for publishing such a salacious piece of trash.

Dottie thought Louella Parsons wrote it. Bogie declared that the whole thing stunk of Louella's boss, William Randolph Hearst—a theory that garnered widespread appeal until Don Stewart pointed out that Hedda Hopper's *LA Times* column was inching further and further to the right.

While the scotch and bourbon, gin and champagne poured like Prohibition was about to return, names of other likely suspects were bandied about. Kay Thompson suspected it was Joseph Breen, head censor of the Hays Office. Her husband suggested it could be someone connected with the right-wing Motion Picture Alliance for the Preservation of American Ideals, which was increasingly vocal in its criticism of Hollywood's liberal leanings.

In the middle of this uproar, Lillian Hellman arrived with Edna Ferber, who immediately pointed out that until her recent success with *The Fountainhead,* Ayn Rand had been a script reader for the studios.

As the sun began to set, the crowd lit the dozens of candles Kathryn passed around until the Garden glowed with a light as gentle as Robert Benchley's nature.

Around midnight, Bette grabbed Kathryn's elbow and led her over to the edge of the patio.

"I've been thinking about you," Bette said, pulling her fur closer around her against the night air. "That malarkey you told me about the FBI."

A wave of panic reeled through Kathryn. They were more frequent lately and were starting to take their toll on her sleep. She kept jumping to wild conclusions, like maybe it was someone at the Garden who'd written *Reds,* someone they'd all snubbed who was intent on revenge. "You didn't mention it to anybody, did you?"

"Of course not." Bette's smile bordered on demure. "I think you're a straight-shooter like me, and a career gal. Marriage and men and lovers are all very well, but they're not what stoke my furnace. Nor yours, I suspect." Bette pulled out a cigarette. "Hollywood is really just a giant game. Learn the rules, when to play by them, and when to break them." She offered her pack to Kathryn.

Kathryn lit one with Bette's struck match. "Are you referring to my marriage?"

"Among other things."

"Such as?"

"Jack Warner and I are constantly at loggerheads, but we both want the same thing: what's best for the studio. I hear that you and your boss don't agree about this Flamingo Club he's building."

"A reckless gambler building a casino is my definition of insanity."

"I know all about difficult bosses and can sympathize entirely." She paused for a moment, her gimlet eyes trained on Kathryn. "Now, about your FBI situation. Have you considered asking Howard Hughes?"

"No." *But it's interesting that you did.* Bette had an affair with Hughes before the war, while she was rebounding from an intense relationship with her *Jezebel* director, William Wyler. "Have you seen him recently?"

"He sent me a telegram after the wedding, and it got me thinking. Howard has connections you and I can barely dream of."

And a grudge against Hoyt. A couple of months before the war ended, Wilkerson drafted Kathryn into a lunch with him and Hughes. While Wilkerson was away from the table glad-handing the newly married Judy Garland and Vincente Minnelli, Hughes admitted to a situation back in the days of Prohibition when Hoyt got the better of him.

Bette smiled. "I see a light going on."

Kathryn killed her cigarette. "Let's get back before they start accusing *us* of writing *Reds in the Beds.*"

CHAPTER 5

With a coffee pot in one hand, a paper tablet and pencils in the other, and her purse jammed under her arm, Gwendolyn shouldered the door to the Garden of Allah's bar and held the door open for Marcus as he headed toward the nearest table with a platter of sliced fruitcake.

He stopped short when he saw every light ablaze. "How come it's so blinding in here?"

The Sahara Room was infamously dark. Its miniature table lamps typically cloaked the Sunset Strip's extramarital encounters in muddy shadows, but not today. An amber stain in the gray carpet caught Gwendolyn's eye. It wasn't the only blotch of booze she could see—just the biggest.

"I want people to take this meeting seriously," she said, "so I told management to turn on every light in the joint."

Oliver walked in, loaded down with plates and dessert forks. "I could run over to Schwab's for some beer?"

"Not at eleven o'clock in the morning," Gwendolyn said. "I want people sober. Help me push these tables together. I need everybody gathered in one spot, not scattered all over the bar."

Everyone was on guard after a string of petty thefts at the Garden. First it was Marcus' missing deviled eggs platter. Then shortly after, New York columnist Lucius Beebe checked into the Garden with his lover, Charles. Gwendolyn liked having Lucius around. He had the well-fed look of a prosperous man-about-town and lent an air of sophistication to the Garden. He could match wits with even the Algonquin contingent.

But then a set of tea towels had vanished from the clothesline in their courtyard, and Gwendolyn could tell they were wondering if they'd chosen the right place to call home.

That same week, Trevor Bergin and Melody Hope moved in. Everybody knew the MGM stars had been asked to leave their Garden Court apartment on Hollywood Boulevard, and now that Bogie had divorced his third wife and settled down with Lauren Bacall, Trevor and Melody were Hollywood's rowdiest couple. On their fourth night, Melody threw all of Trevor's cufflinks out the window in a pique of fury; the next morning, all but one pair were recovered.

But it was a missing silk scarf that prompted Gwendolyn to call this meeting. It had been a present from Madame Nazimova to Gwendolyn's neighbor, Bertie Kreuger, a beer heiress who'd moved in during the war.

Oliver pushed a table against the one at the center of the room, which skidded across the carpet and banged into its neighbor, knocking Gwendolyn's handbag to the floor. Oliver dropped to his knees and collected the scattered contents before standing up with Linc's picture postcard in his hand.

"What is this?"

Gwendolyn looked up. "Mr. Tattler gave it to me. The writing on the back is Linc's; it might be a clue to his whereabouts."

"*El faro*," Oliver said pensively. "That means 'lighthouse.'"

"You speak Spanish?"

Oliver jutted his head from side to side. "I think I've seen this lighthouse before."

"You have?!"

"Maybe when I was doing missionary work."

"Excuse me?" Marcus butted in. "You did missionary work?"

"When I was in junior high, my father and his buddy took a sabbatical to do missionary work for a year. My mother refused to be left behind, so both families hit the road. We spent four months apiece in Mexico, Guatemala, and Cuba." Oliver jiggled the postcard in his hand. "Much of that trip is a blur, but one of the sons from the other family was a good ten years older than me—"

"Do you know where he is?"

"Cincinnati. He's high up at the Catholic Legion of Decency. Perhaps if I took a photograph of this and sent it to him?"

"Could you?" Gwendolyn said, feeling a glimmer of hope. *It's a slim chance, but it's all you've got.*

"Of course." He slipped Linc's postcard into his jacket pocket.

Kathryn and Bertie appeared in the doorway. "Good God!" Kathryn cried out, shielding her eyes with her hands. "Are you trying to blind us?

Gwendolyn was thanking them for showing up early when Trevor and Melody walked in with John Carradine and his wife, Sonia. He'd just hit it big in *Captain Kidd* and was hoping to make the leap to meatier roles.

As everyone pushed the rest of the tables together, Frances Goodrich and Albert Hackett walked in. They lived at the Garden when they were penning *Thin Man* movies before the war, but they'd decamped back to New York, where they felt more welcome, until Frank Capra lured them westward again to write his next movie, *It's a Wonderful Life.* Friends were reuniting among a flurry of introductions when Gwendolyn took her place at the head of the tables.

"Thank you, everyone, for coming."

"And thank you for calling this meeting," Bertie said. "A couple of tchotchkes going missing is one thing, but it's been one after another."

"I must say," Lucius pouted, "if I'd known that we were moving into a den of thieves—"

"Please don't think that," Gwendolyn said. "Some of us have been here since the Garden opened, and we've never seen anything like this."

"Don't mind Lucius," Charles said. "He loves a touch of mystery."

"You wouldn't say that if they were *your* favorite cufflinks," Trevor said.

Melody elbowed him in the ribs.

"If it was just some random stranger on a pilfering spree, all those things would have vanished on the same night," Gwendolyn insisted. "But this has been going on for a while now."

"It sounds like you suspect one of the residents." Sonia Carradine said. "And if this is a new problem, are you saying it must be one of the new residents?"

The door swung open and Kay Thompson, a vision in a white pantsuit and matching nails, burst into the Sahara Room, her arms raised like Christ on the cross. She cut a stark contrast to the shadowy foyer behind her. "Sorry we're so late! Last-minute do-overs on *Harvey Girls* kept me until the wee hours." She spun around, scanning the room. "What happened to Bill?" She flicked her wrists and a throng of silver bangles jangled like wind chimes. "Ah! Coffee!" She poured a cup and fell onto the nearest chair, then reached for cake. "Now, what were we talking about?"

"I'm not sure if you're aware, but the Garden of Allah seems to have a thief," Gwendolyn said, "so we're here to see if we can prevent further pilfering or identify the culprit."

"Well," Kay sniffed, "apparently all you have to do is read *Reds in the Beds.*

"In that case, let's start with you," Melody said, pointing to Kay. "I think we can all assume you're NJN's choir mistress, Dee-Dee Grifter. And we all know what a grifter is, don't we?"

"What the hell do you know, you low-rent Garland?" Kay's husband said from the doorway.

The gathering gasped in unison, as though on cue. Bill Spier was usually the reserved, circumspect half of the Spier-Thompson marriage, so an outburst like this caught everybody in the room by surprise.

They all knew Melody campaigned for Judy's role in *The Harvey Girls*, even after Judy had it and was habitually showing up late. In the end, Judy got it together and Melody's machinations were revealed. All eyes were now on her.

Melody poked her husband in the arm. "Are you going to let him talk to me like that?"

Trevor remained inert. "Pipe down, Nellie Burch."

Melody had risen to fame in *The Pistol from Pittsburgh*, a biopic of nineteenth-century journalist Nellie Bly. In *Reds in the Beds*, Nellie Burch was a tart-tongued harridan movie star, hooked on dope and drinking her way into obscurity.

"You son of a bitch!" Melody snatched up a slice of cake and pitched it at Trevor, then sneered at everyone around her. "I don't know who's stealing your crappy shit, but as far as I'm concerned, you all deserve it."

"That's ironic," Bertie said, "because all this time, my money's been on YOU!"

Melody threw another slice at Bertie, but she caught it and hurled it back, catching Melody on the ear. Bertie leaned her fleshy elbows on the table. "You know the scene where Nellie Burch has a fit on the set of *Versailles* and ends up throwing all of Marie Antoinette's cakes at the director?" She made a sweeping gesture at Marcus' cake platter. "Is this art imitating life, or life imitating art? Sometimes the line gets so blurred."

"I hate to say this," Lucius sniffed, "but that title really is quite clever."

"How do you figure?" Melody demanded.

He raised a shoulder. "All the tabloids have us thinking 'Reds *under* the bed!' but this book ratchets it all up a notch by telling us the Reds aren't under the bed at all — they're *in* bed with us, screwing us nine ways to Sunday. Whoever this Julian Caesar is, he's made sure that if we weren't paranoid about Communism before, we sure are now."

"Please, everyone!" Gwendolyn clapped her hands. "Can we talk about the thefts? Management thinks we should get a house detective."

"We came back to the Garden *specifically because* it's one of the few hotels without a detective," Frances said. "The minute one appears is the minute Albert and I check out."

"We all feel the same way." Gwendolyn said.

"Yeah," Melody snorted. "Name one person in this room who doesn't have a secret."

"Please, Miss Hope," Albert Hackett said. "If you can't contribute something positive to this discussion, perhaps it might be better if you just stayed quiet."

Melody snatched up another slice of Marcus' fruitcake and lobbed it at Albert. It caught him square in the face, knocking his glasses askew.

"ALL RIGHT, MELODY! THAT'S ENOUGH!" Trevor shouted.

"Shut up, *August Vail*," Melody hissed. August Vail was the biggest action hero in Caesar's fictional Tantamount Films — and a secret kleptomaniac called Pinky the Pinko for his fondness for pretty lace panties.

Trevor's wife leapt to her feet.

"Okay, a few things have gone missing. Big whoop! That pile of trash is making us all out to be Commies and subversives and criminals, and Washington is starting to take it seriously. So shouldn't we, too? If you all think some egg platter is more important than our reputations, you're all screwed up." She bolted from the room.

"I hate to admit it, but she's right," Oliver said. "When I first read that damned book, I thought it'd be a tempest in a teacup, but the *New York Times* said yesterday it was mentioned in Congress. Something to do with the House Un-American Activities Committee."

"Aren't they just concerned with rooting out Nazis?"

"Not any longer." He picked up Gwendolyn's postcard and studied the picture. "The war is over. They need a new boogieman, or they have nothing to attack."

CHAPTER 6

By February 1946, Marcus had been in charge for six months and was enjoying guiding his writers through the troughs of apprehension and around potholes of doubt more than he'd expected to. But nothing revved his engine more than coming up with an idea and knowing how to make it work.

The previous weekend, George Cukor invited him and Kathryn to his house for a screening of old silent shorts by one of Hollywood's great silent-era directors. George was talking it up as a celebration of D.W. Griffith's work, but it was obviously a charity fundraiser for someone who'd failed to keep up with the times and was now living at the Knickerbocker Hotel off Hollywood Boulevard. Still, the industry owed a debt to the innovations Griffith introduced, so the crowd of directors, producers, and technicians were happy to pony up.

By contemporary standards, many of Griffith's films were clunky and choppy, the storytelling heavy-handed, the acting overwrought, and the pathos laid on thicker than glue. But a few gems gleamed from the dreck. The final film George screened that evening made Marcus sit up straight.

New York Hat starred Mary Pickford as a girl whose dying mother bequeaths some money to buy a fancy hat more elegant than her miserly father would allow. The whole story was over in sixteen minutes, but not before Marcus grasped its potential as a full-length musical — and not just a musical, but one starring an up-and-comer whose charms had attracted the eye of Louis B. Mayer.

An ambitious hoofer named Ann Miller had set her sights on becoming MGM's next musical leading lady, and to that end, she wasn't opposed to ingratiating herself with Mayer. Nor was Mayer resistant to her sway. The girl could tap like a machine gunner jacked up on a fistful of bennies, but she was under contract at Columbia. It wasn't unheard of for one studio to buy out a rival's contract, but negotiations were smoother if the new studio had a movie lined up. Mayer had sent out word that he wanted a project for Miss Miller. Before *New York Hat*'s credits hit George's screen, Marcus knew he had the perfect idea. He begged Kathryn to leave early so he could get it down on paper before it evaporated.

Ideas for scenes, characters, plot twists, and musical numbers tumbled out of him, and he was up until two filling page after page. The next day he got to work early, his briefcase jammed with scribbled notes, and started banging away at his typewriter before anyone else arrived. Some time later, Dierdre opened his office door with a goofy grin splitting her freckled face. "It's not every day we turn forty!"

He sat back in his chair and pressed his lips into a smile. He was now the same age his father was when he ran Marcus out of town. Adler senior was always so fully in control of his life that Marcus longed to feel that same way. As he sat at his desk with his receptionist smiling at him and his notes for *New York Hat* spread out across his desk, Marcus suspected maybe he finally did.

"How'd you know today was my birthday?"

"I'm pals with Mannix's secretary. She told me he asked her to call personnel and check."

"Why would he check that?"

Dierdre's sly grin returned. "You know about the tradition, don't you?" She took in his blank face. "Oh my! You *are* in for a surprise!"

* * *

The back seat of Eddie Mannix's silver limousine was already filled with expensive Cuban cigar smoke when Marcus climbed in a couple of minutes past six. Mannix, a craggy-faced ex-bouncer who'd made good and was now Louis B. Mayer's right-hand man — the second most powerful guy at MGM — offered up a knowing smile along with a Romeo y Julieta cigar. He leaned back on his soft black leather upholstery and breathed out a pungent cloud.

"It almost makes turning forty worthwhile, doesn't it, Adler?"

Marcus wasn't much of a cigar man; they made him dizzy and a little on the nauseous side. He knocked back Mannix's offer and breathed lightly.

As the car headed east on Washington, he glanced back at the five identical vehicles trailing behind them. Wherever they were going, he hoped they'd be done well before eight. Kathryn and Gwendolyn had put a lot of work into the party they were throwing for him back at the Garden.

"There's only one rule," Mannix said. "The bastard who's turning forty gets first pick." He spat a flake of tobacco on the carpet between them.

As the chauffeur reached La Cienega and headed north, Marcus ran through the list of possible destinations. Restaurant? Casino? Nightclub? Where the hell were they going, and how come he didn't know? It wasn't until they turned off the Strip and started cruising up the steeper inclines of the Hollywood Hills that Marcus' stomach grew heavy with dread.

"I appreciate the gesture and all," Marcus' tongue was sandpaper, "but I'm recently married."

"So?"

"Going to a brothel, it just doesn't sit right with me." Marcus longed for a stiff belt of bourbon. "How about you let me out at the next corner? I can leg it home from here. But you guys go on, have a great time, enjoy yourselves."

The car pulled to a stop in front of an unremarkable two-story house that was painted two different shades of brown. It had a semicircular front porch and a bay window on each side, both upstairs and down, a big shady elm tree, and a row of daisies along the low brick fence that jutted up against the sidewalk.

This is what they look like? Marcus thought.

"You're one of us now, Adler. Think of it as a rite of passage. All senior MGM guys go through it. The only one who turned it down was — *queer.*" He bit the word off like a chunk of sour fruit and Marcus' stomach turned.

Is this his way of finding out if I'm Eugene Markham?

* * *

Marcus and Mannix waited on the porch until eight men in respectable blue suits and ties their wives had probably picked out joined them.

When Mannix rapped the bronze knocker, the door opened, revealing exactly the sort of Louisiana bordello Marcus had been picturing. He ran his eyes around the foyer, which was papered in gold-striped, burgundy-flocked wallpaper. An ornate crystal lamp sat on an intricately carved teak table next to a well-preserved middle-aged woman he didn't want to make eye contact with.

"Gentlemen!" she proclaimed. As she gestured to her left, the sleeve of her gauzy black kaftan swirled like mist.

The men filed into a large, deep, thickly carpeted room that was papered waist-high with the burgundy flock and paneled from there to the ceiling in ivy-patterned pressed tin. Along one wall a table was laid with oysters, olives, caviar, figs, and chocolate-dipped cherries. A sprinkling of Tiffany lamps with rose-and-thorn designs gave the room a muted glow. String orchestrations — the type usually heard behind a tender Hollywood love scene — played through speakers Marcus couldn't locate. As his eyes adjusted, he made out an array of exquisite girls draped with rehearsed nonchalance on sofas, easy chairs, footstools, and against the walls.

—

The woman in the black kaftan greeted Mannix with a kiss to the cheek, her languid eyes trained on Marcus. "Your newest recruit?"

Mannix slid an arm around her waist. "It is."

She wafted another hand in a theatrical arc. "The buffet is open."

Sweet Jesus, I'm going to have to do this.

The girls on offer were as striking as any actress on the screen. Their clothes flattered their figures without resorting to overt exposure, and their smiles gleaming in the lamplight seemed sincere, like they were genuinely pleased to see him. But he wasn't looking for the most attractive of the bunch; he was seeking out the one who seemed most likely to keep his secret.

He spotted a fresh-faced debutant; sort of a Jane Powell type, but with strawberry blonde hair framing her face in soft curls.

"What's your name?" he asked her.

She floated to her feet. "Opal."

He could see her smile tremble around the edges — not obviously, but enough to give her away. "So what happens now, Opal?"

Before the girl could respond, the knot of executives at the far end of the room erupted into applause, and started dispersing toward their choices.

"You follow me." Opal guided him through a door that led to a staircase. He followed her to the top, then down a narrow corridor until they arrived at the end. She opened the door. "Gentlemen first."

The room was small, with enough space to fit a single bed, a side table, and a ceramic basin stenciled with yellow calla lilies. When the girl closed the door, the music playing throughout the house faded away, leaving them in silence.

He was about to launch into his "You don't have to do this" speech when he spotted a narrow desk on the far wall. On it stood a late-model Remington typewriter, similar to the one Marcus used at the office. He chuckled.

The girl threw a red tasseled shawl over it. "You're not supposed to see that."

"Even ladies of the evening are budding screenwriters?"

"Heavens, no!" she giggled. "When Madame Eloise learned that I type sixty-five words a minute—"

"Sixty-five? That's impressive."

"Top of my class—oh, but you didn't come here to talk about typewriters." She gestured toward a hook attached to the wall next to the bed. "If you'd like to hang your jacket up so it doesn't wrinkle. You studio guys get real particular about that, I've noticed."

Now that he had a chance to study her more closely, he could see why he picked her: she reminded him of his sister. She was younger than Doris by maybe five or six years, but she had Doris' cheeky smile. He suddenly remembered that he owed her a letter.

He took Opal by the hand and led her to the bed, where he sat them both down. "How did a girl who can type sixty-five words a minute end up working in a place like this?"

Opal's blue eyes widened and stayed fully open until a wave of understanding washed through them. "Oh, I see," she said, "You don't want to—? You're not interested in—? Because you don't—?"

"Can I trust you to keep this to yourself?" Marcus asked evenly.

"If anybody asks, we screwed like rabbits."

"I'd appreciate that." Marcus felt the lump in his stomach start to dissipate. He nodded toward her desk. "Sixty-five, huh?"

Opal acknowledged him with a crooked smile. "Until a few months ago, I was in legal secretary school. And doing very well, too. But then both my folks fell ill. They came out here for their lungs. Tuberculosis and all that. But they ignored every doctor who told them to give up smoking. Then last winter they came down with TB again. Real bad. Fatal, as it turned out. They died within weeks of each other."

"I'm sorry to hear that."

"Yeah, it was pretty bad. But even worse, they put all their assets in my name after some shyster of a lawyer tried to bilk them out of their money. Daddy did well making those lights the studios use, key lights and what-have-you. Their illnesses dragged on so long that their medical bills stacked up and they died horribly in debt. And as all the assets were in my name, their debts became my debts."

"So you dropped out of secretarial school?"

Opal's debutant veneer evaporated. "If you know of another way a single girl can make a pile of dough in a hurry, then you be sure and let me know."

"And the typewriter?"

"The woman who owns this place found out about my skills, and in exchange for not having to—you know, she gives me office work."

Marcus pictured the woman in the front room, all black gauze and carefully applied mascara. "Madame Eloise has paperwork?"

Opal giggled just like Doris. "No, not her. The one who owns this place. Talk about a dynamo. *That* woman is a force of nature," she whispered. "She owns three different brothels. Can you imagine the money she makes?"

A woman . . . force of nature . . . owns three brothels? How many people in Los Angeles could fit that description? He kept his eyes on the hook in the wall. "Are you talking about Leilah O'Roarke?"

Opal clapped a hand to her mouth, her face suddenly white.

Marcus said, "Your secret is safe with me if mine is safe with you."

She let out a long, jagged breath. "Thank you. If she knew I'd blabbed—"

"What's your name?"

"I already told you."

"Your real name."

The debutant smile reemerged. "Arlene."

"That's a lovely name. It suits you. Tell me, Arlene, exactly how deep in debt are you? And by that, I mean how long will you have to work here until you're free to re-enroll in secretarial school and get your diploma?"

Arlene fidgeted with the tassel on her robe. "Six months, maybe. Why?"

As the controversy over *Reds in the Beds* had swelled from a "Guess Who's Who" parlor game to a storm that threatened to topple reputations, it had dawned on Marcus that it might benefit him to develop a contact inside MGM's legal department who could warn him if any proverbial shit was in danger of hitting any proverbial fans.

"What if I were to advance you the money you need to get back into school?"

Arlene pressed her hands to her chest. "Why would you do that?"

"And when you graduate, what if I put in a good word with the legal department at MGM?"

The trembling smile resurfaced; her eyes glassed over with the effort to restrain her tears. "You don't even know me."

"You don't belong here anymore than I do."

"And in return?" She flicked a finger at him. "I know how this town works. Everyone has a motive, even the nice guys."

Marcus played a hunch. "While you're helping Mrs. O'Roarke with her paperwork, I'd be grateful if you could keep your eyes open."

"For what?"

"I'm not sure, exactly."

"That's not much help."

"I know." He crossed to the narrow desk and wrote *Marcus Adler, Villa 14, Garden of Allah Hotel, Sunset Boulevard* on a sheet of paper. He looked at his watch: twenty of eight. Just enough time to get home. "Is there a back way out of this place?"

"The door at the end of the hallway leads to a fire escape in the alley."

She yanked his tie askew. "If it's too neat, they'll suspect."

His hand lay on the doorknob, then he looked over his shoulder. "A movie character's name has to be just right, otherwise the whole thing doesn't hang together. There's one I'm working on, but I couldn't find one that fitted. Until now. Arlene suits this character. It's perfect."

"You mean there's going to be an MGM movie about a girl called Arlene?"

"You will be in touch, won't you?"

She waved the paper in front of her face.

When Marcus closed the door with a click, he paused for a moment to memorize the details. He had a hell of a story to tell everyone back at the Garden, and wanted to get it just right.

CHAPTER 7

The TWA *Constellation* gleamed blinding white in the sharp February air as Kathryn's mother pulled her beaver coat tighter around her shoulders. "Where are we?" Francine asked. "Burbank? Look at all those lemon trees past the runway. Should I have brought warmer shoes? If it's this cold here, what will New York be like? I've been living in California so long that my blood is thin. They say it happens, you know."

Kathryn let her mother prattle as they crossed the tarmac. She knew it was only nerves causing her verbal dysentery. *This trip is an olive branch,* she reminded herself. *She's still miffed at not being invited to my wedding.*

Kathryn's protests that it was a last-minute justice of the peace ceremony failed to soften her mother's testiness. So when Kathryn heard about Howard Hughes' inaugural nonstop flight from Los Angeles to New York, she figured she could knock off a couple of canaries with one stone.

She was glad she could give her mother such a special experience, and probably would have still brought her along even if Hughes had returned any one of the myriad calls or telegrams she'd placed over the past two months. But he hadn't, so here they were.

As they reached the bottom of the rollaway stairs, Kathryn heard a woman sneeze behind them.

"Excuse me!" It was Paulette Goddard in a knee-length chinchilla. "I grew up in weather like this, but BRRRR! How we stood it, I don't know!"

"I was just thinking the same thing," Francine said.

Kathryn made a round of introductions when Burgess Meredith, Goddard's husband, joined them, and then he swept them into the plane, saying, "Ladies, I think we'll be more comfortable inside."

The cabin held ten rows of four seats—mustard upholstery on the left, olive green on the right—separated by a spacious aisle. William Powell and Cary Grant were already aboard and sipping martinis.

"Gentlemen!" Kathryn exclaimed, accepting kisses on the cheeks from both men. "It's only ten o'clock in the morning."

"Ah," Powell exclaimed, "but it's one P.M. in New York."

"Also known as martini o'clock," Grant said. "At least it is at the Palm Court in the Plaza, which is good enough, isn't it, *Beatrice . . .*?"

Kathryn's *Reds in the Beds* character was as committed to the Communist cause as she was to drinking her way through every bar south of Mulholland Drive. "You know what I'm looking forward to the most? How New Yorkers are capable of talking about something other than that grubby little book."

William Powell warned her not to get her hopes up, and pointed out that *Reds* was now in the top ten best-selling books nationwide. She threw him a weary look; he took the hint and introduced her and Francine to his wife, Diana, and Veronica Lake.

Lake only had eyes for Alfred Hitchcock, who'd come up the stairs behind Paulette and Burgess. The director preferred his blondes icy, and Lake could play it cool better than anyone. This was her chance to make an impression. Cary Grant was about to start shooting a Nazi spy thriller with him, so she asked him to introduce them and leave the rest up to her.

When the movie-star-handsome face of Bugsy Siegel appeared in the doorway past Hitchcock, Kathryn dropped abruptly into her seat.

Howard Hughes' PR department had worked tirelessly to inform America that TWA could fly from one coast to the other without stopping to refuel, thereby slicing hours off the journey. Much had been made of the celebrity passenger list for this inaugural flight and the catering provided by Dave Chasen from Chasen's Restaurant. But at no time had Siegel's name been mentioned. If it had, Kathryn would not have tried so hard for an invite. How would she avoid him if he wanted to talk about the Flamingo Club?

At the end of the war, Gwendolyn blabbed about the fledgling casino to Siegel in the hopes that he'd muscle his way in and shove Kathryn's boss to the curb. But Wilkerson ran out of money and construction had stopped, so she thought Siegel hadn't taken the bait. Unless, Kathryn now wondered, he was biding his time until Wilkerson was even more desperate. Siegel was seated four rows up and across the aisle. A conversation seemed inevitable.

When Howard Hughes appeared at the front of the cabin, Kathryn waved, trying to catch his eye, but he only stopped to nod at his famous passengers before disappearing into the cockpit.

When an air hostess announced they would be taking off shortly, Francine went rigid as a store window mannequin, gripping the armrest and shutting her eyes.

"You'll be surprised how smooth the takeoff is," Kathryn said.

"Let's talk about that after we've left the ground." Francine swallowed her last word whole.

The four engines revved to life, drowning the cabin in a thunderous roar. The aircraft plunged forward; Francine held her breath. Kathryn slipped her hand over her mother's and gave it a squeeze. "We're going to be here for nine hours," she said over the engine drone. "You'll have to start breathing sometime."

* * *

As soon as Hughes announced they were free to move around the cabin, a number of passengers got up and started chatting, Dom Perignon and beluga caviar in hand. Kathryn stayed in her seat, watching the crew duck in and out of the cockpit. After an hour, she asked a hostess if Mr. Hughes would mind a visit.

"I don't know," she said, "it's mighty crowded in there. The cockpit is built for three men and not much else."

"Maybe just the briefest of chats? I'm writing a four-page spread in the *Hollywood Reporter*."

The girl said she'd see what she could do, and wound her way to the nose of the aircraft, then reappeared shortly and told her Hughes would meet her outside the cockpit in five minutes. That was just enough time for Kathryn to recruit Cary Grant to hold Francine's hand. If anybody could charm her mother's nerves away, it was him.

"But remember," Cary told Kathryn, "he's crashed a couple of planes in the last few years, and it's affected his hearing. You'll have to speak up over all this noise."

Edward G. Robinson and Diana Powell were talking with Veronica Lake, who was sitting next to Bugsy Siegel. When Kathryn saw Siegel peer out the window, she squeezed past Robinson and reached the cockpit door just as Hughes was coming out.

He'd always been tall and gangly, but he was more gaunt than when she saw him last year. Still, he'd retained enough of his baby-face appeal. He seemed pleased to see her, but made no effort to greet her with a kiss. She moved nearer to his good ear.

"So you *are* talking to me, then?" she asked. Hughes frowned, clearly puzzled. "I've been leaving messages and sending telegrams, but you've ignored me."

He shook his head. "Been preoccupied with flying nonstop coast to coast, is all. Until I actually pulled it off, I didn't have time for much else. You're one of many people I've been neglecting, if that makes you feel any better."

Kathryn made a deliberate show of reaching up and smoothing down her hair so he could see the charm bracelet he gave her a few months back. It was a thank-you gift for talking Melody Hope into getting rid of the baby he'd unintentionally fathered; Kathryn had arranged an abortion with a trusted doctor and saw to it that nobody was the wiser. The bracelet was solid silver, with nine letters that spelled out *HOLLYWOOD*. He smiled.

"Did you wear that for my benefit?"

She pulled at the cuff of her houndstooth jacket. "I put it on whenever I wear this. It goes so well."

He glanced at the closed door behind him. "I can't be away from the cockpit too long."

"Do you remember that day in La Rue when my boss pitched you his casino idea?" He nodded. "And do you remember pointing out an FBI agent—"

"Did Hoyt talk you into becoming an informer?"

She snorted. "I wasn't given much of a choice."

He bent at the waist, leaning his ear closer to her. "You'll have to speak up."

"I'm kind of stuck," she half-shouted, and hoped that the *Constellation*'s four engines drowned her out in the main cabin. "I need your help."

Out of the corner of her eye, she caught Veronica Lake's blonde hair catching the cabin light. She was huddled at the front of the cabin with Hitchcock now, paying Kathryn no attention.

"What sort of help?"

"I was hoping you might know someone else who works for them," Kathryn said. "Put in a good word for me, maybe? Pull some strings and get them to back off?"

"I see." Hughes gave no indication that he would—or could—help her out.

"You mentioned how you and he tangled over something during Prohibition," she persisted. "Perhaps if you knew something I could use?"

He shook his head. "We made up. We're good now."

"But you said you hated him."

"That was before I wanted Yvonne de Carlo. She was filming in British Columbia, so I flew up to woo her. This was before the end of the war, so I had to break all kinds of regulations. Got myself in a whole heap of hot water over it. I was sitting in a bar in Prince George —"

"I thought you didn't drink."

"Did I say I was drinking? At any rate, he walked in. We were the only two guys in the place, so he came over, sat down next to me. Turns out I made a bunch of assumptions I shouldn't have about that situation down in San Diego. I apologized and he accepted so graciously that I asked if he could help me out of this jam I was in with the Office of Civilian Defense. He said he'd see what he could do, and he did it. I was wrong about that guy. He's a decent son of a gun."

Kathryn stared at Hughes. *And they think women are fickle.* "So he's the FBI agent with a heart of gold?"

He grinned. "Your Mr. Hoyt ain't all bad."

"He's not my Mr. Hoyt!"

"I'll see what I can do." A twinkle lit up his eyes. "Can *you* do something for *me*?"

Kathryn nodded.

"Do you know Lana Turner?"

"Not personally. Why?" He raised his eyebrows as though to say, *Why do you think?*

Bette Davis had co-chaired the Hollywood Canteen with John Garfield, and he had just finished filming *The Postman Always Rings Twice* at MGM with Lana. "I know somebody who knows somebody."

He smiled the goofy smile of a teenager in love. "See what you can do." He swiveled toward the cockpit door, then turned back. "Your boss, do you know where he is? Today, I mean."

"Should I?"

Hughes took a step closer to her, his mouth now inches from her face. "According to a well-placed source" — he jutted his chin toward Ben Siegel — "your boss is meeting with Meyer Lansky."

Meyer Lansky was as notorious a mobster as Lucky Luciano, but he rarely left the East Coast. "Meeting with Lansky? For what?"

"He needs a million bucks to finish his Flamingo Club and he's gone to the mob for it."

Kathryn pressed her hands against the wall behind her, feeling the engine throb through her fingers and up her arms to encase her ribcage. "Why would he do such a thing?" She spoke softly, but he must have read her lips.

"Because he's desperate."

"He's nuts!"

"Desperate and nuts are not mutually exclusive."

CHAPTER 8

The week leading up to the Academy Awards ceremony was always one of the busiest of the year for upscale department stores like Bullocks Wilshire. With so many hats, furs, jewelry, shoes and matching handbags in demand, the store was a frenzy of activity—until the day after the awards, when it became as deserted as a ghost town.

Gwendolyn absently polished her counter's glass top, lulled into the slow rhythm of post-Oscar season. The perfume and lingerie girls had already drifted back to their own stations after an hour of dissecting the Best Actress upset and speculating about why Joan Crawford didn't show up to collect her Oscar for *Mildred Pierce*. There was nothing left for Gwendolyn to do but daydream.

On slow days such as these, Gwendolyn fantasized about her own store. In her mind, she painted the walls pale coral with cream trim and installed matching light fixtures. She designed the signage—currently she favored a typeface she'd seen in a *Life* magazine article about the Paris subway. She calculated the balance of styles she'd sell—fifty percent formalwear, thirty percent daywear, and twenty percent sportswear; and deciding whether or not to carry shoes (no), perfume (maybe), and gloves (definitely).

In her daydream, Oliver's friend had identified the lighthouse in the postcard and she'd tracked down Linc. He'd written back and enclosed her four thousand, and she'd found the most darling little store on Hollywood Boulevard where the rent was affordable, and the landlord was a doll.

But in reality, it had been four months since Oliver wrote to his pal, and he still hadn't heard back. Oliver told her not to give up—"He could have taken a missionary post in Africa or China"—but Gwendolyn's candle of hope had long since burned out.

She returned the polishing cloth to its drawer and pulled out the miniature feather duster. The necklaces and pendants in her counter were high-quality paste that weighed less than their authentic cousins upstairs, so dusting them still required an especially light touch. She was sliding open the back wall of her cabinet when she heard the Wilshire door's brass handle hit the marble wall with a crack that echoed down the central hall. A dozen heads shot in the direction of the sound to see who'd make such a fuss, but only Gwendolyn's ducked out of sight.

She hadn't seen Bugsy Siegel since the day peace in the Pacific was declared. When the news came over the radio that the Japanese had surrendered, Gwendolyn was in the middle of laying out a false trail intended to keep Siegel off Linc's tracks once and for all. She made a break for it amid the clamor, but Siegel caught up to her. Cornered, she pulled out her only ace: Kathryn's boss' plan to build a casino in Las Vegas. She thought for sure he'd take the bait and leave her alone, but it looked like he was coming for her.

Still crouched behind her counter, she heard knuckles rapping on the glass. She arranged her face into the neutral façade that shop clerks adopt whenever a prospective client is on the verge of choosing something inappropriate. She stood up and feigned surprise.

"Oh! Hello."

With his fists perched on his hips, he scowled at her. She'd seen this expression several times before, but the one he wore now seemed hesitant, as though he was still mulling over his options.

"Are you here to buy some jewelry?" she asked. "Because if you are, this here merchandise is phony. The classy stuff is upstairs."

He was having trouble standing still, almost as though he was in a stiff breeze. Benjamin Siegel was known for his meticulous appearance. His obsidian black hair was always combed with the same precision he tied his necktie, wore his suit, and chose his shoes. His tiepin always complemented his cufflinks, and his pinkie ring was buffed to a high shine. But not today. The gunmetal gray suit was neatly pressed, but his tie was a garish raspberry, and he'd pinned it with gold, not silver. His nails were ragged and he needed a shave.

He's drunk. In public.

Gwendolyn took a tiny step backwards, but immediately saw her error as Siegel leaned on her counter and slapped the glass with both palms.

"I sent an associate to Uruguay," he said. "Specifically to San Gregorio, where a pathetic excuse for a lodging house called Hotel Los Medanos sits on Lago Rincón del Bonete. And guess what he found—or didn't."

Gwendolyn lowered her voice. "I told you that day in the Zephyr Room—"

"What you told me," Siegel cut in, his voice now catching the attention of everyone within a hundred feet, "was that you'd bet your last dime that I'd find Linc in that hotel. Guess what. Nobody at Hotel Los *Mierda* has ever heard of Lincoln Tattler. So I'm here to collect." He laid his hand on the counter, palm open. "Your last dime, if you please."

She studied his palm and decided that even drunk, Ben Siegel was far too aware of his image to risk doing anything drastic.

"Surely Linc was just a tiny cog in your machinery," she whispered. "Why are you so keen to track him down?"

"Everything's falling apart." His words came out slurred as his eyes lost their focus. "My casino in the desert."

"Billy Wilkerson's Flamingo?"

"It's *my* place, y'understand? They'll have my head if it doesn't work out."

"I seriously doubt Linc can help you with that."

Siegel nodded slowly. "Oh, he can help, all right. And he knows why. Tell me where he is. I ain't leaving till you do."

"You think he sends me regular telegrams?"

Siegel licked his lips. "Yeah, I do."

"That ocean liner schedule and map of Uruguay were all I had to go on." Gwendolyn glanced around, hoping someone would come to her rescue, but everybody steered clear of her counter.

She caught sight of her boss, but he was keeping his distance. Her hands started to shake. As casually as she could, she started to fan herself with the ostrich feathers in her duster and forced herself not to blink. "If the people at that hotel never heard of him, then I'm all out of guesses."

"I don't believe a single word coming out of that luscious kisser of yours."

"You're Ben Siegel," she said, forcing the words out. Her voice sounded raw and guttural, which she hoped would work in her favor. "I hardly think it would be in my interest to lie to" — she almost called him *the biggest mobster on the West Coast,* but thought better of it— "the likes of you."

He shot out his left hand and gripped her wrist; his fingernails dug into her flesh. "You're coming with me."

"I DON'T—" She stopped when she heard her own voice bounce off the marble wall. "This is where I work. Please don't—"

He stepped around the corner of her counter. "I don't give a pile of pigeon shit where we are."

"Please don't." She tried to tug her arm away, but he jerked her toward him.

"We're taking a walk."

Without thinking, she pulled her arm up, hoping to twist herself free. He grunted, went to grab her other arm, missed it, and instead caught a finger on the sleeve of her jacket. A seam ripped. She used a hip to push him away. The maneuver caught him by surprise, giving her just enough time to bend his arm back. It worked. He let go of her wrist, which sent her hand crashing into the counter.

—

Everything blurred together. A button from his jacket popped off and skittered across the floor. Her gold-plated bracelet broke loose. Her elbow brushed against something hard, then a pinprick of light hit her eye. Her elbow felt it again. A flash of metal. Something dropped to the floor. It hit the marble, dense and heavy. An explosion, deafening. The stink of gunpowder. Another sound — shattering glass. Then screaming. High-pitched, hysterical. Running feet. Someone called "Gwendolyn!" Was it Mr. Dewberry? She couldn't be sure.

Abruptly, both her wrists were free. She pitched back and broke into a sprint, soon passing through the Saddle Shop and into Menswear. She kept on running until she reached the wall, then jumped behind an elaborate display of neckties and slumped to the floor.

She'd barely caught her breath when she heard her boss clear his throat.

Herman Dewberry was a natty sort of man, particular in his grooming, loyal to the store above all else, but kindhearted. He peered at her through circular horn-rimmed spectacles.

"My dear Miss Gwendolyn!" He knelt down beside her. "Are you hurt?"

"Just a little shaken. Is everyone okay? That gunshot and all that shattering glass. I'm so very sorry. I didn't ask him to come here. I'm horrified that I made such a scene."

"Siegel was doing all the scene-making."

She let Dewberry help her to her feet. "Is he still here?"

"As soon as you started running in one direction, he headed in the other." Dewberry held his fingertips to his lips, trying not to laugh. "The floors were polished last night. He fell flat on his hiney. He was mortified. So red in the face!"

Gwendolyn grimaced.

"Well, it's nothing you have to worry about anymore."

"I'm fired? I swear, Mr. Dewberry, I didn't ask him here—"

Dewberry patted Gwendolyn's hand and told her to hush. "I was coming to see you just as he appeared." He smiled at her like a patient uncle. "I have some news."

"You do?"

"Remember when you started here, I said that we require all our staff to work the floor before we promote them to more responsible positions?"

Gwendolyn nodded, feeling a wave of hope.

"We've had two resignations this week in Formalwear. One was a sales clerk."

The wave of hope ebbed. This was hardly a promotion. Same job, different floor.

"We also need someone with superior dressmaking skills who can tailor the couture in the Louis XVI Room."

Gwendolyn pressed her hands together.

"You can start tomorrow."

She grabbed Mr. Dewberry's hand and shook it vigorously until he made her stop. "I could start right now!"

CHAPTER 9

Marcus watched the end of Oliver's cigarette glow in the fading twilight. He listened to his boyfriend drag deeply on it, then directed his attention to the log cabin nestled among a thicket of eucalyptus trees in Mandeville Canyon. He fidgeted with the house key in his pocket to distract himself from the tension between them.

Oliver crushed his cigarette butt into the dirt and finally broke the silence. "Damn it, Marcus, it wasn't my fault. It was a very tense meeting. Breen was stomping around all crazy and shouting, 'We need to regain control of this industry!' How were we supposed to know he didn't read that stupid book until now? You should've heard him. 'We are the custodians of public morals. It is *our* job to protect the innocent from subversive influences. This outrageous book has undercut our work, and we must take evasive action to maintain our authority.' Then he insisted we come up with ideas on how to counter all those insinuations."

Marcus whipped around. "But did you have to suggest a Production Code refresher course?"

The Production Code was a set of "guidelines" the studios had to follow if they wanted their films approved for distribution.

"It was the first thing that came into my head." Oliver flung his arms wide. "And I never said anything about mandatory."

Earlier that afternoon, Marcus had suffered through a spit-and-fury rant while his boss shook a letter in his face informing him that MGM was to be the first studio subjected to the Breen Office refresher course.

Marcus' ears were still ringing.

"We are all too aware of what we're not allowed to show!" He started counting on his fingers. "No profanity. No nudity. No ridicule of the clergy. No drugs. No perversion. We don't need to be sent back to Breen Office School."

At the end of the path that led to the cabin, a hand-painted sign was just barely illuminated by a low-wattage bulb: *Hermit's Hideaway.* "Come on," he told Oliver, "Quentin will already be two drinks ahead."

"We need to—"

"You can join us inside, or you can stand out here and hope for a taxi. But seeing as how we're way out in the boonies, I wouldn't count on it."

Marcus waited for a moment, but heard only the forlorn hoot of a solitary owl. He trudged fifty feet up the path before he stopped.

As he stood alone in the semidarkness hearing himself breathe through his teeth, he faced for the first time the possibility that Oliver was the thief at the Garden.

Marcus' pie tin had gone the way of his egg platter, and Gwendolyn was missing a pair of good shoes. Bertie's childhood photo album and Trevor's favorite cufflinks were gone, too.

Marcus didn't want to believe Oliver was the culprit, but things had begun to disappear when Oliver started spending more time at the Garden after the war ended. All this was circumstantial evidence, but still.

"Aren't you going in?" Oliver's voice was just over Marcus' shoulder.

"I owe you an apology."

Oliver nudged him with a playful punch. "You're a bigwig at the studio now. Jobs like that come with pressure—"

"These thefts at the Garden of Allah, they haven't stopped."

—

"Kay told me she left a novel out by the pool last weekend and the next morning it was gone. She all but accused me of stealing it — as if I would read *Forever Amber* — and said she and Bill were thinking of checking out."

The moonlight made Oliver's hazel eyes paler than they actually were. "What?" he asked.

The woods seemed unnervingly quiet; even the owl was shocked into silence.

"Nothing," Marcus said, turning to go.

"I know your 'nothing' face, and that's not it. You've got something on your mind, so tell me — wait. You think *I* have been stealing — "

"No."

"You wanna go back to my place and look around?" Oliver demanded. "Maybe you'll luck out and find your pie tin and Bertie's scarf."

Marcus reached out, but Oliver pulled back. "It's that book! It's got everyone so damned paranoid. Even at the studio. Everyone's so suspicious."

"I don't care about everyone at the studio." Oliver charged back the way they'd come.

"Please, honey, don't go." Marcus debated the wisdom of running after Oliver. They fought so infrequently that he wasn't sure if Oliver was the *Let's talk it out* type, or more of a *We'll talk after I've calmed down*. He watched Oliver disappear down the path before he headed inside.

* * *

Hermit's Hideaway was the homo bar everybody had heard of but nobody had seen. So when Quentin Luckett called Marcus and asked him and Oliver to meet him there, Marcus had laughed and said it might be easier to hunt down Bigfoot. Even when Quentin sent an address with an elaborate sequence of directions, Marcus and Oliver were skeptical, but there it was, a large cabin set two hundred feet off Mandeville Canyon Road.

It was a simple rectangular room that stretched sixty feet back with a bar of roughly hewn logs running most of its length. The heads of dead animals mounted on mahogany plaques — moose, bears, coyotes, deer — stared down at the patrons with glassy eyes.

The place threw Marcus back to the summer he was thirteen, when his family took a cabin at Yellow Creek Lake, a couple of hours east of McKeesport. His dad was intent on taking his eldest son into the woods to hunt wild turkey, ruffed grouse, and white-tailed, but Marcus was horrified at the thought of killing animals for sport. He tried hard to please his father, but the best he could do was to wing a young turkey. Looking back, things were never the same between them. Assaulted by that awful memory and unnerved by his fight with Oliver, Marcus turned back to the door.

"Where are you going?"

Quentin worked at Paramount, where he analyzed novels and magazine short stories for screen potential. He was the only person Marcus knew whose instincts for a successful story were sharper than his own. They'd done each other a couple of good turns during the war, and had kept up the friendship.

Quentin came charging around the Paul Bunyan cocktail tables. "I thought you'd never get here! I don't know how I could've made those instructions any clearer."

Marcus assured him that his directions weren't the problem as Quentin pulled him through the crowd, which was nothing like the smartly attired writers, costumers, and set designers Marcus usually socialized with. The men at this bar were barrel-chested, sturdy-legged, mountain-man types.

They arrived at a table where several drinks were already lined up. Quentin placed one in Marcus' hand. As far as he could tell in the low lighting, it was a light yellow color. "What is this?" Marcus asked.

"Smirnoff with a splash of grapefruit juice."

He wasn't a big fan of grapefruit, but at that moment he was an avid devotee of anything more potent than sacrificial wine. Vodka had been around before the war, but Marcus had only ever seen it at Bublichki, the Russian restaurant a few blocks from the Garden. But then Russia became the US' ally during the war and suddenly the name Smirnoff was everywhere.

He downed a bracing mouthful. He was taking a second gulp when a tall gentleman approached them. He wore a full dark beard and the complacent smile of someone who knows a secret. Marcus looked at the stranger, then at Quentin, who wore a similar smile.

The light in the bar burned mostly from wall sconces positioned at shoulder height. They were carved out of thick branches and fitted with bulbs no brighter than the one lighting the sign out front. Marcus studied the man's face until he gasped in recognition.

Quentin clamped a hand across Marcus' mouth. "Zip it."

Trevor Bergin was one of MGM's top male heartthrobs. His face on a magazine cover guaranteed vigorous sales; gossip columns had documented his marriage to frequent co-star Melody Hope since the day they met. MGM's PR department made sure nobody outside the industry knew it was a sham, but even they didn't know that Trevor's real love was Quentin.

Marcus touched Trevor's beard. It scratched like a Brillo pad.

Trevor lowered his voice to a whisper. "Not one person has recognized me!"

Alla Nazimova had once remarked to Marcus that anonymity was the most precious thing in the world once it was gone. The only place Trevor failed to raise an eyebrow was at the Garden, which was why, Marcus guessed, he and Melody had moved in, despite the fact that they could afford a Beverly Hills mansion.

Marcus cast around the bar, looking into the hopeful faces of the men clustered at the tables. *I used to look like that. Desperate to connect with a kindred soul, if only for an hour.* But then Oliver came along, and he knew those panting fumbles with nameless strangers was behind him.

"I need to go," he said.

"You just got here!" Quentin protested. "And I have news. You're going to die when I tell—"

"Oliver and I just had a terrible fight." Marcus gulped down his drink. *Of course he's not the thief. What was I even thinking?* "I need to find him. Set things right."

"You're going to want to hear this!" Trevor singsonged.

Marcus started backing away. "I'll call you." He wound his way through the lingering stares. *He can't be far down the canyon. If I run, I'll catch him before he finds a taxi.*

He was only a step or two from the door when it swung open. A flashlight flicked on and a shrill whistle scratched the air. A gruff voice barked out, "EVERYBODY FREEZE! THIS IS A RAID!"

The only sound in the place was Dinah Shore on a radio somewhere singing "Laughing On the Outside."

"HANDS IN THE AIR! YOU'RE ALL UNDER ARREST!"

Thirty pair of hands went up as seven policemen piled into the bar. Marcus was shoved backwards into a knot of men who were a dozen years older than him.

One of them muttered, "I did not survive the Battle of the Somme, the polio epidemic, and thirteen years of Prohibition to put up with this shit." He stepped forward. "ARRESTED?" he shouted. "THE HELL WE ARE!"

The cop reached him in two strides. "What did you just say to me?"

"We're out here in the middle of nowhere, hurting nobody, and disturbing no-one."

In half the time it takes to draw a breath, the cop raised his billy club and struck the man with a hoarse grunt. As the veteran dropped to the floor, the cop faced the crowd. "Any other objections?"

Marcus knelt down.

The cop told him, "Leave him be."

Blood was seeping from the man's ear into the sawdust on the floor. "He's out cold. He may even be dead."

"What's one dead faggot, more or less?"

"He needs medical attention."

"You wanna join him?" The cop jabbed Marcus' shoulder hard enough to knock him on his ass. "Listen up, *ladies.* This is what's going to happen."

While the cop described how they'd be marched to the vice squad paddy wagons outside, Marcus groped for the man's wrist. He found a pulse—weak, but regular. Marcus backed away when he spotted the cop raise his revolver.

As they were herded out of the cabin and down the path toward the vehicles, Marcus heard more than one guy sob. They all knew what lay ahead. They'd be ID'd, fingerprinted, booked on some trumped-up charge, held overnight, then released in the morning to find their names and addresses in the newspaper, heralding public humiliation, eviction, and the loss of their jobs. As he climbed into a cramped wagon reeking with piss and vomit, Marcus thought of Oliver and took solace in the thought that the only man who'd ever made him feel safe had escaped what was shaping up to be a night in hell.

* * *

Marcus' behind ached from the cold concrete seeping through his gabardine pants. The holding cell was bigger than Marcus expected, but with nothing to sit on, the hours crawled by.

The only excitement had occurred outside the lockup on the west side of downtown LA when a scuffle broke out. Desperate to avoid identification, one of the men made a break for it. A fight erupted between the homos and the cops. The cops won, of course, but not before Marcus' favorite watch disappeared.

"What time is it now?" he whispered to Quentin.

"Three o'clock," Quentin replied. "How long can they keep us here?"

"Long enough to make sure the papers spell our names right."

Quentin's head sank into his hands. "I really liked my job; I'm going to miss it."

"Let's not focus on that." Marcus rolled onto his right hip and faced Quentin. "You were about to divulge some big secret."

Quentin's head shot up, his mouth curled into a Cheshire cat smile. He checked the slumbering figures around them for potential eavesdroppers. "I figured out who wrote *Reds in the Beds.*"

"Are you sure?"

Quentin slanted to his right until their shoulders were touching. "Clifford Wardell."

Marcus tilted his head back as he absorbed the name. Wardell was his counterpart at Paramount, and Quentin's boss. He was also an ex-yellow journalist Marcus had discovered snooping around an all-homo party at George Cukor's house years and years ago. He was one of the slimiest toads Marcus had encountered in Hollywood.

He stared at the mottled ceiling. "What did you find? A handwritten draft of the manuscript?"

"No, but close. The first time I read it, there was something that niggled at me, but I couldn't work it out. So I read it again until I found a phrase that the NJN studio boss says to his security chief when he finds out that August Vail takes a powder in the middle of his doughboys picture. He says, 'I don't care if it takes fifty-five flatfoots from Farmington Falls, get me that goddamned Commie!'"

The phrase didn't sound familiar to Marcus, but then again, it could have come up toward the end of the book when Marcus was paying scant attention.

"So?"

"That's what Wardell says whenever he gets mad and starts throwing his weight around. So I went snooping around his desk one night, and found a letter from his mother."

"Wardell has a mother? Human?"

"Ol' Mother Wardell hails from Farmington Falls in Maine. Turns out she's hard up for cash and was begging her son to let her have a grand, which she knows he can afford now that he's swimming in money on account of his—and I quote—'recent literary success.'"

"Jesus!" Marcus sat up. "So it *is* him?"

"What I don't get is why that cunning little prick would include a phrase he's known for. It's a dead giveaway."

Marcus slapped Quentin's chest. "Because he *wants* to be found out. That slimy weasel wants the notoriety of being the mystery author of the big bestseller. When it does get out, I bet he'll act all indignant and betrayed, but you just know he's eating it up." A couple of the slumbering figures stirred. "What are you going to do?"

"I just discovered all this last night—look out!"

A burly silhouette appeared at the steel bars. It moved to the door and shoved a key into the lock. The captives in the holding pen shifted uneasily as the door opened and the warden stepped forward. "Marcus Adler. Identify yourself."

Marcus felt his face blanch as he climbed to his feet and followed the cop down a silent corridor into a bright room where the sergeant on duty sat at a desk raised on a platform twelve inches from the floor—just enough to intimidate.

He had that weathered face of a foot patrolman who'd come up the ranks the hard way. He studied Marcus from behind the flinty mask of stoicism. "Adler?"

Marcus nodded.

"You're free to go."

Marcus felt himself falling backwards and had to catch himself.

"Did you come alone?"

Panic fogged his brain. *Is it better if I came alone? Will I incriminate them?* The desk sergeant lowered a typed list of names. *If they're letting me go, will Quentin and Trevor get released, too?* "Point them out. You got five seconds."

Marcus ran his finger down the list and stopped at Quentin Luckett and Trevor Bergin. The warden disappeared. Marcus asked if someone had posted his bail, but the sergeant didn't budge. When the guys appeared, blinking at the bright lights, Marcus told them they were free to go. The three men left the building without a word and vaulted down the granite steps to the dark and deserted street.

"What just happened?" Trevor asked. "Will our names be in the papers?"

"That was the damndest thing." Marcus glanced back at the police station. "But I'm sure as hell not going back to ask questions."

Trevor picked at his false beard, but Quentin slapped his hand away. "Leave that on until you get home. We need a taxi."

"At three in the morning?"

"We'll never find one," Marcus said. "There's an all-nighter down on Sixth. Coffee and donuts are on me."

CHAPTER 10

Gwendolyn slid her needle into a pincushion and straightened out a heap of pink tulle, then held the outfit to her body as she turned to the full-length mirror to gauge her handiwork. The Pasadena matron who ordered the dress was ten years and twenty pounds past getting away with it, but Gwendolyn had used all the magic tricks in her top hat, and she was satisfied it was as good as it would ever be.

Gwendolyn had been working in Bullocks' couture fitting room for six weeks, surrounded by silks from Thailand, cashmere from India, and lace from France. Now that the war was over and the textile mills were spluttering back into production, the variety of materials was thrilling. She was folding the tulle into a Bullocks presentation box when Mr. Dewberry burst into the room, his hands clasped in front of him.

"I have an important job and I want you to—"

The door opened behind him and a tiny woman with the poise of an Amazon entered. Blunt black bangs sliced across her forehead above horn-rimmed spectacles tinted dark blue. Around her neck hung pearls the size of gumdrops.

She held a knee-length suit of shantung in a striking shade of blue—cerulean was Gwendolyn's guess, but the light in the formal yet cozy fitting room was designed to flatter the customer over the garment. Floor-to-ceiling cream draperies covered all six walls, bouncing gentle light onto the women who scrutinized their bodies in the three-part mirror across from the dressmaker's workbench.

Gwendolyn did her best to make her clients feel comfortable, even though they were usually peeled down to their combinations.

The woman strode toward the center of the room. "Really, Herman! Couldn't you see my hands were full?"

Gwendolyn held her smile in place and prayed that Miss Head didn't recognize her. The memory of that awful night at Mercedes de Acosta's house had retreated into the mists of a half-forgotten life she no longer lived.

"I'm sorry, Edie," Mr. Dewberry said, taking the suit from her, "I thought you were right behind me. This is Miss Gwendolyn, our most expert seamstress."

Edith Head scrutinized Gwendolyn with a lightning-fast down-up-down. Gwendolyn caught a flicker of approval behind the tinted lenses as Dewberry laid the garment out on the table. It was a two-piece suit with a collarless jacket and three-quarter-length sleeves. As Gwendolyn examined the material, Dewberry scuttled out of the room.

"I shall leave you ladies to it."

Gwendolyn groped awkwardly for something to talk about as the woman donned and zipped up the suit. "I'm surprised you need our services," she said, gathering her pins.

Head let out a surprisingly girlish laugh. "Knowing what needs to be done and knowing how to do it at the level I expect are two different beasts."

Gwendolyn gently prodded her customer's arms toward the ceiling. "But you're Edith Head!"

"The *Blue Dahlia* premiere is coming up and I wanted a dress the same shade of blue they've used in the poster. But do you think I could find anything even close? I was complaining to Herman, and he said he had just the thing. So I asked for you."

Gwendolyn dropped her chalk. It bounced across the carpet and disappeared under the table. "Me?"

"You altered a dress for Dolores Hope last week."

"The black sheath inlaid with pearls?"

Before Gwendolyn handed it to the valet for delivery to Bob Hope's wife, she'd made a rough pattern, which was now on her living room floor in preparation for a duplicate.

"I commented on it and she said Bullocks Wilshire has this marvelous girl doing alterations." Head pretended to fiddle with a gold button on her jacket. "You're the girl Bugsy Siegel pawed when he came in drunk, aren't you?"

Gwendolyn closed her eyes. "You heard about that?"

"Is it true the gun went off?" Miss Head whispered. "That must have been *awful!*"

Gwendolyn had heard that Edith Head was as imperious as she looked, but the frowning woman with brows crinkled in concern wasn't what she'd expected.

"Not the best day I've ever had." Gwendolyn went to duck behind Head but was halted by a penetrating look.

"What *are* you wearing?"

Gwendolyn was both flattered and intimidated. She was wearing a scoop-neck dress made of Egyptian cotton she'd dyed a deep teal and accented with pale crêpe around the neck and cuffs. A few months ago, she'd spent a particularly bleak night doubting that Chez Gwendolyn would ever happen, and so to help bolster her spirits, she decided to make an entire new wardrobe for herself comprised of exactly the sort of thing she dreamed of selling in her shop.

"It's something I made myself."

"So you're capable of more than just tailoring?" Miss Head nodded appreciatively as she fingered the tassels Gwendolyn had fashioned out of leftover material and sewn into the neckline. "I could get you a job at Paramount."

The last thing Gwendolyn wanted was to trigger this woman's memory of the night at de Acosta's when someone ran her disastrous *Gone with the Wind* screen test for a titillated audience. She moved around to Head's right arm and tugged at the sleeve. "Thank you, but I'm happy enough here."

"Happy . . . *enough?*" Head pursed her lips. "If I had your skill, I'd open my own salon."

When Gwendolyn drew back with surprise, the woman's eyes widened behind her tinted glasses. "Dolores Hope isn't the only one who's mentioned you. I don't know why, but I had a hunch."

"My plans are barely more than a dream, really."

"Don't underestimate dreams. This whole town's built on them. Does Herman know?"

"Mr. Dewberry?" The chalk nearly slipped from Gwendolyn's grasp again. "Please don't tell him. I'd hate for him to think I'm unhappy here, after everything he's done for me."

Miss Head took Gwendolyn by the chin. "Hollywood is one of the few places where an ambitious girl can fulfill her dreams, but it's still a man's game, and us girls must stick together. Don't you worry about Herman." Gwendolyn expected her to let go of her chin, but instead Miss Head squinted. "Have we met before? You look familiar."

"I don't think so."

"Where do you live?"

"The Garden of Allah."

"Oh, so you're part of that crowd? I imagine you know Trevor Bergin." Gwendolyn admitted that she did. "Would you do me a favor?"

"If I can," Gwendolyn said coolly.

"There's talk at Paramount of remaking Valentino's *The Sheik*, but only if they can borrow him from MGM. I would *kill* to do all those flowing desert robes and belly dancer getups." She let out a snort. "I need a change from pencil skirts and backless ball gowns."

"I know what his first question will be," Gwendolyn said. "Is there a finished script yet?"

"I'm not sure." Miss Head shivered. "I suppose I'll have to talk to that slimy Wardell character."

"Not necessarily," Gwendolyn said. "I know someone — a friend of a friend — who works under Wardell."

"I'd do anything to avoid talking to that awful man."

"Awful doesn't begin to cover it," Gwendolyn said, then caught herself.

—

74

Miss Head slipped back into her own outfit, then pulled a comb from her purse and fixed her austere bangs. "What did you mean? Awful doesn't begin to cover what?"

"Just that he's despicable, from what I hear."

Miss Head grunted. "Or do you mean because he wrote *Reds in the Beds*?"

Gwendolyn slumped. "You know about that?"

"I do now." She picked up her handbag and hung it in the crook of her elbow. "You didn't tell me anything I hadn't already figured out for myself. All you did was provide confirmation."

Gwendolyn laid the cerulean blue suit out on the worktable, smoothing and resmoothing the fabric.

"I need this at the studio no later than noon tomorrow," Miss Head said, mercifully changing the subject. "I trust that won't be a problem?"

Gwendolyn was going to have to work all night.

"Not at all."

* * *

It was just after one in the morning when Gwendolyn heard the music, but she couldn't quite make out the tune—just a brass section blasting out a sassy beat. She laid down her needle and thread and stepped into the empty Louis XVI Room.

Mame kissed a buyer from out of town . . .

It was that song from Rita Hayworth's new movie, *Gilda*.

The crystal chandeliers were dark, but four tall windows let in enough light from the streetlamps on Wilshire to allow Gwendolyn to pick her way around the mannequins and love seats. As she entered the elevator foyer, she could make out the music more clearly, and followed it.

That kiss burned Chicago down . . .

The only light on the floor was coming from Herman Dewberry's office. Through the frosted glass she could make out movement. But who would dare go into Mr. Dewberry's office without him? She crept forward.

She cut a wide arc around display cases filled with hats and scarves and riding gloves to take cover behind a shoulder-high cabinet of black leather boots. She peeked out and looked in through Mr. Dewberry's open office door.

Put the blame on Mame!

Fussy and fastidious little Mr. Dewberry was parading around his office in a floor-length ball gown! Its bateau neckline scooped across his chest from one shoulder tip to the other and cinched down into a princess bodice before sweeping out into a very full skirt that trailed the floor. But that wasn't the problem.

The bold print was atrocious: ivy leaves that were too large, too green, and repeated too often lay against a background of pale rose. It took a vibrant woman like Rita Hayworth or Betty Hutton to carry off something like that, not a diminutive half-pint like Herman Dewberry. Around his waist he'd tied a sash as blue as the Pacific — a pretty color, but it spoiled the whole effect.

He was a man of impeccable taste. How could his infallible eye have failed him? She ventured another peek as Dewberry executed a pirouette, his dress swishing past the corner of his desk, and landed in her direct line of vision.

Their eyes met. Her boss inhaled sharply. After an agonizing moment, he lifted his foot and went to kick the door shut, but his shoe caught his hem and he stumbled to the floor with a dull thud.

Gwendolyn shot forward to help him up, but he cut her off.

"Please don't!" he whispered hoarsely. "I'm humiliated. You have no idea."

"Mr. Dewberry!" Gwendolyn chuckled, hoping to set him at ease. "I'll see you your humiliation, and raise you a mortification that you can't possibly hope to match."

He raised his eyes to meet hers, his face paler than eggshells.

"Maybe one day I'll tell you the story," she said. "But for now, let's get you off the floor."

He took her hand and hauled himself up, turning away from her to marshal his wits. The row of hooks down the back of his dress were unfastened, showing an expanse of lightly hairy skin that shone with perspiration.

He mumbled, "I assumed I was alone."

"Miss Head needs her outfit by noon. I have to work all night." She noticed an array of outfits spread out on his conference table, and recognized them from the display mannequins. "What are all these?"

He began to breathe heavily through his nose. She waited for him to regain his dignity. "There is a bar I go to," he said, pushing each word out like a rock. "It's for gentlemen — such as — myself. You're not expected to dress up, but the first time you do, they call it debutanting. Everyone makes a big fuss, and so . . . ." He ended with a leaden sigh.

"So you want to look your best," Gwendolyn finished for him.

"Uh-huh."

"And these are your choices?"

When he let his hands flop to his sides, she realized for the first time he was wearing opera gloves, the same shade as the sash. She crossed over to the table and waited for him to join her.

"Well," she started gently, "forget the white one. That's the wrong color for you altogether."

"I know." He ran his finger down the skirt. "But it's silk."

"And horizontal stripes? Don't even think of it."

He picked up a bright blue suit like the one she was working on for Edith Head. "I love this."

"And if you had Miss Head's figure, it'd probably love you."

He sighed. "I figured that as soon as I tried it on. I'm surprised I didn't rip it."

She faced him squarely. "Which brings us to what you're wearing."

"What do you think?" He winced.

"It's just a little . . . too much, is all," Gwendolyn said. "And I don't know that opera gloves work with it."

"But they hide my hairy forearms. Plus, the satin feels so nice."

"I won't argue with that."

As Gwendolyn examined her boss' outfit, she took care to avoid meeting him in the eye.

"Here's what I would do," she said. "Lose the sash. It accentuates the waist, which is the opposite of what you want. So we'll broaden the shoulders like Adrian did for Joan Crawford." She tapped her chin. "I do like the rose background. Very pretty. And the ivy, too, but the print is far too bold."

"It's the closest I could find to what I had in my head."

"It shouldn't be hard to track down that shade of pink, then we could stencil an ivy design onto it, but more subtle, like batik. Apparently the Javanese are masters at it. I'm sure we can dig up some textbook to show us how it's done. Then I'll draft a pattern that will camouflage your more masculine traits."

With the hesitance of a panicky kitten, he found the courage to look at her. "You'd make a dress? Especially for me?"

"Mr. Dewberry," she said quietly, "every debutant deserves to look his very best."

CHAPTER 11

Kathryn's desk sat against the western wall of the huge office that housed most of the dozens of people needed to put out the *Hollywood Reporter* every day. Even sitting at the edge of the room, though, gave her little respite from the flotilla of typewriters, telephones, and conversations that were constantly harpooned across the room.

The day the cacophony became too much came late in spring when Wallace Reed, the producer of *Kraft Music Hall*, called to let her know that Bing Crosby had decided not to renew his contract and would be leaving the show in four weeks' time. Yes, that was definite. No, he didn't know who would replace Crosby. No, he couldn't confirm that the show would continue.

Kathryn thanked Reed and dropped the receiver onto its cradle. She needed to think through her options, but all the clacking and jangling conspired to drown her thoughts.

She grabbed her handbag and had almost reached reception as one of the elevator doors slid open. Ben Siegel stepped out. He wore an impeccable dark blue pinstriped suit and a homburg with a matching band.

Kathryn ducked back inside the newsroom and pressed herself against the wall as she watched his shadow cross the linoleum and head up the corridor to Wilkerson's office. She waited another thirty seconds, then darted into the reception area.

Behind the desk was a sharp-eyed honey blonde named Cassandra. Until last year she'd been a waitress in a Harvey House restaurant two hundred miles outside Kansas City. She'd spent five years watching folks heading west until she decided she "oughta go see for myself what all this California fuss was about." Within two weeks she had a job at the *Reporter*, and her five years' experience of sizing people up during a forty-five-minute whistle stop left Kathryn wondering how they'd ever gotten along without her.

Before Kathryn even opened her mouth, Cassandra popped her gum and said, "Did you know he's been coming here twice a week? Sometimes more. Since February."

The last time Kathryn saw Siegel was on that TWA flight to New York back in February when Howard Hughes told her about the million-dollar loan her boss had secured from the mob. She'd managed to avoid him on that flight — mainly because her mother got drunk on whiskey sours and needed help getting off the plane. Kathryn hoped that this million bucks of mob money that Meyer Lansky had loaned to Wilkerson meant that Siegel had been carved out of the picture.

Kathryn started strumming the counter. "How have I missed that?"

"Until recently, it's been after hours," Cassandra said. "Every time Wilkerson expects him, he asks me to stay late in case they need someone to run out and pick up burgers or booze. But the last couple of times he's just shown up here, like he did just now."

She glanced up the corridor.

"Whatever they're working on, it's not going well. Last week, I could hear them — it wasn't quite yelling. It was one notch down, which is probably sensible because the last person you should yell at is Ben Siegel, right?"

The *Kraft Music Hall* news and this Siegel development made Kathryn feel hemmed in on all sides. She reached into her purse for her address book and flipped to D, then bent over the counter and picked up Cassandra's telephone. She dialed a Brentwood number and hoped to hell someone picked up.

* * *

Bette Davis' house on Carmelina Drive was refreshingly normal. Instead of an obnoxious, oversized estate that would stupefy the press and provoke her peers to jealousy, she and her new husband bought a two-story farmhouse with sky blue shutters and a brick patio.

The maid led Kathryn into an airy living room filled with the solid-legged sort of furniture usually found in movies set in the Midwest — comfortable, practical, and free from overly fussy detail. The upholstery matched the drapes — a pattern of cabbage roses and sharp thorns dominated the room and made Kathryn think of Gwendolyn's description of her boss' ball gown.

Bette was seated at the long sofa with a copy of *Life* in her hand, dressed in a brown velvet robe — odd for three o'clock in the afternoon. "I'd get up if I could, but the doctor told me to avoid exertion."

Kathryn sat down beside her. "The doctor?"

Bette took off her reading glasses and rolled her eyes. "I'll tell you if you can keep a secret."

"I'm a gossip columnist," Kathryn reminded her. "It's my job to keep secrets."

"No, it's your job to divulge them."

Kathryn shook her head. "My job is to divulge the secrets I didn't promise to keep." That made Bette smile. "This isn't an official visit. Nothing you say will be taken down and used against you in the court of public opinion." Kathryn had interviewed enough movie stars to know that most of them couldn't resist the opportunity to talk about themselves.

"I'm not pregnant, if that's the scoop you were hoping for."

"I didn't come here looking for a scoop."

Bette made a show of shifting in her seat. "I had a car accident." She shot up her hand. "Nothing catastrophic. I was driving down to our place in Laguna, but I shouldn't have. I was too distracted by this movie I'm shooting."

"*Deception*'s not going well?"

Bette see-sawed her hand. "It's going fine, I guess, but it's all a bit overblown and highbrow. Paul Henreid's in it with me, but if moviegoers are expecting to see a retread of *Now, Voyager*, I fear they'll walk out sadly disappointed. At any rate, my mind was elsewhere and I ran off the road. I'm in better shape than my car, but I'm still a bit black and blue. I was glad to get your call—I could use the distraction."

She rang a little silver bell and her maid came into the room within seconds. Bette asked for tea and cookies to be served, then waited until the maid had retreated to ask, "What's going on?"

"I was told today that Bing won't be continuing with *Kraft Music Hall*, so I'd say my radio career is not long for this world. And that's a shame because I was counting on it in case the *Hollywood Reporter* goes down the plughole."

"It's on shaky ground?"

"Ben Siegel has been visiting my boss at the office. During the daytime."

"That can't be good."

"I did as you suggested, and talked to Hughes. He told me he had it on good authority that Wilkerson has borrowed a million dollars to finish his Flamingo Club." Kathryn fluttered her hands in exasperation.

"He must have been desperate if he turned to the mob. What do you make of it?"

"He's jumped into bed with the mob! At best, they'll shove him out and he'll lose all his dough. At worst, they'll shove him into the nearest cement mixer."

The words gagged her; she felt the sting of tears collect behind her eyes. She reached into her purse and groped around for a handkerchief but found nothing. Instead, she swiped her tears away with the back of her glove.

—

Bette let her gather herself together before she spoke. "He's been like a father to you, hasn't he?"

Kathryn jerked her head up, startled that this had never occurred to her.

"Of course you're worried," Bette said. "If silly Billy isn't going to rescue himself, then somebody's going to have to do something."

The maid appeared with a tray holding a dark blue Wedgwood tea set and half a dozen coconut cookies. She slid the tray onto the coffee table and withdrew without a word.

"It's not like I can go in with my guns blazing like I'm Jimmy Cagney," Kathryn whispered.

"You need to fight fire with fire." Bette handed Kathryn a cup of steaming tea. "If you're going to extricate your boss from the mob's clutches — assuming, of course, you can even pull off something like that — you're going to need someone stronger than you."

Kathryn almost heard the puzzle pieces snap into place. "I see where you're going with this."

"You want to get off the hook with the FBI, don't you?"

"Can I assume that's a rhetorical question?"

"If you do them a big favor, maybe they'll do one in return." Bette clenched as she shifted into a new position. "I'm hardly an expert, but I'd imagine the FBI would be most interested in where that cool million came from."

Kathryn desperately wanted to be rid of this whole mess, but with Wilkerson digging an ever-deepening hole for himself, she could see it wasn't going to fix itself.

"Imagine the points your guy will score with *his* boss if he can say he's got a way in. Just the thought of bringing down the mob will give J. Edgar Hoover a hard-on that won't deflate for *weeks*."

Kathryn laughed in spite of the apprehension swirling inside her. The last thing she wanted to do was give Nelson Hoyt's career a bump, but Bette had a point. She had to play the long game.

CHAPTER 12

The Cadillac Marcus hired for the night was a postwar limousine, midnight black, with a long chrome stripe, factory-fresh leather upholstery, and all the leg room he could possibly need. But the long, luxurious ride he'd been looking forward to would have to happen some other night. Marcus kneaded his temples.

Why didn't I run this past Eddie Mannix?

Being promoted to department head the same week he got married had granted Marcus a double dose of legitimacy in the eyes of social Hollywood. These days, he received all sorts of invitations — galas, premieres, dinner-dances, charity fundraisers. So when the invitation for tonight's reception arrived, no alarm bells went off.

An invitation to a cocktail party aboard a Soviet battleship was unusual, but no more than the one he'd received a few weeks back to a party thrown by former members of the Hollywood Anti-Nazi League to commemorate the first anniversary of Hitler's suicide. And yes, the absence of the words "and wife" or "plus guest" was curious, but he didn't think too much about it when he mailed off his RSVP.

The further south the limo sped, the more he longed for the old days during the war when everything was so clear-cut. The Allies were the good guys, the Axis were the bad guys. The heroes beat the villains and everybody knew where they stood.

But now, the new bad guys were the Commies, and Russia was a Communist nation. During a recent speech in Missouri, Winston Churchill mentioned something he called the "Iron Curtain," and how Eastern Europe now lay inside the Soviet sphere, implying this was not a good thing.

Outside his window, a fog was starting to roll in, blurring the forest of pumpjacks on Signal Hill behind a thickening haze. They made a left and passed a sign: *PORT OF LONG BEACH – 1 MILE.*

I should have picked up the telephone and told Mannix, "I got this invite from Konstantin Simonov. He's the Soviet consul, so it's legit, but I thought you ought to know . . ."

The fog was even thicker when the car swung into a parking lot. Marcus could barely make out the battleship moored along the pier. He showed his invitation to the uniformed sailor, who waved him through wordlessly.

I'll stay an hour, then tell them I'm meeting Mr. Mayer at the Biltmore for a late dinner.

It looked like any other battleship Marcus had seen during the war — about twice the length of a football field, and maybe two stories high at its peak. The whole thing was painted a dull gray, with hand-sized flakes peeling off the hull in several places.

Marcus suddenly wished Oliver was with him.

He had been waiting for Marcus at the Garden when he staggered home at eight o'clock in the morning after the Mandeville Canyon raid. They were both full of regret and apologies, and soon discovered the joys of make-up sex.

A whitewashed wooden gangplank ran from the edge of the pier to the deck. Another taciturn deckhand checked Marcus' invitation and swept his hand toward the ship. A line of tiny electric lights ran aft to an open doorway. The spry notes of Russian gypsy music danced across the air.

He stepped inside to find a chamber not much bigger than his living room. It was square, carpeted, with walls painted a dark cream, and lit largely with enormous candles that were as thick as baseball bats.

A dozen people were gathered into groups of three or four. The first person Marcus saw took him by surprise: Charlie Chaplin dressed in a tux, with his dark-haired wife, Oona O'Neill, by his side. They stood with a wide-faced man in his early thirties who looked like a young Jack Warner with a trim Ronald Colman moustache. Chaplin nudged the man, who looked over his shoulder and smiled. He excused himself and headed straight for Marcus.

He shot out his hand. "Mr. Adler!" he exclaimed. "What a pleasure that you could join us tonight. I am your host, Konstantin Simonov."

Marcus shook his hand, surprised that this amiable Ruskie would recognize him. "Have we met before, Mr. Simonov?"

A waiter appeared with a tray of shot glasses. Simonov took two and handed Marcus one. "Authentic Russian vodka. One swallow. Bang! Yes?"

They threw back the drinks and waited for the euphoria to warm them. Taking him gently by the elbow, Simonov guided Marcus over to Chaplin and his wife. "Charlie tells me you've met before."

Marcus shook hands with the actor and his young wife. "I'm flattered you remember."

Chaplin's vodka-infused smile widened. "Of course! That was quite a night for you."

It was the triumphant premiere of MGM's *William Tell*, which Marcus had written. Chaplin had gone out of his way to greet Alla Nazimova, who introduced him to Marcus. He then insisted that the two of them have their photo taken in front of a striking portrait of Napoleon Bonaparte on horseback. Marcus assumed that what had been a heady experience for him was a forgettable moment for the star.

Simonov excused himself when another guest appeared in the doorway, leaving Marcus with the Chaplins. Oona turned to her husband.

"Isn't that John Garfield who just walked in? What's his wife's name?"

"Roberta," Charlie replied.

It was then that Marcus realized Chaplin was here with his wife, and John Garfield had brought his. *Why then,* he wondered, *was my invitation not addressed to Mr. and Mrs. Adler?* An innocuous oversight? Or because Kathryn was a member of the press? Marcus wondered if he was getting paranoid.

The waiter appeared with more shots and everybody downed them as an intense man with black wavy hair approached them.

Chaplin greeted him with a bear hug. "Lewis Milestone, may I present Marcus Adler."

Marcus shook the director's hand. He'd admired Milestone's *Of Mice and Men* before the war, as well as *All Quiet on the Western Front.* They also had a personal connection in Marcus' sometime neighbor, Lillian Hellman, who wrote the screenplay of a pro-Soviet/anti-Nazi picture called *The North Star* that Milestone directed for Goldwyn.

Milestone rolled his eyes. "Don't look now, but that lump of horse hockey from Paramount just walked in."

Whereas everybody else was in a tuxedo, Clifford Wardell had shown up in a rumpled gray suit. His necktie, a noxious shade of brown, hung loosely outside his jacket, and his hair, though combed, shone greasily in the candlelight.

"Who's that?" Oona asked.

"My counterpart at Paramount," Marcus said. "Runs the writing department, though how he managed that coup is anyone's guess."

"I tangled with him during *The Strange Love of Martha Ivers,*" Milestone said. "After every meeting, I wanted to run home and scrub myself raw."

The conversation drifted onto the recently opened Tokyo war trials, but Marcus kept an eye on Wardell as Simonov congenially led the guy around to various guests.

It had been more than ten years since that day at George Cukor's brunch when Marcus exposed Wardell as a muckraking journalist looking to dig up dirt. Marcus' actions had cemented his friendship with George, but he never knew what became of the grubby slob until he met Quentin.

By the time John Garfield and his wife joined them, the conversation had moved on to Walter Winchell's report on how Howard Hughes had dared to file a lawsuit against the Motion Picture Association charging restraint of trade over his Jane Russell picture, *The Outlaw*. But Marcus was barely paying attention.

He kept thinking of his post-arrest breakfast at the Nite Owl with Quentin and Trevor. When Trevor pointed out that Quentin couldn't reveal Wardell as the author of *Reds in the Beds* without incriminating himself, he reminded them that Wardell was a nasty drunk, easily given to losing control. Quentin suggested that someone needed to get Wardell tanked-up and then needle him enough to push him too far. With all the vodka flowing around this second-rate tub, Marcus thought, that shouldn't be too difficult. And if he could get Wardell to spill in front of all these Hollywood witnesses . . .

He watched Wardell knock back shot after shot, to no effect. He stayed as rumpled and slouched as he had coming in, and eventually Marcus returned to the conversation. John Garfield's wife was making a lengthy speech about the pitfalls of unintended consequences as illustrated by her husband's recent movie, *The Postman Always Rings Twice*. She'd obviously made her speech before — she barely paused to draw breath — but it was so eloquent that Marcus lost track of Wardell altogether until a sailor tugged on his elbow, asking him if he could join Mr. Simonov out on deck.

The sailor led him to the other side of the ship into a small space that was hemmed in with chain fence. The fog was even thicker now — Marcus couldn't see six feet past the edge of the ship, let alone the lights of Long Beach. Simonov and Wardell were waiting for him.

Simonov clapped his hands. "I know it's a bit cold out here, but I wanted to talk business." He motioned to Wardell with a gloved hand. "Marcus Adler, allow me to introduce to you Clifford Wardell." If he caught the contempt that crossed the faces of his guests, Simonov ignored it. "Mr. Adler, I have been a fan of your work since *Free Leningrad!*"

Like all studios, MGM had made a number of pro-Allies propaganda movies during the war. *Free Leningrad!* was MGM's most successful effort, both critically and commercially. "Is that right?" Marcus asked Simonov.

"Back when I was a journalist, I covered the Siege of Stalingrad during the early part of the war. I knew firsthand what it was like to live in a Russian city under siege during the wintertime. I thought you captured the Leningrad experience with great realism."

Wardell helped himself to a bottle of Smirnoff tucked away in the shadows nearby. "You mentioned something about business." The words came out slightly slurred.

"I was wondering if either of you have ever considered making a motion picture of the life of our great Anna Pavlova."

Wardell grunted. "Ballet dancer, right?"

"She was Europe's greatest prima ballerina!" Simonov declared.

"But did she have a dramatic life?" Marcus asked. "Or survive through circumstances that could be dramatized?"

"Most certainly! When she entered ballet school, they said her arches were too high, her ankles too thin, and her arms too long. What she endured to become Russia's greatest ballerina is the stuff of dramatic motion pictures."

Wardell threw back another vodka shot. "We'll be the judge of that." He announced. "And I judge your idea to be . . ." He let out a long, spittly belch, then struck a match along the handrail and lit a bitter, cheap Cuban.

"I disagree," Marcus said, just to needle Wardell. "Ballet is a highly dramatic art form, and if Pavlova suffered for her art, it could make a great story."

Wardell swept his arms into two wide arcs. "A bunch of boney foreign hoofers prancing around on stage to some boring music? Yeah, you got yourself a winner there, Adler." He made a dismissive wave, causing his cigar to fall between his fingers. As he stooped to pick it up, he lost his balance and fell against a wall.

Simonov went to help, but Wardell pushed him aside. He gripped both sides of the metal doorjamb and stumbled through the opening. Marcus followed.

"You don't look so good." He kept his eyes on Wardell and sensed everyone in the room turning toward them. "We don't want you falling overboard."

"Your concern is inspirational," Wardell threw over his shoulder, then blundered into a steward carrying a tray of crackers loaded with black caviar. The steward recovered quicker than Wardell, losing only a couple of hors d'oeuvres.

"Holy mackerel!" Marcus exclaimed, just a bit louder than necessary.

The only scene in *Reds* that made Marcus laugh was when someone dubbed Luther Mackerel — an obvious caricature of Louis B. Mayer — "Holy Mackerel." Wardell spun around, his eyes flaring.

"You better watch your step," Marcus pressed, "lest you fall and cut yourself. Then this ship will be awash with *red* and someone will need to put you to *bed*."

Wardell let out a low grunt and stomped toward the exit. Marcus followed. By the time he got to the door, his prey was staggering along the gangplank toward a green pre-war Nash at the edge of the pier. Marcus caught up with Wardell near the car.

"What's the matter, Wardell? Seeing red yet?"

Wardell considered Marcus through a heavily lidded eye. "What the hell are you talking—" He raised a hand as though to swipe away a bug. "You know what? I don't give a crap."

Marcus stepped forward. "Blood. Henna. Poinsettia. Paprika. Ketchup."

"Shut ya trap, Adler, before I shut it for you."

"Maraschino. Cranberry. Tomato."

Wardell swung faster than Marcus expected. Marcus ducked as the fist swished through the air several inches off its mark. "Apples. Mars. Rhubarb."

Wardell yanked at his tie, pulling it away from his collar. "What're you yapping about?"

Marcus cut a wide arc around Wardell, hoping to get between him and his car before Wardell caught on. "Answer me this, Clifford: How exactly do you find fifty-five flatfoots from Farmington Falls?"

The two men faced each other. Realization didn't drop onto Wardell as Marcus expected; it was more of a slow burn, like an unrushed sunrise. He knew his taunting had taken hold when Wardell bunched his right fist.

"We both know it was you," Marcus jeered. "I just want to hear you admit it."

Wardell wiped a glob of spit from the edge of his mottled lips. "Yes, it was me. Okay? The best-selling book of 1946 was written by Clifford Wardell from Farmington Fucking Falls. Happy now, you pansy-assed faggot?"

"But why?" Marcus lowered the heat from his voice to catch Wardell off-guard. "You've made this whole industry paranoid. You know we're not all Commies."

"An expert on what I do and do not know, are you?"

"Come on, Clifford," Marcus said quietly. "What were you hoping to achieve?"

Wardell shoved him aside. Marcus' grabbed the edge of Wardell's jacket and they tumbled to the pier, clenched like a pair of pugnacious lobsters. They rolled over, and then over once more, ending with Marcus on top as they gripped each other's arms. Marcus felt his sleeve rip — then suddenly, they stopped. Their heads jerked in the same direction as they realized they'd reached the edge. One more rotation and they'd plunge into the freezing Pacific.

"Let's quit now," Marcus panted, "before both of us end up —"

"FUCK YOU!"

Clifford Wardell let out an almighty grunt as he heaved himself over the side of the pier, taking Marcus down with him.

CHAPTER 13

Gwendolyn stood with Marcus and Kathryn at the corner where Sunset and Hollywood Boulevards intersected. It was eleven o'clock at night; hardly any traffic in any direction. They said nothing until the Vista Theatre's yellow-green neon lighting switched off, cloaking them in shadow.

"That's our cue," Gwendolyn said.

Sewing a gown for a man had turned out to be far more straightforward than she expected. Her favorite fabric store carried exactly the shade of pale rose quartz silk Mr. Dewberry liked. Stenciling the ivy pattern was tricky to begin with, but she got the hang of it, and the end result was exactly as she'd envisioned. Dewberry's chest, waist, and hips were the same measurement, which eliminated the trickiest part of a formal outfit, so the whole thing was ready within a week. Mr. Dewberry cried when he saw his reflection in the mirror.

A week later he reported that he'd caused a sensation at the bar, and that his pals wanted to meet her. As happy as she was to make the gown for her boss, Gwendolyn wasn't sure she wanted to march into a cross-dresser bar by herself, so she asked him if she could bring a couple of friends. She saw the hesitation in his eyes, but then it faded, and he gave her the address.

The Midnight Frolics was located a couple of buildings behind the Vista Theatre. He told her to wait until the lights were switched off, then go around the rear where she'd see a black door with a gold handle. She was to knock on it three times, and when the little window in the door opened, tell the guy, "The widow sent me."

The door handle glowed in the light of a shoe store across the street. When Gwendolyn knocked three times, a picture-postcard-sized window opened to reveal a pair of overly mascara'd eyes. When Gwendolyn gave the pass code, the eyes looked each of them up and down, then slid the window shut. A moment or two later, the door opened.

Gwendolyn, Kathryn, and Marcus squeezed into a small foyer whose walls were all painted black. A bright orange poster featuring a line drawing of a nude fan dancer advertised a San Francisco nightclub called The Music Box.

The six-foot doorman was in a knee-length cotton sundress, dark brown with bursts of bright yellow California poppies. Unlike Mr. Dewberry, this guy knew what he was doing. It sat across his chest in a way that accentuated his shoulders, making his waist look slimmer than it probably was. The color suited his Mediterranean complexion, too. He prodded them through the arched doorway.

The nightclub was larger than the Sahara Room back at the Garden. Its walls, too, were painted black, with gold silhouettes of voluptuous women in burlesque poses.

Four-top tables were set around a T-shaped stage that jutted out into the square room. A trio of musicians—piano, drums, saxophone—played softly at the end closest to the bar. A third of the tables were occupied.

"You ever been to one of these places?" Kathryn asked Marcus.

"I didn't even know they existed. Reminds me of the old speakeasies."

Gwendolyn grabbed the first table they came to. "Maybe this wasn't such a great idea." She picked up a black cardboard coaster with the letters "TMF" stenciled in white and threaded it through her fingers. "Everyone's staring."

"Dewberry said his friends wanted to meet you," Marcus murmured. "He wouldn't have invited you if we weren't welcome."

A gaggle of eight men arrived, all gussied up in the sort of dresses usually seen on showgirls in the saloons of Westerns, their bright satin ruffles layered in purple, pink, and blue. They beelined for a pair of tables closest to the runway and didn't notice the three new patrons until they were seated.

"I thought Mr. Dewberry would be here already," Gwendolyn said.

An elfin waiter appeared, tall as the doorman, wearing a tawny poplin dress with an empire waist. With narrow eyes holding more than a smidge of suspicion, he ignored the women and looked at Marcus. "What'll it be?"

"Manhattan, straight up, hold the cherry."

The waiter took in the girls' outfits before raising his eyebrows at them. They ordered the same.

"Do you know Herman?" Gwendolyn asked.

Suspicion ratcheted up a notch. "I don't believe so." He left before Gwendolyn could form a second question.

"I wish Oliver could be here," Marcus sighed, "but when Bertie came knocking, he felt he should volunteer."

The petty thefts around the Garden of Allah had continued unabated through the spring of 1946—scarves, booze, magazines; there appeared to be no rhyme or reason to it—so Bertie had organized a night watch. "Speaking of blowing the whistle." Marcus motioned for them to lean in closer. "I heard from Arlene today."

Gwendolyn eyed the arrival of four redheads dressed in identical black silk gowns that would look stunning on Hedy Lamarr. The guys' lumberjack shoulders spoiled the effect they were probably going for, though. "Who's Arlene?"

"The girl from Leilah O'Roarke's house of ill repute," Marcus whispered. "She called to tell me about a screaming match Leilah and Clem had in the back alley. She only caught the odd phrase, but Leilah was throwing things at him. Arlene waited until she was off duty to sneak outside."

"Did she find anything?"

"A piece of paper caught up in some weeds."

"What was it?"

"She didn't say, but she thinks it's incriminating."

Gwendolyn and Marcus agreed with Bette Davis: If Kathryn could help Hoyt connect the O'Roarkes' laundered brothel money to the land they bought around Vegas, the FBI could make some high-profile arrests. And then maybe Hoyt would let Kathryn go.

"She promised to get it to me," Marcus continued, "but then got panicky and hung up."

Kathryn went to say something, but it got stuck in her throat because three of the saloon showgirls were approaching. They all looked like bouncers from a rough part of town. The one in front with the Mediterranean complexion was not tall, but was impressively wide. He pulled his straps back onto his hairy shoulders. "We don't mean to be inhospitable, but perhaps you three are in the wrong place?"

The guy behind him was less swarthy, less hairy, and looked more at home in his pink-and-black-striped can-can dress. He planted his hands on his corseted hips. "Maybe you're looking for the Midnight Moon. Coupla miles down Sunset." He pointed east.

Feeling herself go pale, Gwendolyn beseeched Marcus and Kathryn. *Let's just go?*

Marcus got to his feet and held up his palms. "Look, fellas," he said placatingly, "I understand your qualms, but—"

"I doubt it," said the one in the can-can outfit.

"Did you read about that vice squad raid up in Mandeville Canyon?"

"Hermit's Hideaway?" the first one asked.

Marcus nodded. "I was there that night. Got caught up in their net and only just managed to get off scot-free. So I know all about the chances guys like us take to come to places like these—"

"Stop right there." Mr. Mediterranean tipped forward. "You think this is a faggot club?"

Marcus' jaw dropped an inch. "I—er, kinda assumed—"

"You can take your assumptions and shove them up your ass." He gripped his petticoats with hairy-knuckled fingers and rustled them. "Just because we enjoy getting into these, don't mean we're a bunch of queers."

"My mistake, fellas," Marcus said, leaning back. "I jumped to a conclusion I shouldn't have."

The waiter approached their table with the doorman in the poppy dress trailing behind him. The waiter pointed to Marcus, Kathryn, and Gwendolyn and addressed the doorman. "They asked about Herman. Clearly, they ain't never heard the rule."

"They knew about the widow," the doorman put in.

"Gentlemen." Gwendolyn stood up. "We were invited, but it seems our presence here is causing anxiety." The band had stopped playing and everybody in the bar was now rubbernecking at them. She pulled Kathryn to her feet. "We'll be going now. Please accept our apologies." She picked up her handbag.

"Gwendolyn," Marcus said, "perhaps you should leave a message? He's going to wonder—"

"No," she said, "I'll talk to him on Monday."

They went to step around the growing crush of patrons when the can-can guy held up an accusing finger. "Are you *Miss* Gwendolyn?"

She eyed him. "I could be."

Mr. Can-Can's taut lips melted into the first hint of a smile she'd seen since walking into the place. "Miss Gwendolyn who made Hermione's ivy dress?"

Hermione? Hermione! "Yes," she smiled, "that was me."

The guy with the hairy shoulders intertwined his fingers as though in prayer. "That dress! We all drooled with envy when he walked in."

"I'll say!" One of the redheads in the black cocktail dresses sidled up behind her and pointed to the runway in the middle of the room. "We made him walk the walk three times."

Gwendolyn found herself surrounded by men of every size, coloring, and body shape, but not many of them wore a dress that did them any favors. The redheads should have been in emerald green; Mr. Hairy Shoulders needed sleeves.

The group suddenly directed its attention to what Gwendolyn was wearing: a full-skirted shirtwaist dress in periwinkle blue with tiny polka dots that she'd adapted from an outfit in Bullocks' casualwear department.

An older gent in too much blue eye shadow pinched the hem of her skirt and ran the fabric between his fingers. "Crêpe de chine?"

"Close," Gwendolyn replied. "It's georgette, but heavier than they used to make before the war."

He was transfixed by the fabric. "I'd love something like this, but in large polka dots. Huge ones, the size of plates."

The crowd purred in approval, but Gwendolyn threw up her hands. "No! No! No! Very few people can get away with large polka dots." The crowd gaped at her as though she'd just revealed the location of the fountain of youth. "Tall people shouldn't wear vertical stripes because it only makes them look even taller. By the same token, short or wide-hipped people shouldn't wear horizontals. You want to camouflage your flaws, not emphasize them."

"Like when we were in Bataan," one of the redheads piped up. "Remember? The wrong shade of green and you were done for."

Several heads nodded in comprehension, so Gwendolyn did too. "You must think about color," she told them. "What color are your eyes, your skin, your hair?"

"But I *like* yellow." The doorman bunched his skirt in his fist.

"The question isn't 'Do I like yellow?'" Gwendolyn told him. "But 'Does yellow like me?'"

"For instance," Kathryn put in, "with my brown hair and hazel eyes, yellow loves me, and so does green. But blue? Especially light blue?" She tsked. "Not good. I stick to either very dark blues, or skip it altogether."

"And your doorman," Gwendolyn added, "see how the puffy sleeves give him a Crawford look. They create a V-shape, which conjures the illusion of a slender waist."

She watched comprehension sift through the crowd. By now, even the band had joined them, and they were the worst offenders of all. One of them had the pale complexion of a Scandinavian but had chosen to wear a blouse whose horrible shade of apricot drained away all his remaining color. She was about to launch into another lesson when one of the Western showgirls pointed at Kathryn.

"Say," he said, his gravelly voice thick with hostility, "ain't you Kathryn Massey? From the radio and the *Hollywood Reporter?*"

Gwendolyn sensed the tide of suspicion turning against them.

"You're with the press?" The doorman seemed to grow three inches in every direction. "That's a rule we do not break." He started to squeeze his hands into fists just as Gwendolyn heard Mr. Dewberry's voice bellow from somewhere in back.

"All right, everybody, you can put away your knives!"

The Midnight Frolic's patrons moved aside to reveal Herbert Dewberry, resplendent in his rose-quartz silk gown with the delicate ivy print. He'd added matching gloves and a necklace of paste sapphires. He raised his arms like Aimee Semple McPherson. "Or at least stick them in *my* back."

"She brought a member of the press," someone growled.

"I told Miss Gwendolyn it would be okay," Mr. Dewberry declared. "Anyone who is a friend of hers is a friend of mine, and is therefore a friend of ours."

Gwendolyn took a purposeful stride toward him. "Look at this ivy print." She ran her fingers along Mr. Dewberry's torso. "He wanted a bold pattern, with leaves the size of his hand. But I convinced him to go with a smaller leaf and stencil it in pale green. You'll do well to remember three little words: LESS IS MORE!"

The room was so quiet Gwendolyn heard a truck rumble along the street outside. The first person to speak was one of the redheads.

"I was on my way to work the other day and I passed a fabric store on Wilshire."

"Famous Fabrics?" Gwendolyn asked. "I go there all the time."

"In the window I noticed a bolt of—I don't know what it was. Velvet, maybe? Real dark pistachio color with stars in gold thread. Embroidered, like. I've always wanted a dress with stars on it, but I pictured royal blue with silver stars. Now I think green and gold is more my coloring." The guy stepped into a light. "What do you think?"

Gwendolyn had never seen so many freckles on one face before. They were packed in so densely they almost made for a new shade of complexion. "I think it sounds perfect for you."

He looked at her shyly, like a teenager. "If I bought a whole bunch of it, would you make me something?"

"I'd be delighted."

A current of excitement shot through the crowd.

"Me too?" shouted a lumberjack in an atrociously misshapen gown of cheap satin.

You need me most of all, Gwendolyn thought.

Mr. Dewberry stepped in front of her and waved his arms. "As you can see, Miss Gwendolyn does superb work, but I have to warn you, she doesn't come cheap. If you want an outfit as lovely as mine, you'd better be prepared to pay for it."

He spun around, sweeping the hem of his dress behind him with such panache that she knew he'd practiced it. He looked her in the eye unblinkingly, a knowing smile on his lips. *Go get 'em!*

CHAPTER 14

Kathryn planted her hands on her hips, arranged her lips in an exaggerated pout, and winked at the radio audience. "Really, Edward! Any more cracks like that, and I'm going to get the folks at Kraft to take away your cheese allowance."

The audience hooted as Edward Everett Horton pulled his trademark shocked expression. He wagged a finger at her. "Nobody gets between me and my Velveeta!"

"You better watch out," Kathryn volleyed back, "or I'll have to use my Miracle Whip."

The audience broke out into applause as the red light on the back wall of Studio 2 lit up.

"And that brings us to the end of the all-new *Kraft Music Hall*," Edward announced.

"A big thank you to the ladies and gentlemen of our wonderful studio audience," Kathryn said. "To our radio audience wherever you are, thanks for tuning in, and as we here in California say, see you at the beach. Goodnight!"

The audience was still cheering as Edward escorted Kathryn off stage.

"That went awfully well, I must say." He pulled a handkerchief from his pocket and wiped it across his forehead.

"You sound surprised," Kathryn said.

He gave a dismissive shrug. "Let's face it, I'm no Bing Crosby."

When Kathryn got the call that Crosby had decided to exit *Kraft Music Hall*, she'd expected the show to fold. She wasn't prepared to hear that Kraft and NBC's market research revealed that after Crosby, Kathryn was the second most popular reason the audience tuned in each week — and that they wanted her to co-host.

At first, Kathryn wondered if Eddie was such a great choice as a replacement for the universally loved Crosby. Their first meeting was pleasant enough. He was polite and deferential, but palpably nervous. But when he and Kathryn stepped in front of a studio audience, their chemistry began to fizz like a Bromo-Seltzer and they were soon bubbling with adlibs.

Kathryn nodded toward the bustling audience. "Sounds like they didn't care you're not Bing."

He squeezed her hand. "Thank you for making it so easy to slip right in. But I must say, I never knew we in California say 'See you at the beach.' Mind you, with my Scottish heritage, going to the beach is not advisable."

Kathryn steered them along the backstage corridor to their dressing rooms. "I was trying out a new signoff. I figured it's time to freshen things up a bit."

"See you at the beach," Eddie said, nodding. "Very Californian. Let's keep it and see if we can't score a catchphrase."

Kathryn kissed her co-host goodbye and closed her dressing room door with a nudge to the hip. She stood in front of her mirror. "Oh, the lies you tell," she sighed.

See you at the beach was code to tell Nelson Hoyt where to meet her that night.

When Marcus' hooker friend sent him the paper she found in the alley out back of Leilah's brothel, Kathryn placed a classified ad in the *Hollywood Citizen-News* saying what day and time she wanted to meet him. Fearful that someone may have figured out who they were, Kathryn refused to nominate the place, so they came up with a code she could use in her next radio broadcast. "See you at the beach" meant "See you at Don the Beachcomber."

——

It was just past seven, which gave her an hour to walk up to the nightclub. She could easily have asked reception to call her a cab, but the apprehension that Arlene's back-alley discovery might be her ticket out of the FBI was starting to hit home. She needed the walk to calm her nerves.

* * *

Don the Beachcomber was one of the first bars in Hollywood to ride the Polynesia wave. From its South Seas shanty décor of bamboo shutters, wicker furniture, and glass buoys strung up with fishing nets, to the Hawaiian ukulele playing over the loudspeakers, a thirsty patron could walk into the place and almost believe he'd been cast away onto a Pacific island with nothing but bracing rum concoctions like Missionary's Downfall and Vicious Virgin to keep him going.

The back bar was called the Cannibal Room; its low lighting made it a popular place for clandestine meetings between people who perhaps ought not be clandesting.

Hoyt was in the most distant booth when Kathryn arrived. He'd taken the liberty of ordering drinks in matching twelve-inch bamboo trunks.

She sat down and pulled off her gloves. "I hope those aren't Zombies." The first time she tried the bar's signature drink, she lost about six hours.

Hoyt slid one toward her. "It's a Cobra's Fang."

He flashed one of those smiles she was sure was intended to disarm her. On someone else it may have worked, but not from the guy she wanted most to evict from her life. She pretended to take a sip, and pulled a piece of paper from her purse.

"I have something for you." She laid it out in front of her, covering it with splayed hands. "I'm not going to tell you how I got this, but it *is* on the level."

"Okay."

"Have you heard of something called the Nevada Project Corporation of California?" Despite the Cannibal Room's low lighting—mostly from sconces that flickered like flaming torches—Kathryn could see the name meant something to him. "Did you know the principal stockholder is Benjamin Siegel?"

"No, I didn't."

"Do you know what the corporation is for?"

When his eyes blinked several times, she knew she'd scored a direct hit. *For an FBI agent, you're really not that great a poker player.* She could see the cogs rotate behind his eyes until three Kings lined up in a row. *Bingo!*

"Are we talking about the Flamingo Club?" he asked.

Kathryn nodded and took another pretend sip.

"I thought your boss was building that."

She thumped her bamboo cup onto the table. "My boss is so determined to build a casino that he accepted a million-dollar loan from the mob." She pressed a fingertip to the center of the paper in front of her. "And this shows where he got it."

"Get a load of you, Nancy Drew."

"My money is on Siegel aiming to take over the whole kit and caboodle."

Hoyt's eyes were now on the paper. "But where would that leave Wilkerson?"

"Hopefully out in the cold."

A pause, then, "I have something to tell you. I probably shouldn't, but I'll take a chance that you'll keep it to yourself." He made a deliberately casual sweep of the Cannibal Room. "For a while now, Hoover has wanted to wiretap all of Siegel's telephone lines."

"He hasn't already?" Kathryn was being flippant, but made sure her question was hard-edged enough to remind Hoyt of the time during the war when the FBI wiretapped Bogie's villa at the Garden. She wanted to believe that Hoyt hadn't known about it at the time, but she never knew for sure.

"In his own strange way, Hoover has a moral code. He'll only wiretap somebody when he feels justified."

Kathryn went to push the paper toward Hoyt, but stopped. "Are you planning on wiretapping Wilkerson too?"

His gray-blue eyes were back on hers now. "It's Siegel and the mob we want, not Wilkerson."

Suddenly, Kathryn wanted to down her whole Cobra's Fang. She took a deep swig. "I'm not cut out for all this lying and sneaking around." He said nothing but she could see the acknowledgment in his eyes. "I know you can't let me off the hook for no reason, so I want to earn my freedom by giving you something so good that you, or Hoover, or whoever makes these decisions thinks, 'Well now, *this* is great stuff. That gal has done her duty to this nation's security, so let's thank her and send her on her way.'" She hoped for a response, but got nothing. "Does it even work that way?" she prodded.

"Depending on how I sell it." He jutted his chin toward Arlene's paper. "And depending on what that says."

Kathryn extended both index fingers and used them to push the paper across the table. He kept his eyes on her until he picked it up. As he read it, she scanned the room. It was now getting close to eight o'clock and parched customers were starting to file in.

"This isn't the O'Roarke who heads up security at Warners, is it?"

"It's his wife."

Hoyt tapped the paper. "So this Linden Holdings Company — that's hers?"

"They live on Linden Drive in Beverly Hills."

"That's where Siegel's girlfriend lives."

"Virtually across the street. Convenient, huh?"

Kathryn reached into her purse for cigarettes. She needed something to camouflage the kick she was getting at beating Mr. FBI at his own game.

"I strongly suspect that if you dig into Linden Holdings, you'll find it's being used to launder money from brothel gravy." Kathryn knew the address, but she wasn't going to give it to him until she knew that Arlene was out and safe from arrest. "You'll also find it connected to a company called Primm Valley Realty, which has been buying up all the land around a little Nevada desert town called—"

"Las Vegas."

"See how it all fits?"

He pointed to the handwritten number at the bottom of the sheet. "This figure here."

"Four hundred and seventy-five thousand, six hundred and ninety-one dollars?" When she saw the way his eyes lit up, she was pleased she'd taken the time to memorize it. "It's a very specific number. Easier to identify than, say, a round five hundred grand."

She took a long drag and listened to the plinkety-plink ukulele version of the "Hawaiian Wedding Song" wafting over them.

Eventually he said, "This is very good work, Miss Massey."

She arched an eyebrow. "But is it good enough?"

* * *

Their standard procedure was to leave separately, usually with Kathryn going first. But this time she told him, "Maybe we should switch for once."

She counted for sixty seconds, and then slipped outside. In front of Don the Beachcomber was a patch of yard crammed with ferns and banana palms. She gently pulled one back to see Hoyt round the corner on foot, then head west along Hollywood Boulevard.

She wondered if shadowing an FBI agent was such a good idea. But as a gossip columnist who'd spent years developing a sixth sense for secrets, she'd learned when to play a hunch. And this, she told herself, was one of those times.

She watched him cross Hollywood and head south past the Max Factor building. It was coming up to nine o'clock, and the warmth of the summer day had all but dissipated, leaving her chilled and wishing she'd had her hunch earlier in the day when she could have planned for it better. Hoyt ambled along Highland Avenue so slowly it was almost annoying. *Don't you have some place to go?* When he lit a second cigarette from the butt of his first, she grasped that she'd given him a lot to think about.

He turned left at Sunset and headed east.

She hurried down the street, then peeked around the corner. He stopped outside a store and looked in the window. Above his head, an orange neon sign flashed on and off. He waved to someone inside, then disappeared through the front entrance.

Kathryn peered into the brightly lit store window. Tiffany lamps, desk lamps, bedside reading lamps, wall sconces, and chandeliers filled the display. An older gentleman behind the counter beamed when he saw Hoyt. They approached each other and met in the middle, embracing with a heartfelt hug.

Kathryn pulled back. *He's like Marcus! My FBI agent is queer!* She tipped back against the glass of the neighboring florist and breathed in the sweet scent of roses lingering in the air. Passersby crossing in front of her blurred into nebulous blobs as her mind whirred with ways she could exploit this information.

Then something popped into her mind. *But what about that flirting? Those knowing smiles. The way he touches me, real casual like. That can't be in the FBI Agent Rule Book.*

She stole another look inside the store. The two men stood side by side, discussing a floor lamp with a long brass stem and a black fabric shade. Both men now stood in profile, and she caught something else: they shared the same high forehead, the same sharp nose, and the same cleft chin. In fact, they had the same hair—the only difference was the amount of gray flecked through it.

That's not Hoyt's lover — it's his father.

The realization that Nelson Hoyt had a family struck Kathryn like a mallet to the chest. It had never occurred to her that a guy like that had actual parents. And if he had parents, did he have a regular childhood? With a pet dog and a little red wagon and Boy Scout meetings and summer camp?

He's a regular person!

Suddenly, she wasn't so afraid of him anymore, not so daunted by the power he held over her.

The blinking orange neon sign above the window caught her eye as it flickered on and off. Sunset Lamps and Lighting.

There's irony for you, she thought. *Here I was assuming this Nelson Hoyt guy had a shadowy past I had no hope of discovering. Turns out, all I had to do was follow the light.*

CHAPTER 15

A meteor struck Hollywood on the Friday before the July fourth weekend, when Walter Winchell unveiled that the author of the best-selling roman à clef, *Reds in the Beds*, was Clifford Wardell, head of Paramount Pictures' writing department. The news sent scandalized Angelenos into bars and nightclubs to cluster for endless rounds of "Have you met him? Would you ever have guessed? What will happen now?"

Marcus was relieved that the truth was out. "Now that the mystery's been solved," he said to Kathryn over the scotch and soda somebody conjured that weekend by the pool, "maybe we can all get back to whatever passes for normal."

But they both knew the ripples in that particular pond had swelled too far for that. Hollywood knew that the Divine Oasis was supposed to be the Garden of Allah, that NJN was really MGM, and that their head of the writing department, a senior member of the Communist Party called Eugene Markham, was a thinly veiled Marcus Adler. "Quite honestly," Kathryn said the night after the Winchell show, "I'm surprised Mayer and Mannix haven't hauled you across the coals already."

The call from Mayer's secretary, Ida Koverman, came before Marcus had finished his first cup of coffee the morning after the long weekend. "Your presence is expected at ten. Do not be late."

With one minute to spare, Marcus let himself into the executive reception area. Ida pressed a button on her desk and the walnut door swung open.

Long before the name Benito Mussolini took on pejorative implications, Louis B. Mayer had decorated his office all in white to replicate the dictator's. The fact that Mayer had chosen not to renovate mystified Marcus. He braced himself as he approached Mayer and his right-hand man, Eddie Mannix. Seated with them at the round conference table were two men Marcus had never seen before.

Skipping any perfunctory shaking of hands, Mayer asked him to be seated. He waved a hand. "This is Tanner and Ritchey from Legal." He didn't bother to distinguish one from the other; not that it mattered. To Marcus they both looked like they'd spent too much time preparing legal briefs in the office and not enough honing their tennis volleys.

Marcus took a seat as Mayer gripped a copy of *Reds in the Beds.* "You read this?" he asked.

Marcus nodded.

"I was told it was trash and to not waste my time," Mayer said. "But of course, after Winchell . . ." He flicked the pages with his pudgy fingers. "It's trash, all right, but it's dangerous trash."

"It's dangerous," Mannix added, "because it's believable."

"Only to those who want to believe it," Marcus said.

"Are you a Commie, Adler?"

Mannix had seven inches and fifty pounds on Mayer, but they had the same beady eyes, which looked at Marcus with accusatory distrust. Meanwhile, Tanner and Ritchey maintained their professionally trained neutral lawyer faces.

Marcus took his time studying each of them before he picked up the book. "Would you be asking me if it wasn't for this three-hundred-page pile of horseshit?"

"Of course not," Mannix said, "but since Winchell's show on Friday, it's become an issue we can't just hope will go away."

One of the lawyers cleared his throat. "Mr. Adler, we need you to answer the question."

"Jesus Christ! This isn't NJN and I'm not Eugene Markham."

"Mr. Adler—"

"NO!" Marcus didn't mean to shout, but it got his point across. "I am not, nor have I ever been a member of the Communist Party. Is that legalistically succinct enough for you?"

He wished he hadn't been quite so terse. He needed to curry favor with these lawyers when he put a good word in for Arlene. She'd really come up with the goods for Kathryn and it was time to return the favor. "I'm sorry, gentlemen," he said placatingly, "but that blasted book has made my life thorny since the day it came out."

"How so?" Mannix asked.

"I live at the Garden of Allah."

Four pairs of eyes stared at him, then almost as though they'd rehearsed it, they blinked together in comprehension.

"The Divine Oasis," Mayer said, almost to himself. "I didn't make the connection."

"I wouldn't say this book has pitched neighbor against neighbor, but it's made life there less than congenial." Marcus placed his hands on the table in preparation to stand. "But I'm sure it'll pass. So if that's all you require of me, I have a story conference. The *Holiday in Mexico* script isn't coming together as well as it ought, so—"

"No, Adler, that isn't all," Mayer said. "Since Winchell's announcement, the shit's been hitting the fan over at Paramount. Do you know Quentin Luckett?"

"As a matter of fact, I do."

"Did you know he's been promoted to head up their writing department?"

"I did not." Marcus was so pleased for his friend that it was hard not to smile. *Quentin and I are now both heads of writing. And THAT calls for a long boozy celebration. Maybe the Sahara Room would be safe.* Since the night of the Hermit's Hideaway raid, Marcus, Oliver, Quentin, and Trevor had been warily avoiding each other's company in public. "But what about Clifford Wardell?"

"Banished from the lot. For life."

Maybe there is some justice in the world.

"We hear you know each other." That mix of suspicion and accusation had crept back into Mannix's voice.

"Me and Wardell?" Marcus pedaled softly. "It would be an overstatement to say 'know each other.'"

"What would a more accurate statement be?" Tanner asked—or was it Ritchey?

Marcus took a moment to consider his response. The only sound he could hear was Ida Koverman's typewriter clacking away in the next office. "We both attended the same cocktail party recently."

"Thrown by—" the lawyer paused to consult his notes— "Konstantin Simonov. Who's he?"

"The Russian consul. Also a playwright. He said he invited me because he admired my work on *Free Leningrad!* but Wardell and I were there so he could pitch an idea."

Mannix snorted. "Everybody's got an idea for a movie."

Marcus and Simonov had corresponded a couple of times after the Russian sent him the Pavlova outline. It was a thoroughly professional piece of work, and Marcus was still waiting for a response to his offer.

Mayer and Mannix looked at the two lawyers, who nodded.

"There's something we need you to do," Mannix said.

This doesn't sound good.

"We want to secure the rights to *Reds in the Beds.*"

"Are you out of your mind?" Marcus thundered. "It's bad enough the book's done so well to convince half of America that there's a Pinko in every bed in Hollywood. Film it and that message will find its way to every corner of the country."

"Don't be an idiot," Mayer snapped. "Nobody said anything about making a movie out of that donkey shit."

"You want to make sure *nobody* makes a movie out of it."

"And you need to get it for us."

Evidently, nobody in the room had heard about the brawl down in Long Beach. Marcus chose his words carefully. "I'm not the best guy for that job." *Because Clifford Wardell hates my guts with a rage that Hitler would envy.*

"I put a call through to that bastard's publisher," Mannix said, "and they told me Wardell's contract gives him the power to conduct all screen right negotiations."

"I assure you," Marcus insisted, "our best chance at scoring those rights will be if someone else does the negotiating."

Mannix crossed his arms. "Adler," he said, his voice low and growly, "did I give you the impression you had a choice in this matter?"

Marcus had played office politics long enough to know when to beat a hasty retreat. "I'll do my very best."

"You'll do whatever it takes."

Marcus nodded and headed for the walnut doors. He kept his eyes glued to the floor until he was in the elevator, facing a recent portrait of Mayer looking smug and detached. Marcus tapped the glass.

"If you were doing your job properly, you'd have jumped on this eight months ago when the book came out. Our chances here are somewhere between zilch and zero."

CHAPTER 16

Gwendolyn's sewing machine was so old that Prohibition was still the law of the land when she bought it. It was a basic model, black with the Singer logo in gold. She'd used it to stitch together hundreds of outfits over the years, and it had never once failed her. There were newer models capable of executing much fancier work, but until this one fell apart in her hands, she was happy to rely on the Singing Beast to get her work done.

And what work there was to be done! She walked out of the Midnight Frolics with fifteen orders. After Mr. Dewberry warned the men they'd better be prepared to cough up good dough if they wanted something classy, Gwendolyn quoted as high as she dared, and nobody fainted from shock. Several of them demurred, saying it was beyond their present budget, but most offered to pay the whole amount up front. Gwendolyn told them she'd be perfectly happy to accept half as a deposit, and then take the balance when they came for a fitting. The words "for a fitting" sent most of them twitching in anticipation.

Bent over the Singing Beast, she could feel the heat radiating from the motor and knew it was time to give it a rest. She looked up to see her new volunteer assistant, Arlene, standing in front of her portrait.

"You done with that hem?" Gwendolyn asked.

Arlene nodded. "Those ruffles weren't too bad, once I got the hang of it."

A moon-faced accountant type with pudgy fingers and a double chin had requested a Carmen Miranda outfit. Gwendolyn was daunted at first, but when he sent her a photo from *That Night in Rio* clipped out of *Modern Screen* showing Miranda in a pale yellow dress with large panels of crimson zigzags, she was relieved. The trickiest part was the puffy sleeves, and they could tackle that after lunch.

When Marcus first told Gwendolyn about his strawberry blonde hooker from Leilah's brothel, she pictured a hard-bitten Warner Bros. gun moll with a bad henna rinse and a shoddy manicure.

She was taken aback when Arlene moved into one of the inexpensive rooms in the main house and shyly joined the cocktail party Bertie threw to celebrate the navy's first successful atomic blast in the Pacific.

Gwendolyn doubted Bertie could even find this Bikini Atoll on a map, but she knew she'd been looking for an excuse to throw a party. Bertie invented a new drink and called it a Gilda after the nickname the military gave the bomb.

Gwendolyn couldn't have been more surprised when Arlene asked Kathryn who the Deanna Durbin in the cashmere sweater and ballet slippers was. By the time the party was over and everybody was smashed on Gildas, Gwendolyn had recruited Arlene to help. Gwendolyn had rashly promised to finish two dresses a week and was already starting to panic that she would fail her first-ever paying customers. Thankfully, Arlene turned out to be as skilled with a needle as she promised.

But as much as Gwendolyn needed the help, she didn't want to continue under false pretenses. It took a special sort of person to be okay with making dresses for men, and Arlene deserved to know what she was doing.

Gwendolyn headed for the kitchen past Arlene, who was still looking at Gwennie O'Hara. "What do you think?"

"You should rig up a spotlight on it," Arlene said.

"To be honest, I find it narcissistic to have one's portrait hanging in the living room. Are ham and cheese sandwiches okay? I might have some chutney."

Arlene trailed after her. "If you think this is narcissistic, you should see what I've just escaped from. Oh, brother."

Gwendolyn pulled bread, cheese, and ham from her little Frigidaire and spread them along the counter. "It must have been dreadful."

"Could've been worse. I figured out ways to avoid the actual work as often as I could."

Gwendolyn flipped on the radio. After the warm-up static abated, the smooth strains of Perry Como's "I'm Always Chasing Rainbows" filled the kitchen.

"You mean like doing Leilah's paperwork?" Gwendolyn asked.

"Yes, that, and fixing buttons and zippers and hems for all the girls. They were pretty as all get-out, but Lordy, what a bunch of dummies. They couldn't do a thing for themselves — not sew, not cook, and forget about balancing a checkbook. Honestly, I'm surprised they figured out which hole to use."

Gwendolyn looked up from her sandwiches.

The girl rolled her eyes. "After working in a brothel, nothing shocks me anymore."

Gwendolyn eyed the half-finished Carmen Miranda on the dining table.

"Pretty much the only thing those dumb gals knew how to do was keep the weight off. Mrs. O'Roarke insisted everyone stay movie-star thin, so black coffee and Benzedrine is all I saw any of them have. I guess I'd gotten used to it because when I saw the measurements of this outfit we're making, my first thought was, *Sheesh, how big is this woman?* Then I realized, *Maybe she ain't fat, she's just normal.*"

Gwendolyn sliced their sandwiches into triangles and slid them onto plates. "There's something about my clientele I haven't shared with you."

Arlene wiped up an errant spatter of chutney with a finger. "Oh yes?"

Gwendolyn was still deliberating where to start when four loud beeps sounded from the radio.

"We interrupt this broadcast for a news flash. Aviator and movie producer Howard Hughes was testing his new XF-11 photo-reconnaissance plane this afternoon when he experienced propeller trouble over Beverly Hills. Eyewitnesses report he tried to reach the Los Angeles Country Club. However, he lost altitude short of the golf course and made a crash landing on Linden Drive at the western edge of Beverly Hills."

"Oh my!" Arlene exclaimed. "Do you think he's dead?"

They moved closer to the radio.

"The giant aircraft tore the roof off 803 North Linden Drive then sliced through the upstairs bedroom of the home next door. Mr. Hughes was pulled from the wreckage alive; however, initial reports state that he hovers near death, with a punctured lung and multiple broken ribs. We shall bring you updates when they come to light."

As Perry Como filled the kitchen once more, the two women bit into their sandwiches.

"Do you know who lives on Linden?" Gwendolyn asked.

"Who?"

"Leilah O'Roarke."

"No!"

There was a knock at the door.

Gwendolyn pulled it open to find Marcus and Oliver; Marcus had a large book and Oliver held a letter. She ushered them inside. "You've heard the news, then? Can you *imagine*?"

The guys frowned at her.

"We've come with news," Oliver said, "but something tells me it's not the same news." He held up a letter. "My friend was on a mission down in Colombia."

Linc's postcard had been stuck to the refrigerator so long, Gwendolyn barely even saw it anymore.

Marcus held up the book in his hands. *A Detailed Atlas of the Americas.* He laid it on the counter and cracked it open to a map of the west coast of Mexico.

Oliver pointed to a spot about halfway down.

"Mazatlán. My pal recognized it straightaway. *'El faro'* means 'the lighthouse,' and apparently the Mazatlán lighthouse is pretty famous, at least in Mexico."

Marcus flipped over a few pages until he came to a more detailed map of the town. On the opposite page was an alphabetical list of streets. He ran his finger down the first column; Gwendolyn read the name where his finger stopped.

Marcus took Gwendolyn's left hand. "It's quite possible that you'll find Linc living on a street called Emilio Barragán down south of the border."

Between the Hughes bulletin and this Mazatlán place, Gwendolyn's mind had gone to mush. She didn't know what to think, or how to feel, or what her next move should be, or if she even had a next move.

She studied the atlas again. "Looks kinda remote."

"We made some enquiries and it seems you have three options. Take a series of buses—"

"How many is a series?" Arlene cut in.

"Five. And it takes three weeks."

"What's option number two?"

"Fishing boats. They start out at San Diego and go all the way down to a place called Acapulco, stopping at every port along the way. They don't often take paying passengers, but apparently you can talk your way on board if you show them *mucho dinero.*"

Gwendolyn jacked her fists on her hips. "So your plan is for me to spend weeks at sea on a boat full of lonely sailors with nothing to do but—" She waved away the rest of her sentence. "Option number three?"

"Hire a pilot with an aircraft and fly down there."

Gwendolyn looked past the boys to the half-finished Carmen Miranda dress on her dining table. She had no idea how much it cost to hire a pilot and get him to fly down to Mexico, but she was pretty sure it was at least a month's work. Maybe more. Probably more. Probably a lot more.

Maybe you've moved on.

The thought took her breath away.

Even if I did find a way to get down there, what if Linc no longer lives on that street? And even if he's still there, what're the chances he's still got your dough? I've now got a list of clients almost begging me to charge as much as I want for a gown. Even so, fifteen clients won't generate what you need to open a store, but they're still paying you to do what you love.

"Guys," she said, "Arlene and I are fighting an uphill battle, so you'll need to excuse us. We must finish this dress by tonight so we can start the next one tomorrow. Thank you for your help, but—"

"We know none of these options are practical." She could see the disappointment in Marcus' face.

"I want you to know that I love you for trying." She nudged them toward her front door. "You've certainly given me food for thought, but meanwhile, you got to scoot. Carmen Miranda is calling."

She closed the door behind the guys and rested her head against the cool wood. *But what if he is there?*

She heard Arlene pointedly clear her throat. "Do you need to be alone?"

"No," Gwendolyn insisted, crossing back the Singing Beast. "Tomorrow we have a much more complicated ball gown. I hope you're fast with sequins, because there's going to be lots of them."

At least you'll know why Linc did what he did.

Arlene sat down at the dining table and picked up another panel of zigzag. "We were talking about your clientele. Is there something I should know?"

Gwendolyn lifted the dress off the table. "Let me describe the person who will be wearing this little number."

CHAPTER 17

Kathryn lingered in the corridor outside her boss' office, nervous as a turkey in November. She fanned herself with two versions of her next column. She had already put off this confrontation for three days and was all out of procrastination.

She strode toward his secretary, faking nonchalance. "Is he free?"

Vera didn't look up from her typewriter. "Yep."

"Today's mood?"

Vera tugged out the letter and screwed it up into a ball. "On a scale from white to black, I'd say battleship gray."

Kathryn found Billy Wilkerson standing at a teak credenza against the large windows that looked north across Sunset Boulevard toward the Hollywood Hills. He was using a blue checked handkerchief to wipe down a plaster statue painted a striking shade of pink.

"What's that?" she asked.

Wilkerson stepped aside to give her a full view of a two-foot-tall flamingo with a downward curving beak tipped in black, long spindly legs, and tiny eyes of yellow glass. "Inspiration." He returned to his desk.

Kathryn took a seat. "How goes it in the casino-building department these days?"

Kathryn and her boss had never actually agreed out loud that the subject of his desert folly was off limits. She'd already made it sufficiently clear that she thought the whole project was a reckless waste of time and money, and he'd made it clear he didn't care about her opinion one way or the other. It made for an easier working relationship if they simply didn't talk about it.

Wilkerson sat down to the mess of papers littering his desk. "You need me for something?"

She held up both sheets of paper. "I'm doing a piece on the Busby Berkeley situation."

The director and choreographer had been suffering through a tough time lately. His mother, with whom he'd been particularly close, had died, and he was floundering in a sinkhole of debt. Still, everyone was shocked when the *LA Times* reported that he had attempted suicide.

"Got some news to add?" Wilkerson asked without looking up.

"LA General is releasing him to a sanitarium."

"Probably the best place for him. So what do you need me for?"

I need you to wise up and get out of business with the mob.

"It's a delicate situation, and I don't know whether to go with just the hard facts, or softball it into a puff piece."

She knew how to read his scowl: *You've never needed my opinion before.*

"Whatever you've got up your sleeve must be a humdinger," he growled, "if you think you need to come up with a ploy as feeble as that."

She lowered the papers. "I know about the million bucks."

His face froze over. "I didn't know your sources were *that* good."

She looked at the tacky plaster flamingo while she steeled herself. "This time my source was the top of the food chain."

On the credenza behind him, a barrel-shaped mahogany humidor sat on a shelf out of the sunlight. Wilkerson reached back, flipped open the lid, and pulled out a Montecristo. He closed it, but made no attempt to light the cigar. Instead, he ran the length of it under his nose. "Which food chain might that be?"

Kathryn felt a line of sweat pool along the underwire of her brassiere. "The FBI."

Wilkerson remained as still as the garish statue behind him. Eventually, he said, "You want to explain that?"

I don't want to, but I'm going to have to.

"About a year before the end of the war, an FBI agent approached me about becoming an informer for them. I told them no, but they can be persuasive."

"So they had something on you?"

"No, but they could see I was hostile to the idea, so they said, 'We only want you for the duration.' Then they changed their story. 'We really just need you for one thing.' They were trying to build a case against Humphrey Bogart. They had some crazy idea he's a Commie, so they wanted me to befriend him because he lived at the Garden before he married Betty Bacall."

"And did you?"

Kathryn rubbed her forehead. "It got complicated. The long and short of it is that I'm still on their radar. He's the one who told me that their main area of interest is a particular Nevada casino."

"And who is this 'he'? Your super-secret spy FBI agent G-Man?"

"It's not like that." Kathryn thought about their convoluted method of contacting each other through classified ads. *Okay, so maybe it is.*

"And what have you been able to tell him?"

"I thought I'd given him a solid line on where Ben Siegel got the extra money to fund the rest of the project."

A cheerless smile curled his lips. "I had no idea Mata Hari was on my payroll."

"Apparently, I'm not a very good Mata Hari—my lead on Siegel's dough went nowhere."

"Why is this the first I've heard of it?" The dour smile had already disappeared.

"I figured the best policy was a 'need to know' basis."

"Are we having this conversation because I now need to know?"

Kathryn couldn't get a grip on whether or not he approved.

"You need to know that the FBI recently started to wiretap all of Siegel's domiciles and offices."

Wilkerson's poker face dropped away. His hand trembled as he lit his Montecristo. "You think they're wiretapping me?"

"He said they're not."

"Do you believe him?"

She pictured Hoyt greeting his father inside the lamp store. "I'd like to, but he only knows what Hoover chooses to tell him. Either way, I felt you should know."

He blew out a plume of gray-blue smoke. They both watched it shoot toward the ceiling.

"I appreciate your sharing this with me."

Kathryn breathed more easily. She'd been expecting fireworks, maybe some desk thumping and ashtray throwing. But he sat across from her, puffing like a banker. "They don't care about you," she said. "The whopper they're hoping to land is Siegel." She perched at the edge of the seat and gripped the corner of his desk. "Boss, don't you think it's time to let this one go? I know it's your dream, and I know it could become the ultimate moneymaker for you, but it's put you a million bucks in debt to the mob. I know you don't want to hear it, but this might not end well for you."

She let herself fall back in the chair, sapped. His eyes wandered aimlessly around the messy office until they landed on a framed photograph on his desk. It was of Wilkerson and his fifth wife, Vivian, who he'd married only two months before. He was still contemplating the photograph when someone from the typesetting room burst through the door. He was a short guy, thickset, with Popeye forearms and a perpetual five o'clock shadow.

"Here you go, boss." He rushed to Wilkerson with a galley proof. "Gimme a jangle when you're sure it's exactly what you want."

"Thanks, Perc," Wilkerson said, and waited for the guy to leave the room. "You know I can't walk away," he told Kathryn. "I've got too much invested, and I don't just mean the money."

I gave it my best shot.

His telephone rang. She went to get up but he waved her back down. "There's something I want to ask you," he said as he picked up the receiver.

Kathryn's eyes fell onto the galley in front of her as Wilkerson took the call. The fresh black ink was drying in the afternoon sun that was slanting through the panoramic window behind Wilkerson. She blinked when she saw the headline: *A VOTE FOR JOE STALIN*

For a number of years now, Wilkerson had been using his editorial column, "TradeView," as a soapbox for his deepening hard-line views. Whenever anyone — especially the more politically active liberals at the Garden — brought them up, Kathryn was quick to point out that she rarely agreed with anything her boss had to say. She would then add that he seldom censored anything she wrote in her "Window on Hollywood" column, and reminded them there were worse things than being given free rein to write whatever she wanted by someone who wrote whatever he wanted.

But "A Vote for Joe Stalin"?

Preoccupied by the phone call with his new wife, Wilkerson flung his feet up on the credenza. Kathryn perched herself forward and swiveled her head to the left to read the column.

He's actually going to name names! In print!

She recognized many of them. She'd briefly met Dalton Trumbo at the Academy Awards banquet the night he was nominated for *Kitty Foyle*. She'd met Howard Koch a couple of years later when he won for *Casablanca*. And Ring Lardner Jr. — Hoyt had asked about him the night the Hollywood Canteen closed down.

By the time Wilkerson got off the telephone, Kathryn was on her feet.

"Are you insane?" She pointed at the galley. "This is libelous. You'll be sued all the way to bankruptcy court!"

He stared back at her, infuriatingly nonplussed. "I can only be sued if I publish a false statement that is damaging to a person's reputation."

"Exactly!" Her voice hit a strident pitch.

"In that case, I've got nothing to worry about."

"How do you figure that?"

He ran a finger down the list of names. "Every one of these men are members of the Communist Party. They won't be able to deny it."

"You'll ruin careers!"

"Whose careers?" Wilkerson's voice had thickened with contempt. "A bunch of fellow travelers hard at work slipping their Communistic message into our movies? If those careers get ruined, then I consider that 'mission accomplished.'" He got to his feet. "I'm not the only one who thinks Clifford Wardell did Hollywood a favor by expos—"

"*Reds in the Beds* is a pile of drivel written — atrociously, I might add — by a two-bit hack with a chip on his shoulder the size of Cleveland. You cannot use it as the basis of some" — she waved her hand over the galley — "manifesto declaring war on talented people who may or may not be members of the Communist Party, which, I should remind you, is not illegal. It's called the First Amendment. Look it up!"

"I'm not concerned with constitutional legality."

"You should be!"

Kathryn stepped away from the desk, wanting to throw something at him.

"I'm concerned with the moral question here," he said. "Our motion pictures exert a huge influence on the values of this country. If there is any danger — and there is — that the fabric of American society might be compromised by the Communist principle, then I consider it my duty to fight it where I see it. To sit by and let that happen is un-American." He held up the draft of tomorrow's column. "This is how I fight the fight."

She opened her mouth, but he cut her off.

"Don't get me wrong. I appreciate the information you came in here to share with me. But I'm warning you, Kathryn, when it comes to this Commie issue, you either get on board, or get out of my way. This is war."

Kathryn backed out of her boss' office, past Vera's desk, and into the corridor that led to the elevators. The doors opened, and she was whisked to the ground floor. When she stepped out onto Sunset Boulevard, the heat of the July sun shocked her out of her stupor.

I'm standing here in public, she realized. *No hat, no gloves, no handbag. People will think I'm a homeless person.* Then she thought, *Just walk, Kathryn. If this is war, you're going to need a clear head.*

CHAPTER 18

Marcus tugged at the sweetheart neckline of the lilac shot-silk dress he was wearing. "Is this thing *supposed* to be uncomfortable?"

Gwendolyn slapped his hand away and pulled out the three pins clamped between her lips. "It's not lined."

"And my shoulders are cold," he added.

"That's what cashmere wraps are for," Arlene scoffed. She handed Gwendolyn more pins. "And besides, it's August—how cold can your shoulders be?

When Gwendolyn invited him over for drinks and nibbles with Arlene, he'd thought nothing of it. Oliver was at some official city function commemorating the first anniversary of Hiroshima, and Kathryn was at a soiree to welcome Marlene Dietrich back from entertaining the troops. Trevor Bergin was drafted into attending the same party with Melody Hope, so Quentin had dropped by and they were about to pour their first whiskeys when Gwendolyn came knocking.

"Stop fidgeting," she scolded him. "We'll never figure out why this darned thing isn't hanging properly if you keep squirming."

"I think you look terribly fetching." Quentin raised his glass in salute. "Lilac suits you so awfully well."

Marcus shot him a stink eye. "You're not helping."

"Then please, dear Marcus," Quentin said, "tell me: How I may help?"

"By tracking down Clifford Wardell."

It was now nearly a month since Mayer and Mannix ordered him to secure the rights to *Reds in the Beds*. The Herculean task was made all the more impossible when the news of Wardell's authorship and subsequent dismissal drove the little skunk underground. Quentin pulled in a favor and got Wardell's home address, so Marcus sent a series of ever more urgent telegrams, but they generated no response. So then he went to Wardell's little bungalow south of the Wilshire Country Club. His incessant knocking drew a nosey neighbor who sent Marcus to Wardell's favorite bar, a seedy joint called the Round Up. The bartender knew who Marcus was looking for, but hadn't seen him.

Quentin scooped up Arlene's French onion dip with a celery stick. "I already did my bit. Perhaps he hightailed it back East to visit Mother Dearest."

"That's more than possible," Marcus said. "Hand me my drink, will you?"

"Not till you're out of this dress!" Gwendolyn pulled on the front hem. "Don't move. The drape is perfect now." She took the piece of chalk Arlene handed her and ignored Marcus' awkward position. "You did a wonderful job, Arlene. Marcus should have gotten you a job in Costuming, not Legal."

When Marcus sent Arlene a message to meet her at C.C. Brown's ice cream parlor on Hollywood Boulevard, he knew she'd be pleased to hear that the secretary for Ritchey in Legal had found out she was pregnant, and the job was hers if she wanted it.

But he wasn't prepared for the flood of tears that erupted amid the high schoolers and out-of-work actors. It was the only nice-girl-happy-ending story he'd heard in a while.

Quentin raised his whiskey glass. "Here's to Clifford Wardell!" He downed the rest of his Four Roses in a swift gulp.

"What does this creep look like?" Arlene asked.

"As a matter of fact . . ." Quentin reached into his jacket and pulled out a clipping from *Variety*. "I cut this out to show Trevor because he was asking, too." He unfolded the article and handed it to Arlene.

"HIM? *This* is the guy?" She started to laugh. "I wish someone had showed me that a month ago."

Gwendolyn stood up. "Okay," she told Marcus, "you can get out of it now. But be careful — there's two dozen pins in this thing now." She lowered the zipper at the back.

Marcus snaked his way out of the dress and reached for his shirt. "You recognize him?" he asked Arlene.

She nodded, and made with the Betty Boop eyes.

"HOLY MOSES!" Quentin shot up in Gwendolyn's loveseat. "Clifford is a regular at Leilah's house of ill repute?"

Arlene nodded. "That's Mr. Ketchup, all right. He's got a thing for redheads. It's red or nothing with that guy."

"Puts a whole new spin on *Reds in the Beds*, doesn't it?" Gwendolyn observed.

Marcus looked at Arlene's strawberry blonde hair. "Does that mean you had to . . .?"

Arlene threw up her hands in horror. "No, thank the Lord. His preference was Rita Hayworth red, or Lucille Ball red. I didn't qualify."

"How often would he visit?" Marcus asked.

"Tuesdays and Fridays. He preferred the cathouse up on Benedict Canyon. She would swap us around from house to house if one of the girls had the day off, or called in sick because Aunt Flo had come for a visit."

"And you're sure it was him?" Marcus asked.

"We all knew about Mr. Ketchup. Mrs. O'Roarke would even pay girls to have their hair dyed extra red, and then charge him a premium. He never hesitated."

"Tuesdays and Fridays, you said?" Marcus asked. "What time?"

"Ten o'clock."

Marcus looked at his watch. It was a quarter of ten on a Friday night. He looked at Quentin. "Feel like taking a ride?"

* * *

It was a wide, single-story house spread out along a hairpin curve high up in the Hollywood hills. To the east, the Sunset Strip glowed, and farther up the canyon a single streetlamp lit the intersection with Mulholland Drive. Finding a place to park along this deserted stretch wasn't difficult, but locating a furtive cranny from which Marcus and Quentin could observe comings and goings proved more of a challenge. In the end, they agreed that it would be best to park a little ways uphill.

By the time Marcus embedded himself among the mammoth fronds of an old banana palm across from the brothel's front door, it was almost ten thirty.

Marcus wondered if a pig like Wardell was the type to get in, do his business, and get out in fifteen minutes. But Quentin insisted that he'd take his time and get his money's worth. "If he shows up at ten, there's no way he'd be gone already."

So Marcus stood under the broad leaves and waited and waited and waited.

At a couple of minutes to eleven, the left side of the double doors opened and Wardell slipped outside and rummaged through his pockets for a cigarette. Marcus was barely a couple of feet away before Wardell saw him.

Marcus jutted his head toward the house. "Enjoy yourself?"

Wardell didn't answer straightaway. He took in Marcus' appearance while he tried to figure out what was going on. "I did. But don't let me get in your way." He stepped to one side and jerked his hand toward the double doors. "Oh yeah, that's right, you're not interested in anything that goes on in there. On account of your *wife* an' all." He blew a smoke ring into Marcus' face and went to walk around him.

Marcus stepped in his path. *This might be your one and only chance to put this deal across. You need to keep this calm and contained, no matter what he says.*

"You never responded to any of my telegrams."

"You've got a high opinion of yourself if you think you've got anything I wanna hear." The jerk was pale as a wraith.

"Actually, Clifford, I think there is."

"After what you did to me?"

"What did I do to you?"

"Down at Long Beach. Goading me into admitting I was Julian Caesar."

"Someone broke the news to Winchell, but it wasn't me."

Wardell jabbed a finger toward Marcus' face. "I'll tell you this for nothing. You did me a favor. Since Winchell blabbed the big secret, *Reds* is selling more than ever. And the publisher has offered to buy my next book. Whopper of an advance like you wouldn't believe. I got money, I got fame, and I got out of that job I hated. I'm sitting mighty pretty and I owe it all to you. So thanks, buddy-boy."

"I'm telling you, it wasn't me."

"Well, in that case —"

Wardell shot out his right fist and slugged Marcus in the temple. Marcus staggered back with a deafening buzz in his ears. "And that's for calling me Clifford. I don't recollect inviting you to use my first name."

"You better watch that right hook of yours," Marcus said calmly. "Whacking people like that might affect your movie deal."

"Shovel that shit someplace else. Ain't no studio going to touch my book with a ten-foot pole."

Marcus looked Wardell in the eye, willing himself not to blink. "The movie deal I'm about to offer you."

A pair of headlights rounded the corner behind them. The two men split apart, backing onto opposite sides of the road while a late-model Pontiac slowed outside the brothel, then disappeared up the hill.

"What movie offer?" Wardell said, suspicious as hell.

Marcus pulled the contract from his jacket pocket and held it up in the moonlight. "Fifty grand. Standard deal. Sign it now and you'll have a cashier's check by Monday afternoon."

Even in the dim light, Marcus could make out the gleam of greed in the man's eyes. Marcus jiggled the paper. "Fifty grand's pretty good for just writing your name."

Marcus heard a window open; honky-tonk poured from the brothel as they stood in the murky moonlight, staring at each other. Eventually, Clifford hawked up a wad of spit and shot at the patch of dirt between them. "A hundred," he said.

Marcus whistled as though he was dismayed to hear him aim so high. "We both know this is the only offer you're going to get. And it's a one-time-only deal. If I walk away without your signature on the dotted line, Mayer told me to set fire to it. Come on," he pushed, "be realistic."

Eventually, Wardell said, "Seventy-five. And not a dollar lower."

"I'm authorized to go to seventy, and not a dollar higher."

Mayer had told him to go as high as a hundred grand, but Marcus knew that if he secured this deal for substantially less than that, it'd land him big kudos.

Wardell crossed his arms. "How about sixty-eight?"

Marcus blinked with surprise. "Didn't you hear what I said? I can go to seventy—"

"I'll take sixty-eight if you do me a favor."

"A favor worth two grand?"

Marcus searched Wardell's face for traces of sarcasm, or deception, or anything that indicated a hidden agenda. The honesty he found looked out of place, but genuine.

"I figured if I put a price on it, you'd take me seriously."

Oh, this I've got to hear. Marcus suddenly wished Quentin was hiding under the banana palm fronds witnessing this bewildering exchange. "I'm listening."

"There's this guy. Name of Anson Purvis. Son of my best pal growing up back home. He signed up to the marines right after Pearl Harbor. Bravest son of a bitch I ever met. Spent the whole war in the Pacific until Iwo Jima."

"What happened there?"

"Got a leg blown off, all the way up to his ass. Couldn't walk for nearly a year, but never complained. Not for a second. Now he's up and at 'em like a champ. And guess what he wants to do?"

"What?"

"Write movies. Can you beat that? You could've knocked me over with a cotton ball. So I ask him if he's actually ever written a screenplay. The next day he's on my doorstep with three of them all typed up, neat as can be."

"Were they any good?"

"Not bad. Needs a guiding hand, but then who doesn't?"

"So why not get him a job at Paramount?"

Wardell grunted. "I don't know if you've heard, but I'm persona non grata around there these days. Nobody wants to know me. Personally, I don't care one way or the other, but I promised the kid. He's had a rough time but is keen as all get-out and I'd hate to let him down."

"It must be killing you to ask me for a favor."

"Let's get one thing straight." Anger flared in Wardell's eyes before he wrestled it under control. "I don't like you. Not one little bit. But when I saw *Free Leningrad!* I thought to myself, Jesus, that annoying little twerp knows how to craft one damn fine story. Anson needs a strong hand, and if you give it to him, he'll churn out some great stuff for you. And I'll have done at least one decent thing in my life."

Screw you, Marcus thought. Screw you for snow-jobbing me with a sob story. He snorted. "This business sure makes for deadly bedfellows."

"What does that mean?"

"Sixty-eight grand, and I'll see this Purvis guy."

"Deal."

It was now time for Marcus to jab a finger in Wardell's face. "I'm making no promises that I'll give him a job."

"Anson understands that it's up to him to get the ball across the line. Now gimme your pen and tell me where to sign."

* * *

Marcus opened the door to Quentin's Chevy. He said nothing while he closed it and let his head fall onto the back of the seat.

"So?" Quentin urged. "What happened?"

Marcus pulled the contract from out of his jacket and dropped it into Quentin's lap.

"Shit! You actually got him to — wait, why aren't you smiling?"

Marcus closed his eyes. "I think I just made a pact with the devil."

CHAPTER 19

Kathryn sat her empty champagne coupe on the concessions counter of Grauman's Chinese Theatre. She let out a quiet burp and wondered if that had been her second or third glass as Bogie and Bacall approached her.

"Did you manage to get it all off?" she asked Bogie.

He held up his hands to show her that they were clean of wet cement.

"He had a hell of a time," Bacall said. "Damn near got it all over my new suit!"

"You're a part of history now," Kathryn told him. "Your handprints and footprints will outlast us all."

She grabbed the edge of the counter. *Three. That was definitely my third.*

Bogie pulled at his necktie. "I don't know how I managed to get cement inside my collar. Would it be rude if we just left?"

"But you're the guest of honor!" Kathryn pointed out the two dozen people gathered in the red and gold foyer to toast the latest recipient of the ceremony that was becoming the measuring stick of a star's worth.

"Kathryn's right," Betty said. "They're all going to want their five minutes with you."

Bogie curled a lip.

"Why don't you make one lap?" Kathryn suggested. "Wave and say hi without actually stopping, then slip out the back."

"This wet sand is driving me nuts."

"It's the price you pay for landing at the top of the mountain." Betty tugged at Bogie's sleeve. "One lap." She turned to Kathryn. "We're having a bite at Chasen's if you want to meet up later?"

"After we make a pit stop," Bogie interjected, "for a change of shirt."

But Kathryn had a pit stop of her own to make. Three champagnes had given her enough pluck to follow her original plan. "Maybe a rain check?"

* * *

On the sidewalk outside Grauman's, a Warner Bros. flunky asked her if she needed a taxi. She told him that home was within walking distance, thanks all the same.

She headed for Sunset toward a store whose orange neon sign flashed on and off with clocklike rhythm.

Kathryn had spent two months rethinking every presumption she'd made about Nelson Hoyt. FBI agents weren't supposed to have families or personal lives or childhoods. And they certainly weren't supposed to have kindly fathers who ran lamp stores that anyone could walk into at any time of any day, like for instance a late-summer Wednesday evening.

The shock of seeing Hoyt with his father had hurled Kathryn through such a loop that she hadn't even mentioned it to Gwendolyn or Marcus. She couldn't articulate the emotions duking it out inside her every time she thought of him. He was the face of the FBI. The one she wanted to get away from. The one who had her best interests at the bottom of his list.

But watching him greet his father with a hug, observing how the two men spoke to each other and made each other smile, was a disturbing jolt.

You need to know that your Mr. Hoyt ain't all bad.

Sunset Lamps and Lighting had two display windows on either side of a glass door. On the left, half a dozen antique lamps were arranged on two levels. The vibrant jewel tones glowing through the stained glass lampshades carpeted the sidewalk. The opposite window held only a matching pair of bedside lamps with bases made of eye-catching aqua crystal.

The tinkling of a small brass bell above the door brought Nelson's father from behind the long counter at the rear. A rush of lightheadedness forced Kathryn to wonder whether she'd downed an extra champagne without noticing.

As the man approached, she was struck by how much his son resembled him. Nelson was a carbon copy.

The gentle light of an elaborate crystal chandelier fell across his face. He looked like one of those character actors who played the wise father able to set things straight whenever Mickey Rooney or Jane Powell got themselves into a scrape. "If you're looking for something in particular, I'm here to help. Otherwise, take your time, browse around."

"I have a friend," Kathryn said. He almost looked startled. "A seamstress. She does a lot of work at home, but her place is kind of dark."

"So she needs something with a downward-facing bulb?"

"Uh-huh."

"With a goose neck so that she can direct the light?"

He smiled knowingly — as Andy Hardy's father might do when Mickey Rooney had confessed his latest calamity — and led her through a maze of lamps that pointed beams of light in a rainbow of hues. They arrived at a brass lamp with a clamshell shade on the end of an adjustable neck shaped like a question mark.

Kathryn beamed. "Perfect!" Gwendolyn's birthday was months away, but she'd had tired eyes and headaches ever since she took on her Midnight Frolics clients. The poor thing had been making do with a coffee-table reading light.

"I'll take it."

He ushered her to the counter along the back wall. "It's rather heavy," he said. "Do you have your own vehicle?"

Kathryn admitted that she didn't, so he suggested she leave her name and address so they could deliver it the next day. He pushed some paper across the counter to her while he made out her receipt. When she was done, she slid it back and started making out the check. As she was signing her name, she became aware that the gentleman was staring at her, almost bemused.

He handed her the receipt. "Do I pass muster?"

"Excuse me?"

"You are the girl, aren't you?"

She wondered if he recognized her voice from *Kraft Music Hall*. It happened from time to time.

"Which girl?" she asked lightly, slipping the receipt into her pocketbook.

"The one my son is keen on."

What?

She tried to keep her face noncommittal. "Am I?"

He rummaged through one of his drawers until he pulled out a photograph. He held it under the light of a frosted glass Art Deco fixture suspended from the pressed metal ceiling and studied it for a moment. He nodded silently as he handed her a photo of herself on the stage of the Hollywood Canteen on its closing night.

"Nelson has talked about me?"

She jumped at the sound of a slamming door at the rear of the store.

"DAD?" Nelson called. "I know I said I'd drop by tomorrow, but we just heard The Hoov will be in town." The door swung open. "So I went to the Gotham Deli and —"

Nelson's face fell when he saw Kathryn. It only took him a moment to recover, then he dumped his homburg and a brown paper bag on the countertop. He shouldered the office door open. "If you don't mind?"

She thanked Hoyt Senior for his help, then trailed behind Junior as he led her through a windowless office to a back door that opened onto a service alley.

He thumped the door behind him. "What the hell are you playing at?"

Kathryn regretted her third champagne. "My ex-roommate, Gwendolyn, is doing a lot of sewing these days, so I thought I'd surprise her with a new lamp." She crossed her arms. "Coincidences do happen. People need lamps. Not everything is a conspiracy."

The two of them faced each other like a pair of dueling musketeers for what seemed like an hour until he jutted his head toward the store. "Did he say something?"

She heard the old guy's voice again. *Do I pass muster?* This back alley was neither the time nor place she needed to digest that question. "Are we done here?" she demanded.

She went to walk past him, but he blocked her path. "What did he say?"

Kathryn opened her mouth but nothing came out. Even at the end of the day, Hoyt Junior's clothes were crisp and clean; his jacket fit snugly across his broad shoulders. "He asked me if he passed muster."

Without warning, Nelson leaned over and kissed her on the mouth. He pressed his lips — *so warm! so soft!* — and a full second — maybe even two — slipped past before she yanked her head away and pushed against his chest until he let go of her waist. "What the hell was that?"

"You've never been kissed before?"

She sputtered with indignation. "Let's get things straight, mister. You're the enemy." *An enemy who sure knows how to land a kiss.*

He crossed to the sagging wooden fence on the other side of the alley and thumped it with the side of his fist. A flock of seagulls on a telephone line overhead flapped away.

You've gone from kissing me to punching fences in no time flat. That makes you a little bit scary, but at least you've dropped the façade.

"Tell me, who exactly is the enemy?" he demanded. "And how can you be so sure?"

"Because *you* coerced *me* into ratting on my friends and neighbors. From where I'm standing, the whole situation is pretty black and white."

"Have you really failed to notice that we no longer live in a black-and-white world of easy answers?" He hung his fists on his hips and jutted out his chin, but had regained control of his voice. "That changed the day we bombed the Japs. Sure, if we hadn't, we might still be at war, wasting thousands more lives. But we unleashed a holy hell most of us never thought possible. You've seen the photos of Hiroshima and Nagasaki."

Like most people, she'd rationalized those bombs as the necessary evil that ended the war. But those photos out of Japan were haunting and painful to look at. *How the hell did we go from that kiss to atomic bombs? Is he trying to confuse me?*

"That may well be," she stalled, "but unlike Louella and Hedda, who jumped at the chance to inform on their peers, I really wasn't given much option. You, on the other hand, *chose* to join the FBI."

He spun away from her, then turned back. "I joined the FBI for the right reasons."

"And what might they be?"

"Ten years ago I saw war coming. I knew the military wouldn't accept me because of a twisted aorta, but I still wanted to do my bit. The Nazis and Japs aren't the only bad guys trying to defeat our way of life, and I happen to think that the American way is worth fighting for."

"You can rationalize what you do any which way you see fit, but don't go pulling some cornball stars-and-stripes routine. Not on me, buster."

"Then stop making me out to be the bad guy."

"I hate to break this to you, but you *are* the bad guy. You had me cornered since that day you walked into my dressing room at NBC. I even got married because you threatened me with vicious rumors if I didn't do something!"

"That order came from Hoover."

"Now you're sounding like one of those Krauts at the Nuremburg trials. 'It wasn't my fault. Hitler made me do it.'"

He let out a long, low whistle. "Where does that leave us?"

A flicker of movement flagged her attention in the corner of her eye. Hoyt's father was watching them through the office window. "That bank statement for Linden Holdings Company, the one I gave you at Don the Beachcomber. Any news?"

"I've seen some tangled webs in my time, but that one's a humdinger. It's going to take us time."

"Let me know when you do. And for the record there is no 'us.'"

She walked past him down the alley. It was the wrong direction for the Garden of Allah, but this was Hollywood where a great exit is sometimes all a girl needs to make her point.

CHAPTER 20

It was hard for Gwendolyn not to stare at the blonde sitting next to her in the starched white suit. She tried to train her eyes on the cab driver's head as he negotiated the hairpin curves in the woody folds above Beverly Hills. In a city teeming with beauty, Gwendolyn was used to encountering exquisite women of all kinds, but this creature was something else again.

Lana Turner opened her alligator skin purse and pulled out a compact to study her reflection. "I can't believe how nervous I am," she muttered.

"Haven't you and Howard been dating?" Gwendolyn was glad for an excuse to look right at her. *That flawless skin! And I always thought it was just good lighting.*

Lana snapped the compact shut. "We were, thanks to Miss Massey."

Kathryn turned around in the cab's front seat. "Guilty as charged."

She'd kept her promise to Howard Hughes and teed up a date between the two of them. Things started cooking quickly, and news of the romance circulated at Ciro's and the Mocambo until the day Howard crashed his plane. He'd refused all visitors until he called Lana a few days ago. Scared of what state she might find him in, she asked Kathryn to go with her, and even to recruit a friend as backup.

Gwendolyn was still working her way through her list of cross-dressing clients — there were still five outfits she hadn't even started — so she could scarcely afford to take a whole Sunday afternoon off.

On the other hand, what fool would pass up an opportunity to meet Lana Turner, Howard Hughes, *and* Cary Grant?

The cab pulled up in front of an eight-foot wrought iron gate that stretched between columns of creamy concrete. Kathryn paid the driver and the three women got out of the taxi and lined up across Cary Grant's driveway.

"Why is he recuperating here?" Gwendolyn asked.

"They're very good friends," Lana said. "Howard's always taking Cary up in one of his planes. They have lunch in San Francisco, or fly over the Grand Canyon. I guess he didn't want to be alone." She fanned herself with her purse and adjusted a wide-brimmed sunhat, white as her suit. "What if he's banged up real bad?"

The horrific shots of Howard's mangled aircraft made all the papers and newsreels. How anybody survived was beyond Gwendolyn's comprehension. Had Leilah and Clem O'Roarke lived one house over, they'd be waiting for the Hughes Aircraft Company to build them a new home.

"If he was still that bad, I doubt he'd have asked to see you," Gwendolyn pointed out.

The fanning stopped.

"If it's really too awful to bear," Kathryn said, "tell him your Aunt Cora is leaving for the East Coast tomorrow and you promised to visit with her."

Lana let out a smirk. Cora was the role in *The Postman Always Rings Twice* that made Lana an even bigger star. "I like that," she said, nodding. "Oh and girls, thanks for coming. I've never been great around doctors and hospitals. Gives me the heebie-jeebies."

She pressed the intercom button built into the pillar and identified herself to the haughty voice that answered. A long buzz sounded and the gate glided to the left.

* * *

Cary Grant's house was every bit as tasteful as Gwendolyn expected. Lots of teak and mahogany, drapes in warm maple brown, thick carpets in hunter green, bookshelves neatly stocked and spotlessly dusted. But there was no evidence that Grant was at home, leaving her more than mildly disappointed.

At the rear of the house, a uniformed butler drew open a glass door that led to a spacious back patio. Beyond the glazed terracotta tile, an expanse of lawn half the size of a football field stretched, and to the left stood a guesthouse bigger than three Garden of Allah bungalows combined.

A courtyard shaded by jasmine jutted out into the grass. Underneath it, Howard Hughes reclined on a chaise lounge angled to take in the panoramic view of the Pacific. A magazine was in his lap, but he seemed to be asleep.

The butler asked them to wait. He approached Hughes and tapped him on the shoulder. Hughes looked up and smiled, then beckoned the women to come join him.

Gwendolyn was relieved to see that Hughes wasn't nearly the appalling mess Lana had feared. Red jagged scars crisscrossed his face, but they looked like they'd fade with time and the help of a skilled plastic surgeon. While his skin was puffy and blotched in places, the bruising was mild, and there was no sign of burns. His brooding eyes were sharp and clear. He accepted Lana's kiss and Kathryn's handshake, and nodded politely when Kathryn introduced Gwendolyn.

"Have a seat," he told them. "I've sent my man to fix us some coffee."

The women sat down in the three patio chairs that were discreetly arranged on the side of his good ear. Kathryn and Gwendolyn let Lana take the seat closest to him.

"Why, Howie," Lana exclaimed a little too brightly, "don't you look wonderful?"

"I don't know that 'wonderful' is quite the word I'd use." He kept his eyes on Gwendolyn. "But I appreciate you saying so."

"All I had to go by was the papers and newsreel footage." She laid what struck Gwendolyn as being a territorial hand on Hughes' arm, but he recoiled so she pulled it away. "It's a wonder you survived at all."

"Things look different from this side of the bed. Thank you for coming. I've been a mite short on company lately."

From the nascent pout starting to form on Lana's mouth, Gwendolyn could see she wasn't very happy that her banged-up beau was focusing on someone else.

"I'm sure Mr. Grant hasn't left you alone." Gwendolyn made a show of looking at Lana. "Don't you think, Lana?"

The man glanced Lana's way, but only for a few seconds. "I don't know what I would've done without his support. But there comes a time when a guy needs companionship of the tender kind."

Lana shifted in her seat so that Hughes could see her more clearly without having to twist his neck at too great an angle. "When I got your call," she said, "I took it as a sign that your recovery was on its way. I can see now that it is. You're not in the most terrible pain, I hope?"

His eyes lingered on Gwendolyn. "So you're Gwendolyn Brick." She smiled but didn't know what to make of his comment. Hughes couldn't see the glare blooming on Lana's face. Or he was ignoring it. "I knew Linc pretty well," he said.

"Is that right?" *Please look at Lana. Pay her some attention. I didn't come here to distract you from her.*

"Linc and his head tailor used to make house calls." He pulled his shoulders back, flinching from the pain. "Whenever I needed a new suit or tux, they'd come over, loaded up with tape measures and cloth samples."

"He never mentioned that to me."

"Glad to hear it," Hughes said. "I insisted on full privacy — he was the only bespoke tailor who didn't go running to the tabloids and gossip columns." He flickered a sardonic eye toward Kathryn, who crossed her heart and held up her hand like a Girl Scout.

"Even if he had," she said, "I'd hardly consider it newsworthy. Especially with all the other sorts of things you get up to. Skywriting, for instance?"

Earlier that spring, Hughes hired a biplane to fly over Los Angeles and spell "THE OUTLAW" and draw two giant circles with dots in the center. He wanted Jane Russell's breasts back in the news, and for the days that followed, he achieved exactly that.

Hughes smiled, but it didn't last long. He let out a low groan.

"Howie, darling!" Lana exclaimed. "Are you all right? Can I make you more comfortable? How about some painkillers? Where are they? Shall I get—what's the butler's name? Can we get him to fetch you some?" She looked up. "Gwendolyn, how about you scoot inside and see what you can find?"

Gwendolyn was grateful to relinquish Hughes' focus. She stood up, but Hughes waved her down onto her patio chair.

"Stop fussing," he told Lana. "He'll be out with the coffee any minute. And anyway, I took my last fistful less than an hour ago; it'll be a while before I can have any more."

He looked at Gwendolyn again. She expected a lascivious gleam, but he seemed to be studying her with objective, almost scientific detachment. "Linc was always the gentleman," he said. "A real class act. I was surprised to hear of his disappearance."

Kathryn let out an involuntary snort. "You and the rest of the world."

"You know where he went?"

Gwendolyn hesitated long enough to be rescued by the butler's arrival with a large sterling silver tray loaded with a coffee pot, cups and saucers, and a plate of macaroons. Lana asked him to set it down on the table next to Hughes' chaise lounge and took it on herself to play hostess.

As they all sat back, Hughes said, "I don't suppose he went to Mexico?"

Gwendolyn and Kathryn exchanged looks.

"Why do you say that?" Kathryn asked lightly.

"The last time he came to see me, his head tailor was out with the croup, and he showed up with a replacement. A distinguished looking chap, clipped moustache, gray at the temples. Linc explained he came from down south of the border and *no hablo inglés*. I was impressed with how good Linc's Spanish was; his accent was impeccable. So when I heard he'd vanished and nobody knew where to find him, my first thought was, *Isn't anybody looking in Mexico?*"

"I went to Mexico once," Lana announced. "A place called Ensenada. We stayed at the Hotel Riviera del Pacífico. Every chance they got, the staff told us it's where the margarita was invented, on account of that was the name of the owner. I don't know if that's true or not, but I remember thinking their margaritas were the best thing about the place."

Hughes waited for Lana to finish her monologue. "Have you thought about looking for him there?" He must have seen the hesitation on Gwendolyn's face because he added, "Or should I not assume that you care?"

Lana crossed her arms and sat back with a huffy sigh.

"I do care," Gwendolyn said. Linc had been on her mind more and more since Oliver had heard from his missionary friend. "In fact, I think I might know where he is."

"Oh?"

"A town called Mazatlán. It's on the—"

"West coast, about halfway down. Been there a bunch of times."

"We hear it's a devil of a place to get to," Kathryn said.

"Not if you fly," Hughes replied, as though he was wondering why it was so necessary to state the obvious. "I have some property in Guadalajara, so I often stop at Mazatlán to refuel."

Gwendolyn eyed Kathryn and watched her friend subtly tilt her head. *If you want to know what happened to Linc, this might be your only chance.*

Hughes fell back on his lounge, suddenly looking gaunt and fragile. "I could fly you down sometime."

Lana let out an exasperated "Oh!" She strode out onto the plush lawn and headed for the oval pool at the end.

"That's very kind," Gwendolyn said, "but I can't imagine you'll be taking to the skies any time soon."

"Perhaps not," he said grimly.

"Honestly!" Kathryn asked. "How many times can you tempt the devil?"

"I'm an aviator. Flying is what I do. This last crash was a bad one, I'll admit, but it certainly won't prevent me from going back up the first chance I get." He eyed Gwendolyn. "You're at the Garden of Allah, right?"

Gwendolyn nodded slowly.

Mazatlán seemed so very far away and so impenetrably inaccessible that Gwendolyn had all but put out of her mind the possibility she could ever get there. So she was surprised to find how thrilled she felt at even the vaguest prospect that she might see Linc again.

Don't get your hopes up, she told herself, looking at Hughes' shattered body with a more detached eye. *It's going to be a very long time — if ever — before that man can even cross the yard unassisted, let alone fly an aircraft down to Mexico and back.*

"Think about it," Hughes said.

"I will," Gwendolyn promised. "Meanwhile, perhaps Kathryn and I should take our leave." She eyed Lana Turner's lone silhouette by the pool. "I believe you have an ego to soothe."

CHAPTER 21

Marcus dropped the *Hollywood Reporter* onto his desk and shook his head. He'd always thought of Kathryn's boss as a blowhard whose bonnet always had room for more bees, and his column confirmed that day after day. His now infamous "A Vote For Stalin" column where he'd named names had been bad enough. But then he decided to take his feud to the Screen Writers Guild and started throwing around words like "Catholic" and "Pope" and "Communist" and "Russia" as though he was running for president.

Marcus personally knew many of the screenwriters Wilkerson had listed — some of them at MGM, and some from the Garden of Allah. By printing these names right after posing questions like "Were they Communists or commissars of thought? Were they party-liners or fronters?," Wilkerson was signaling to Hollywood that he expected everyone to take sides.

Either get on board with me, or get out of my way. This is war.

He caught sight of his receptionist at his office door, squinting at him. He folded his *Reporter*. "You need something?"

"Security called. Said they've got someone asking to see you, and want to know if they should let him in."

"Did they get a name?"

Dierdre consulted a slip of paper. "Anson Purvis."

Marcus dropped his face into his hands. He had been expecting a letter or telegram or phone call from this wannabe screenwriter with the hard-luck story, and was planning to fob the guy off with the standard "Sorry, but our roster of writers is full."

"You want them to send him on his way?"

Marcus thought about the two thousand bucks Wardell had sacrificed to get this guy through the door. "Send him up."

* * *

Anson Purvis' beefed-up, outdoorsy frame filled Marcus' doorway. His white-blond hair was cropped in a military crew cut that suited the sharp angles of his open, mid-Plains face. His Scandinavian blue eyes were ice-pick sharp, the type to take in every detail — a handy quality for a screenwriter.

Marcus reached out to shake Purvis' hand.

"I didn't realize I was supposed to make an appointment first." Clutching a black leather satchel like a security blanket, Purvis took the closer of the two chairs.

"I was expecting to hear from you before now," Marcus said.

Purvis nodded. "I was going to come the day after I got the call from Cliff, but I took a nasty tumble on the steps out front of my apartment and ended up in the veterans hospital down on Wilshire. Did Cliff tell you about this?" He rapped three times on his leg — a dull, heavy thud. He offered Marcus a pained smile. "Took a while to recover."

"I hear you saw some heavy action. Iwo Jima, wasn't it?"

"Uh-huh. Land mines have a way of knocking a guy out but good." The pained smile persisted. "Here's a tip. If you're going to get blown apart, make sure you do it next to the most experienced medic in the Pacific."

A month before Pearl Harbor took the world by surprise, Marcus tried to sign up for the navy but was rejected on account of his poor eyesight. In the intervening years, he'd wondered what might have happened if the navy had rubber-stamped him. But sitting opposite this burly amputee with the vigilant eyes reminded Marcus how narrowly he'd avoided that kind of fate.

"But that's my past," Purvis said. "I came here to talk about my future."

"Yes, about that. I don't know what Clifford Wardell promised you, but we don't have—"

"I know I don't have any practical experience to speak of, but we've all got to start somewhere, right? And there's a lot to be said for growing up around Leonard Purvis."

Marcus sat up like a jack-in-the-box. Leonard Purvis was legendary. His career straddled the silent and sound eras, during which he wrote some of the most successful Westerns to come out of Hollywood, including nearly all the biggest hits for Hoot Gibson, Harry Carey, and Tom Mix. If you were a producer who wanted to make a Western, the first thing you did was try and convince Leonard Purvis to write the screenplay.

"He's your father?"

Anson Purvis blinked. "Cliff didn't tell you?"

Marcus wondered why Wardell failed to mention the single most persuasive detail that would've convinced him that their deal was on the up-and-up. "No, he didn't."

"Good, 'cause I don't want to ride into town on my father's horse," Purvis said. "Dad instilled in me two things: a strong sense of good ol' American patriotism, and what it takes to put together a good story. Before the war, I used to work construction. It paid well, especially for a guy with no college education. But I was like one of those fountains, always gurgling up a constant stream of ideas. The fellas on the crew used to kid me a lot on account of the fact I used to sit up there and dream up all these tales."

This big lug is just like me. "My teacher would yell at me in front of the whole class for staring out the window all the livelong day."

"You too, huh?" Purvis smiled, showing two rows of milk-fed teeth the size of movie posters.

Marcus pulled himself up short. *This guy is here because of Clifford Wardell. If something goes wrong and the brass asks you where the hell you found this schmuck, do you really want to say he came from the guy who wrote* Reds in the Beds?

"That's all well and good," he said, "but here at MGM, we don't make many Westerns."

"Fine, because I don't want to write 'em."

"What do you want to write?"

"War pictures. The way I figure it, people want to know what it really was like in the war. We fought the fight and won—that makes for heroes, and if there's one thing the American moviegoer loves, it's a hero."

The guy had obviously thought through his argument.

Purvis shifted forward until he was perched on the edge of his seat. "I can see you don't want to hire me. And that's okay—as long as you're saying no because I haven't convinced you I'm good enough for MGM, and not because you associate me with Clifford Wardell."

Outside Marcus' window, somewhere on the lot, gunfire pelted the air from the set of *Courage of Lassie*. Marcus didn't think much of the story—Lassie improbably ends up on the battlefield of the Aleutian Islands—but the volley of bullets helped to underscore Purvis' point about war pictures.

"Go on," Marcus said.

"You've met Wardell, right? Not exactly an upstanding example of American citizenhood."

"I thought you were a friend of his."

"He and my dad were on the college debate team that won the national championship three years running. My dad's a real loyal kind of guy. He knows Cliff ain't exactly war-hero material, but in his book, a pal is a pal."

"What about in your book?"

"In mine, a schmuck is a schmuck. Clifford Wardell is an A-1, first-class schmuck. And that novel he wrote proves it, right?"

The guy got to his feet, wincing from a sudden pain that Marcus could almost feel shoot through his own body. "Lookit, the truth is I didn't take any tumble outside my apartment. I didn't contact you because I didn't want you to think that I was any friend of Cliff's."

"What changed your mind?"

"I was visiting my dad and he brought it up. Told me you were the guy who wrote *Free Leningrad!* and that was the best goddamned picture to come out of Hollywood during the whole war. A nod from you would mean a whole lot to me."

Marcus was starting to thaw.

Purvis got to his feet. "You're a busy guy and I don't want to take up any more of your time."

Marcus stared at the guy's huge hands. "You must've been very good at construction work."

"I'm better at constructing a meaty plot."

"Can you prove that?"

"I brought some with me." Purvis lifted the flap of his satchel and pulled out three stacks of paper.

"Which is the best one?"

The guy dropped the top script in front of Marcus.

THE FINAL DAY

AN ORIGINAL SCREENPLAY BY ANSON PURVIS

Marcus looked up at the hopeful face. "A hundred words or less. Convince me."

"Okay, so it's the final day of the war in Europe before Germany surrenders. The audience knows this, and the Germans know it, but our hero doesn't. He's an American infantryman whose entire company has been cornered by a last-ditch Kraut offensive intent on killing as many Americans as they can before they have to endure the humiliation of surrender. He's almost out of ammo and food and water, but he learns there's a cache of supplies in the basement of a house at the edge of Berlin. It's a race against time to hold out for the official surrender, and it's a race for the last stockpile that might save the lives of his buddies."

Purvis extended his hand. This time, the handshake was firmer, more earnest.

Marcus asked, "How do I contact you?"

"My address is on the second page."

"Let me walk you out."

Purvis waved away Marcus' offer. "I've taken up enough of your day, Mr. Adler. I can make my own way."

As Marcus stood at his window waiting for Purvis to emerge from the building, he saw Mickey Rooney hurry past. Production had started on *Love Laughs at Andy Hardy*. Rooney was twenty-six now and could scarcely be expected to play the love-struck teenager much longer. As Rooney stopped in front of a mirror parked outside Soundstage 16 to check his tan woolen army uniform, Purvis walked past with a distinct limp that he'd been able to hide in front of Marcus. He watched Purvis trek to the front gate, wave at the security guard, and disappear around the corner.

Marcus stayed at the window and rubbed his chin. He wanted to go with his gut, and his gut said this Anson Purvis was the real McCoy.

CHAPTER 22

Kathryn threw a wooden spoon into her kitchen sink.

"I am working for an insane person!" she told Marcus and Oliver.

The spoon bounced out of the sink and clattered to the floor.

"He's going around naming names while he's building a casino with mob money. What if he starts naming *mob* names?"

The day after Billy Wilkerson accused twenty-three screenwriters of being Communists, Kathryn could tell she was falling prey to that ridiculous sort of female hysteria that her male counterparts found sneerworthy. But she was dealing with a boss who seemed to have lost his grip on what constituted acceptable risk, so a part of her felt justified.

She strode into her living room, leaving Marcus and Oliver to trail in her wake. "I can't even bear to look at this thing!"

She rolled the *Hollywood Reporter* into a baton, yanked open her front door, and threw it onto the landing. She kicked the door closed and headed for her purse on the telephone table.

It was too early for a drink, so a cigarette would have to do. She lit a Chesterfield and took a deep drag.

"After he published that Stalin column, I held my tongue for nearly a whole month. Then yesterday he made the mistake of asking what I thought of it." She rolled her lighter around in her hands. "We've gone ten rounds before, but that was a darn-tootin' doozie. And when I told him how disgraceful he was, being so cavalier with the professional livelihoods of so many people, he said I ought to be grateful. What the hell for? I asked him."

"What did he say?"

"That he was tempted to include the name of Marcus Adler—"

"What?!"

Kathryn tried to take another drag but found she'd already finished her cigarette. She flicked the butt into an ashtray. "He said he'd learned about the Simonov affair."

"It's officially an affair now?" Oliver asked.

"That's why I called you over here. Because Charlie Chaplin and John Garfield were at that party onboard a Russian ship, he strongly suspects you're a Commie. But— and this is where I'm supposed to be grateful—he omitted your name in deference to me."

She took comfort in the way Marcus suddenly looked like he could do with a drink, too.

"What did you say to that?" he asked.

"I started throwing around *How dare you?* and *How could you?* when he cut me off with marital advice!"

Oliver grunted. "From a guy who's on his fifth marriage?"

Kathryn didn't remember lighting another Chesterfield. "He said that marrying you was a mistake that could lead to professional ruin, and that I ought to start divorce proceedings immediately."

Kathryn flopped onto her armchair and Marcus joined Oliver on the loveseat. She closed her eyes. *If he wants to run his company like a fascist, then he can find someone else to fill his paper.* "What time is it?"

"Nearly noon."

Kathryn leaped to her feet. "Already?" She started straightening the newspapers and magazines sprawled over her dining table. "My mom's coming over."

Francine had called earlier that morning saying there was something she wanted to tell her. Kathryn tried to put her off, but Francine ignored her blatant hints.

She shooed the guys out of her apartment and was wiping down her kitchen counter when she heard her mother and her husband and her husband's lover greet each other at the bottom of the stairs. She walked into the living room just as Francine let herself in the door.

"Hello, dear." Kathryn's mother was starting to look every inch the late-fifties matron now. She'd taken to wearing conservative dresses in somber browns and muddy yellows with lace lapels and no jewelry save for her double strand of pearls. She started pulling off her gloves. "Who was that with *your husband?*"

Kathryn flinched. She could never tell whether Francine was still miffed at not being invited to the wedding or just disapproved of Kathryn's choice of spouse.

"Some new pal," Kathryn said, crossing the room to hug her mother hello.

"A fellow *writer?*" There was that tone again.

"You can put your gloves back on. We're not staying in."

"You said you'd make us a bite of lunch." Francine regarded the fallen wooden spoon with disapproval.

Kathryn picked it up and dropped it into the sink. "I'm not in the cooking mood."

"A grilled cheese sandwich will be fine."

"I need to get out of here. We'll go to the Cock'n Bull."

"That British place?"

"They serve Welsh rarebit. It's like a grilled cheese sandwich, British style." She picked up her handbag. "I've been fighting with my boss over — well, everything. I need sunshine, I need exercise, and I need . . ."

Francine stopped at the front door. "What else do you need?

"Either a stiff drink or a bicarbonate. Maybe both."

* * *

Kathryn was in no particular rush to get to the Cock'n Bull —
she wasn't sure they even served Welsh rarebit — but the
Saturday afternoon strollers and window shoppers
crowding the Sunset Boulevard sidewalk conspired to annoy
the hell out of her.

All she knew was that she needed to keep moving. She
half-led, half-dragged Francine around oversized baby
carriages, errant dogs, and women loaded with so many
shopping bags that they took up half the goddamned space.

"Gracious!" Francine panted, "if I'd known we were in
training for the London Olympics, I'd have worn different
shoes."

It took some effort for Kathryn to slow down.

"Isn't this lovely?" Francine nudged her toward an arty
window display of fifty-one silk scarves arranged like flags
to represent the recently convened first General Assembly of
the United Nations.

Kathryn barely took it in. An overloaded shopper ahead
of them had a man in tow who reminded her of Nelson. She
couldn't stop thinking about that kiss in the alley.

"You *are* in a mood," Francine said. "You going to tell
me what's on your mind, or is it something you only share
with *your husband?*"

Oh, that tone!

Kathryn could normally glide over it, but today it felt
like her well of patience had run Death-Valley dry. They
arrived at the three-story building with a matching pair of
chimneys right before Sunset curved into Beverly Hills.
"Have you tried their Moscow Mule? Scott Fitzgerald
introduced me to it. They call it 'the Drink with the Velvet
Kick' and boy, do I need one of those."

* * *

Kathryn had forgotten how dark it was inside the Cock'n Bull. The owner had tried to mock the place up as an English pub with straw scattered on the floor and antique hunting prints and brass plaques decorating the walls. Most of the seats were wooden armchairs called captain's chairs, which Kathryn didn't find terribly comfortable, but rumor had it that they kept the drunks from falling out.

The weekend lunchtime crowd was drinking tall glasses of a dark brown Irish beer called Guinness, which Kathryn had heard about but never tried. When the waitress warned Kathryn it was a tad strong, she ordered one, plus a Moscow Mule for her mother and a couple of Welsh rarebits.

Across from them sat a pair of nattily dressed studio executive types — fashionable suits, tasteful ties, gold pinkie rings, and jackrabbit eyes that were perpetually in motion. On their table lay a copy of yesterday's *Hollywood Reporter*. Kathryn looked away. "So," she said, "you have news?"

Francine shook her head. "No, dear, I didn't call you because I have something to tell you. There's something I want to ask you."

Kathryn could feel a headache coming on, and rubbed her forehead.

"I finished that book." Francine said, thin-lipped. "I assume Eugene Markham and Beatrice Kahn are supposed to be you and *your husband*?"

"It's the general consensus."

"Not very flattering, I must say."

"The whole book is not very flattering."

"I'd have thought it's the last thing *your husband* needed, what with all these Communist allegations flying around town."

"That hideous book is half the reason for all those Commie rumors."

The waitress arrived with their drinks. Kathryn was surprised how thick and creamy her Guinness was. There was a hint of chocolate, but bitter and dark, like a cold, foggy night. She wasn't sure she liked it, but she didn't hate it enough to send it back.

"We're just trying to ignore the whole thing."

"That can't be easy," Francine said. "Not when your boss is the one pointing his crosshairs at all those Pinkos. I do hope it's not placing a strain on *your marriage.*"

"What's with that tone you always use whenever you mention Marcus nowadays?" Francine looked at her as though she didn't understand the question. "You said it just now. The last thing *your husband* needs; a strain on *your marriage.* Are you still miffed I didn't ask you to the ceremony? Because I explained that to you. It was all very spur of the moment."

"It was your ceremony, Kathryn, you're allowed to conduct it in any way you please."

"You didn't miss anything. Just the four of us with a justice of the peace."

"My beef isn't that you didn't invite me to your wedding."

"But you do have a beef." Kathryn took a third sip and decided she enjoyed the yeasty, molasses flavor. "Just come out and say it."

"Do you think your husband is a Communist?"

"Oh, mother, if you only knew how laughable that is."

"They're saying the Hollywood Anti-Nazi League is a Communist Party front, and we both know that it was founded by Don Stewart and Dorothy Parker, both of whom have lived at the Garden of Allah. So it's not entirely outside the realm of possibility."

"Marcus is no Communist, I know that for damned sure."

"All I know is that your husband is no heterosexual."

Kathryn gaped at her mother.

The waitress appeared with their lunch, giving Kathryn a minute to consider how to handle this curveball.

It turned out that Welsh rarebit was an extra-thick slice of toast smothered with a gooey cheesy-mustardy sauce. Not quite a grilled cheese sandwich, but close enough.

Francine spoke again. "That chap he was with when he came out of your apartment, is that his *special friend?*"

The blood pounded Kathryn's temple. She scrambled to formulate a response that wasn't a lie and wouldn't compromise Marcus' private life, but the words evaporated somewhere at the base of her throat.

Francine drew herself up ramrod straight. "I've sat on the sidelines withholding my opinion about your marriage, but this Communist thing has brought out all the daggers. When I read your boss naming names in his column, I felt it was my duty to say what none of your friends have the courage to."

"Which is what?"

"You're lucky to live in Hollywood, because this is one of the few places where it's not the worst thing in the world to get a divorce."

"A divorce?" Kathryn nearly had to spit out the chunk of rarebit. "We've only been married a year!"

"In the eyes of God, you haven't been married at all."

"Since when do you care about the eyes of God?"

"I've started to attend services lately." Francine wiped the edges of her mouth. "The Church of the Good Shepherd."

That was the one in Beverly Hills with the most celebrity worshipers west of Central Park. Everybody from Valentino to Bing Crosby went there, some of them to be seen rather than to be pious.

"Thank you for your advice, Mother, but I'm not about to get a divorce because your vicar's been preaching from his pulpit—"

"He's not a vicar," Francine cut in, "he's a priest, and give me some credit, please. I'm telling you because this anti-Communist thing has every sign of becoming a witch hunt. Don't forget—I hear things. Not intentionally, of course, I don't go snooping, but I do hear things."

Francine was the head telephone operator at the Chateau Marmont Hotel. "What sort of things?"

"Suffice it to say that if the House Un-American Activities Committee comes to Hollywood, they're going to start digging around. If you've got any skeletons in your closet, now is the time to sweep them out."

CHAPTER 23

Oliver and Kathryn peered into the mixing bowl while Marcus lit the pilot light in his oven with a kitchen match.

"Do you think it's going to work?" Oliver frowned.

"During the war, I made this cake a ton of times."

"I know, but—"

"Without butter, eggs or milk, it tasted just fine. It can only be better *with* them."

Kathryn risked a sniff. "Without a recipe, how are you sure you've added the right amounts?"

Marcus elbowed the amateurs out of the way and started aerating the batter. "You just know, you know?"

"No, I don't." Kathryn crossed her arms. "I'm a working woman who's next to useless in the kitchen—"

"—which is precisely why I'm divorcing you."

Marcus waited a moment before checking to see how his zinger landed. He was relieved to see Kathryn smile. He filled the cake tin with batter and slid it into his oven.

"You ready to talk about it?" he asked Kathryn.

Marcus had been at home reworking a problematic screenplay for *Lady in the Lake* when he heard Kathryn arrive home from her lunch at the Cock'n Bull. He listened to her stomp around upstairs, slamming cupboards for a while until she started swearing like a longshoreman. He then mounted the stairs and asked her what in tarnation had got her all riled up. He didn't help her mood when he hinted that perhaps Francine had a point. He left her apartment, telling her she was welcome to talk about it when she was calm.

It took a week.

However, she more than made up for it by arriving with a tray of Marcus' favorite appetizers — crab-stuffed celery, liverwurst on rainbow rye, sliced tongue, pearl onions — and the three of them decided it was enough for dinner with Marcus' modified War Cake for dessert.

He set his oven timer to thirty minutes and poured out three glasses of champagne. "So," he said, "the D word."

Kathryn tsked. "I'd feel like a failure."

"But as your mom pointed out, this is Hollywood," Oliver said. "Lana Turner's got three under her belt and she's, what, twenty-five?"

Marcus grabbed her hand and kissed her fingers. "My darling wife, if this were a real marriage, then maybe you'd be right to feel that way. We did this because it suited us. Between your FBI association and my" — he jutted his head toward Oliver — "predilections, we both have skeletons which could threaten not only our own careers, but each other's. Perhaps we ought to quit while we're ahead."

Oliver drained his champagne coupe. "You could get an annulment. Technically, you've never actually consummated the marriage, have you?"

After a long pause, they all burst out laughing.

Marcus crossed over to the kitchen to pull out some plates. There was a knock on the door. "Could you get that?" he asked Kathryn. "I've already got crabmeat all over my fingers."

The next thing he heard was Kathryn exclaiming, "Why, Mr. Mannix! What brings you here?"

Marcus and Oliver exchanged looks of panic. *Go! Marcus* mouthed at Oliver. *Bedroom!*

"Your husband at home?" Mannix asked.

Oliver dashed into the bedroom and jumped into Marcus' closet just as the second most powerful man at MGM invited himself in.

Marcus threw his hand towel into his sink and crossed the room. "This is a surprise. Something up?"

——

"Don't tell me the studio just burned to the ground" Kathryn let out a nervous twitter of a laugh.

Mannix looked at the coffee table, where three champagne coupes sat amid Kathryn's hors d'oeuvres. He looked around for the owner of the third glass.

"Our neighbor's moving out, so a little farewell was in order." Kathryn said.

"I'm here about an urgent matter." Mannix took off his hat. "However, we're gonna need privacy."

"Our guest has gone," Marcus said, offering Mannix a drink that was declined.

Kathryn shot Marcus a wide-eyed look: *An awful big pile of shit must have hit an awful big* fan *if HE has come to see YOU and doesn't even want a drink.*

"So what's going on?" Marcus asked.

"I got some questions to ask you and didn't want to do it at the studio."

And apparently, Marcus thought, *it's so urgent that it can't wait till Monday.*

Mannix glanced warily at Kathryn. "We don't mean to kick you out of your own home, but it's confidential. Do you think you could make yourself scarce? An hour, maybe?"

"I do believe I have a strong hankering for a Schwab's chocolate malted, so if you'll excuse me." Kathryn picked up her handbag and started heading out, then returned to give her husband a wifely goodbye kiss. As she bent over, she whispered into his ear, "Briefcase!"

Oliver's light-brown leather briefcase sat against the end of the sofa nearest the bedroom. His name was stenciled in gold leaf above the clasp.

"See you soon, dear," Marcus said, taking a seat on the far end of the sofa to draw Mannix's eyes away from the briefcase. "What's going on?"

"I need to know everything that happened at Konstantin Simonov's cocktail party."

Oh Jesus, the Simonov thing again?

Mannix pulled a pad out of his jacket. "First off, why did you go?"

Marcus poured himself some champagne. "I get invited to all sorts of things. I'd never seen a Soviet battleship before. I was curious."

"You went because you were curious about some ship?" Mannix seemed far from convinced. "Okay, so you get on board. Was Chaplin there?"

"As a matter of fact, yes, he was."

"How did he behave?"

"He was very cordial—"

"Cordial with who?"

"He came right over to say hello. We met the night of the *William Tell* premiere. He—"

"How did he seem with the Russians? What about Simonov? And the crew? Did he know them? Was he friendly with them?"

"He was friendly with everyone."

"Okay, so who else was there?"

"His wife, Oona. And John Garfield, and his wife."

"Forget the wives. Chaplin and Garfield. Who else?"

"Lewis Milestone."

The way Mannix bit into his lip and scribbled something on his little pad made Marcus uneasy. This was all leading to something.

"Was there any talk of Communism?"

Marcus wondered if Oliver could hear all of this. "Not around me," he answered. "But then again, Simonov took me outside at one point to talk about business."

Mannix shifted in his seat. "What business?"

"*The Russian Swan*. You know, that Anna Pavlova biopic we're doing."

"What's that got to do with Simonov?"

"It was his idea. The outline we bought was his."

"FUCK!" Mannix's face deepened several shades of red. "I'll take that drink now. Whiskey."

As Marcus rounded the end of the sofa, he gave Oliver's briefcase a quick kick, but only managed to get it halfway underneath. By the time he'd returned to the coffee table, Mannix had loosened his collar and was tapping his foot on the rug.

"Surely we could have had this conversation at work," Marcus said.

"L.B. just learned that the FBI's got all of Bugsy Siegel's places bugged, so now he's paranoid about the studio."

"That's a stretch, isn't it?"

Mannix made a grunting sound like he agreed but wasn't willing to say it out loud. "L.B. and I were having dinner at Romanoff's tonight when Hedda Hopper walked in. She made a beeline for us, couldn't wait to tell us about her piece in tomorrow's *Times* about our union trouble."

Over the past summer, the unions representing carpenters, painters, and set designers went on strike. It was settled after a few days, but not before police squads were called in and the firemen turned hoses on the picketers. Rumors had been swirling around MGM that more trouble was on its way.

"So Hedda's now on the politics desk?" Marcus asked.

"The bitch has decided to saddle up her high horse and take us to task over our so-called heavy-handed tactics. Now she's referring to us as Metro-Goldwyn-Moscow. Between *Reds in the Beds* and Billy Wilkerson's list of Pinkos, it's the last thing we need." Mannix held out his empty glass for a refill. "Then she starts in about this Simonov character."

Marcus retrieved a bottle of Four Roses and brought it to the table, kicking the rest of Oliver's briefcase out of sight. "What did she say?"

"First, she had to explain what it was, because she could tell from our what-the-fuck mugs that we were in the dark."

"She must have got a kick out of that."

"And then she mentioned *your* name."

Marcus felt lightheaded, but not in a champagne-with-a-whiskey-chaser way. "In what context?"

"This."

Mannix pulled a strip of paper from out of his pocket and handed it over. It was a list of about twenty names, commencing with Lewis Milestone and Charlie Chaplin. Immediately following them was Dalton Trumbo, one of MGM's best screenwriters—his *Thirty Seconds Over Tokyo* was one of the highest-praised movies during the war. Then Lester Cole, a screenwriter whose work for studios all over town Marcus had long admired. He ran his eyes down the list. Some names he knew, some he didn't. He stopped when he got to Ring Lardner Jr. and thought of the conversation Kathryn had with Nelson Hoyt outside the Hollywood Canteen. But it was the last four names on the list that made Marcus twitch: Lillian Hellman, Donald Ogden Stewart, Trevor Bergin, and Dorothy Parker.

Marcus only started breathing again when he realized his own name wasn't there. "Whose list is this?"

"Hedda's, but it looks like Wilkerson's. You see why we asked your wife to leave the room?"

"My name's not here," Marcus said.

"That's what bothered Hedda, seeing as how you were on board that Ruskie tub. That's when we got into the whole Simonov thing. Who else was there?"

Marcus shrugged. "The rest were strangers to me."

"What about when Simonov was pitching the Pavlova movie to you? Anyone else hear that?"

Oh boy. I thought I was going to be able to skate past this one.

A rustling noise came from the bedroom, like heavy shoeboxes tumbling over. Mannix's eyes shot toward Marcus' closet.

"Is somebody else here?"

"The plumbing," Marcus said as blithely as he could. He poured some more whiskey. "It's got a life of its own."

Mannix kept his eyes on the bedroom.

"Clifford Wardell," Marcus blurted out.

The name was enough to cause Mannix to lose interest in Marcus' closet. "What about him?"

"We both got invited because Simonov wanted to offer up his Pavlova idea."

"What did Wardell think of it?"

"Said it was a piece of crap. That's how we got it. But it's shaping up to be a fine picture. Got class written all—"

"Kill it," Mannix said darkly.

"We've spent a decent amount in preproduction."

"The time to make that movie was when the Ruskies were our allies. Since Churchill dropped his Iron Curtain, those fakakta Bolshies are now the enemy. Cretins like Wilkerson and Hopper have seen to it that anything associated with Russia is now painted with pink and red stripes."

Marcus thought of his greatest success as a screenwriter. *Free Leningrad!* was set in Russia during the first part of the war. Were agitators like Wilkerson going to start applying their slanderous labels retroactively?

Mannix squinted over his cigar. "We got any other Russian pictures on the slate?"

Marcus' mind was hazing over. "I'll double check on Monday."

"You'll go into work tomorrow and triple check," Mannix told him. "L.B.'s ordered that anything remotely connected with Russia be shut down."

Ironic, considering Mayer was born in Minsk.

"We need to find a picture with an all-American hero," Mannix continued. "Tough as nails and braver than shit." He glowered at Marcus. "I don't care if you have to pull it out of your ass, Adler, but you need to find us something so patriotic it'll make every lousy Pinko on the face of the planet shrivel up and die. I'll be damned if we're gonna let that bitch call us Metro-Goldwyn-Moscow and think she can make it stick."

Marcus' closet emitted another shuffling sound, louder this time. Mannix got to his feet and stepped inside the doorway, cocking his right ear toward the room. "What you got in there? A gorilla?"

"I've got exactly the picture we need," Marcus said shrilly.

"Yeah?"

Marcus hadn't read Anson Purvis' *The Final Day* yet; it was still languishing on the outer edge of his desk because he thought of Wardell every time he reached for it.

"It takes place on the last day of the war. It's got patriotism, bravery, an American hero, the whole bit."

"And it's good?"

It'd better be. "I'll have a detailed synopsis on your desk first thing Monday."

Mannix threw back the last of his drink. "All this bullshit's giving me a fucking headache." He put on his hat and started for the front door. "Tell your missus sorry to boot her out of her own house."

"She understands," Marcus said. "She enjoys her chocolate malteds at—" Mannix slammed the door behind him.

Marcus ran into his bedroom and yanked open the closet door. Oliver toppled out.

"Are you okay?"

"Let's just say I'm in no hurry to do that again."

As Oliver hauled himself to his feet, the two of them sniffed the air.

"Do you smell something burning?" Oliver asked.

"My cake!"

They raced into the kitchen and Marcus yanked open the oven door. A bloom of pungent smoke enveloped him as he retrieved the cake tin and set it on the counter. Marcus fanned away the smoke. The edges were moderately, but not irreparably, singed.

"Is it salvageable?" Oliver asked.

"That depends," Marcus replied, "on whether you're asking about my cake or my career."

CHAPTER 24

Gwendolyn stepped out of the empty store and into the harsh sun, barely registering the early afternoon traffic that was sailing past.

"Well," Kathryn said behind her, "that was certainly a slap in the face."

Gwendolyn faced the store she'd hoped might soon be Chez Gwendolyn. "It would've been perfect."

"The rent!" Kathryn exclaimed. "Talk about highway robbery. Did you see that realtor's face?" She took on the guy's haughty Connecticut accent. "'Obviously you haven't been keeping up with the times.'"

The papers were all reporting how Los Angeles was undergoing the biggest boom since the transcontinental railways arrived in the 1880s. Article after article detailed how rents were spiraling ever upwards, as were costs for construction, labor, and raw materials. But cloistered inside the walls of the Garden of Allah, Gwendolyn hadn't paid much attention.

After she'd delivered all fifteen dresses for her Midnight Frolics customers, they were so happy with them that she got orders for four more. After paying Arlene for her time, she had nearly a thousand dollars stashed in her Girl Scout cookie tin. She'd been so thrilled when she walked past that empty store last week.

It was exactly what she'd been picturing all these years. Two spacious windows, lots of good light, and she could walk there from the Garden. But if that's what they were asking for in rent, and without her black market stash . . .

Damn Linc Tattler and his thieving little fingers. Without Chez Gwendolyn, what have I got to look forward to?

"If Linc were here, I'd slug him in the guts."

"Howard offered to fly you down."

"Humpty Dumpty has a better chance of flying an airplane than he does. Can we please change the subject?"

"Shall we talk about tonight?" Kathryn suggested.

Gwendolyn knew it was only a lavender marriage, but now that Kathryn and Marcus were unraveling their bonds, she felt a sort of grief. And now that Chez Gwendolyn had withered on the vine, it was as though her whole life were dwindling to a standstill. The last thing she felt like doing was hosting the Gay Divorcée party she'd offered to throw.

"Schwab's is delivering the booze at six," she said. "Are you sure you want to do all the hors d'oeuvres?"

"Haven't you heard?" Kathryn said proudly. "I'm queen of the hors d'oeuvres now."

"I didn't hear from Dottie. Is she coming?"

"Yes! Universal is doing a picture called *Smash-Up* from some story she wrote with the guy who did *The Corn Is Green*. I saw her at the Nickodell after my show last week. She'd been angling to write the screenplay, but they've given it to John Howard Lawson."

"Isn't he on Billy's blacklist?"

Wilkerson's list of suspected Commies had become so notorious, everybody now referred to it as "Billy's Blacklist."

Kathryn nodded. "Which is why I told her she'll have dodged a bullet if she doesn't get the job. Lillian was with her, so of course she was agitating that Dottie ignore me."

"She wouldn't be Lillian Hellman if she didn't."

By the time they walked through the Garden of Allah's main building and out into the pool area, it was just after five. That gave Gwendolyn two hours to freshen up and organize her place for the dozen guests. But that plan flew out the window when she spotted her brother sitting in the foyer.

"MONTY!"

Gwendolyn's brother was a life-long navy man who'd survived Pearl Harbor and ended up serving on a battleship in Tokyo Bay the day the Japanese signed the peace treaty. Gwendolyn was proud of her brother's service, but she hardly ever saw him.

She launched into his outstretched arms and breathed in the starch of military discipline, mingled with briny sea air. She hugged him until her arms ached.

"Typical navy," she sobbed. "Never give a girl any notice. You appear, you stick around, you vanish, then three years later you pop up again."

"You should be used to it by now."

She looked into his sky blue eyes. He seemed older than his thirty-four years now. "How long have I got with you?"

"Seventeen hours."

"Not even a full twenty-four? Monty!"

"What can I tell you? It's typical navy. I'm on tomorrow's Sunset Limited to San Francisco."

"You've timed it well," Kathryn said, stepping forward. "You can be the special guest at the wingding Gwendolyn's throwing me tonight."

Monty's weathered face lit up. "Birthday?"

"Come with me," Gwendolyn said, "and I'll try to explain."

* * *

Monty wasn't as impressed with being in the same room as Trevor Bergin and Melody Hope as she'd thought. After five movies, the two were MGM's most successful pairing since Katharine Hepburn and Spencer Tracy, but Monty was clearly bored with Trevor's talk of his upcoming Valentino remake at Paramount.

Monty looked horrified as Melody teetered into Gwendolyn's apartment with a bottle of bourbon in each hand, superfluously announcing that she was already half-soused. She made a point of spilling a full glass on Quentin, who did his best to laugh it off, but Gwendolyn could tell he was on the verge of leaving. She wished she could grab Monty and find some quiet restaurant to spend a long evening just the two of them.

"Hey! Pinky the Pinko!" Melody called out. Trevor's face congealed at the mention of the kleptomaniac in *Reds in the Beds* that was based on him. "Ain't you gonna pay me any attention?" Melody whined. "Even if it's just for show?"

"Take it easy, Mel." Bertie made a grab for Melody's drink but Melody pulled it away and launched the contents of her glass onto the wall several feet behind her, missing Gwendolyn's portrait by inches.

"Everybody grab something!" Gwendolyn announced. "We're taking this party outside!"

The party was soon relocated to the far side of the neglected patch of dirt that had once been a victory garden, and an impromptu bar was set up on the periphery of a small fountain.

"Hey, Melody!" Quentin said. "Now you can toss around your hooch without ruining anything."

Melody attempted a wisecrack, but inspiration failed her, so she made do with a sneer instead.

"Surely you're capable of more than pulling a face," Quentin persisted. "Nellie Burch would have cut me down with a real whammy."

Please, everyone, Gwendolyn thought, can't we just have one night without that book?

"Did I hear someone say Dee-Dee Grifter?"

Kay Thompson looked dazzling in a pantsuit swathed in orange bugle beads. "Bill's show ran into technical difficulties tonight. Sends his apologies, and best regards for a blissful divorce, and insisted I stop off with these."

She held a couple of bottles of champagne aloft. "Imported!" She set one down on the fountain's ledge and tackled the cork on the other.

"You know what I heard at CBS tonight?" she asked nobody in particular. "That Clifford Wardell spent a week here at the Garden to get veris — verisimilit — what's the word I'm searching for?"

"It's verisimilitude, you big knucklehead."

Dorothy Parker had arrived with Lillian in tow, and the two of them were wearing virtually identical outfits of mildew blue. "That Wardell prick sure got around, didn't he?"

"Don't believe a word of it," Marcus said. "I'd have seen him, and then strung him up by his balls — if I could find them."

"I think it took balls to write what he did," Melody said. "He knew exactly the sort of blowtorch he was lighting."

"Melody!" Trevor looked like he was about to wallop his lavender wife across her strident yap. "You don't know what you're talking about, so pipe the hell down."

Gwendolyn grabbed up a plate of Kathryn's liverwurst on rainbow rye. "Everyone, you ought to try these."

"I hate to say it," Lillian said, "but I agree with little Miss Movie Star over there."

Dottie Parker looked as horrified as Gwendolyn felt. "Oh, Lil, you can't mean that."

Lillian Hellman had been tenacious in her criticism of Billy's blacklist, mainly because she was an unapologetic member of the Communist Party herself. "Now that we've vanquished the Nazis and the Japs, America needs a new enemy to rail against. What gets my goat is that someone seems to have decided that our new nemesis should be the Communists."

"Please don't stand here and defend that book."

Gwendolyn could tell from the steely mien in Marcus' eye that he was getting steamed up and ready for a fight.

"Of course not," Lillian said. "That book is atrocious, but it's pushed the issue onto center stage where we shall all be forced to grapple with it, come what may."

"I'll tell you what may come," Marcus said. Oliver laid a placating hand on his shoulder, but he jerked it away. "If we don't play this very, very carefully, we're going to find ourselves blackballed."

"Oh, Marcus!" Kay fluttered her hand at him. "I hardly think it's going to come to that. And even if it does, you're no longer actually writing any of these movies, so it's hardly going to affect you."

"What affects one of us, affects us all," Kathryn put in.

"Says the gal who works for the guy who wrote the blacklist that kicked it all off," Melody said.

"My boss didn't start it, Wardell did," Kathryn said.

"Yeah, but he sure as hell picked it up and ran with it," Dottie said.

"COULD WE PLEASE JUST DROP IT?" Gwendolyn exploded. "I asked you all here tonight because Marcus and Kathryn are getting divorced. All of us here know why they got hitched in the first place. Not the most ideal reasons, but under the circumstances, practical and necessary. And now it's practical and necessary that they *un*hitch, and I thought we might gather together and wish them well. Is that too much to ask?"

Bertie stepped forward. "Quite right, Gwennie." She lifted up the filled champagne coupe in her hand. "Here's to Marcus and Kathryn, the happiest married couple I know, which is ironic, all things considered."

Everybody disposed of whatever liquor happened to be in their glass, and started chatting among themselves. Gwendolyn was starting to feel like she'd managed to prevent the party from turning into another philosophical slugfest when Dottie piped up.

"Can I just say one more thing? The fact that Wardell portrayed the Garden of Allah as a hotbed of subversive—"

"JESUS!" Gwendolyn felt the last wisps of patience dissolve between her fingers. "I'm so sick of hearing about, and talking about, and arguing about the lousy Reds in the lousy Beds. I wish we could pile up every last copy, and set fire to the whole dang thing!"

Gwendolyn hung her head while an uncomfortable hush rendered the group immobile.

It was Oliver who broke the silence. "Why don't we? Let's make a funeral pyre and burn the lot."

"A Viking funeral!" came from Arlene. "If we could get a sheet of metal—"

"There's some corrugated metal in the parking lot," Trevor put in.

"We could sit it on the life preserver next to the pool, then pile it high with as many copies as we can find. Then flambé the whole thing, push it out into the middle, and watch it burn."

"Like Clifford Wardell's soul in hell!" Lillian declared. "How positively cathartic!"

Everybody looked at each other, waiting for a dissenting voice, but nobody could conjure a single one. Arlene was first to dash off to her apartment, and the rest scattered to their corners of the Divine Oasis.

Minutes later, they gathered by the pool clutching their books. Marcus laid the Garden's life preserver on the ground and covered it with the corrugated metal. Everyone placed their books onto it, forming a pyramid with Marcus' copy on top, standing upright, its pages splayed open.

Marcus doused the whole thing in brandy, then Oliver gingerly placed it on the water. Kathryn stepped forward and struck two matches, saying, "A pox upon you, and all who sail in you!" and tossed them onto the pyre.

Gwendolyn felt the heat of flames as it flared to life. Someone shoved a rake into her hands, and she pushed the burning pile toward the center of the pool. The crowd let out a cheer, raw and purgative; the pent-up tension dissipated in the night air.

"Where thine enemies have been vanquished," Dottie intoned, "Where the brave shall live forever."

"What the hell was that?" Lillian asked.

"A Viking funeral prayer," Dottie said. "Or something. This is my fourth bourbon, so don't put any money on it."

The group stood in silence, watching their floating bonfire.

"I must admit," Kathryn said, "there's something satisfying about seeing that mound of excrement burn."

Several others agreed with her, consigning Wardell to the hellhole from which he crawled.

Gwendolyn turned to her brother. "And that's the way we do things at the Garden of Allah."

Monty let out a long, low whistle.

"I don't expect you to get it," she said. "But in this town, that book has been the bane of every person with the God-given sense to know the difference between right and wrong."

"It's just that—well—y'all just participated in a book burning. Isn't that what the Nazis did?"

A heavy silence fell over the group as they watched the charred rubble subside into a faintly glowing heap, then, finally, extinguish altogether.

CHAPTER 25

Marcus loved the way Oliver looked when he got up in the morning — his undershirt wrinkled and his brown hair tussled like he was a Dead End Kid. On weekend nights when Oliver slept over, they usually lolled around in bed, snoozing away their hangovers. Now that September had given way to October and the night air was growing cooler, those half-asleep, half-awake hours snuggling under the covers were among Marcus' favorite. He looked forward to them all week.

But not that first weekend in October. When Mayer read Purvis' *The Final Day* screenplay, he gave the picture top priority and decreed a February release. It was a tight schedule, but achievable, chiefly because most of the costumes and sets from previous MGM war pictures were camera-ready.

However, while Marcus thought the screenplay was good, he saw a slew of ways to make it better. He'd given nearly every waking moment to polishing the script, and with the next day's deadline looming, had already spent several hours on his sofa smoothing out lines that still needled him.

Oliver appeared in the doorway holding the *LA Times* Marcus had left for him at the foot of the bed. "Looks like Hedda's at it again." He patted down his wayward hair. "Her whole column is about the union skirmish. Said there was rioting."

"I know some punches were thrown, but I don't think anyone could call it a riot."

"She used 'Metro-Goldwyn-Moscow' three times."

"That's a record."

"You need some peace and quiet, don't you? Shall I go?"

Marcus looked up at Oliver and smiled. It was already eleven o'clock and he'd made little progress. "I don't ever want you to go, but I must have this on Mayer's desk by nine o'clock tomorrow morning, otherwise — there is no 'otherwise.'"

Marcus returned to his script. One of its main problems had been lack of a love interest. Not that every picture had to have a pretty girl, but the hero needed some sort of character to play off to show his vulnerability and humanity. In war pictures, the hero's army or navy buddies usually filled that role, but this guy was alone. So Marcus wrote in an Austrian kid hiding in the deserted house where the ammunition stockpile was hidden. The kid had lost his whole family in the Anschluss, so he had no love for the Nazis, but Marcus was having a hard time nailing the dialogue. The hero didn't know much German and the kid didn't know any English, so it was a delicately balanced *pas-de-deux*.

"Yoo-hoo!"

Arlene stood with Oliver at his front door. He waved at her but made no move to get up.

"You look like you're real busy, but I have some news you ought to hear."

Marcus kept his eyes on the script. "Can it wait?"

Arlene took a few steps into the room, her face twisted with ambivalence. "It's not great news, so you won't actually *want* to hear it. But forearmed is forewarned."

Marcus threw *The Final Day* to one side. "Okay, out with it."

Oliver headed into the kitchen. "I'll put on coffee."

When Arlene sat down beside him, the morning sun caught her light red hair. Despite everything she'd been through, she'd retained that fresh-faced look, as though her innocence about the world and the way it worked was still intact. It was refreshing to see, and always reminded him of his sister, Doris.

Arlene pressed her hands into her lap. "Actually, I have three pieces of news. The first two are noteworthy in a 'That's interesting to know' sort of way. The other is less, well, we'll get to that."

"Tick tock, Arlene."

"I spent yesterday going through everybody's contracts."

"Why?"

"Ever since these IATSE strikes and clashes started up, and with Hedda calling us Metro-Goldwyn-Moscow, Mayer has been super sensitive to the whole Pinko thing. So yesterday, the instruction came down from Mannix to review all contracts for loopholes, especially any involving language they could twist if it becomes necessary to fire someone for being a Commie, or a Socialist, or even just a possible Pinko." She cleared her throat. "You didn't hear it from me, but there's a list of targeted employees."

"Have you come to tell me I'm on it?"

"I managed to sneak a peek, and your name wasn't there." Marcus slumped into the sofa. "But," she added, "it doesn't mean you can't be included later, so you might want to tread carefully."

Marcus took in this news, wishing he had more time to think about it. But the script was nudging his elbow. *Finish me . . . finish me . . .*

"Thanks for the warning. Was there something else?"

Before Arlene could reply, there was another knock on the door. "Christ!" Marcus hauled to his feet. "What is this, Union Station?" When he opened the door, he found Kathryn in front of him, holding up a paper sack.

"I got farewell Danishes!"

"What's the occasion?"

"I'm off to Reno tomorrow to divorce you, remember? I've narrowed it down to either mental cruelty or habitual drunkenness. You got a preference?" She read the dark look on his face. "Bad timing?"

The smell of fruity pastries filled his nose. "You might as well come in, you Danish-bearing, book-burning Nazi, you."

Everybody at the divorce party knew that Monty had made a very good point about becoming the thing you hate most, but by week's end they'd all dealt with the accusation in the same way: calling each other a book-burning Nazi at every opportunity.

Marcus arranged the Danishes on a platter while Arlene filled Kathryn in on her news. By the time everything was set out on his coffee table, Arlene was ready with her second revelation.

"While I was down in the filing room, I came across a thick folder filled with copies of the minutes from every meeting held by the Motion Picture Alliance for the Preservation of American Ideals."

The Alliance was a group of right-wing conservatives who'd come together during the war, convinced that Hollywood was crawling with Communists determined to pervert the movies "into an instrument for the dissemination of un-American ideas." Nobody on the left-hand end of the spectrum had taken them seriously, but they'd held fast to their belief that Hollywood was going to the dogs.

"How does this affect me?" Marcus asked.

"I noticed a frequent name among the attendees: Leonard Purvis."

"The guy who wrote all those Westerns?" Kathryn asked.

Marcus pointed to the unfinished script, which was still calling *Finish me . . . finish me . . .* "His son wrote that."

"I thought you'd want to know that the Purvis apple doesn't fall far from the tree," Arlene added. "Sonny boy was there, too."

Since joining Marcus' department, Anson Purvis had proven himself to be hardworking, punctual, and dependable. Although he lacked a well-developed sense of humor, he did take Marcus' revisions squarely on the chin.

The fact that he was a member of the Motion Picture Alliance wasn't news Marcus welcomed, but it wasn't surprising, either. Marcus would give it some thought when he had time, but for now *The Final Day* was tapping its wristwatch with an impatient finger.

"Was there something else? I've really got to get back to work."

Arlene stiffened. "You might want to put some Irish whiskey in that coffee."

"Just tell me, Arlene."

She interlaced her fingers and squeezed them together. "When I was in legal secretarial school, I made this friend. She's a bit of a wild card, likes to drink, carry on with men. I doubted she'd ever hold a job, but she ended up at Doubleday."

"The publisher?"

Arlene nodded. "She and I get together once in a while, just to catch up. She told me in the strictest drunken confidence that Clifford Wardell has written a sequel."

"Jesus H. Christ! That lousy little worm!" Kathryn said.

Arlene wagged a finger. "It's all very top-secret hush-hush, so don't breathe a word to anyone."

This must be the book Wardell mentioned that night outside the brothel. "Did she tell you the title?" Marcus asked. "Or what it was about?"

"It's called *Deadly Bedfellows,* and apparently it's about the head of a Hollywood movie studio writing department—"

"Please tell me you're kidding."

"—who actively recruits fellow-traveler screenwriters into the Communist Party with the aim of teaching them how to incorporate the Communist message. In fact, what it's really about is how a freelance journalist gets wind of this and foils the Commie plot."

Marcus pushed his glasses to the top of his head and pressed his fingers to his eyes, blacking out everyone in the room. "So it's about me."

"It could be Quentin," Kathryn pointed out. "He's head of writing at Paramount. Wardell probably hates you both."

The four of them sat in silence while Marcus cast his mind back to the night he convinced Wardell to sign over his screen rights. "This book isn't about Quentin Luckett."

"How can you be sure?"

"Because the last time I saw Wardell, he was trying to sell me into agreeing to see Purvis. And I said to him, 'This business sure makes for deadly bedfellows.'"

CHAPTER 26

Kathryn surveyed the dining room of the Reno hotel she'd been living in for the past two weeks. The proprietors had tried to gussy up the place with orange and yellow wallpaper, pink curtains, and fresh-cut daisies and tulips, but there was nothing as dispiriting as a restaurant of tables set for one. The Liberty Hotel, Kathryn decided, was the most depressing place in the world outside of a federal penitentiary.

She left a tip for the frowzy waitress and headed outside to thread her way through the usual throng of pedestrians along Liberty Street until she got to the post office.

Kathryn was astonished by how much work she could get done sitting alone in her hotel room with nothing to distract her. In three days, she'd banked a whole week's worth of columns, a bunch of movie reviews, and two interviews. The clerk at the post office promised her the new airmail service would get her package to the *Hollywood Reporter* by the following afternoon.

She stepped out of the post office and into the cool October breeze coming off the Truckee River to face a day in which she had nothing else planned.

Back home, her life was such a kaleidoscope of work, parties, premieres, and weekly radio appearances that time off with nothing to do sounded heavenly. But she'd been here for two weeks now, and more weeks stretched ahead of her like a prison sentence. She wondered how she was going to fill them.

Perhaps take in a movie? *The Jolson Story* was playing at the Majestic on First Street. Right before she left Los Angeles, she'd heard from one of her spies, a lighting guy at Columbia, that Larry Parks had put on a hell of a performance.

Kathryn loitered in front of the poster for a few minutes while she finished off a cigarette and worried about her radio job. Bing Crosby's new show, *Philco Radio Time,* was going to debut the following week with Bob Hope as his first guest. It was bad timing for *Kraft Music Hall* — the show was on an enforced hiatus while Kathryn was in Reno. *Kraft's* rating were strong, but would their audience desert them for this new show now that Bing was back on the air?

A shadow fell across the glass. "May I buy you a ticket?"

He sounded like one of those amorous ranch hands who spent his days off roaming the town in search of lonely women keen to experience matrimonial emancipation with the first decent stud to present himself. She wasn't prepared, then, to find herself face to face with Nelson Hoyt.

That ironic, knowing smile of his — part wily shrewdness, part mocking indulgence — was nowhere to be seen. There had been times when it infuriated her, but now she missed it. In its place was a dour mask, all business.

"What are you doing here?" she asked.

"I've been sent to escort you to the Riverside."

The Riverside was the grandest hotel in town, geared specifically for the high-end divorce trade. Kathryn had purposefully avoided it for fear of bumping into someone she might know.

"Why? Who's there?"

Hoyt stepped to one side and made a gallant sweep of his arm in the direction of the Riverside.

A cold shiver goosefleshed Kathryn's skin. "I'm not going anywhere with you until you tell me what's going on."

"I'm to take you to a meeting." Finally he looked at her, his gray-blue eyes blank. "With Hoover."

Kathryn looked around for eavesdroppers. "Is this about my boss and his casino? Because I can tell you right now Wilkerson doesn't talk to me about that cockamamie project."

"He's applying for a loan with the Valley National Bank of Phoenix for $600,000 to keep the Flamingo from going into bankruptcy. But it's only a drop in the ocean; he's in far deeper than that."

"See? That just proves there's nothing I can tell you that you don't already know."

"Kathryn!" She saw the veneer of stoicism slip, but for only a moment. "Do you really want me to go back and report to J. Edgar Hoover that you refused?"

Kathryn fidgeted with her handbag while she weighed her options. It didn't take long to see that she only had one.

* * *

The door to the penthouse at the Riverside Hotel was carved mahogany and featured a brass plaque announcing the Henry G. Blasdel Suite. The polished metal reflected back to her the deer-in-headlights fear in her eyes as she adjusted her blue velvet fastener hat.

Hoyt rapped on the door three times. "Whatever you do, keep calm. He'll try and—"

"Enter!"

The door opened onto a spacious parlor done out in Victorian décor—brown and gold wallpaper in a horseshoe pattern, heavy drapes in dark aubergine with matching carpets, and a Tiffany lamp on every other table.

The director of the FBI had the face of a French bulldog with a graying hairline receding over a box-shaped head. Kathryn guessed him to be around fifty, but he wore the frown of a man ten years older. He was seated in an armchair, his eyes on a one-page report in his hand. He motioned for Kathryn to take a seat in the chair opposite him. Kathryn wondered what Hoyt was going to say out in the corridor. *He'll try and . . . what?*

Eventually, Hoover let out a dissatisfied "hmm" and inserted the sheet into an unmarked folder on the coffee table. He offered his hand. She was surprised to find it soft and warm.

"Thank you for meeting with me."

Like I had a choice. Kathryn could no longer see Hoyt in her peripheral vision. *Has he left me alone?* She laid her handbag on her lap and pressed her hands against the alligator skin to stop them from giving her away.

Hoover pulled a cigar from the breast pocket of his navy blue pinstripe and bit off the end. "Hoyt tells me you're unhappy about your association with the Bureau."

It was one thing to bitch and moan to Marcus and Gwendolyn within the safety of the Garden, but to admit it to Hoover himself? She nodded and gripped her purse tighter.

"Do you want to sever ties with us?"

She nodded again.

He seemed in no hurry to light his cigar, but instead threaded it in and around the fingers of his left hand. "Benjamin Siegel has been a huge thorn in our side for years, and he's only becoming thornier. We want you to bring us as much information on him as you can procure."

"What sort of information do you think I can get?" Her voice came out a strange blend of hoarse and squeaky.

"Your boss is close to him, and you're close to your boss. I can see the panic in your eyes, so let me put your worries to rest. We're not concerned with Billy Wilkerson; Siegel is the big prize. If you could furnish enough rope to swing Siegel, I'd be more than happy to cut you loose."

Kathryn felt a noose tightening around her throat. "What kind of rope?"

"Bring us anything you can find, and let us decide if it's rope."

Kathryn dropped her gaze onto the gold clasp of her handbag. *What does he think I am? One of his super-spy double agents?* It took all the courage she had to look him in the eye, but she forced herself.

"Mr. Hoover, I don't wish to be uncooperative. Truly, I don't. But you're barking up the wrong tree. That Linden Holdings Company bank statement I got a hold of? That was a once-in-a-lifetime fluke."

Hoover let out another dissatisfied "hmmm" before he returned to the folder on the table and withdrew the paper he'd been reading when she walked in. "I have here a tax bill from the IRS totaling ten thousand dollars."

Kathryn blurted out a "ha!" before she could help it. "You don't work for Billy Wilkerson without witnessing the consequences of neglecting your taxes. I am meticulous when it comes to submitting—"

"I didn't say it was *your* tax bill."

Kathryn dropped her eyes to the paper in Hoover's hand. Marcus and Gwendolyn both used Kathryn's rigorously boring accountant. Hoover passed the paper to her with an achingly slow flourish. She ran her eyes down the page. The guilty party wasn't named until the halfway mark.

Francine Massey.

"My mother is a telephone operator. There is no chance that she could owe the IRS this much."

Hoover made a show of sucking something out from between his teeth before he said, "According to my investigation, your mother has never paid her personal income tax."

Kathryn heard a soft gasp behind her. It was the first indication she had that Hoyt was still in the room.

"Never?" Kathryn scoffed, knowing how hollow it sounded.

He extended one of his pudgy index fingers and pushed the paper until it was back in front of Kathryn. "I have instructed the IRS to hold off bringing charges." He jutted his double chin toward the bill, his dark eyes bowling-ball hard. "You should know that I have the power to make that disappear."

* * *

Kathryn left Hoyt floundering in her wake until they reached the Liberty Street corner. "I want to hear the words coming out of your measly little mouth."

"What words?" he asked

"Tell me you had no idea of the ambush you were leading me into."

"I only half knew."

"What a crock!"

She dashed across the intersection and went half a block before it dawned on her she was going in entirely the wrong direction, just like the last time she'd seen him in the alley behind his father's store when he jumped her with that kiss. She'd tried not to think of it, but once in a lonely while she found herself reliving how soft his lips were, and how her whole body had reacted to its touch. But then she'd swat the memory away.

The first she knew that Hoyt had followed her across Liberty Street was when he grabbed her by the wrist from behind. "He's desperate to collar Siegel."

His hold was disturbingly firm.

"How did my mother even enter the picture?"

"He wanted leverage, and asked for a full report on you detailing every fact in my possession. When he read it, his first question was, 'What about the mother?' I told him she's just a telephone operator so there was no leverage to be had, but he said, 'We'll see about that.'"

Her heart gave a yip of hope. "So that tax bill, it's bogus?"

Hoyt shook his head soberly and let go of her wrist.

Kathryn stood on the busy sidewalk, too flummoxed to speak, while locals and divorcées dodged around them.

Eventually she said, "What is Hoover even doing here? Surely he didn't come all the way to Reno just to see me."

Hoyt flicked the brim of his homburg toward the back of his head. "He did. Which should indicate how desperate he is to get Siegel. You need to take this seriously."

She felt weak at the knees. A little farther down the street, she spotted a bus stop and headed for it. She sat down on the bench and closed her eyes, unsure what to say, or even how to feel.

"You ought to consider yourself lucky," he said.

"How do you figure?"

"He talked about strong-arming you into pressing your husband into service."

"Marcus? Squealing for the FBI?"

"He's a man of some influence and position in the movie industry, and not without his — skeletons?"

Kathryn opened her eyes to narrow slits and looked at him askance. "Jesus, you people stop at nothing."

"But I talked him out of it."

"So you say."

"Did you know he was light in the loafers when you married him?"

How come there's never a ten-pound brick around when you need one? "Why? Did you?"

"No." He ignored the disdain in her voice. "Not until the night of the . . . Mandeville Canyon incident."

The way he paused for the briefest split-second before he said "Mandeville Canyon incident" made Kathryn's antenna quiver. "What?"

"The desk sergeant at that station is a college buddy of mine. We get on the horn once in a while to shoot the breeze. We were yakking away one night when a bunch of queers got hauled in. In case there was anything I could use, I got him to read out the list of names. When he got to Marcus Adler, I asked him to do me a favor and let him go, as well as anybody with him."

Kathryn felt a cool breeze waft off the Truckee River a few blocks north of them. It was the first hint of the winter to come and it afforded a brief, albeit fleeting, respite from the heat of the desert that lay just beyond the city limits. "Why would you do that?" she asked him quietly.

"Because I'm the bad guy, remember?"

She let his sarcasm float past her. "Whatever your motives were, thank you."

"What do *you* think my motives were?"

"Quite honestly, you confound me beyond all comprehension."

She was thankful when he said nothing further. They let the traffic jostle past them — cars, buses, bicycles, even a horse or two. Eventually, she asked, "Do you think Hoover meant it when he said that if I come up with the goods, he'll let me go?" When Hoyt didn't respond, she pressed him. "Well, do you?"

He scowled. "I didn't hear him give you any choice."

The two of them sat there, knee brushing knee, saying nothing. His scowl softened into something less officious, more contemplative. She watched the way his eyes roamed her face, as though memorizing every detail.

He's going to kiss me again. Isn't he? He is. No, he's wavering. He wants to. I want him to. He knows he shouldn't. Not with Hoover so close. Not with anyone so close. And yet. There's something there. Let's stop pretending there isn't.

Abruptly, he shot to his feet. Tipping his hat to her, he pivoted on his heel and charged back the way he came. She watched him retreat down Liberty Street until he turned a corner and disappeared without once looking over his shoulder.

———

CHAPTER 27

Gwendolyn was shocked when Howard Hughes called to say that his doctors had given him the go-ahead to start piloting again. A couple of months back, when she and Kathryn visited him with Lana Turner, she thought it'd be a miracle if the man could reach the bathroom by himself before Christmas. But there he was on the line telling her he had a quick business trip to Guadalajara planned for the second week of November, and it'd be his pleasure to drop her off at Mazatlán on the way down and pick her up the following day.

She arrived at the Hughes Aircraft hangar and found he walked with a hesitancy that gave her pause, but he ran through his preflight checklists as though there'd never been a horrific crash three months earlier.

When they climbed into the silver S-43, Hughes offered her either a passenger seat in the main cabin or the copilot seat up front. Kathryn had told her that if he offered her a chance to sit in the cockpit, she must take it, promising, "You'll never see the world in the same way again!"

So Gwendolyn chose the cockpit . . . and regretted it the moment they took off.

Her stomach cartwheeled as the ground dropped away at an alarming rate. The endlessness of the Pacific to her right seemed to want to surge up and swallow her whole. And when an air pocket shook them around like lifeless dummies at Bullocks, she snapped shut her eyes and kept them that way until Hughes told her she was missing the best part.

He was right.

The sight of the ragged coastline far outstripped her expectations. It even exceeded Kathryn's promise that she'd be overwhelmed so much that she was happy to pass the rest of the flight in silence.

Hours later, armed with only a postcard and a snapshot inside her overnight bag, Gwendolyn alighted from the plane repeating the phrase Howard had taught her: *Estoy buscando. I'm looking for.*

* * *

Plazuela República was a medium-sized plaza half the size of Pershing Square, dominated by the Cathedral of Mazatlán. Its twin spires pointed toward a cloudless sky dominated by a bright sun that burned hotter than it did in LA. Even the wide-brimmed straw hat she'd grabbed at the last minute offered scant protection, so she took refuge under the shade trees surrounding the central rotunda.

She pulled out Linc's photograph and used it to fan herself while she repeated, "*Estoy buscando . . . estoy buscando . . .*"

"You spent ten years approaching strangers at the Cocoanut Grove," she told herself. "This should be a piece of cake." When a middle-aged gent in a white linen suit entered the square and started heading toward her, she put on her professional cigarette-girl smile.

"*Hola!*" She held up Linc's photo. "*Estoy busca*—no, *es*—*estoy bucansca*—oh, crap!" The man cut a wide arc around her and was thirty feet away before she got it right. "*Estoy buscando!*" But he was already beyond earshot.

The next passerby was an elderly woman loaded with half a dozen bundles tied together with string. She looked at Gwendolyn as though to say, *Oh honey, you've caught me on such a bad day.*

A pair of giggling teenage girls just shook their heads. A nurse about her own age in starched white cotton and sensible shoes didn't even break her stride. The burden of hopelessness pressed on her.

But then a trio of nuns barely scraping five feet tall and dressed in black habits stopped when she held up Linc's photograph.

"*Estoy buscando,*" she said, pointing at the snapshot.

"*Es muy apuesto,*" one of them said, nodding her head in approval.

"Have you seen him?"

The three women looked at her blankly. She felt her underarms go damp.

The name on the back of the lighthouse photo popped into Gwendolyn's mind. "*Emilio Barragán?*"

"Sí," they chorused. "Emilio Barragán. Sí."

Gwendolyn threw out her hands. "Where? Where? Where is Emilio Barragán?"

A glimmer of recognition sparked in the face of the oldest woman. "*El tejedor americano,*" she said to the other women, and they all started nodding.

"Ah! *Sí, sí. El tejedor americano.*"

The oldest nun took her by the hand, her skin rough as sandpaper. She tugged at Gwendolyn, beckoning her into the oppressive heat. Skirting down one of the streets bordering the cathedral, they came to the rear where Gwendolyn saw a line of taxicabs, all of them battered Fords punctured with rust.

The nun marched Gwendolyn to the driver lounging against the door of the cab at the front of the line. She launched into a stern speech in rapid Spanish. Gwendolyn caught the words *americano* and *Emilio Barragán,* but that was all. The harangue ended with a pointed finger directed toward the church. "*Jesucristo!*" The driver leapt away from his cab and pulled open the door, motioning for Gwendolyn to step inside.

* * *

The one-story adobe reminded Gwendolyn of the houses around Olvera Street in downtown LA. With its fresh coat of cream paint and its fire engine red flower box filled with bright purple geraniums, it certainly had its charm. But was it Linc's?

The wooden door was the same color as the flower box, with a wrought iron handle fashioned into the shape of a feather. Gwendolyn took off her sun hat, wondering if she looked like a wilted daffodil. Had her lipstick worn off? Were her underarms stained?"

"Stop procrastinating," she told herself, and knocked before her nerve deserted her.

She heard the sound of a wooden chair dragging along tile.

"Un momento, por favor."

There was no mistaking Linc's voice. She put the hat back on, then took it off in an attempt to look as though she just happened to be in the neighborhood and thought she'd drop in. She quickly realized how ridiculous that looked, so she jammed it back on her head, only to realize she'd put it on backwards when the door flew open.

Linc was astonishingly tan. She'd been used to his Black Irish pale skin and dark, dark hair, but this bronzed version brought out the deep blue in his eyes. But more than that, she'd never seen him so gosh-darned relaxed. The worry lines accumulated from fifty-hour working weeks and the puffy bags from marathon Mocambo nights were erased. Instead, a clear-eyed, beaming Lincoln Tattler stood before her.

You haven't come all this way to collect your money, she realized. *You're here to understand why he took it.*

"Gwendolyn!" He stretched his arms out wide and enveloped her in a lung-crushing hug. "My darling girl!" He released her and grabbed her hand. "I never imagined—! Come in, come in. That sun today is gruesome!"

The house was just one big sparely furnished space—living room on the left, kitchen and dining area to the right. At the rear, a double bed was pushed up against the wall, and to its left was a worktable covered with long, thin brown reeds. The walls were all painted terracotta with a dark green trim.

Gwendolyn took off her hat and held it to occupy her jittery hands.

———

"You sure know how to surprise a guy," Linc said, still beaming. He headed into the kitchen area and opened a small icebox to pull out a blue glass jug. "I just made lemonade."

She waited until he'd filled two glasses before she said, "You're not easy to find."

But all he said was "Gosh, it's good to see you!" while he handed her a drink. She took a sip. It was just the right balance of tangy and tart. And deliciously cool.

He led her to the sofa and sat down next to her, so close she could smell the salt in his hair. He looked into her eyes unblinkingly. "You always were a resourceful little dickens. I'm flattered. And surprised. Shocked, even." He took her hand; she wanted to pull it away, but it felt so nice to feel his skin again. "I've often wondered if I should let you know where I was, but I was concerned others might get wind of my location. But now that you're here in front of me, I can see I should have told you. We might've spent the last year and a half living in this paradise. Well, you're here now."

"LINC!" Gwendolyn pulled her hand away. There was no coffee table so she set the lemonade on the tiled floor. Even his bare feet were tan. "Aren't you curious about why I tracked you down?"

As he glanced at the small overnight bag she'd left at the door, she saw the gears of his mind grind to a halt. "Gwennie, I—"

"How could you do that to me?" she yelled. "You knew how hard I worked to get that money. I was saving every penny to open my store. I was so damned close, but then you decided to go on the lam. I guess you had your reasons, but did you have to steal my money, too?"

"WHOA!" he cut in. "Your money? Went missing?" He sat upright. "And you think *I* took it? Why the hell would you think that?"

She fell back into the sofa and crossed her arms. "I flew all the way from LA to find out. I'm not leaving until I do."

He stopped pacing and jammed his fists onto his hips. "The last time I saw your money, it was in that ratty pillowcase inside Bertie's safe. I'm sorry, Gwennie, but I don't know where your dough is."

His eyes darted back and forth between hers. He took her hand again; this time she didn't want to pull away. "Now I really wish I'd told you where I went, if only to stop you from spending a year and a half wanting to stab me in the throat."

Gwendolyn stroked the tops of his long fingers. "You are telling me the truth, aren't you? 'Cause if you did, now's the time to come clean, even if you've spent it."

"Do you know how far three grand can go down here? I could live on that in style for years." He jutted his head behind him. "I live in a shack. It's hardly the life of Riley I'm leading here."

Gwendolyn felt her body sag as she tilted her head against his shoulder. *It wasn't him. Linc isn't a thief. He didn't go on the lam and take my money, my hopes, and my future with him. He's the decent guy I always thought he was. I'm not such a terrible judge of character, after all.*

His hand stroked the back of her head until she sat up and wiped her cheeks clean of tear tracks she hadn't been aware she was making. "Your shack is charming."

"Now that I've plastered and painted the whole thing, laid this tile, and put in running water and electricity. You should have seen it a year ago — to call it a hovel would've been generous."

"It's a far cry from Beverly Hills."

"The farther, the better," Linc replied darkly.

"That bad, huh?"

"Worse."

"But why did you up and leave like that?"

"I left a note."

"You mean the one where my sackful of money should have been? It was hardly self-explanatory, Linc. All you said was something about Ben Siegel and the O'Roarkes. Linc, honey, I've come all this way to hear why you left. I want an explanation."

"No, Gwennie, you really don't."

"How bad can it be?"

He nodded as though it hurt, and pointed to her overnight bag. "Any American cigarettes in there?"

"Chesterfields. Four packs." She watched him lick his lips. "You're welcome to them. *If.*"

"All right." Linc let out a long, raggedy breath. "Remember that theory I had, about the O'Roarkes laundering their money through my dad's company? I spent weeks looking for proof. I'm not the world's smartest accountant, but I'm no muttonhead either. I knew what to look for, but those bastards covered their tracks well, and I didn't find much." His eyes lost their focus. "I got so frustrated that I snuck over to the O'Roarke's house one night and started going through their trash cans."

"What did you find?"

"Nothing. But while I was pawing through their stinky garbage, I heard them starting to argue. And let me tell you, when Leilah and Clem O'Roarke have a fight, the Marquess of Queensberry rules do not apply. They go at it with flying brandy snifters, face slapping, and cuss words to make a sailor blush. Those two do not hold back."

"What were they fighting about?"

"One of those little metal boxes that hold filing cards. They couldn't find it and were each accusing the other one of hiding it. Oh boy, were they ever both blowing a gasket. I sat in the dirt listening to them going at it for a while, and finally they convinced each other this precious box wasn't anywhere in the house. So they both jumped into Clem's Oldsmobile and roared off. They didn't even bother to lock their window, so once they were out of sight, I climbed in and took a look around."

"You didn't!" Gwendolyn started to fan herself, scandalized, impressed, and fearful in equal measure.

"The funny thing is that it didn't take me long to find the box. It'd fallen off the back of Clem's desk in his downstairs study. So I grabbed it, jumped out the window, and hightailed it home before I even looked at what was inside."

"What did you find?"

"Details of every visit made to their brothels by each one of their clients." Linc tilted his head and squinted at her, his eyes tinged with disappointment. "I recognized every single name on those cards. Movie stars, studio chiefs, directors, politicians, policemen, captains of industry, diplomats — I knew them all, either socially or I've done business with them. It was all there. Dates, fees, preferences. The O'Roarkes were keeping records as a way to blackmail their clients if they ever needed to. Can you beat that?"

I might have known it was something as down and dirty as this. "No wonder they were going bananas."

"Imagine that file falling into the hands of the vice squad? Or worse, Bugsy Siegel."

Gwendolyn let out an involuntary groan. "Speak of the devil, he's been moving heaven and earth to find you."

"It wasn't me he wanted; it was the O'Roarke's filing box." His smile fell away. "After reading through all those cards, Hollywood suddenly seemed so tawdry and sordid that I was repulsed by the whole place. I talked my way into Bertie's room to get my money out of her safe, went home to throw together the bare minimum of what I could get away with, and left town. I kept driving until I reached Mazatlán."

Gwendolyn opened her bag and pulled out the picture postcard Linc's father had given her. She handed it to him. "Your father found it while he was packing up your house. He had to sell it, by the way."

"Why?"

"He's broke." Linc looked up in surprise. "And divorced. Last I heard, he was living at the Hershey Arms. Write to him, Linc. Even if it's just to tell him you're okay."

"I'm more than okay." He led her to the worktable covered in reeds. "I'm a weaver now! Wicker and rattan, mainly. I sell baskets and furniture and hats all over town. They call me *el tejedor americano*." Linc sounded like a native. "*Tejedor* means weaver. There's a store in Puerto Vallarta that wants to stock my humble wares." He cast a fatherly eye over a half-finished basket. "I don't earn much from them, but then again I don't need much."

Without warning, he pulled Gwendolyn into a full-body hug, just like he used to. It felt so familiar and so comforting that she allowed herself to melt into his arms. They stood there for a while, molding themselves into each other's bodies, listening to the tinkle of a brass wind chime outside Linc's kitchen window.

After a few minutes, she felt him raise his hand and begin to stroke her back. "Stay." He whispered the word so gently she barely heard him. "Here. With me."

"Linc, I—"

"You're good with your hands. I'll weave baskets while you make dresses. The local señoritas will flip their sombreros over your stuff."

Gwendolyn thought of the creations she'd built for her Midnight Frolics boys. She'd made everything from slinky body-huggers like something out of Lena Horne's closet to overblown explosions of sequined ruffles with rhinestone cockatoos perched on Crawfordesque shoulder pads. They were a hell of a lot of work, but enormously rewarding.

"I'm sorry, Linc," she whispered back, "but this isn't the place for me."

"How much time do I have to convince you?"

"I've got to be at the airstrip at noon tomorrow."

She'd forgotten how tender Linc's kisses were—unhurried, and soft like rose petals—until he pulled her tighter and pressed his mouth against hers. His lips invited hers to open with a gently tantalizing promise of passion lurking in the shadows. When her knees buckled, he lifted her off the cool tiles and carried her to the bed.

CHAPTER 28

The Chateau Marmont Hotel was built in the style of a French chateau from the Loire Valley transplanted to the Sunset Strip. As the head telephone operator, Kathryn's mother qualified for subsidized housing in one of the employee bungalows at the rear.

Despite the fact that Francine lived within spitting distance of the Garden, Kathryn and her mother rarely saw each other. They got together for birthdays and Christmases, and the occasional lunch when time and opportunity permitted, but they both worked jobs that devoured most of their waking hours — or at least that's what they told themselves. However, the truth was there'd always been a wedge of sandpaper chafing the tender points of contact whenever they came within scraping distance of each other.

As she rapped on her mother's front door, Kathryn knew this encounter wouldn't be any different. In fact, it would probably be a whole lot worse.

Francine answered the door in her uniform. It wasn't a "uniform" as such — Francine was allowed to wear whatever she wanted, as long as it was a tasteful mixture of black and white. Now that she was steaming into her late fifties, Francine had given up obscuring the fact that her hair was going gray. It suited her, especially in her black-and-white ensemble, and Kathryn made a point of telling her.

"Thank you, dear," Francine said, closing the door behind her. "I must say, life's a lot easier now that I only have it styled without bothering to dye it, too. But you'll find that out for yourself soon enough."

Francine headed straight for the kitchen and offered her the usual. Kathryn wasn't particularly fond of brandy and ginger ale, but it was her mother's favorite, so she went along to keep the peace.

They took their drinks to the sofa, which sat amid a forest of potted dahlias whose leaves glowed with vibrant colors embracing the entire rainbow. Whatever maternal instincts Francine Massey lacked, she made up for by nurturing bulbs and seedlings to verdant ripeness.

"I have some news," Kathryn said. "I've been handed a bill from the IRS."

"Back taxes?"

"Ten thousand."

Francine nearly choked on her drink. "But you've always boasted about how persnickety you are with your taxes." Kathryn bristled at "boasted" and "persnickety," but swallowed her resentment with a mouthful of brandy.

"Should I pay it?"

"Darling, with the IRS, it's pay up or else."

"Or else what?"

Francine strummed her nails on her glass. "Jail, I expect."

"So you're saying I should pay this ten-thousand-dollar tax bill I was handed in Reno?"

"When you were getting your divorce? So they aren't yours alone? They're Marcus' too? Well, then, that's quite different."

"So *he* should pay the bill?"

"If he incurred the taxes. That's only fair."

"So the person who incurred the taxes should pay them?"

"Naturally —" Francine broke off when she caught the triumph in Kathryn's eyes.

"This tax bill was neither mine nor Marcus'."

As comprehension bloomed on Francine's face, the color drained away. In equal measure, an unexpected surge of disillusion supplanted the gratification Kathryn expected to feel. By the time she left Reno, she'd decided that the tax bill was probably just a ruse. But her mother's blanched face told her the head of the FBI had all the edge he needed.

"You've never paid your income tax, have you, Mother?"

"I — uh . . . guess I never got around to it."

Kathryn placed her drink on the coffee table. "The sort of people who never get around to paying their income tax are usually the ones whose mug shots we see pinned up on post office walls." Kathryn paused long enough for Francine to picture herself under a sign proclaiming *Ten Most Wanted.* "How can you not have paid your taxes?"

"What I want to know is if it's my tax bill, then why is the IRS handing it to you?"

"It wasn't the IRS, mother. It was the FBI."

"The — ? Why would they involve themselves in something like this?"

"During the war they recruited me as an informer." Kathryn watched closely, but Francine's face scarcely registered a flicker. "Did you hear what I said?"

"I'm fifty-eight, not deaf," Francine snapped. "I was thinking about a conversation I had with Louella a little while after Pearl Harbor. We bumped into each other at the Hollywood Brown Derby. She told me the FBI had approached her, and I asked if she thought that meant they'd asked Hedda as well. She said it was likely, so I wondered about you. You never said anything, so I assumed they hadn't, which I thought was a trifle insulting."

The labyrinthine logic of her mother's mind often baffled Kathryn. "Insulting?"

"You're every bit as well connected as Louella and Hedda, and you're certainly a lot sharper. I'd have thought you'd make a more useful spy."

"So it doesn't bother you they asked me to snoop on my friends and colleagues and neighbors?"

"Not if it was for the war effort."

"But at the end of the war they all but forced me to continue."

"With all these Communists coming out of the woodwork, I'm sure they need you."

Francine's lack of outrage illustrated just how different they were. Most people Kathryn knew would be appalled at the FBI's tactics. "I don't share your brand of patriotism, Mother. I've been trying to disassociate myself, and they've tried to keep me tied to them. They must really be getting desperate because the person who showed me your tax bill was no less than Hoover himself."

There was no cloaking the dismay that blew across Francine's face.

Kathryn said, "I have to ask: How did you think you could get away with not paying your taxes?"

"You have to remember, I came to California with a new name, and an illegitimate baby. I told nobody back home where I was going, and I planned to stay hidden for the first year and then slowly build my new life. But one year bled into the next, and then the one after that, and before I knew it so many years had flown by that it seemed ridiculous to poke my head up. Remember, we didn't have income tax back then."

"But did you really think they wouldn't notice?"

The lively notes of a jazz quartet floated in from the hotel's dining room. They were playing one of those *Let's all pick ourselves up and dust ourselves off* tunes popular for keeping up everyone's spirits during the Great Depression, but Kathryn couldn't put a name to it. The jaunty melody brought into sharp relief the awkward silence permeating Francine's little bungalow. Kathryn silently begged her mother to say something as the tea dance crowd applauded the musicians, but Francine stayed tight-lipped.

"So about this tax bill. Do you *have* ten thousand dollars?"

Francine threw Kathryn a withering look.

"I have a theory he's using your tax problem as leverage," Kathryn said.

"Against what?"

"Hoover wants me to supply them with information that will help get Bugsy Siegel behind bars."

Francine laughed dismissively.

Kathryn jumped up from the sofa and headed for the kitchen. Pulling an ice pick from a drawer, she hacked at a brick of ice, cleaving chips in all directions. Marcus' advice came back to her:

You have a very public profile now. If Kraft learns that your mother is a tax dodger, you'll get dumped faster than a mob witness in concrete shoes.

"You think that's funny?" Kathryn asked.

"I mean to say, what could you possibly know about Bugsy Siegel that'd land him in jail?"

"My boss is in cahoots with him over the building of that casino in Las Vegas."

Kathryn took a measure of satisfaction in seeing her mother's jaw drop. "He is?"

"Siegel's been coming into the office. Frequently. So it's not as preposterous as you might imagine."

In truth, Kathryn still found the whole idea preposterous. What did Hoover expect her to do? Sneak into Wilkerson's office and scour it like some private eye in a halter neck? She returned to the sofa.

"What are we going to do?" Francine asked.

"Obviously we have to play nice with the FBI so they can make your tax bill go away."

"But Kathryn, dear. Bugsy Siegel?"

"It's either that or come up with ten grand to pay off the IRS. Got any banks we can rob?"

The two of them sat on the sofa, mute as clams.

Eventually, Francine said softly, "I've put you in an awful predicament, haven't I?"

A lump rose in Kathryn's throat. Her mother was usually so brittle, and defensive, and used her voice like the ice pick Kathryn had left on the sink. She laid her hand on top of her mother's and said, "We'll think of something," though she couldn't imagine what the blazes that might be.

CHAPTER 29

Marcus sharpened his red pencil while he stared in despair at the script on his desk. The five screenwriters who'd worked on *Song of the Thin Man* had done their damnedest, and William Powell and Myrna Loy would try hard, but it was clear that the movie series had run its course. All Marcus could do was make a few suggestions where plot logic could be improved, and warn Mayer not to expect the colossal profits its predecessors had enjoyed.

He was still drafting the memo in his head when Arlene called him from the legal department.

"I heard from my pal at Doubleday," she whispered down the line. "*Deadly Bedfellows* arrived the other day."

Marcus curled his finger around the telephone cord and squeezed it until his knuckles hurt. "Is it really about the head of a studio writing department?"

"Uh-huh."

That miserable son of a prick. "What else?"

"The lead character's name is Mathias Addison."

"He's about as subtle as he is original," Marcus said. "Quentin will be pleased to know it's not about him."

"He hasn't escaped untouched. The plot revolves around how this Mathias Addison guy recruits into the Communist Party a talented new screenwriter by the name of Quinn Lubbock."

"That bastard's not going to be happy until he's pissed off every last person in Hollywood, right down to the guy who peels the potatoes in the commissary." He was going to ask Arlene if her pal could write up a synopsis of *Deadly Bedfellows,* but before he could, Anson Purvis marched into his office.

"Here's your goddamned pile of cockeyed baloney." He slammed a screenplay onto the desk and thundered back to his office.

Marcus told Arlene he'd call her back.

Months ago, when Marcus informed Purvis they'd not only be buying *The Final Day,* but offering him a generous contract, the guy was happier than a puppy with his first bone. He arrived at the studio in a gray checked suit with the price tag intact, all handshakes and thank-yous and yes-sirs. His face darkened, however, when Marcus told him that he wouldn't be polishing *The Final Day* but had been assigned to adapt a picture from a *Saturday Evening Post* short story called *Happily Never After.* It was about a commitment-shy divorce lawyer and the girl in the newsstand out front of his office building, and Marcus pointed out that if he did a good job, it could be the first postwar movie Gene Kelly made after his discharge from the navy. And if that happened, his co-star would probably be Judy Garland or Melody Hope or June Allyson—not bad for a first movie.

But Purvis had just stared at him, his mouth curved down in a sour huff. In the end, Marcus told the guy, "Just write the damned movie," and figured his best tactic was to give him enough time to realize how childish he'd acted.

An hour and a half after Purvis slammed *Happily Never After* onto his desk, Marcus finished the script and buzzed Purvis on the office intercom. "Get in here." When he heard the guy's footsteps stomp toward him, he thought, *You picked the wrong fucking day, mister.*

Purvis appeared in the doorway, his arms crossed.

Standing five foot nine to Purvis' six foot three, Marcus needed all the intimidation he could mount, so he told the guy to take a seat while he stayed on his feet. He glanced down at *Happily Never After,* then looked up, glad he'd had the chance to rehearse this scene with Yip Wainright. "You got one thing right. It's baloney."

"I told you." Purvis bristled.

"Let me clarify," Marcus said. "It's not baloney because you think it's a frivolous love story set to music. It's baloney because you've handed in a shoddy piece of work. *The Final Day* wasn't perfect, but it pole-vaults what you've done here, and that's a problem."

Look at you, you big pouting baby. You're only here because I went against my instinct, and you don't even have the decency to do your best. You'll be lucky if I don't can your ass.

"No," Purvis said, "that's not the problem here."

"Oh, yeah, Mr. I've Been In The Business Two Minutes? Why don't you give me your considered assessment?"

Purvis slid forward to the edge of his chair and started tapping Marcus' desk.

"The problem isn't that this movie's a waste of time. As far as a Kelly and Garland musical goes, it's fine. Guy meets girl; guy ignores girl; girl gets guy. This studio—this whole industry—has been churning out this junk since Edison invented the Kinetoscope. They know exactly how to nip-and-tuck it so the thing'll mint money. That's not the issue. The problem is that folks like you think the people who went to the movies before the war are the same ones going to the movies now."

"Of course they're the same," Marcus said.

Purvis sat back in his chair, smirking. "You don't come out of D Day, or Guadalcanal, or the Battle of the Bulge, or Iwo Jima the same person you went in."

"Stories about people falling in love will never go out of fashion," Marcus countered. "War or no war, people still love to love. Look at how well *Anchors Aweigh* and *Meet Me in St. Louis* did. Both those pictures made back three times their budget."

"Maybe that's the difference: You're still looking to the past, and I'm looking to the future. I tell you, it's hard to fall in love in a world where we drop bombs that can kill hundreds and thousands in a matter of minutes. Guys like you fail to recognize the world has changed."

"What the hell's that supposed to mean? Guys like *me?*"

"I'm talking about ones who stayed behind, safe in their offices while real men risked life and" — he reached down and struck his knuckles against his wooden leg — "limb."

Marcus was about to launch into a lecture about how after the navy knocked him back he helped write the speeches that helped sell millions of dollars of war bonds. But a word of advice from Jim Taggert, his outgoing predecessor, came back to him: *Never excuse, never explain.* "Are you aware of how close you are to being fired?"

"Are you aware of how little I care, if this is the sort of dreck you're going to waste my talents on?"

Dierdre buzzed Marcus' intercom to say that a Mr. Gessler was on the line. Gessler was the code name Marcus and Oliver had agreed on — after the villain in *William Tell*, the movie that brought them together — if Oliver needed to call him at work. It didn't happen often, but they felt they couldn't be too careful.

Marcus wanted to toss Purvis out on his behind and jump on the line to Oliver. But Purvis might well have a point. Suddenly he longed for the good old days when all he had to do was show up and write movies, and then go home to Oliver's chicken pot pie. He told Dierdre he'd call Gessler back.

Marcus sat down and glared at Purvis with what he hoped was an intimidating scowl, but the guy's glacial blue eyes stared back at him as though to say, *Now what?*

"This studio," Marcus said, "needs versatile writers capable of pulling together a top-notch screenplay from whatever material I throw at them. However, I recognize that some writers excel at particular genres and it's to the studio's advantage that we utilize each employee's talents."

Purvis lifted his hands to the skies like a tent-revival preacher. "That's all I'm saying."

"I don't have any war movies on the boil right now, and I can't have you sitting around tiddly-winking your day away, so—"

"I've got one."

Of course you do.

Purvis leaned forward, elbows on knees. "Okay so there's this navy pilot—Jimmy Stewart would be ideal—and he's downed in the Pacific. He's alive, but pretty banged up and thinks he doesn't have much time left. His microphone is still working and the guy on the other end is his best buddy on the battleship heading for him. So that Jimmy doesn't lose hope, the best buddy—Peter Lawford or Van Johnson, maybe—gets Jimmy to talk of his love for his girlfriend. The buddy links Jimmy's speech across the whole navy network and everybody listens in to his big 'This is what we're fighting for' speech. Civilian radio picks up the story so that by the time he's rescued, he's this big war hero."

"Skip to the part when trouble sets in."

"His girlfriend—I'd cast Gloria DeHaven—has up and married some other guy. So the military brass finds this lookalike actress to play the girlfriend, but that bugs the bejesus out of the girl's new husband—Jack Carson, if we can get him."

"Is there a twist?" Marcus asked.

Purvis' face lit up. "The hero agrees with the husband that all this playacting makes a mockery of the sacrifices the boys are making out there, fighting for truth, justice, and the American way."

"Please tell me it's got a happy ending."

"A boffo happy ending that'll leave the women crying and the guys cheering."

"You got a title for this masterpiece?"

"*Pacific Broadcast*, but I'm not married to it."

"That's a great title," Marcus admitted. "I can see the poster already."

"So . . .?"

"I need a detailed outline by the end of the week."

Purvis jumped to his feet and shook Marcus' hand.

Outside his window, the tops of the oak trees bent and snapped. It was the first of the Santa Ana winds blowing in from the desert. Angelenos liked to believe the hot, dry Santa Anas brought restlessness and dissatisfaction, shorter fuses and wilder tempers. It was said that the murder rate in LA went up when the Santa Anas were blowing dust along the boulevards.

His intercom buzzed. "Gessler again?" Marcus asked Dierdre.

"No, Arlene from Legal."

Marcus picked up his phone. "Lemme guess—in the end, Mathias Addison gets snuffed out by a posse of gun-happy G-men?"

"My friend just called. Are you sitting down?"

"Do I need to be?"

"Mathias Addison is toppled in disgrace by his protégé, an ex-navy man awarded the Medal of Honor for his service during the war."

Marcus felt his body go limp. "If the protégé's name is something like Andrew Purdue, I'm going to punch a hole in my wall."

"He's only ever referred to by his nickname—Amp."

"What kind of name is that?"

A gust of Santa Ana whipped the branches outside Marcus' office, scraping them against the glass.

"It's short for 'Amputee.'"

CHAPTER 30

The ambulance came to a halt at the curb in front of the Garden of Allah's ten-foot sign on Sunset Boulevard. The driver with the Randolph Scott eyes looked into his rearview mirror.

"This is where you said, right?"

"Thank you, gentlemen." Gwendolyn tried not to slur as she gathered up her red and gold gypsy shawl, taking care none of its foot-long tassels caught on the equipment. "Are you sure giving us a lift wasn't against the rules?"

Kathryn opened the back door with a grunt. "Of course it's against the rules! But mum's the word, fellas." She pressed a finger to her lips—or at least tried, but missed by half an inch.

Gwendolyn nudged her drunken friend out of the vehicle. "If it hadn't been for you," she told the driver and his partner, "we might still be waiting outside Paramount."

As the ambulance sped off, she found Kathryn sitting astride the low brick fence that ran around the Garden's perimeter.

Gwendolyn sat next to her and brushed away a dried leaf that was caught in the elaborate lace of the dancing-girl outfit Gwendolyn had put together for the evening.

In fact, it was an abandoned ensemble she'd made for one of her Midnight Frolics clients whose instruction had been "Make me look like Salomé!" She knew that his beer belly would do him no favors once he donned the seven-layered skirt. Even camouflaging his pudgy middle with the shawl that was now around Gwendolyn's shoulders couldn't disguise the fact his fantasy outfit should have lived only in his imagination. But when he saw himself in the mirror, he paid Gwendolyn and promptly ordered a full-length gown encrusted with as many diamantes as it took to "Make me look like Mae West!"

Kathryn laid her head on Gwendolyn's shoulder and let out a terrific belch. "Well, that was certainly a night to remember."

For weeks now, Paramount's PR department had been convulsing over how their remake of *The Sheik* would be the top picture of 1947. As if to prove their boasts, they invited half the Hollywood press corps to the wrap party.

The studio had secured one hundred Persian rugs from a dealer who claimed his family had woven carpets for a thousand years. Whether or not this was true, the set was an impressive tent palace with half a dozen rooms divided by dazzling fifteen-foot-high rugs in crimson, azure, and vermillion that photographed gloriously in Technicolor. Against this background, Trevor Bergin as Sheik Ahmed carried off Yvonne de Carlo's feisty British socialite Lady Diana to have his wicked way with her—or at least as wicked as the Breen Office would permit.

Even the fake desert was impressive, with two tons of Santa Monica sand and papier mâché palm trees so realistic that everyone joked that Paramount should sell them to the Cocoanut Grove to replace the trees they'd procured from the Valentino version.

The night of the wrap party, an unending supply of liquor flowed alongside a bounty of unpronounceable Arabian delicacies. The party carried on past two o'clock, by which time no one was in any condition to drive home. The taxis were gone by the time Gwendolyn and Kathryn reached the front of the line. That's when the ambulance driver took pity on them. He'd been called to treat an especially exuberant partygoer who had decided to scale one of the palm trees only to drop on his head.

The November night blew through Gwendolyn's shawl. She nudged Kathryn awake. "Come on, my champagne queen, 'tis time you headed to bed."

Kathryn lifted her face. "I'd forgotten what real French champagne from real France tasted like."

Gwendolyn pulled Kathryn to her feet and lead her around the Garden's main building. "Do you have any BC Headache Powder? You're going to need it come morning."

Kathryn had been hitting the sauce a little heavily lately. Not that Gwendolyn blamed her. The poor thing thought she was going to Reno to get a divorce and have a nice break, but ended up with J. Edgar Hoover shoving a tax bill in her face. Gwendolyn had an inkling something else happened in Reno, but Kathryn clearly wasn't ready to talk about it.

The gravel path was sparsely lit, and Gwendolyn was taking care not to slip. She managed to negotiate the pool patio, but on the approach to Kathryn's villa, she spotted a figure kneeling in one of the flowerbeds. It was hard to make out in the meager light of the new moon, but it looked like someone was hunched over and . . . *digging?*

She squeezed Kathryn's shoulders tighter and shook her. "Wha . . .?"

"Someone is gardening," Gwendolyn whispered.

"This *is* a garden."

"At two in the morning?" She shook Kathryn again. "I need you sober!"

Kathryn drew in a deep breath and straightened up. "What's going on?"

Gwendolyn's eyes had adjusted enough to make out a woman in a cotton nightgown tilling the soil in the old victory garden. The girl stopped for a moment to brush a wily lock of hair away from her face.

"It's Bertie!" They walked up to the edge of the plot. "Sweetie? What are you doing?"

Bertie ignored them as she plowed the dirt with her right hand, then patted it down with her left. "Buried and safe."

"Bertie?" Gwendolyn repeated, this time more loudly.

"Is she sleepwalking?" Kathryn whispered.

Gwendolyn slipped off her Arabian sandals and stepped onto the cool, damp earth. It stuck to the soles of her feet as she crouched down. "Bertie honey, wake up!"

Bertie's head jerked back and she took in a jagged gasp. Her eyes were open now, darting wildly. "What the hell—?" she panted. "I'm outside! Why am I—Gwendolyn! Kathryn!" She looked down at her dirty hands. "Oh, Christ! Not again!"

Gwendolyn went to lay a comforting hand on her arm, but Bertie brushed it off. "I thought I was done with all that business."

"Bertie?" Kathryn said gently. "What's going on?"

"I CAN'T!" Bertie staggered to her feet and started backing away. "I JUST CAN'T! In the morning—I'll—I can explain—not now—please—the morning."

Gwendolyn and Kathryn watched her retreat into the shadows of the main building.

"What do you make of that?" Kathryn asked.

"She was burying something." Gwendolyn peered down at the ground. "Do you still have your shovel from the victory garden days?"

"Uh-huh."

"I still have that big flashlight. Meet you back here in five."

* * *

When Gwendolyn returned to the victory garden, flashlight in hand, she found Kathryn in a pair of dungarees and a work shirt. She arrived just as Kathryn's shovel struck something in the dirt with a dull clang.

"Shine it here." Kathryn started digging faster. "I'll be damned!" She pulled on something with a grimace until it gave way, then brushed off the dirt and positioned it in the beam of Gwendolyn's flashlight.

"It's Marcus' platter." Gwendolyn fell to her knees and started to excavate the damp earth with her hands. "All this time it's been Bertie?"

Kathryn pulled free a silk scarf Alla Nazimova had given her. "Oh, look at this." She poked a finger through the rotted material and it gave way in shreds. "Damn it! That was a favorite." She tossed it aside.

They kept digging until Gwendolyn touched something small, sharp, and hard. She burrowed around it until she could pull it free and hold it to the light. It was a square gold cufflink with rows of tiny diamond chips set along the top. "This must be Trevor's."

They kept clawing at the earth. The smell of freshly turned dirt reminded Gwendolyn of the happy days she'd spent planting and harvesting the victory vegetables. They were rare and precious bright spots in the otherwise gloomy days of the war when she didn't know if she'd ever see Monty again.

"Look!" Kathryn pulled a wad of material out of the ground and held it in the light.

It took Gwendolyn a moment to register why the pastel yellow and orange stripes looked familiar, then gave out a yelp. "It's my pillowcase! My money!"

She pulled it out of Kathryn's hand, but it tore along the seam. She groped around inside for bills, and pulled a handful into the light. Her heart dropped. Her black-market money was in tatters.

"Oh, darling," Kathryn said softly. She reached over and placed a hand on Gwendolyn's wrist at exactly the same moment Gwendolyn let a handful of mulched bills fall into her lap like confetti.

"So that's the end of that."

"Is it?" Kathryn asked. "Sleepwalking or not, Bertie took your money and buried it where the bugs could eat it. That makes her responsible, if you ask me."

"But it just doesn't seem right."

"Do you know how much her allowance is from dear ol' dad, the canned beer king?" Kathryn started brushing dirt from Trevor's cufflink. "We should go see her. She looked real upset."

Gwendolyn shook her head. "Let's give her the night to calm down. I'll slip a note under her door inviting her to breakfast at Schwab's tomorrow morning."

* * *

Schwab's was its typical hive of activity — unemployed actors chatting with barely employed writers schmoozing with studio-employed musicians looked after by overemployed waitresses. The place rang with the clanking of empty dishes, the fizz of the soda fountain, and the whir of the cash register bell.

Finding an available table was a hit-and-miss affair — all the regulars had eaten standing up at one time or another — but that was part of the place's charm.

One of the waitresses waved at Kathryn, Gwendolyn, and Bertie. "If you want a booth, you better grab it while you can." She pointed to the only vacant one left in the place. Sitting next to the soda fountain, it was the noisiest booth in the place, but they were lucky to get it.

After they ordered coffee and toast, Gwendolyn said, "So, last night . . .?"

Bertie had been uncharacteristically taciturn on the walk over from the Garden. She raked her fingers through her hair. It was such an unmanageable tangle of corkscrew curls that she'd dubbed it her Wild Man of Borneo. "I was thirteen when the stock market crashed and Dad lost everything. I started to sleepwalk. I'd take vases and wooden spoons and sweaters, and bury them in our backyard."

"Did your parents know?"

"Sure, but they didn't want to tell me. So every morning after I left for school, mom would send the chauffeur out and dig it all up again. It went on for nearly a whole year until one night I was out digging under the plum tree when the Great Dane next door barked so loudly he woke me up." She cast her gaze down at her hands. "I had a minuscule breakdown over the whole thing. Oh yes, it was high drama in the Kreuger household there for a while, but I got over it eventually and life went back to normal. Or so I thought, until last night. I'm so sorry you had to see that."

"It must have come as such a shock, huh," Gwendolyn said.

Bertie pulled at her hair. "I nearly died! When I got back to my room, I thought *Thank God it was Gwennie and Kathryn*. Imagine if it'll been Melody!"

"But Bertie honey, when all those things started disappearing, didn't it occur to you that maybe history was repeating itself?"

"Of course it did!" Bertie exploded, then calmed herself. "Actually no, not at first. I guess I didn't want to believe it. But after a while, I started to worry. So every now and then, I snuck out in the middle of the night and started digging around. But like a dope I just checked the flowerbeds near my place. It never occurred to me I'd bury all that stuff way over in the victory garden."

She started to tear her napkin into shreds. *Just like my money*, Gwendolyn reflected.

"Never mind," Kathryn said placatingly, "what's done is done. But I'm curious to know why you're doing it again?" Kathryn asked. "Something must have set you off again."

Bertie nodded slowly until their waitress refilled their coffee cups. "It's my dad."

"He's not sick, is he?"

"No, nothing like that."

She dropped her shoulders with an exaggerated sigh. "Kreuger canned beer did great during the war with all those thirsty servicemen looking to get all liquored up. But now he's got a whole bunch of competitors and it's been sending him slowly broke. Anyway, the long and the short of it is, Dad's cutting my allowance."

"To what?" Kathryn asked.

"From a thousand a month to zilch."

Gwendolyn looked at Bertie's long face and started to smile. *Couldn't you have let us find you digging around in the dirt a couple of months ago?*

Bertie wadded up her paper napkin and threw it onto the table. "I'm glad you think it's funny."

"Darling, I'm not laughing at you," Gwendolyn said. "That's a heck of a tough break. I was laughing at myself. Really I was."

"What about?"

"Nothing much. Just something silly. So, how long can you last on your savings?"

Bertie let out a honking laugh. "What savings?"

"You've been blowing through a grand a month?" Kathryn asked.

Their order arrived. Bertie started slathering her toast with butter. "There was always going to be another check next month, so what did I care? Now I care plenty. God, what a dunderhead I am!"

"So you'll do what we all do: get a job."

"I'm thirty-two and never had to work in my life. I don't suppose there's much call for an ex-heiress whose sole skill is picking up the tab?"

"It's been a while since I've read through the want ads," Gwendolyn said, "but I can't imagine there's much call for that sort of thing. Maybe I could put in a good word for you at Bullocks."

"Would you? That'd be terrific."

Gwendolyn nodded, but knew it wouldn't do much good. High-toned stores like Bullock's required all their flawlessly groomed sales girls hold themselves with a degree of poise that a free spirit like Bertie could only dream of.

A solemn silence fell over the table until Bertie said, "So all those things that have been going missing around the Garden, I guess they're all still where I buried them?"

"They were," Kathryn said. "After you ran back into your room, we dug it all up."

"So you found everything?"

Gwendolyn looked at Bertie's face mottled with red blotches, her eyes bleary and her Wild Man of Borneo in its usual state of mutinous chaos.

"Yes," she sighed, "it was all there."

CHAPTER 31

Kathryn stared at the empty bottle and crushed cigarette packet on her dining table with the same question running through her mind as she'd had when she started: *Was I in the right place at the right time, or entirely the wrong place at the worst possible time?*

Earlier that afternoon, she'd been in the stacks room where the *Hollywood Reporter* archived old issues to track down their review of Valentino's *The Sheik.* That gargantuan party at Paramount had made anything connected to the remake hot news.

She'd just found the review when she heard Wilkerson's heavy footfall. She listened to him take a seat at the front desk on the other side of a wall of filing cabinets, then pick up the telephone and tell someone to "put it through."

Wilkerson's terse side of the conversation was enough to scare the bejesus out of her. Amid the gruff "yeps" and "nopes," she caught enough to know it was Bugsy Siegel on the other end of the line. Wilkerson's voice coarsened. "Ambassador. Six o'clock. Yes, I *will* be there."

Kathryn jumped when he slammed down the phone and thundered from the room, then waited a full minute to ensure there was no danger she'd encounter him again.

She stopped by her desk long enough to reschedule an interview with Betty Grable before heading straight home. She didn't want to leave the house until she'd decided what to do. Fortunately, Schwab's delivered anything at any time—even to girls damp with sweat, numb with worry, and on the verge of losing their minds.

When there was a knock on the door, Kathryn grabbed her purse.

"Are you there? They said at your office you went home early."

What is Nelson Hoyt doing here?

She laid a hand on her doorknob and took a deep breath before opening it. "Whatever today's threat to the nation is, can it wait?"

He pierced her with his blue-gray eyes and walked inside. "I know what's going on."

She could feel the walls of her defenses start to crack, but she pulled herself together and kicked the door closed behind him.

"We know about Siegel's phone call to Wilkerson," he said. "Siegel thinks your boss has been sabotaging the Flamingo, and he's ready to take it over completely."

"I want to go down to the Ambassador and stop him. He might never—" She stumbled over the words *walk out alive.*

"My car's out front. If we catch a good run along Wilshire, we'll be there before six."

* * *

The lobby of the Ambassador Hotel was preposterously huge, like the living room of a rich maiden aunt who expects regular visits. Well-padded loveseats upholstered in fraying velvet and damask were spaced around wood-paneled columns and potted ferns.

Kathryn looked wildly around.

"You'd never make a good agent," Nelson said.

"What have I been trying to tell you all this time?"

He led her behind a square column that was close enough to the reception desk to see who approached, but far enough to avoid detection. A string quartet filled the air with a light waltz while guests milled around waiting for taxis, checking for messages.

"What if we miss him?" she whispered.

"He's probably taken a suite. The elevators are over there." Hoyt pointed to the right. "Wilkerson has to pass this way."

"What if he doesn't show?"

"Hoover met with him last week and warned him about Siegel. Wilkerson got all hotheaded and refused to believe Hoover, calling him an alarmist old biddy—there he is."

Wilkerson's dark brown suit made him look like a funeral director. With the homburg she bought him for Christmas last year dangling from his hand, he walked through the lobby, and stepped inside the first elevator that opened.

"It'd help if we knew which room he was heading to," Hoyt said.

A squeal of relief almost flew from Kathryn's mouth. "You're not the only one with contacts."

She dashed toward the ornate doors of the Cocoanut Grove, assuming he was following her.

She hadn't been to the nightclub in a while, and never as early as six o'clock. It was jarring to see the cavernous place so deserted; the papier mâché palm trees looked desolate and forgotten. She was relieved to see a familiar face behind the bar.

Back when Gwendolyn was the Grove's cigarette girl, she was pals with the head bartender, who'd always looked out for her in a big-brother sort of way. Chuck Bellamy had the blond charm of a matinee idol, but had witnessed the shortcomings of fame firsthand too often to ever be tempted onto the screen.

Kathryn explained what she needed, knowing Chuck was too jaded to ask questions. He made a phone call to his pal in housekeeping: Siegel was in Room 505. Room 503 was taken, but 507 was available. He slipped a passkey into her hand, made her promise not to tell a soul where she got it, and pointed her toward the service elevator.

Minutes later, they had their ears pressed to Siegel's wall.

She could distinguish between her boss and Siegel, and a third voice she suspected was Mickey Cohen, but she couldn't catch everything they were saying.

" . . . damned lie . . . million bucks' worth of incompetency . . . construction costs . . . FBI . . . coulda done a better job . . ."

Then, suddenly, Wilkerson yelled, "PUT THAT FUCKING THING AWAY!"

Kathryn clenched her fist and pressed it against the wall, missing what Siegel's, or maybe Cohen's, response was.

Then Wilkerson yelled, "Fine! Wave it around like a flag on the fourth of July if you want. It's not going to intimidate me. I have every right to decide what happens to the Flamingo. It was *my* goddamned idea in the first place!"

"You weren't dreaming big enough!" Siegel yelled back.

"I didn't get where I am today by dreaming small."

"You canned my crew and replaced them with a bunch of knuckleheads who wouldn't know a plank from their peckers. That place is a shambles and you know it."

"There's nothing wrong with my casino that can't be fixed."

"This is *our* project and — "

An agonizing silence followed before Wilkerson let fly with a piercing yelp. "Go ahead, Cohen, stick your peashooter wherever you think it'll do the most good, but I've worked too long and too hard to sign this piece of shit."

Something heavy fell to the floor, followed by a rasping grunt, and then another. A vase — or maybe a bottle — smashed against the wall Kathryn and Nelson were listening against. Wilkerson was in his mid fifties, no match for the much-younger Mickey Cohen, who was probably pummeling — or worse, pistol-whipping — Wilkerson right now. Kathryn closed her eyes.

The fight didn't last long. The next voice they heard was Siegel's — hard-edged and remote, as though he was on the far side of the room.

"I don't need you to sign it right now, but you will sign it. Or I'll kill you myself and sign it for you."

Kathryn heard only silence until the hotel room door slammed. Hoyt ran to the door, listened for a moment, then cracked it open. "They've gone."

She followed him into the hallway and into Room 505.

Wilkerson sat on the floor with his back against the foot of a double bed, holding a hand to his nose. The floral bedspread was half-dragged off and all of the pillows scattered. Blood had oozed onto his sleeve and spattered the cuff of his silk shirt. His eyes were unfocused and registered little surprise to see Kathryn there.

In the bathroom, she doused a face towel in cold water, then kneeled beside her boss.

"What are you doing here?" Wilkerson's face was parchment gray.

"You need to get out." Kathryn squeezed the compress to his nose. "And I mean out of town."

He steeled himself against the pain. "There's this lodging house in Connecticut. It's so out of the way I'm surprised they do any business at all."

"It's not far enough," Hoyt said.

Wilkerson registered mild surprise. "And who might you be?"

Hoyt consulted his watch. "The Super Chief leaves Union Station in an hour and a half. You'll make it if you jump into a taxi and go straight there. You'll arrive in Chicago in time to catch the Twentieth Century. That'll put you into New York with three and a half hours to spare."

"Spare for what?" Kathryn asked.

"The *Ile de France*."

"You think he should go to Paris?"

Hoyt helped Wilkerson to his feet. "Siegel's network extends to every corner of the country."

"Now just hang on a minute." Wilkerson had had time to collect himself. "Who's Mr. Charlie-in-Charge here?"

"This is John Mandeville," Kathryn replied, saying the first name that came to her. "He's the Hollywood correspondent for the *New York Times*."

"What happened to the old one?"

Hoyt had Wilkerson's jacket in hand, and helped him into it. "Take him downstairs and ask the bellhop to hail a cab. I'll get the concierge to book the connection to New York and the passage to France."

Kathryn grabbed her boss by the arm. "Come on, we need to step on it."

By the time the elevator doors pinged open, Wilkerson's color had started to return, along with the astute look in his eye. Luckily, the elevator was empty. He waited for the doors to close before he said,

"I met with Hoover on the weekend." He paused for her reaction, but she refused to budge a muscle. "He warned me about Siegel, but I paid no attention, and look at me now, on the lam like I'm goddamned Dillinger. Anyway, your mother's tax bill came up."

A part of her wasn't surprised. There didn't seem to be any secrets left in Hollywood. Maybe that was good. Everything out in the open, flapping in the Santa Monica breezes on laundry day.

The elevator pinged again and the doors opened onto the busy hotel lobby. They stepped out and Wilkerson led her into a quiet alcove.

"I was hoping that tax thing was just a ploy," Kathryn told him, "but it turns out my mother is a genuine, dyed-in-the-wool tax dodger. There are no good options."

"What if I paid the ten grand?"

Kathryn flung her arms around Wilkerson's waist and hugged him tighter than she'd ever hugged anyone in her life, and squeezed her eyes shut to stop from gushing like a sob sister. There would be time enough for that later. "You don't have ten grand, do you?" she said into his chest.

"I barely have two dimes to my name," he chuckled, "but there are ways around that. Of course, arranging it all the way from Paris might present problems."

"Thank you," she said, "but I need to solve this mess soon. I appreciate the offer, though." She unhooked herself from his embrace. Deep red welts were starting to appear across the side of his face. "Let's find you a taxi." She went to pull him toward the Ambassador's front entrance, but he resisted.

"I need a favor," he said darkly.

"Sure. Anything."

"When the Flamingo opens next month, I want you to be there."

"You want me to walk into that lion's den?"

"After everything I've been through, it kills me that I can't be there for the opening. I'd feel better if someone I trusted was there to see it all and report back to me."

The thought was almost enough to give her the dry heaves. *Anything but that.*

Blood began to drip from his nose again. He dabbed at it gingerly. "At least think about it?"

"Look, there he is." She pointed to Hoyt. "And yes, I'll think about it."

As they walked outside into the early evening, Hoyt handed him a sheet of the hotel's stationery. "Stateroom numbers, confirmation numbers, it's all there. I took the liberty of booking you a room at the George V Hotel in Paris."

Kathryn decided it was a fortunate coincidence that Hoyt chose Wilkerson's favorite watering hole. Before she knew it, she was watching his cab pause at the end of the Ambassador's driveway and wondering when they'd see each other next.

"He wants me to go to the Flamingo opening," she told Hoyt.

"Will you?"

"Fat chance."

She headed back into the hotel in search of a martini at the Cocoanut Grove. Chuck knew exactly how she liked them, but Hoyt stopped her. "I have something to tell you."

"Okay."

"But not here."

He led her through a maze of passageways and corners until they stepped outside where a long, covered walkway stretched before them. There was nobody about.

She watched the rapid rise and fall of his chest and realized she'd never seen Hoyt nervous before.

He ran his finger down a concrete column. "I'm thinking of leaving the Bureau."

"That's an awful big step."

"I believe in the ideals that make this country great. I wanted to protect and preserve them."

"And what do you want now?"

He rocked onto his toes, then back onto his heels. "I want to get away from the diseased carcass that's eating away at every principle I value. All I ever do is eavesdrop and maneuver. Those who I can't maneuver, I manipulate; those I can't manipulate, I bribe; and the ones I can't bribe, I threaten." He kept his eyes on the traffic along Wilshire.

"Not exactly what you signed up for, I imagine," she said.

"Did you hear about that series in the *Chicago Tribune*?" Following the midterm elections, the paper ran a rabble-rousing series of articles alleging a Communist takeover of Hollywood, with FDR as the instigator. "I want out before Hoover burns everything to the ground."

"From what I've heard, he's real big on loyalty, and makes it hard for anyone to leave."

"If I was no longer with the FBI, wouldn't that remove your objection?"

"My objection to what?"

She knew what was coming, but felt powerless to stop it. She knew she didn't *want* to. Even more deeply, she knew she couldn't ignore the thrill welling up inside her. As she felt Hoyt's warm breath on her face, she closed her eyes. This time, he didn't hide his ardor by brushing her lips with tentative kisses. Instead, he pulled her to him, and pressed his mouth to hers until she succumbed.

———

CHAPTER 32

The Florentine Gardens nightclub was like that girl who thinks just a touch more lipstick and a brush more rouge will fool everybody into thinking she's more attractive than she actually is.

Gwendolyn doubted that the real villas on Capri had painted papier mâché grapes pretending to climb up balsa wood columns sprayed to resemble Carrera marble. She also doubted they had dusty burgundy velvet drapes, clouds painted on their ceilings, or balsa wood busts of Roman generals. Like the girl with too much makeup, it worked as long as nobody inspected the details.

And on the day after Christmas, 1946, nobody was intent on inspecting the details of the Florentine Gardens — they were too thankful to have dodged a bullet.

The Flamingo Hotel's opening day had been hanging over Los Angeles like a zeppelin in a lightning storm. Bugsy Siegel had chartered an all-Pullman train from Union-Pacific and invited every celebrity between the Hollywood Hills and the Mexican border, but his luck had finally run out. That morning, a squall swept across Los Angeles, grounding all transportation. Hollywood breathed a sigh of relief and cancelled.

Subsequently, everybody found themselves with nowhere to go.

Kathryn told Gwendolyn that she'd heard Lana Turner called Peter Lawford and suggested they go out. So he called Judy Garland, who proposed the Florentine Gardens and hooked Joan Crawford into coming along. Crawford called Gable, who was about to start a movie about New York advertising men with Ava Gardner, and invited her. Ava talked Cesar Romero into joining them, and he in turn roped in Veronica Lake. By the time Gwendolyn walked in with Kathryn, it felt as though half the town was there.

"If everybody's here," Gwendolyn asked Kathryn, "who's in Las Vegas?"

Kathryn shrugged. "Hopefully no one, and maybe Siegel will close the place down and let the Mojave Desert reclaim the whole rotten thing."

Since its halcyon days during the war, the Florentine Gardens' reputation had frayed. The comics were getting coarser, the girlie shows scantier, and the drinks weaker. The furs and twinkling jewels peppering the place that night lent a diverting pearls-before-swine air, but it wasn't enough to pull Gwendolyn out of the blues she'd had since the night they discovered Bertie's stash.

Kathryn argued that Bertie needed to know what she'd done, but Gwendolyn couldn't work up the nerve. Now that she was broke, Bertie had moved into the cheapest room at the Garden of Allah and had spent more than a month looking for a job. But with no experience, no skills, nor the slightest idea of what it took to interview well, her search was fruitless.

So Gwendolyn decided that what's done was done, and there was no undoing it. She resolved to put it all past her. Sewing outfits for her boss' cross-dresser friends wasn't lucrative enough to fund a whole store, but it commanded enough of her attention to prevent her from sinking completely into the doldrums about how LA's postwar boom was passing her by.

Kathryn, too, had been subdued since the night she helped ship Wilkerson off to Paris.

"Have you heard from him?" Gwendolyn asked.

Kathryn blinked away her preoccupation. "Heard from who?"

"The *Ile de France* . . .?"

"Nope."

"You've been awfully quiet lately."

Kathryn nodded as though she'd been anticipating a question Gwendolyn hadn't asked, and led her into a corner of the room. She sat them down at a tiny cocktail table and gripped the edge.

"Something happened. Twice. And I don't know what to make of it." Gwendolyn knew that when Kathryn clipped her sentences into bite-sized chunks, something big was about to come out. "That FBI agent. He made a pass at me."

"HE WHAT?"

"A couple of months ago. I followed him—"

"YOU WHAT?"

"I met with him about what Arlene found. Afterwards, I had a hunch. So I followed him. His father has a lighting store. On Sunset, east of Highland."

"Is that where you bought my lamp?"

Kathryn nodded. "And while I was there, Hoyt showed up. You should have seen his face! Dragged me out into the back alley. We had a huge argument."

"You had a huge argument, so he made a pass at you?"

"No, he kissed me, so we had a huge argument."

"About his kissing you?"

"About me calling him the enemy."

"But he kind of is."

"Not to his way of thinking. Remember that raid up in Mandeville Canyon? He was on the phone with the desk sergeant as they were getting hauled in. When he heard Marcus' name, he asked the sergeant to let the three of them go."

"Why?"

"I'm not sure. To demonstrate that he's not all bad, I expect. It's hard to discern his motives."

Something moved across Gwendolyn's line of vision. Even in a crowded, smoky club, she knew one of her outfits when she saw it. And not just any outfit. It was the trickiest one so far, with alternating diamond-shaped black-and-white sequined silk panels, a scalloped neckline, and a calf-length hem. The damned thing had taken Gwendolyn and Arlene a full ten days to build, and the result was spectacular.

Gwendolyn snapped her attention back to Kathryn. "Have you seen him since?"

"He helped me get Wilkerson out of town. And then he kissed me again."

"Did you kiss him back?"

"I did!" Self-doubt puckered Kathryn's face. "But not for long."

"Bad kisser, huh?"

"The opposite! I kissed him because it felt so good. But I put a stop to it before I started doing something I'd regret. I'm not even sure why I let him kiss me in the first place."

"I think that's what they call 'forbidden fruit.'" Gwendolyn watched Kathryn grasp the obvious.

Kathryn fumbled to light a cigarette. After three attempts, she gave up and just waved it around. "I'm starting to wonder if he's everything he says he is."

"Which is what?"

"He maneuvered me into marriage to a guy who he then turns around and saves from professional ruin. He tells me he joined the FBI because the military wouldn't have him and he wanted to do his bit for the war, and the next thing I know, he's saying how he's disillusioned with the FBI and wants out." She tried her lighter again. This time it fired up; Kathryn took a long drag. "Is it any wonder I don't know what to think anymore?"

Gwendolyn slanted her head to the left. "Did you enjoy kissing him?

While Kathryn pondered her question, Gwendolyn stole a glance around the crowd, looking for her black-and-white dress. She spotted it ducking behind Betty Hutton and Edith Head.

Kathryn said, "I mean, let's be honest. It's been pretty slim pickings for me since Roy. And he was married. Then there was Orson, and we know what he's like in the keep-it-in-his-pants department. So all in all—"

"That's not what I asked."

Kathryn kept up her bravado until she'd sucked the last half inch out of her cigarette, then she sheepishly admitted that she did enjoy kissing the guy back. Part of her wished they'd run inside and gotten a room.

Gwendolyn said, "Maybe you should set up another meeting and probe him some more."

"Probe him?"

"Don't listen with your ears, or your heart, or your lips. Listen with your guts, and see what happens."

Kathryn made a brave attempt at a smile. Before either of them could say anything more, Bette Davis came charging at Kathryn like a runaway bulldozer.

"We must speak!" She was practically seated at the table before she realized Gwendolyn was there. "Oh good!" she exclaimed. "You're here too." She flagged down a waiter and ordered a double martini. "I've got a scoop for you, dear Kathryn."

"Boy or girl?" Kathryn asked.

A month ago, Bette announced that she and her new husband, Bill Sherry, were expecting. Kathryn didn't admit it out loud, but Gwendolyn knew she was miffed at not being slipped the news first. But such was the pecking order among Hollywood's gossip columnists; Jack Warner had probably insisted the news go to Louella Parsons.

"I haven't the faintest idea." Bette blew a long plume of smoke into the air. "Just before Christmas I had a meeting with Jack Warner about my new contract."

"Did you reach an agreement?"

"After eight hundred years of indenture, I have only a year and a half left to serve, and then I'm free!"

Kathryn squinted in a way that Gwendolyn knew meant she was memorizing every detail. "Did he play hard?"

"It was all so shockingly civil!" Bette lifted a martini glass off the tray that appeared beside her. "I think I simply wore him down. However . . . "

The house band struck up a lively version of Nat King Cole's "I Love You For Sentimental Reasons" and suddenly dancers were jostling for space.

Gwendolyn was barely listening anymore. She couldn't leave without being sure that was her dress. She was rubbernecking the crowd when she felt Bette touch her arm.

"This is where you come in," she said. "After I signed my new contract, I headed over to Costuming to see Orry-Kelly, who's overseeing my alterations — I'm having some of my favorite clothes let out. When I walked in, he was standing at one of the tables with an assistant and they were examining a rather odd gown."

"Odd in what way?"

"The shape of the thing," Bette said. "It was made for a woman who was not exactly the slimmest girl at the ball. We measured the waist — thirty-eight inches! And there was no shape to it. The bust, the waist, the hips — all thirty-eight."

Kathryn cast an unblinking gaze at Gwendolyn, who tried to mask her shock with her champagne coupe.

A month or two ago, she'd received a parcel from an anonymous customer who'd said that he'd heard about her work. Along with a generous check, he sent her the material, the measurements, and the pattern, and asked that she follow the specifications exactly. The dress itself wasn't difficult to make, but its measurements were 38–38–38.

"What did it look like?" Gwendolyn asked.

"It was a dark emerald green overlaid with a sort of rainbow pattern in various shades of blue gathered together over the left hip."

That was the dress all right. But what was it doing at Warner Bros.? "Why did you think of me?"

"When I was examining it, I noticed the tiny "G" embroidered inside the right sleeve. That's your trademark, isn't it?"

The trademark was Kathryn's idea. Gwendolyn wasn't sure why it was necessary, but Kathryn's instincts were astute, and she went along with it.

She nodded. "But why would Orry-Kelly have it?"

"They decided it was a mistake. The parcel had simply been addressed to 'Jack.' Even though his name is really Orry George Kelly, he's known around the studio as Jack. Nobody had any idea who it belonged to, but then I saw your little 'G.' I just thought you might like to know."

When the conversation drifted on to Bette's first post-pregnancy movie, Gwendolyn saw her chance to seek out her black-and-white diamond dress. The crowd was well on the way to being liquored up by now, and the din boomed across the club. Betty Hutton and Edith Head had lassoed Cesar Romero and Peter Lawford onto the dance floor, where they were attempting the jitterbug under the influence of several rounds of scotch. They were only somewhat successful.

Gwendolyn honed in on every scrap of glistening fabric until she caught sight of her handiwork behind a series of Roman busts along the wrought-iron balustrade leading to a mezzanine level. She carved her way through the crowd, straining to catch a glimpse of the wearer, who looked like a heavy-browed hood from an early Cagney picture. *Surely he wouldn't be wearing it here?* She followed it to the bar and positioned herself for a better view.

It was a woman, but her face was turned away.

Then she heard her name shooting across the music.

"Goodness gracious!" Leilah O'Roarke said. "You've been scuttling all over this place like a crab. Who *is* that woman in the black and white dress?"

"I made that outfit," Gwendolyn said, "but her husband still hasn't paid up."

During the war, Leilah had been her biggest nylons customer, and Gwendolyn had grown to admire her. But now that she knew Leilah was one of LA's most successful madams, the woman's matronly maternal swell had taken on a shabbier air. It was almost as though the tawdry nature of her business had seeped into the veneer she presented to the world.

"I've been thinking of you lately," Leilah said. "We both have."

"You and Clem?"

"Me and Dorothy di Frasso." Leilah craned her head around the room. "She's here somewhere. At any rate, she told me she'd heard on the grapevine that Linc had been spotted somewhere down south. Argentina, I think. And I was wondering if you'd tracked him down and cleared up that mess about his making off with all your dough."

Leilah's dark brown eyes seemed clear of collusion but Gwendolyn couldn't be sure. Was she fishing for information? Gwendolyn decided it was best to stick vaguely to the truth.

"Linc and I have cleared up that misunderstanding," Gwendolyn said.

"You found him?" Leilah managed to look pleased for her. "That must have been a relief. Where in heaven's name did he decamp to?"

"His letter arrived with no return address." She scanned the revelers for her dress, but it had disappeared.

"I always liked that boy. But weren't you counting on that money to open your store?"

"I've put that dream on hold for the time being."

"Oh, but you mustn't! We should never let something as easy as money stop us from realizing our dreams. I'm a big believer in putting one's money where one's mouth is. If it's a backer you need, then here I am."

Gwendolyn felt the air in her lungs escape in a silent *whoosh.*

"What do you need?" Leilah asked. "Five thousand? Ten? Just say the number and it's yours."

For the briefest of moments, Gwendolyn was tempted to say yes. But it was brothel money, and she'd heard enough of Arlene's stories to know that the only hookers with a heart of gold were the ones in the movies.

"Are you as surprised as I am that Siegel managed to get his Flamingo up and running?" Gwendolyn asked. "From what I've heard, the East Coast cut him off and he magically came up with the money to finish the job." When a sly smile blossomed across Leilah's face, Gwendolyn thought about what Linc told her in Mazatlán and added, "I don't suppose *you* know anything about that?"

Leilah's eyes bulged, making her look like a girl with a schoolyard secret. She looked around to ensure nobody could hear.

"A while ago, Ben came to Clem and me and told us he was aware that the FBI had bugged all his telephones, so Clem offered our place for his meetings. I had my hesitations, but it's Ben Siegel so . . . you know. And of course Dorothy is over at the house simply all the time, so I should have seen it coming."

"Seen what coming?"

"Dorothy and Benjamin rekindling their romance! Right there in our guesthouse!"

Any remnants of temptation to accept Leilah's offer flushed away. "Did Clem know about this?"

"He *encouraged* it. Although Ben was doing a terrible job building that place, Clem could see that once it was up and running properly, it'd rake in cash, even if the East Coast couldn't see it. So he bided his time until Ben was at the end of his financial rope and stepped in."

"You lent Siegel the money? But that was a million dollars!"

Leilah let fly an unguarded double take. "How did you know it was a million?"

Gwendolyn flagged down a passing waitress and ordered another champagne. "Remember Howard Hughes' TWA flight? That inaugural nonstop coast-to-coast? I heard that Bugsy was bragging about the fact that Wilkerson went to Mayer Lansky, but Lansky knocked him back, so he got the money together himself." It was a bald-faced lie, but nothing on Leilah's face told Gwendolyn she was way off the mark, so she plowed on. "A cool million was the amount that got floated around."

When Leilah told Gwendolyn yes, it was a million, Gwendolyn pressed further. "What did you do, sell all that land you bought around there?"

Leilah's cagey eyes stopped a whisker short of suspicious. "Did Linc tell you about that?"

"It was more of a read-between-the-lines sort of thing."

"Yes," Leilah admitted after a long pause, "that's exactly what happened."

Kathryn emerged from the dance floor, pointing to her watch and then pressing her hands against her face to show she was tired and heading home.

It wasn't until she'd made her excuses to Leilah and started weaving her way back to her ex-roommate that Gwendolyn realized she'd just gotten what Kathryn needed to extricate herself from the FBI.

CHAPTER 33

Marcus got his hands on the manuscript for *Deadly Bedfellows* in the middle of January. He spent all day Saturday plowing through it, and by Sunday morning he was finished. He slammed it shut with a thud and tossed the piece of crap against the bedroom wall.

Oliver bent his *LA Times* along the fold. "That bad?"

"He drowns Mathias Addison in a vat of red ink used for printing the Communist Party newspaper."

"Wardell's use of symbolism is remarkable," Oliver said drily.

Marcus glanced at Oliver's paper. "Tell me some news that doesn't involve death by cliché." Then he saw the headline.

BLACK DAHLIA'S LOVE LIFE TRACED IN SEARCH FOR HER FIENDISH MURDERER

The appalling discovery of the surgically dissected body of a two-bit wannabe had shocked a jaded Los Angeles. Taking its cue from the victim's dyed hair, the press had dubbed her the Black Dahlia, transmuting Elizabeth Short from a talentless nobody into a film noir femme fatale whose unspeakable fate now obsessed everybody in a two-hundred-mile radius of the grisly murder scene.

Each day that passed without a suspect or arrest meant a field day for newspapers who overlooked no opportunity to remind the populace that a monstrous butcher roamed the streets unfettered to strike again.

Directly below was an article heralding the House Un-American Activities Committee promising that a "top priority" of the new Congress would be an investigation of Communist influence in Hollywood. Marcus dropped the paper and ran his hand down Oliver's arm. "Because this town isn't paranoid enough."

"There's champagne and orange juice in the ice box." Oliver threw back the covers and headed for the kitchen. "Go to the Vehicles for Sale section. The head of MGM's writing department shouldn't be taking streetcars."

Marcus heard Oliver flip on the radio; a light waltz filtered through the doorway.

"We've got the greatest public transportation network of any city in the world," Marcus called back. "I can get anywhere I want and get work done while I'm at it." He received no answer save the pop of a champagne cork. "Did you see Kathryn's column yesterday? For the first time ever, Paramount, Warner, and Fox have all started to out-gross us."

Oliver returned to the bedroom with a tray holding two filled flutes, a half-empty bottle of French champagne, and a pitcher of orange juice. He slid it onto the bedside table, handed one of the flutes to Marcus, and rejoined him in bed.

They clinked glasses.

"Be that as it may," Oliver continued, "you work for a prestigious company and I doubt that it would look good for their writing head to arrive for work on the same streetcar as the kewpie dolls from the typing pool." He grabbed the *Times.* "Did you know there's a massive surplus of Jeep Willys and they're selling them off for a song?"

Oliver's mimosa was exactly what his funk needed. *Who did Clifford Wardell think he was fooling?*

Anson Purvis professed to be no fan of Wardell either, but did he know about *Deadly Bedfellows*? Marcus decided to call him into his office first thing Monday. The guy was a man of high principles and didn't strike Marcus as being the type to take character assassination lightly.

———

With Paramount, Warner, and Fox now starting to outgun MGM, Marcus needed every one of his writers to be firing with both pistols fully loaded, and Anson Purvis was proving to be his secret weapon. He'd just handed in his detailed treatment for *Pacific Broadcast*, about the downed navy pilot whose speech gets replayed across the country. It was a humdinger.

"I doubt that a surplus Jeep is going to enhance my standing at the studio," Marcus said.

"They're going for cheap, they're reliable as hell, you can get them painted in any color you want, and now they're putting on these retractable roofs. Can you imagine rolling up the coast to Malibu or even Santa Barbara with the wind in our faces? How much fun would that be? And besides, there's a homicidal maniac out there. I don't want you taking the streetcar late at night."

Marcus had never had anyone worry about him the way Oliver did, and the concern etching Oliver's face touched him deeply. Sure, Kathryn and Gwendolyn had always had his back, but it was different with Oliver. "Thank you." He pressed his forehead against Oliver's and kissed his nose. "But it seems this killer has a thing for marginally pretty, tarted-up tramps."

The late morning sun peeked over the roof of Lucius Beebe's villa and streamed through the window, filling Oliver's face with a shaft of light more typically seen in Renaissance paintings of religious ecstasy. Oliver glanced at the paper sprawled at their feet. "That Elizabeth Short woman could have been any arbitrary stranger unlucky enough to be the next passerby. LA's not as safe as it used to be."

Deadly Bedfellows still lay crumpled at the foot of Marcus' dresser. "You can say that again." He drained his glass. "How about we finish these off and head on out to whoever is peddling these Jeep Willys?"

A volley of sharp knocks against Marcus' door slayed their romantic spell.

"MARCUS!" It was Bertie. "IF YOU'RE HOME, OPEN UP!"

Marcus wrapped himself in his robe as he padded over to the door. He opened it to find Bertie in a surprisingly tasteful two-piece suit of navy blue with a matching fastener hat that struggled to restrain her chaotic mop.

"What is it?" Marcus asked.

"I've just come from a job interview—"

"On a Sunday?"

"I stopped off at Schwab's for eggs, and who should I see that Wardell rat!"

Marcus slumped against the doorjamb. "Bertie, everybody in this entire city has probably sat at a Schwab's booth at least half a dozen times—"

"He was sitting with Anson Purvis."

Marcus stood up straight. "How do you know that?"

"Buzz cut? Walks with a slight limp? Nods when the guy in the next booth says, 'Say, ain't you Leonard Purvis' youngest?'"

Marcus reflexively shifted his focus past Bertie's shoulder to the corner of Crescent Heights and Sunset and thought of what Purvis told him that day he showed up unannounced.

"You think they're still there?"

Bertie nodded so hard her fastener slipped off the back of her head, propelling her curls into a frenzy. "They'd just ordered burgers when I vamoosed."

Marcus sensed Oliver behind him. He was already dressed.

* * *

The rattle of cutlery and crockery vied with the burble of spirited gossipmongering. Schwab's rarely had a slow time, but late Sunday mornings were especially crowded with hungover Angelenos recovering from the aftereffects of a boisterous Saturday night.

Marcus searched the faces until he spotted Wardell and Purvis, and headed straight for them. Purvis caught sight of him and alerted Wardell with a jut of his head.

"Well, now," Marcus goaded, "isn't this a fine sight? Niccolò Machiavelli sitting down to break eggs with Benedict Arnold."

If Wardell was surprised to see Marcus, he hid it well, taking his time to sink his yellow teeth into a cheeseburger. "Lemme guess. You've read *Deadly Bedfellows*. I've heard it's one of those books you can't put down."

"What did I ever do to you?" Marcus demanded. "This can't be all about that time at George Cukor's party."

"Oh, it couldn't, huh?"

Marcus ignored the stares of the people around him. "You were a yellow muckraker who snuck into a private party with every intention of exposing the private lives of decent and talented people whose only crime was—" He faltered when he realized he'd painted himself into a corner.

"Was what?" Wardell asked. "Getting married to cover up their perverted inclinations? I've got a newsflash: It's not about you."

"The hell it isn't!" Marcus could feel half a bottle of French courage pumping through his heart. "Mathias Addison? Could you *be* any more obvious?"

"It's about every last prissy fag, and loudmouthed lesbo, and Commie-loving traitor who thinks his puke don't stink because he earns a thou a week and got nominated for an Oscar. You and everybody like you make me wanna heave. *Reds* and *Bedfellows* aren't about you, Adler; you're just the sap I chose to represent everything I hate in this swamp of a town."

"Then why don't you just go crawl back into whatever hellhole you slithered out of?"

Purvis chose this moment to release a snort of laughter.

"Last I heard, you thought this jerk was an A-1, first-class schmuck," Marcus barked. "Your very words, as I recall."

Purvis wiped ketchup from the corner of his mouth. "Since then, I got to know him better."

"And when did that happen?

"Last month's meeting of the MPA."

Marcus had half-forgotten that Oliver and Bertie had followed him until he heard Oliver's explosion over his left shoulder. "You belong to the Motion Picture Alliance?"

Purvis looked at Wardell and jerked his head toward Oliver. "Who's this?"

"I wouldn't swear to it in front of the HUAC," Wardell said, "but I suspect this one and Adler are . . . you know."

"You're not going to be happy until I get hauled up in front of Congress, are you?!"

"Sir?" Marcus swung around to the twitching face of a Schwab's waitress. "If you don't lower your voice, I'll have to ask you to leave."

"I'm going." He swung back to Purvis. "I don't know the first thing about the Communist Party, but even at their worst, they'd have to be a darn sight better than the hate-peddling chumps at the MPA. Falling for their jingoistic bullshit makes you the worst kind of fool."

Purvis propelled himself out of the booth and drew himself up to his full six foot three. "I've decked men for saying less."

"And I've *fired* men for less," Marcus spat back.

"Then I suggest we take this outside and settle it man to man."

Marcus shouldered through the crowd and stepped out onto the sidewalk along Sunset. He let three cars roar past, then spun around. Before him stood Wardell, pudgy and pale, looking like he hadn't exercised since high school phys ed. After the surprise right hook outside the brothel, Marcus knew he shouldn't underestimate the guy. But next to Wardell loomed a tower of lean Scandinavian muscle with fists clenched like hunks of raw beef. Behind them, the two long windows of Schwab's Pharmacy filled with dozens of expectant faces.

"Mr. Purvis." Oliver stepped between them, his voice low and controlled. "In the heat of the moment, all this may seem justified, but someone needs to remind you of the imprudence of slugging your boss."

Marcus gently nudged Oliver aside. This was his fight to win or lose.

"Do you know what Wardell did?" Purvis shook his head. "He's got a new book coming out. *Deadly Bedfellows*. And he's got this character, a returning war hero who becomes a screenwriter. This guy is referred to only by his nickname, Amp. Short for Amputee."

Purvis side-eyed Wardell. "You used me as inspiration for a character?" Marcus couldn't tell if he was impressed or repulsed.

"You know what he has Amp do?" Marcus pushed. "He drowns his boss, the studio writing department head, in a vat of red ink. Yeah, real classy. Is that how you want people to see you?"

"Just 'cause he's your boss," Wardell said, "doesn't give him the right to belittle you in public."

"And don't let this weasel tell you what to think," Marcus told Purvis. "He invited you to join the MPA, didn't he? What did he say? Just come along to a meeting and see what happens? I'll tell you what happens. Unless you keep your smarts about you, you'll get hoodwinked into thinking their brand of narrow-minded intolerance makes sense."

"I can make up my own mind." Purvis raised his fists.

"You're not at work now, Anson." Wardell's upper lip curled back. "This is just a couple of guys settling a difference of opinion on a public street. Don't let him call you an idiot."

"The law for assault and battery is quite clear," Oliver warned. "The party who throws the first punch — "

"Shut up!" Purvis's fist missed Oliver's chin and instead connected with his nose.

Oliver staggered backwards into Schwab's front window. Blood ran down his neck in wide streams, dripping onto the pavement.

Marcus felt the twin stallions of outrage and adrenaline stampede through his veins. "You can take a poke at me if you want," Marcus shouted, "but nobody hits him and gets away with it."

Purvis rapped on his wooden leg. "Don't let this stop you."

Marcus flew at Purvis, who had fourteen years on him, not to mention fifty pounds, and landed a punch dead center in his sternum. It didn't wind the guy, but it made him totter backwards a step or two. Marcus' knuckles burned, but he stepped forward, thrusting an uppercut into the guy's diaphragm. Purvis rotated just enough to avoid the blow.

Marcus saw a fist as big as a T-bone shoot toward him. He didn't even feel the pain when it connected with the midpoint between his eyes. Instead, he felt the disorientation of the sidewalk rushing toward him before he blacked out.

CHAPTER 34

Kathryn knew she was taking an awful chance asking
Nelson Hoyt to meet her at the Midnight Frolics.

Its patrons had made Gwendolyn their darling, and last
time Kathryn was there, someone said to her, "Miss
Gwendolyn makes us look as glamorous as we've always
dreamed." They'd be horrified to know that an FBI agent
was in their midst.

And there was no way of telling how Hoyt would react
when he realized he was sitting among perverts. Not that
Kathryn saw the Frolics crowd as perverts, but Hoyt might.
The last thing anybody wants is to be near a guy blowing a
fuse when he's within arm's reach of a gun.

The last time Kathryn saw Hoyt was the previous
December when he kissed her at the Ambassador.
Afterwards, anxiety and indecision compelled her to keep
him at a distance, but then a couple of things transpired that
could only be dealt with face to face. "Pick somewhere out
of the way," he'd told her. "Someplace unexpected."

She strummed her fingers on the table, chain-smoking
Chesterfields while she watched Gwendolyn work the room
with her boss, Mr. Dewberry.

The regulars liked to call this joint The Licks and referred
to themselves as Licketysplitters. As soon as she and
Gwendolyn walked in, the Licketysplitters gathered around
her like gazelles at a watering hole. *Does this color suit my
complexion? What are your thoughts on diagonal stripes? Could
you make me a copy of that black-and-white number Gene Tierney
wore in* Leave Her to Heaven?

After Gwennie's disappointments about Linc, her money stash, and her store, it warmed Kathryn's heart to see she had found her niche. It wasn't one she could tell many people about, but it paid well, and her clients adored her.

Kathryn went to light another cigarette, but realized it would be her fifth inside ten minutes, so she slid it back inside the pack. She glanced at the entrance. It wasn't like him to be late. She pulled the cigarette out again and tapped it on the table. *Were my instructions not clear enough? Did the door guy send him away? Maybe he already knows this is a cross-dresser bar.*

The drumming of a microphone pounded through the loudspeakers. Onstage stood Miss Julie, the Midnight Frolics manager, a gangly Charlotte Greenwood type.

"We have a hell of a treat tonight," he announced. "Miss Vilma is back in town from his six-month stint at the Brooklyn Navy Yard" — he paused to let the Licketysplitters wolf-whistle their appreciation — "and is here to entertain us with a few songs."

Miss Vilma made a passably attractive woman. With a sun-ripened olive complexion accentuated with dark red lipstick and a hint of eye shadow, he took the stage in a gauzy floor-length gown of apricot chiffon that Kathryn immediately recognized as a Gwendolyn original. He launched into "I Could Write a Book" with a purring, gravelly voice, and was barely sixteen bars in when Hoyt plopped himself on the chair next to her.

"Sorry I'm late, but this Black Dahlia thing has us working overtime since we ID'd the body with fingerprints." He fished out a cigarette and asked the approaching waitress for a bourbon on the rocks, then studied him more closely as he wound his way back to the bar.

Over Hoyt's shoulder, Miss Julie pointed to Hoyt and mouthed *Is that him?*

Kathryn had felt it only fair to secure the manager's okay to bring an FBI agent into the club. Understandably, Miss Julie almost imploded with horror, until Kathryn pointed out that a vice squad raid was not an altogether unlikely event for a cross-dresser bar, so if push ever came to shove, it might be handy to have an FBI agent in his corner.

Hoyt wrested his attention from Miss Vilma's song styling. "You look pretty tonight."

Part of her stirred. Having spent so long in the company of a head-turner like Gwendolyn, she had convinced herself that she was perfectly fine with not being the center of attention. Then this guy comes along and pitches a compliment like that in her direction, and suddenly she was a sixteen-year-old virgin.

"How's your father?" she deflected, then wished she had stuck to a less personal topic.

He ducked his head. "Not so great, actually. He came back from the Great War with TB, which is why we moved out West. It flares up every now and then. This one is particularly bad."

He didn't look at her in his usual direct way, but averted his gaze to a blank spot on the wall. She could see the worry in his eyes as he shifted in his seat. "But you didn't ask me here because of dear ol' dad."

Kathryn straightened her spine, all business now. "I've come across some information that you and your boss will find interesting."

Kathryn related Gwendolyn's conversation with Leilah O'Roarke at the Florentine Gardens, when Leilah admitted that she and Clem had sold blocks of land to fund Bugsy Siegel. Gwendolyn wisely cautioned Kathryn against bringing this news to Hoyt without some independent verification, so Kathryn sent her freelance snooper to Las Vegas to do some nosing around.

Lenny didn't strike gold, but he struck silver in the form of an upturn in real estate sales along the Los Angeles Highway, where the Flamingo now stood. According to his calculations, the total sales came to $989,600. When he dug for names, he was stonewalled, but Kathryn figured she had enough information to take to Hoyt, and that he'd have the resources to uncover the missing pieces.

"So what do you think?" Kathryn pressed. "Is it enough to cut me loose?"

"If all this checks out, you've given us more than enough to lasso Siegel and the operators of the most profitable brothels in California. They all kick back to the LAPD to allow them to stay open, but the O'Roarkes don't."

"How the hell do they get away with that?"

"Our theory is they've got bigger muscle behind them."

"The mob?" Kathryn whispered.

Hoyt nodded. "But we've never had any proof of a link. Until now."

Kathryn started to feel lightheaded. She tried to tell herself not to count her chickens, but it was hard to keep a lid on the excitement rising in her chest.

Hoyt accepted his bourbon and lit a Viceroy. "Mr. Hoover is a lot of things, some of them unsavory, but he is a man of his word. When I told him your mother's tax bill had been paid in full, he laughed."

"What kind of laugh?"

"The touché, well played kind."

While Miss Vilma brought his sultry rendition of "I've Heard That Song Before" to a close, Nelson surveyed the crowd. "What sort of club is this? Not one of those private lodges with nutty initiation rites, is it?"

He watched some more. A group of four couples walked through the arched entryway. Half of them were dressed in tuxedoes tailored to look like something Marlene Dietrich used to shock audiences with; the other half wore identical ball gowns of silver lamé tipped with white fox fur. Hoyt scrutinized them as they waved and kissed their way through the thicket of tables until they found their seats.

When Miss Vilma made a big finish, his spotlight went out, and the Licketysplitters filled the room with the thunder of their applause.

From the way Nelson chewed his lower lip, it was clear Kathryn had succeeded in throwing him. She wondered how many people had managed to pull that off.

He looked away from the Dietrich-tuxedoed quartet and flashed an impish Errol Flynn type grin. "Why do I get the feeling I'm being tested?"

Because you are. On paper, you're quite a catch. Good-looking, dresses well, speaks nicely, treats his father with respect, has a real job, and a set of principles I can't help but admire the more I get to know you.

"We have another item on the agenda," Kathryn prompted. "That post office box I asked you to look into." She watched Hoyt's wall of G-man neutrality rise between them. "Did you get anywhere?"

One of the things this guy had going for him was his sense of humor, which he managed to maintain regardless of what was going on. She watched it drain from his face, and was shocked at how different he looked.

"I want to know why you asked me to look into it," he said.

She shifted in her seat so their faces were closer together. Not that anybody could hear them over Miss Vilma's "Summertime."

"There was an impromptu gathering at the Florentine Gardens the night the Flamingo opened."

"I knew you'd find a way to get out of that."

"I bumped into Bette Davis, who told me about an odd garment that arrived when she was visiting Orry-Kelly at Warner Brothers. It turned out to be something Gwendolyn had made."

"She works there now?"

"No. It was a freelance job for an anonymous customer who asked her to mail it back to the same post office box. Nothing to do with Warners, and yet that's where it appeared. When Bette told Gwendolyn about it, I got a strong hunch. The measurements for the dress Gwendolyn made were 38–38–38. Women don't have those sorts of measurements."

Nelson's eyes looped around the nightclub. "But men do."

"That post office box was where Gwendolyn sent the dress." The audience burst into applause. Gwendolyn glanced over to Kathryn and frowned. Kathryn made a *keep away* hand signal. "Did you find out who that box belongs to?"

Hoyt started to knead his forehead. "The Ding-a-ling Toy Company."

Kathryn felt her heart drop. *So much for my hunches.*

"But they've only had it a month or so," he continued. "Prior to that, it belonged to a Jack Humboldt."

"That name doesn't ring a bell."

The Flynn grin resurfaced. "A few months back, Hoover came into town with a full agenda. All the anti-Commie stuff with the studios, the HUAC, Chaplin.

"When he got there, he had trouble with his briefcase. He's got this huge thing he totes around — like the ones doctors carry on house calls. It has these two big locks that open with separate keys, but one of them jammed. He messed around with it but couldn't get it open. His assistant, Clyde, had a go, but he couldn't do it either. Hoover got more and more frustrated, but none of us dared volunteer until finally he said, 'There's got to be at least one man here who's good at picking locks.'"

"You?"

"I'm good with mechanical stuff. The damned thing refuses to budge, so I get more physical with it. I start to break a sweat when suddenly, it bursts open—boom! Krakatoa! So naturally I get on my knees to pick it all up. You should have seen the way he threw himself on top of all these papers and folders and letters. I only managed to pick up a few things before he ordered me back to my seat, but I saw a pile of envelopes bound up in an elastic band, and the top one was addressed to . . ." He gestured toward Kathryn.

"Jack Humboldt . . . J.H. . . . John Edgar Hoover."

" . . . who is very friendly with Jack Warner."

Kathryn thought about Bette's story about the package landing in Orry-Kelly's office marked "Jack." She shook her head as things started to fall into place. "So the head of the FBI likes to—" She couldn't bring herself to finish such an outrageous sentence.

"Everybody has a personal life," Nelson said, "but not him. Leastways, none that I've observed. He's the most tightly closed book I've ever encountered."

They let Miss Vilma's gravelly final note of "Summertime" waft over them.

"You said you wanted to leave the Bureau." Kathryn fancied she could see Nelson's eyes harden as the lights of the club dimmed. "Was that just a heat-of-the-moment declaration, or did you mean it?"

"I think maybe I've found my way out."

"Blackmailing the head of the FBI?" Just the thought of it made Kathryn's innards churn.

"I'm going to have to play it smarter than that."

As the Licketysplitters thundered their applause, Kathryn felt Nelson's breath fill her ear.

"This is a transvestite joint, isn't it?"

"You said to pick somewhere unexpected. Are you mad?"

"I probably should be." She heard him chuckle. "You really are one hell of a gal."

A part of Kathryn melted. Nobody had ever said that to her before. It wasn't the most flattering compliment a typical guy could pay a typical girl, but here she was sitting with an FBI agent in a cross-dresser bar talking about hoodwinking J. Edgar Hoover. Kathryn Massey had passed "typical" so far back it wasn't even in her rearview mirror.

CHAPTER 35

Gwendolyn ran her nail around the edges of the brown paper package sitting on her dining room table. The last time she received something like this, it contained an anonymous request to make a dress measuring 38–38–38.

The possibility that she'd sewn a dress for J. Edgar Hoover made her cringe; the prospect of making another horrified her. If this client really was him, she probably wasn't in any position to refuse. And besides, it was just a theory, she told herself. Kathryn could be wrong.

She peeled back the Scotch tape and opened the contents. A letter fell out. Gwendolyn read it, then read it again before inserting it back inside the package, folding up the sides, and charging outside.

* * *

When Kathryn answered her door, Gwendolyn held the parcel aloft, then brushed past her. "He wants a replacement, same as the first." She pulled out the letter.

"He wants a second one because he never got the first," Kathryn said.

Gwendolyn pointed to the return address. "This isn't the same post office box."

"He'd be careful not to leave a trail. Are you going to make it?"

Gwendolyn shrugged as she eyed the package. *It was kind of exciting when I didn't know who it was for. But now, it's just flat-out scary.* "I won't be deciding tonight. I'm on my way out to visit Bertie at work."

"At nine thirty on a Tuesday?"

"She said the evening shifts are horribly boring after nine o'clock, so I told her I'd keep her company."

Gwendolyn hadn't been there the Sunday afternoon that too many whiskey sours around a cribbage board resulted in Kathryn blabbing to Bertie about the pillowcase full of shredded bills buried in the old victory garden. To her credit, Bertie ran straight to Gwendolyn's door and promised she'd do everything she could to pay off her debt. After moving to the Garden's cheapest room, she sold her DeSoto to Marcus and pawned all her jewelry. Gwendolyn could barely believe it when Bertie arrived on her doorstep with a check for ten dollars and a solemn promise to repay every last penny. At ten bucks a month, it would take her twenty-five years, but the gesture was touching, sincere, and admirable, so Gwendolyn accepted the check.

"You're not walking there, are you?" Kathryn asked.

"It's just the other end of the Strip."

"The hell you will!" Kathryn grabbed her pocketbook. "Until they catch the Black Dahlia killer, no single woman walking the streets of LA at night can assume anything. I'm coming with you."

* * *

Bertie had always been a night owl, so she happily took the evening shift at the new ice cream parlor at the western end of the Sunset Strip. With its vivid red, pink, and white décor, Wil Wright's reminded Gwendolyn of the one she used to visit as a kid back in Florida. The white metal chairs had red and white striped leather cushions and the round tables were topped with pink and cream marble. At night, extra-bright lighting lit up the bold red and white awning so that nobody on the Strip could miss the place.

When Gwendolyn and Kathryn walked inside, the only person in the place was Bertie.

"You came!" She threw aside her copy of *The Snake Pit* and beamed a mouthful of crooked, oversized teeth. "This place has been a graveyard since seven thirty. They've started this new campaign — 'Tonight, leave the dessert to Wil Wright's' — but they needn't have bothered. The Black Dahlia killed off all our evening traffic. So, girls, what'll it be?"

Kathryn chose a fresh peach sundae, and Gwendolyn ordered a dish of chocolate burnt-almond ice cream.

"You picked an auspicious night," Bertie said, preparing their orders. "Howard Hughes should be here soon. You've met him, haven't you?"

By the time Bertie was finished with their orders, a pack of teenagers rushed through the door. The tallest one waved a five-dollar bill and instructed his pals to order "anything and everything you want. We ain't leaving till there's no change left!"

"Hey, moneybags." Gwendolyn nudged him. "Don't forget to leave a tip for the gal behind the counter. She's a real trouper." She took their orders to a table in the bay window that looked out across the Strip.

Over the past months, Gwendolyn had come to understand that Licketysplitters didn't necessarily want to look like women; they wanted to *feel* like them. She was wondering now if Hoover was like that, and if sewing a second 38–38–38 dress would lead her into darker, deeper waters than she'd prefer to wade through, when Kathryn launched into an entirely different subject.

"Did you read Winchell today? That excruciating piece about Communist infiltration of Hollywood?"

"He's so spiteful, isn't he?"

"Meaner than a schoolyard bully with a slingshot, but at the end of yesterday's column, he included a blind item about how a certain 'Loaded Lou' and 'Separated Sue' are carrying on their white-hot affair at the sprawling home of 'Retired Rita' but warning them they'd better be careful because both Separated Sue's boss and her soon-to-be-ex have set two different teams of private eyes on her."

"Someone's asking for trouble," Gwendolyn said.

"I have a theory that Separated Sue is Rita Hayworth. Her boss is Harry Cohn and her soon-to-be-ex is Orson."

Gwendolyn thought about the affair Kathryn had with Welles before the war, and wondered if a vestige of jealousy was fueling this conversation. Kathryn had always maintained she was long over anything she'd felt for Orson, and if she was going to start something with this Hoyt guy, maybe she really had.

"Who do you think Loaded Lou is?" Gwendolyn asked.

"Howard Hughes. He's pretty chummy with Marion Davies, and she hasn't made a picture since way before the war."

"Retired Rita?"

"Exactly, and she hardly ever uses that huge white elephant down on Santa Monica Beach. It all fits. And Howard is about to walk in here, so—"

"Did anything happen after that kiss?" The question felt like it shot out of Gwendolyn's mouth on its own accord.

Kathryn reared back. "What kiss?"

"The one with Nelson, that night at the Ambassador." It was hard to tell if Kathryn was blushing, or was it just the light reflecting off the pink marble table tops. "I know it's none of my business," Gwendolyn added. "I'm just a mite concerned, is all."

Kathryn screwed her face up like a child begging forgiveness. "Would it make me the worst person in the world if I wanted it to?"

"Hardly." Gwendolyn tried a smile designed to soften Kathryn's guilt. "He's handsome and all, and that whole forbidden fruit thing is tempting. I get it. But I was watching you that night at the Frolics. I saw the way you two were with each other."

"What did you see?"

"Heat. Electricity. Temptation."

"I hated him when I first met him." Kathryn shoved a spoonful of peach into her mouth. "And for the longest time after."

"But now?"

"He's disillusioned and wants out. That's what all this dress stuff is for. Finding him a way to leave the FBI."

"But have you thought about how Marcus will feel when he learns of this? He loves you more than anybody, but aren't you afraid this will cause more damage than it's worth?"

"Of course I've thought about it." Kathryn toyed with her sundae. "The HUAC is out for Hollywood's blood, and the FBI is supplying the ammo. This whole industry could go under, and Marcus right along with it. Believe me, I've thought about all that."

"Where we stand in this will count for a lot."

"I KNOW!" Kathryn's outburst captured the attention of the teen boys, who gawked at them for a moment, then burst into stifled giggles. Gwendolyn heard the jangle of the store's front door bell and watched Kathryn's eyes as she saw who'd entered. They tracked Hughes' path to the counter, where he ordered a scoop of coconut, a scoop of peppermint, and four macaroons on the side.

While Bertie put on the finishing touches, Hughes surveyed the boys for a while, then noticed Gwendolyn and Kathryn. To Gwendolyn's surprise, he smiled.

"Mind if I join you ladies?"

He winced slightly as he sat down on one of the wire chairs. Kathryn drew in a breath to go fishing for gossip, but his attention was fixed on Gwendolyn. "I never did ask you how things went in Mexico."

For the flight back from Mazatlán, Hughes took on a copilot and three aviation engineers, and had been so preoccupied with airplane talk that he barely even acknowledged her.

"It went fine, thanks," Gwendolyn said.

"Did you track Tattler down?"

Gwendolyn swirled the spoon around her dish of melting ice cream. "Turns out he was innocent of any wrongdoing, so that trip put my mind to rest. You were busy on the flight home and I never really got a chance to thank you."

"I got your note," Hughes said around a macaroon.

"Still," Gwendolyn said, "thank you very much."

"But what about your missing three grand?"

Gwendolyn glanced at Bertie. "I've kissed that money goodbye."

"But you were hoping to fund your store with it, right? Dresses, if I recall."

"Uh-huh," she said, mildly. "But that's life, isn't it? Some things work out perfectly, while others fall apart."

Hughes dropped his spoon. It clattered onto the ceramic dish, splashing green peppermint ice cream onto the marble. "You have a dream, you make it happen. And you don't stop until it comes true. Sometimes that means you enlist the support of someone who can help."

He pulled a paper napkin from the metal box and wiped his mouth. "I'll send you a check for five thousand next week." Hughes dropped his wadded paper into his empty dish.

Her vision of how Chez Gwendolyn would look — the window display, the sign, the clothing — swam into view. "Thank you," she said slowly. "But I need time — "

Hughes hoisted himself to his feet. "No deadline. It isn't a loan. It's a gift." He clutched his hip as he disappeared into the night.

Kathryn landed her hand on top of Gwendolyn's. "Honey!" she cried. "You've done it! Chez Gwendolyn's a go!"

Gwendolyn stared at the abandoned dessert and shook her head to clear her mind. "I don't know that I feel comfortable taking his money."

"You were right to knock Leilah back. But this is completely different! Hughes earns his money honestly. Half the girls in this town have been the recipients of his generosity, so why not you too?"

Gwendolyn nodded absently, but wasn't convinced. Obviously the man could afford to fund a hundred Chez Gwendolyns and not even miss a dime. If she was going to accept his money, she wanted to know there were no strings attached. The problem was that when it came to Howard Hughes and girls and money, there were always strings attached.

CHAPTER 36

Kathryn was thankful Bette Davis had told her to not put herself out. "I'm eight and a half months pregnant," she drawled over the telephone. "I can't stomach anything more exotic than saltine crackers with peanut butter, and a pineapple Jell-O chaser."

She switched on the radio; an old Harry James tune — "I've Heard That Song Before" — started to fill her living room when the doorbell rang. An alarmingly pregnant movie star huffed to catch her breath.

"Maybe this wasn't such a good idea," she said, taking Bette by the hand and guiding her to the sofa, taking as much of the weight as she could while Bette lowered herself.

Bette expelled a harsh breath as she arranged the cushions to support her back. "Cover model for *Maternal Monthly Magazine,* I am not."

"Are you drinking?" Kathryn asked.

Bette barked out a laugh. "I shouldn't."

"Which means — ?"

"We should probably stick to milk and pray it might induce Barbara to pop out early."

"So you're having a girl?"

"Barbara Davis Sherry," Bette replied. "BD for short." She rubbed her stomach like a farmer might pat a cow. "And don't you dare print that until I pass this watermelon."

Kathryn crossed into the kitchen. "I hope you were serious about the saltines and peanut butter."

Bette's eyes lit up when Kathryn returned with two glasses of milk in one hand and a platter in the other. "Perfection! Now, sit yourself down and tell me what's on your mind."

Kathryn should have known Bette was far too canny to not see through her breezy invitation. The night at Bertie's ice cream parlor had unnerved her. She was worried that every last crumb of willpower would rot away before she knew Nelson meant what he said.

But it was Gwendolyn's question that kept haunting her: *Have you thought about how Marcus will feel when he learns of this?*

Until that moment, Kathryn had assumed that Marcus would support anything she did. She'd never given him any grief over his romance with Oliver. But didn't the Breen Office obstruct Hollywood's freedom of speech as much as the FBI? Surely they were in the same boat. How could Marcus see it any other way?

But Nelson was with the FBI, and the FBI was in league with the HUAC, which was out to bring Hollywood to its knees over something that scarcely even existed. Nobody doubted there were Communists in Hollywood, but the idea that they were sneaking Commie dogma into every movie was laughable.

The questions swirled around Kathryn's head like dishwater circling the drain until she didn't know which way was up. She couldn't talk to Gwendolyn about it — she was too close. So she'd decided she needed someone to put her straight — someone who wasn't afraid to tell her that she was a mercenary she-devil.

Bette sat before her, wide-eyed with expectation. "Is it man trouble?" she prompted.

That was all the prodding Kathryn needed.

To her credit, Bette tsked and smiled in all the right places, and never interrupted the flood of words that came pouring out.

"Well!" she exclaimed once Kathryn reached the end of her story. "That's one mighty sharp pickle you've gotten yourself into."

Kathryn bit into another saltine. "Maybe Gwendolyn's right—it's just the fleeting temptation of forbidden fruit."

Bette laughed. "I'm the world's greatest expert on the subject of forbidden fruit."

"Did you ever wish you hadn't given in?" Kathryn asked.

"Every single time." She caressed her belly. "Including the one responsible for this, sad to say. Let me take a wild stab in the dark here. You rarely find yourself on the receiving end of romantic attention from men, so when it actually comes along, you don't know who—or what—to trust." She held out her glass for a refill and stared at Kathryn, daring her to deny her hypothesis.

That's it exactly, Kathryn thought. *Ask me to interview a star who doesn't want to share anything, and I know exactly what to do. Give me a moral dilemma about censorship, or tell me the boss blew the payroll at Santa Anita, and I'll swing into action. But when a nice guy with a soft pair of lips smooches me in the moonlight, I'm senseless as a bobby soxer.*

"That's the trouble with women like us," Bette said. "We're not the white-picket-fence type, nor do we want to be. We're intelligent, capable go-getters who want more out of life than knitting circles and meatloaf recipes."

"Says the woman who's minutes away from motherhood."

Bette ran her hands over her stomach. "I'm thankful for the chance to experience motherhood and I fully intend to embrace it, but it's not the be-all end-all. I don't want a husband to take care of me; I want a partner, an equal who will take care of and look out for me as I will for him. However, we live in a world where men like that are a rare sighting. And when one comes along, it's like catching the abominable snowman."

"So what do we do?"

"We make a decision, then deal with the consequences. What else can we do? But if he *is* a good guy, you be sure to grab him with both hands."

"I'm starting to think he might be," Kathryn confessed.

Bette rested her chin on a palm. "If you've learned to tell the difference, I'd love to hear how."

Kathryn confided what Nelson had discovered about the post office box used for the dress that turned up in the Warner Bros. costume department, and how wonderful it would be if they could track down the dress itself.

"What would you do with it?"

"Persuade Hoover to let Nelson leave the FBI. I even tracked down his favorite tailor in LA and double-checked: Hoover wears a 38 suit jacket, so it all fits."

Bette started to laugh. "I always knew that little shit had a dark secret, but I never suspected *that!*"

Her laugh was infectious and soon Kathryn was giggling, too. "Can you imagine? Hoover? In a dress?"

"That's not why I'm laughing." Bette flung her arms out. "You've got it!"

"Got what?"

"I'm *wearing* it!"

Kathryn took in Bette's maternity dress. It was dark green, shiny, and too tight across the chest. "This is the one that arrived in the office when you were visiting Orry-Kelly?"

"I got Jack to insert some side panels for extra room, but Gwendolyn could take them out easily enough." Bette extended her right wrist and reversed the cuff to reveal the tiny embroidered G on the inside. "You can have it back if you get Gwendolyn to make me something new to wear once I've expelled BD from my loins."

Kathryn's head spun as she gave Bette a roomy old robe and hung the Hoover dress in her closet, and over pineapple Jell-O, they moved on to how MGM's rivals were starting to out-gross them, and if now was not the best time for Bette to be leaving Warners. Bette told her not to worry.

"There's more than one game in town. Scrappy old battle-axes like me and Miss Crawford will always find work."

* * *

After Bette departed, Kathryn decided Hoover's dress would be safer in the closet. But as she lifted it off the top of her bedroom door and turned toward her room, the dress caught the edge of a statue she'd set on a small credenza against the wall. The sculpture wobbled for a moment, then crashed to the floor. She was picking up the pieces when she noticed a black wire coming from the statue's foot.

Kathryn yanked the wire free and found something at the other end: a heavy device about the size of six quarters stacked together, black with red stripes and had two wires sticking out. It was warm in the palm of her hand.

She took two steps at a time down to Marcus' villa, and banged on his door. When he opened it, she thrust the device and the statue into his face.

"Is this what I think it is?"

Marcus looked from the broken statue of Mercury, Roman god of communication and luck, to the device, then back again. His eyes hardened. "Remember Bogie? And now they're doing the same to you?"

She snatched it out of his hand and started to march away.

He followed her. "I'm coming with you."

A near-full moon peeked through the branches of the eucalyptus tree that shaded both their places. It was light enough for Kathryn to see how fearful Marcus was for her.

"I'll be fine," she told him.

"Alone? I'm sure the Black Dahlia thought that too."

She thought about all those tawdry Black Dahlia headlines.

GIRL TORTURED AND SLAIN
SEX FIEND VICTIM IDENTIFIED
BY FINGERPRINT RECORDS
DAHLIA KILLER TAUNTS POLICE

"I don't know that you coming along is such a good idea. I can take a cab."

"And what if the Black Dahlia killer is a cab driver?"

* * *

Nelson's apartment at 5905 Fountain Avenue was one of a mini-court of four whitewashed bungalows a few blocks north of the cemetery next to Paramount. She wasn't surprised to see that he had his own back door allowing him to slip in and out, unobserved from the street.

She tapped on his back door, then knocked louder until he opened it.

He smiled when he saw Kathryn, but his lips thinned when he spotted Marcus behind her. She held the bug in her palm and raised it to his face. He looked at it, then said, "You better come inside."

Nelson's living room was warm and light, with dark orange drapes against apricot walls. Two sofas faced each other across a walnut coffee table. Over the fireplace hung an old California booster poster produced to convince people to move to the West Coast back in the days before the movie industry took over that role.

Kathryn gestured to Marcus. "I'm sure you know who this is," she said.

Nelson nodded. "Yes, Mr. Adler, it's—uh . . ."

"Good to meet me?" Marcus asked, thick with sarcasm.

"Please, take a seat."

"I don't want a seat," Kathryn said. "I want the truth."

"And I want to know how you found out where I live. I'm not in the book."

"Maybe you're not quite as mysterious as you think you are." Kathryn had spotted Nelson's address on a telephone bill on the counter of his father's store the day she bought Gwendolyn's lamp. Accustomed to reading upside-down papers scattered on the desks of movie moguls, she only needed a glance to memorize it. "And maybe your father should be more careful what he leaves laying around on his desk." She lifted the bug up to face level again. "Can we stick to the subject, please?"

"Where did you find it?"

"Exactly where you put it!" Marcus jeered.

I knew it was a bad idea, Kathryn thought. *If this is where I find out he's been stringing me along, I'd rather not have an audience. Not even Marcus.*

"I knocked over a sculpture," she said, "and found it attached to the base."

"I can assure you, that thing did not come from us."

"The FBI bugged Bogie's villa and you claimed to know nothing about it," Marcus said. "Your assurances don't mean diddly."

Kathryn placed a gentle hand on Marcus' pounding chest. "Let's hear him out."

"We haven't used those since before the war," Nelson said. "The newer ones are smaller and much harder to find."

Kathryn felt a ripple of tension leave her shoulders. She looked at Marcus. *That does make a certain amount of sense.*

"I don't buy it." Marcus muttered

Nelson turned toward the desk in the corner. "Let me show you what we use nowadays. You'll see they're nothing like that old dinosaur you've got there."

"So you admit that you do use bugs?"

"You know we do," he said quietly.

"So who's to say that you didn't just decide to use some old bug you had lying around from the old days?" she asked. "Nobody at the Bureau would miss it. You could listen away to your heart's content."

"Because *I'm* saying it, Kathryn. I give you my word."

"Your word!" Marcus scoffed, but Nelson ignored him.

"Tell me, Kathryn why would I go to the trouble of bugging your apartment and risk getting caught out by the one person whose trust I'm trying to win?"

"What do you know about trust?" Marcus demanded. "What do you care about what happens to people? Just as long as the FBI gets what they want."

"I cared enough the night of that raid," Nelson shot back.

Marcus turned to Kathryn. "What's he talking about?"

"You never told him?" Nelson asked.

"Told me what?"

"That raid up in Mandeville Canyon," Kathryn said.

"What of it?"

"Didn't you ever wonder why you guys were released?"

Kathryn threw Hoyt a *Shut the hell up!* look, then turned back to Marcus.

"He was on the phone with the desk sergeant when you were hauled in. He convinced the guy to release the three of you."

Marcus twisted his neck just far enough to bring Hoyt into his peripheral vision. "Why would you do that?"

"I figured it'd encourage her to trust me."

"To get her to do what you wanted."

Nelson had been soft-peddling his voice, keeping it aw-shucks friendly. But now it turned harsh. "If I'd known you'd take this attitude, I probably wouldn't have bothered. Did you read what happened to everybody else?"

The raid had made front-page news for days afterwards. Every man arrested that night was listed along with his home address and current employer.

Nelson stepped up and poked Marcus in the chest. "Within a week, all those homos were out of a job, and most of them evicted from their homes."

Kathryn threw her hands up. "What did you say?"

"You heard me. Oh, come on! Let's lay all our cards on the table. That was a homo bar. You married a homo. Knowingly, I assume. You had your reasons. But what I did that night saved your friend from public humiliation that would have cost him his career. And what do I get for it? A thank you? No. I get accused of manipulating you to get what I want."

"And how is that any different from what you've been doing since the day you walked into my dressing room at NBC?" she challenged.

"It's different now because I want out. And I want you."

Nelson had done a damned decent thing getting Marcus and the others off the hook, and he deserved to be thanked for it better than he was. Kathryn wanted to be nobody's fool, but was Marcus right? Had he done it just to curry favor with her?

Hoyt broke the silence.

"And as long as we're laying our cards on the line, you want to know the truth? Okay then, here's the truth: That time during the war when we bugged Bogie's place? We were supposed to be bugging *yours*."

Kathryn reared back. "What?"

"You told her you didn't know about that," Marcus said.

"I didn't. Not at the time. I didn't learn till much that later those agents who broke in, they got the wrong place. Nobody knew until we started listening and discovered it was Bogie's. You should've heard Hoover when I told him. He sounded like he was literally dancing a merry jig. Bogie was his ultimate target, but he wasn't convinced the bugs we used back then could do the job, and didn't want to take the chance with such a high-profile subject."

Something inside Kathryn gave way. It was almost like she could feel the muscle and sinews in her chest pulling apart.

"My life was fine till you came skulking in!" she yelled. "And it's been a bottomless rabbit hole ever since." She pitched the bug at him. It slugged him squarely on his forehead.

She stomped past him, brushing away his attempt to grab her arm, and headed for his door. She clutched the tarnished brass knob to steady herself, and threw over her shoulder, "My mom's tax bill is paid, and you've got your information about the O'Roarkes' real estate dodge." She jerked the door open. "I'm out, and if Hoover's got a problem with that, he knows where I work. Don't contact me again — ever."

She hurried down the gravel path that led to the side street where they parked the DeSoto. The night air chilled the damp sheen of sweat coating her face. As she hit the sidewalk, she kept expecting Nelson to open the door again, but it stayed shut and the path remained dark. Part of her was glad he hadn't followed them; another part couldn't help but be disappointed.

They said nothing as Marcus opened the passenger door for her. She nodded her thanks as she slid onto the front seat. By the time they pulled away from the curb, she could barely see it through the tears pooling in her eyes. Marcus headed north toward the Hollywood Hills, away from Nelson's bungalow, away from Paramount, away from the cemetery. She didn't open her eyes again until she saw the lights along Sunset.

CHAPTER 37

Marcus thought he had his share of problems until he learned about the bug in Kathryn's apartment. She'd tried to pretend she wasn't a teary, snotty, shaking mess when she came home that night, but that pretense only lasted until the second whiskey he put in front of her and the pair of Nembutals he left on her nightstand.

Since then, she'd been a far cry from her forthright, chatty self. It was like someone had turned down the volume and mislaid the dial. So when Marcus learned that the last day of filming the new Clark Gable movie, *The Hucksters*, was also the start of production for *The Final Day*, he arranged an all-day visit to the studio, where she didn't need to be followed around by a clingy staff member from Publicity.

The Hucksters featured an all-star cast — Gable, Adolphe Menjou, Sydney Greenstreet, Deborah Kerr, and someone Marcus had his eye on: Ava Gardner.

She'd been at the Garden a few times during her disastrous marriage to Artie Shaw, where she'd endeared herself with her free-spirited bawdy humor. She'd acquitted herself very well on loan out to Universal in *The Killers* with Burt Lancaster, and now the studio was giving her screen time with Gable — a landmark moment for any up-and-comer.

She was now on Marcus' *Actively Seek Properties For This Player* list, which was the next rung on the ladder to Hollywood heaven.

Marcus and Kathryn walked down the laneways between soundstages, nodding and saying hello to workers and performers they knew. As they passed under the enormous *METRO-GOLDWYN-MAYER STUDIOS* sign, they found a rare pocket of privacy. He was about to ask her how she was doing, but she spoke first.

"That Purvis guy, the one who sucker-punched you."

"What about him?"

"I still don't get why you didn't fire him."

Marcus flapped his lips. "In a perfect world, I'd have canned him on the spot. But this is Hollywood, where we only pretend it's perfect. Fact is, he's the new golden-boy writer around here. Our two biggest pictures during the holidays are shaping up to be *The Final Day* and *Pacific Broadcast*, and he wrote them both. I hate to say it, but he knocked them out of the park, which means I need him more than he needs me."

Kathryn watched a group of extras costumed in voluminous eighteenth-century dresses for *Green Dolphin Street* pass by. "How can you trust him?"

The humiliation still stung. He didn't blame her for bringing up the subject, but the sooner he could put it behind him, the better. "We've got to be able to trust some people. And others like Purvis and Wardell, you keep your eyes and ears open."

She shrugged and walked in through the soundstage door.

The last scene to be filmed was one in which Gable and Menjou meet their biggest advertising client, Sydney Greenstreet, in his teak-lined boardroom. The actors were on set, waiting for their next take. Greenstreet, wearing a dark velvet jacket and a tall white homburg, was seated in an elevated, elaborately carved throne at the head of a conference table long enough to seat twenty. At the other end of the table, Gable and Menjou sat chatting in three-piece suits.

When Gable spotted Marcus and Kathryn, he smiled and stood. As they approached, he cheek-kissed Kathryn and thrust out his hand for Marcus. "I was just thinking of you," he said. "I want my next one to be a war picture. Got anything up your sleeve?"

Marcus mentally searched through the scripts on his desk. "We've got something called *Homecoming*, about a guy who joins the Army Medical Corps."

"Sounds promising," Gable said. "I wanted *The Final Day*, but Mayer flat-out told me I was too old."

"Isn't that character supposed to be a greenhorn fresh out of boot camp?" Kathryn asked.

Gable grinned. "Mayer's never heard of rewrites?"

Kathryn elbowed him in the ribs. "I shall have a stern word with him the next time I see him."

Marcus was happy to see that Kathryn could still switch on the charm when she needed to. He'd never said anything — not even to Oliver — but he couldn't help wondering if she'd started to fall for that FBI guy. After her trip to Reno, a girlish quality had seeped into her voice whenever she talked about him. He'd been praying something might come along to jolt reality into her, and was relieved when she appeared at his door with that listening bug in her hand.

He felt someone catch him by the elbow. It was Arlene, and she wasn't smiling.

"I told my boss I needed to see the nurse," she whispered.

Kathryn was deep in conversation with Gable and Menjou about Mayer's recent divorce, so Marcus and Arlene stepped away.

"You're going to be called into L.B.'s office today," she told him.

"What for?"

"One of the typing pool gals just told me she spent the last two days working on dozens of copies of a declaration they're going to ask employees to sign."

Marcus swallowed hard. "Declaring what?"

"That you are not, nor have ever been, a member of the Communist Party."

"For the love of Mike!" The soundstage suddenly felt suffocating.

"They're taking this real serious, Marcus. But remember, you're protected under the First Amendment. You're free to belong to whichever political party you choose."

"I'm not a fucking Commie!"

"They have no legal grounds to force you into signing a declaration like that. Whether you sign it or not, they can still subpoena you."

"Subpoena? Who the hell—?" Her look of *Surely you can't be that naïve?* arrested him. "The House Un-American Activities Committee?"

Arlene stared at him. "Your receptionist, the one with the red hair. Dierdre?"

He turned to see her approach him, her eyes wrinkled with trepidation. "I was told to track you down. You've been summoned."

* * *

When Marcus entered his boss' office, everyone was already seated around the table: Mayer, Eddie Mannix, and three humorless lawyer types he'd never seen before.

Marcus shook Mayer and Mannix's hands, but Mayer didn't bother to introduce the others.

"As you know," Mannix said, "the HUAC have made it their business to root out subversives in any position to influence government policy or public opinion."

"You mean Communists," Marcus said, crossing his arms.

"Exactly so," Mayer said.

"It seems fairly clear to us"—Mannix gestured toward the lawyers—"and our equivalents at other studios that the HUAC are planning to campaign Washington to interrogate key Hollywood contributors about the Communist influence here."

The whole thing sounded like a rehearsed speech; Marcus wondered if he was the first audience. "If the HUAC get their hearings, it'll be one long, tortuous succession of political grandstanding. Just because they set up their sandbox doesn't mean any of us have to play in it."

"Maybe it does, maybe it doesn't," Mannix replied. "However, we feel that if we can present them with declarations of loyalty signed by everyone in the industry, they will, to use your phrase, pack up their sandbox and leave us all the hell alone."

Marcus thought about *The Hucksters* and its plot about how advertising men will say anything to get their product sold.

He eyed the sheet of paper on top of the stack in front of the lawyers. He could only make out a single word across the top: "DECLARATION."

"You want me to declare, in writing, that I am not a member of the Communist Party?"

Mayer's face brightened up. "That's it." He pushed his glasses back up his nose.

Marcus addressed the table. "You gentlemen have heard of the First Amendment, yes? As American citizens, we're allowed to belong to whichever political party we choose. That's kind of the whole point of the Constitution. I seem to recall that in among all that business about the right to freedom of religion, of speech, and of the press, there's something about political freedom, too."

"This is simply an evasive tactic," Mannix said expansively. He gestured toward his bank of lawyers. "We're looking to head the HUAC off at the pass. Nothing more."

The stuffiest-looking lawyer in a bow tie slid the paper in front of Marcus. His pale blue watery eyes belied a hard-edged shrewdness. "If you're not a Communist, signing this form will abrogate nothing."

"Nothing but my constitutional rights. I shouldn't have to sign anything, because you shouldn't feel as though you need to ask me." Marcus pushed the paper away.

"Look, Adler." Mannix's voice had grown curt. "If the HUAC hearings get up and running, and you don't sign this form, you might be treated as an unfriendly witness. In front of cameras, and microphones, and reporters. Trust me, that is not something you want to experience."

"Now listen here," Mayer said, more softly now. "I admire your high-minded principles, and wish more people had them these days."

Before Marcus could say anything, Mr. Watery Eyes pushed something else across the table toward him. "Besides," he said, "there's a bonus in it for you."

The check lay just out of reach. A thousand dollars. "Why do you guys always make everything about money?"

"Don't look at it that way," Mayer told him. "You're a company man, aren't you? We've looked after you, haven't we?" *Except for that time when you fired me then rehired me into the B unit.* "This is a 'lesser of two evils' type situation. Either you sign a piece of paper now and help us avoid a public nightmare, or you don't sign it and face the all too real possibility of testifying before the HUAC in Washington. That's what it comes down to."

"The signing bonus is just our way of saying thank you," Mannix added.

Marcus' eyes darted back and forth between the loyalty oath and the check. *If you're just going to throw money at me . . .* "All right," he said.

Outside Mayer's window, far off in the distance, a muffled boom hit the glass, rattling it for a moment. "That must be *The Final Day*," Mannix said. "They've started shooting."

Marcus asked the group if there was anything more. They told him there wasn't. He held the check in his hand as he took the long walk to Mayer's office doors, past Ida Koverman to the elevator, down the elevator to the foyer, and out into the harsh May sunshine. The first person he saw was Kathryn standing in the shade of an oak tree.

"Where'd you go?"

"To hell." He headed for the first trashcan that came into view.

"What's that?" she asked.

Marcus wondered if it was the opening salvo in a war he should have seen coming. He ripped the check in half, then in quarters. He kept ripping until the pieces were so small he couldn't tear them anymore, then let them flutter from his damp palms.

CHAPTER 38

Kathryn adjusted the brim of her straw Breton after closing the taxi door. "Is this on straight?" she asked.

Gwendolyn paid the cabdriver and reassured her the hat was fine, but Kathryn didn't believe her. "It hasn't felt right since we left home."

"Good gravy! How come you're so nervous when I'm the one who's auditioning?"

Gwendolyn had been fluttery ever since Kathryn told her Bette wanted her to make something. Only a handful of people had to ask Bette, "Wherever did you get that lovely outfit?" and she'd be on her way.

She'd gone all out with this creation: a sheath in reddish-pink moiré silk with matching ruffles in Chinese organza. She claimed it was a beast to sew, but she was thrilled with the result.

Bette had given birth eight days after her visit to the Garden. A month later, she was on the phone telling Kathryn she was antsy and begging her to come visit. When Kathryn asked if she could bring Gwendolyn, Bette had roared down the line, "Of course! Just *come!*"

Bette's maid ushered them into a conservatively appointed living room—lots of fresh flowers and pastoral landscapes—and told them Miss Davis would be down in a moment.

Several minutes passed before they heard footsteps on the stairs.

They rose to find a slimmed-down Bette Davis in a snug wool suit. Kathryn glanced at Gwendolyn, whose eyes were on the cream ruffles at the hem, and watched her exhale in relief. She'd been unsure about ruffles on such a shoot-from-the-hip type.

Bette greeted them with hugs and thrilled exclamations over the new dress. She insisted on "taking it out for a road test" and disappeared upstairs. It only took her a minute to change and she came down with a delighted smile. "I didn't think I'd lost enough baby fat, but look!" She spun on her heel and proclaimed the dress "Glorious!" Kathryn hadn't been convinced that the deep pink suited Bette's coloring, but she could see now that Gwendolyn's choice was inspired.

They sat down. "How's motherhood?" Kathryn asked.

Bette rolled her eyes. "It's fine. No, really, it's lovely. But I'll be happier when the little darling can actually talk back. Our conversations are one-sided, and even *I* get sick of my own voice. I've never been holed up inside the same four walls, day in, day out. For the love of all things adult, tell me what's been happening outside."

Kathryn's mind went blank. Since that horrible scene at Nelson's place, she'd hardly been the most social butterfly.

"You know what I want to hear," Bette said slyly. "That situation we talked about over your peanut butter crackers?"

"Things took a turn for the worse."

"So it wasn't your dress, after all?" Bette asked Gwendolyn.

"Oh, it was mine, all right. But something else came up that put a whole different spin on it."

The maid walked into the room with tea and sugar cookies. Bette told her she'd pour, and waited until the woman was through the swinging kitchen door before pressing Kathryn for more information.

When Kathryn launched into her story about how a fallen statue resulted in her discovery of the hidden bug, she expected Bette to be appalled, but when Kathryn was done, Bette simply said, "Are you positive it was him?"

"He works for the FBI!" Kathryn exclaimed. "It's what they do."

"Correct me if I'm wrong, my dear, but I got the distinct impression that the two of you had taken a shine to each other."

"Finding a bug has a way of changing everything."

Bette took a couple of contemplative sips, and said nothing. At least, nothing with her mouth . . . but those famous large eyes said plenty.

"What?" Kathryn demanded. "Out with it."

Bette set her cup down on its saucer. "I've made a career out of exploring human relationships, both on-screen and off. And if there's one thing I've learned, it's this: When someone is about to betray someone else, there are signs. So indulge me, just for a moment. Looking back with the benefit of hindsight, can you think of any signs he was about to do this to you?"

"I was completely blindsided!"

"So," Bette continued patiently, "maybe he didn't."

Bette's measured tone was starting to grate. Kathryn wanted shock and outrage, but was getting Spring Byington in *Little Women*.

"To be fair," Gwendolyn put in, "didn't he say that the bug you found wasn't the sort the FBI used anymore?"

"Interesting!" Bette took a wide-eyed sip of her tea. "Another subject I'm well versed in: enemies. I have mine, and I'm sure you have yours. What if we were to draw a line and call it The Scale of People Most Likely To Wiretap Kathryn Massey? Wouldn't the guy who is falling for you most likely rate only a one or two?"

"Don't forget, he wants to leave the FBI," Gwendolyn said. "I got the impression that he's partly doing it for you."

Kathryn had spent days upon days reliving that night. She wished they could do it over.

This time, Marcus would be more gracious about Nelson saving his career; Nelson wouldn't have said "those homos" in such a harsh tone; and she wouldn't have let everybody's outrage overwhelm her ability to distinguish bullshit from bombast. She stiffened as she considered for the first time in a long, dark month that maybe Nelson was telling her the truth. "Possibly," she admitted meekly.

"If that's the case," Bette continued, "who hates you enough to rate an eight or nine?"

The possibility that Nelson wasn't the culprit fogged her muddled brain so densely that she couldn't conjure a name.

"Or perhaps hates someone you're close to?"

Gwendolyn cracked a cookie between her teeth. "What about Wilkerson?"

Kathryn's teacup clattered onto the coffee table.

The silence that followed was so profound that Kathryn could hear the screams of young children playing in a swimming pool over the other side of Bette's back fence.

Gwendolyn was shaking her head. "Your Billy Hothead has tangled with a lot of people over the last few years, but there's only one person who scared him so much it sent him scuttling all the way to France."

* * *

Before she got out of the cab, Kathryn peered into Sunset Lamps and Lighting. When she spotted Nelson's father behind the counter, she forced herself to walk through the door before she lost her nerve.

A flash of surprise crossed Wesley Hoyt's face.

He almost looks pleased to see me. Obviously Nelson hasn't told him what happened.

"Are you here to see my son?"

"I need to speak with him on a matter of some urgency. Do you know where he is?"

"Not for certain."

"Could I leave a note with you?"

"Or you could come back at seven. Since the whole Black Dahlia thing, he's been walking me home at night. I think he's being a bit alarmist, but that's always been his way."

Kathryn looked at her watch. It was only four thirty. "I'll come back then."

"Ever been to the Radio Room?" The barest hint of a smile curled his mouth.

"Over on Vine?"

"By the time you get there, it'll almost be five o'clock, and today is Friday. Some men have their routines."

* * *

The Radio Room was a small place with a bar along the southern wall, a dozen tables, no dance floor, and a tiny stage with room for a jazz trio. It was dark, with just enough lighting to help a girl find the end of her cigarette. Kathryn was two Chesterfields down when Nelson walked in.

He found a table and signaled the guy behind the bar. As the bartender prepared the biggest manhattan Kathryn had ever seen, she slid up to him. "Mind if I take that?" The bartender had the grizzled face of a grumpy walrus. He raised his eyebrows, suspicious. She dropped a ten-spot on the counter. "He's a pal. I want to surprise him. Make me one of those, too."

She was careful to keep to Nelson's back until she was close enough to lead with the manhattan. His head shot up, his mouth gaping.

"I brought a fat slice of humble pie with me," she said. "Thought we might go halves?"

Eventually, he said, "You are the most confounding woman I have ever met."

"Does that mean I can join you? These drinks are heavy."

He nodded at the empty chair next to him. She placed the drinks on his table and dumped her handbag on an empty chair. She felt like she was sitting on eggshells and if a single one cracked, he'd bolt. She decided to open with humor.

"How's your forehead? Who knew I was such a good shot? Not me."

"Did my dad send you here?"

She angled a shoulder toward him. Not close enough to spook him, but it was a move that always worked in interviews when she was trying to establish a connection with a star on high alert. "I think you're a dear for walking him home every night."

"And I think Wesley Hoyt talks too much."

He lit a cigarette from the smoldering butt of his last one. "Why are you here?"

"I've had time to think."

"Four weeks' worth, by my count."

"I had a lot to think about."

A ghost of a smile pulled at his mouth. "Yes, you did. Are you here because you've come to a conclusion?"

"Maybe you weren't the only one with a reason to eavesdrop."

"I'm surprised that I satisfied the minimum requirements of 'beyond reasonable doubt.'" He started tapping his cigarette rapidly so she let him finish his thought. "Glad to see it though, I must say. What about your pal? Has he seen the light, too?"

"You leave Marcus to me," she said.

"Gladly." He sipped his drink. "So you were saying that you think I wasn't lying?"

"I told someone about what happened. She pointed out who had more to gain by bugging my place than you did."

"And who's that?"

"Bugsy Siegel."

She watched the name pierce the chrysalis of his professional surface. "Shit." He killed his Viceroy. "SHIT!"

"It makes more sense, doesn't it? After all that business about the Flamingo and the Nevada Project Corporation—"

"I'm such a fool. Why didn't I see this before?" He faced her with a mocking smile. "You're the girl!"

"What girl?"

He drew his face close enough to put him in kissing distance. "We've been listening in to Siegel's conversations. Most of it's been about Wilkerson and how he stabbed them in the back. They've been looking all over for him. For a long while they thought he was in the Poconos."

His breath was the manliest thing she'd smelled in a long while—a heady mixture of whiskey, vermouth, and burned tobacco.

"When they came up blank, they thought maybe they could squeeze it out of 'the girl' and how they could use her to get to him. We thought Wilkerson had found himself a little gold-digging mistress."

"You think *I'm* the girl?"

"There was talk of kidnap and ransom."

She took a sip. A long one. And then a second, even longer. The manhattan didn't seem near strong enough now.

"We weren't convinced they'd take it that far, but now I'm not so sure. I can't believe they managed to bug your place."

"You guys did it to Bogie," Kathryn pointed out. He clenched his hand on top of hers. It felt like a security blanket without which she'd slide under the table.

"Siegel blames Wilkerson's meddling in the Flamingo and he's out for blood. After we shipped him off to Paris, did you ever talk about Wilkerson's whereabouts when you were at home?"

"I don't think so."

"But are you sure?

She shook her head. "I—I don't—I can't be sure. This has got me all rattled."

"They snuck a bug inside your place once, they could do it again. You need to go to a hotel."

"What?!"

"Right now. Don't go home. I know this place in Pasadena. Real quiet and discreet."

His palm had gotten clammy. She wanted to grab her purse and hightail it into the night, but she knew she couldn't keep Ben Siegel at bay for long. She had no choice but to put herself in the hands of the guy who a month ago had her convinced he was the embodiment of evil. She closed her fingers around his.

CHAPTER 39

Gwendolyn no longer cared about her store, or job, or her dressmaking business. She had no time for tanked-up neighbors or needy coworkers. All she could think of was Kathryn.

Ten days ago, she found a note slipped under her door.

When you hear a story about my burst appendix, don't believe it. That bug wasn't placed by the FBI, but most likely Siegel. He's intent on tracking Wilkerson down and might very well come after me to do that. At Nelson's insistence I've gone into hiding. I'm at a hotel but will move every three days. Look for a classified ad in the usual place. BURN THIS MESSAGE!

"The usual place" was the *Hollywood Citizen-News.* Back when they were roommates, they would read the obituaries out loud over breakfast. Whoever wrote them had a wicked sense of humor, usually managing to insert a backhanded compliment to the recently deceased. A private joke evolved between them that if either of them should die unexpectedly, the other must contact the *Hollywood Citizen-News*, which in time became "the usual place."

Three days later a classified ad appeared.

Lassie wants Wick to know that she's comfortable at the Happy Duke.

Lassie rhymed with Massey and Wick with Brick, but it took Gwendolyn and Marcus nearly an hour to figure out she meant the Gaylord Hotel on Wilshire. They were tempted to go see her, but what if Siegel was having them followed, too?

Three days later:

Sassy wants Slick to know she's lonesome at Mr. Goodbar's.

Gwendolyn figured that one out in less than ten minutes: the Hershey Arms Hotel, near MacArthur Park. She was tempted to call Kathryn there — especially as that's where Linc's dad now lived — but even a public telephone seemed like a risk.

Then, yesterday, a third ad appeared.

Cassie wants Slick to bring books number one two three to the Hamilton.

Gwendolyn decided that one meant that Kathryn was so bored out of her noodle that she wanted her to bring the top three bestsellers to the Alexander Hotel downtown. And that meant she felt safe enough for Gwendolyn to drop them off. So she put together a care package that included *The Miracle of the Bells*, *The Moneyman*, and *Gentleman's Agreement*, along with some lipstick, cold cream, four packs of Chesterfields, half a dozen back issues of the *Hollywood Reporter*, and a couple of Mr. Goodbars for a laugh.

The Alexander Hotel had once been the classiest joint in town. So many huge deals had been struck during the silent era that the rug in its Palm Court room was called the "million-dollar carpet." But its heyday lay behind it, and it was considered a neglected relic — which made it a perfect hiding place.

Gwendolyn approached the front desk and asked for a guest by the name of Cassie. The clerk confirmed they did, but the guest had left word not to be disturbed. Gwendolyn handed over Kathryn's valise and fled outside into the comforting crowds.

Without caring much where she was going, she charged up Fifth Street until she almost collided with a newsboy. He held up a copy of the *Examiner*, whose hysterical headline reminded Angelenos that it had been five months since the Black Dahlia was found, and the killer was still at large.

At Pershing Square, she turned down Olive Street in search of a tranquil tea lounge she remembered. She was trying to recall its exact location when she heard her name.

Edith Head was in a black linen suit and a silk blouse with large black-and-white checks. She was holding a bolt of material, four feet long and nearly a foot wide, wrapped in brown paper; it looked dreadfully heavy. She let it slide from her arms as Gwendolyn approached.

"How nice to see you," Edith panted.

They exchanged cheek kisses, and Gwendolyn asked her what she was doing downtown on a Sunday.

"I'm working on a new Burt Lancaster picture, *I Walk Alone*. His love interest is this new femme fatale they've found, Lizabeth Scott." Edith rolled her eyes. "Nice enough, but they're grooming her to be the new Bacall. Big mistake, if you ask me, but what do I know? I've only worked on a hundred and fifty pictures."

She thudded her package with a finger. "I couldn't find the material I wanted for her big scene, so I went looking." She peered up at Gwendolyn through her tinted glasses. "That story about Kathryn Massey and her appendix, is it true?"

Gwendolyn feigned surprise. "She had a tough time of it at the hospital, but she's fine now. Or will be, once she's recuperated in Palm Springs."

Edith nodded, not entirely convinced. Something behind Gwendolyn caught Edith's eye; she looked at it a moment and frowned. "It's just that I heard the wildest rumor at work this week. That Kathryn was the next victim of the Black Dahlia killer."

Gwendolyn didn't have to fake her surprise. "How ridiculous!"

"That's what I thought. But you know how feverish the rumor mill can be." She looped a fingernail around a button on Gwendolyn's coat and pulled her closer. "Come with me."

She herded Gwendolyn inside the Biltmore Hotel. The grand foyer soared two stories up to a vaulted ceiling that resembled a Spanish cathedral; the floor was dotted with gold velvet loveseats. Edith led her to one under an ornate staircase and laid her heavy package on the floor.

"I saw an Imperial roll to a stop at the curb not far from us," Edith said conspiratorially. "It only stayed there a moment, then took off. A minute or so later, it came around the block again."

Gwendolyn blinked. "Did you see who was in it?"

"Tinted windows. But between the Black Dahlia and the subpoenas the HUAC keeps issuing like they're parking tickets, a girl can't be too careful." Her pale face took on a pinched look. "Is there any chance someone could be following you?"

Gwendolyn shook her head. "Not that I can think of. But like you said, these days, who knows? I wonder if they're still there."

Edith called a waiter over and asked him to check whether a black Imperial limousine was parked out front. He reappeared a few moments later and reported that it was.

"Take the doors on Grand Avenue, out by the Biltmore Bowl." Edith hefted the roll of material into her arms. "I'll go back the way we came in and make out like I'm looking for you. Are you *sure* you don't know who they are?"

Gwendolyn avoided replying to Edith's question by thanking her and hurrying up the stairway. She followed the signs to the Biltmore Bowl and headed for the double doors that opened onto Grand.

It was late Sunday afternoon now and the crowds were thinner, and no taxis in sight. She headed down the hill, crossing over Sixth Street, then Seventh, breathing a little bit easier at every intersection.

A black limo, large and expensive, crossed Seventh Street in a hurry, then jammed on the brakes as it came to a stop a little ahead of Gwendolyn. She walked past without acknowledging it. It sped up again, passed her, then came to a stop ten feet down the street.

The driver — a barrel-chested Italian with the florid face of a heavy drinker — stepped out from behind the wheel, around the front of the car, and opened the rear passenger door. He stared at her sullenly.

Fear contracted Gwendolyn's chest as she approached the car, gripped the top of the open door, and bent down. Inside, Benjamin Siegel motioned for her to join him.

She slid inside; the chauffeur slammed the door behind her.

Siegel chewed on a toothpick, sucking it noisily as he pushed it from side to side with his lips. The car took off. Soon they'd be out of busy downtown and in an industrial area south of the city. On a Sunday. When the factories and streets were deserted. She sat motionless, waiting for him to initiate what was bound to be an uncomfortable conversation.

They'd gone several blocks before he said, "Now that the mob has seen fit to take the Flamingo out of my hands, I have only one goal: to find Billy Wilkerson. Has Kathryn told you where he's gone?"

"No." The word popped out a shrill squeak.

"I've had someone check every hospital south of Santa Barbara, and not one female under the age of fifty has been treated for appendicitis. I'm going to ask you again, but only once more. Where is Wilkerson?"

He still hadn't looked at her, but kept his eyes on the front window.

Gwendolyn gripped the armrest. "I asked her where she was, but she refused to tell me. Said it was for my own good."

He spat his chewed toothpick onto the carpet. "Tell her she's to be at Virginia Hill's house in Beverly Hills before midnight tomorrow. Is that clear?"

"But what if I can't find her?" The question brought no response, so she tried a different tack. The sweet ingénue act had worked with him before. "I'm not trying to get in your way here, truly I'm not," she said, raising the pitch of her voice and softening it at the same time. "But I'm no Mandrake the Magician. If Kathryn doesn't want to be found, there ain't a whole lot I can do about it."

A hard silence cut the air in the cabin. Siegel didn't move. He didn't even appear to be breathing. Without the slightest flicker of warning, his right hand shot out and wrapped around her throat. He pulled her toward him, his mouth barely two inches from her ear. The fuggy stink of cigar swamped her.

"I want her there before midnight. If she's not, I will come after every person she holds near and dear." He squeezed her throat a little bit tighter. "Gwendolyn Brick. Marcus Adler. Francine Massey. Oliver Trenton. Bertie Kreuger." The limo's shadowy interior started to blur. "I could go on, but the clock is ticking."

Gwendolyn managed to yelp, "I get it."

Siegel released her as the car screeched to a halt. Gwendolyn lurched forward and slipped off the seat. Her knees gave out and she crumpled at his feet.

"Get the fuck outta my car."

When she pried open her eyes, she caught sight of the late afternoon sun slanting in through the open door. She wrapped her fingers around the leather handles of her handbag and crawled on her knees until she tumbled to the unforgiving curb. She felt a *whoosh* of air, then heard the *whamp* of a car door. A second or two later, the Imperial's engine roared and she listened to it recede into traffic. The only thing she could feel was her pulse throbbing in her ear.

CHAPTER 40

Kathryn yanked off her gloves and twisted them around her fingers until they burned. A streetlamp flashed past the window of Marcus' DeSoto. "I think I'm going to puke."

As Marcus rounded the gentle curve where Sunset Boulevard entered Beverly Hills, she swallowed hard and focused on the back of his head.

When they passed the brown and gold Beverly Hills shield, Gwendolyn laid a hand on top of Kathryn's. "We can pull over. Or we can just go home."

Going home wasn't an option, and all three of them knew it. She tilted her watch toward the light outside. Nearly eleven thirty. She wished she hadn't cut it so close, but it had taken all evening to screw up enough courage to simply get into the car.

Marcus pulled to the curb.

Kathryn gripped the back of his seat. "What are you doing? It's nearly midnight."

He held up a silver flask and unscrewed the top before handing it to her. The smell of expensive whiskey filled her nostrils.

"I need to keep my head clear." She brushed the flask away. "Who knows what he might pull."

"But you've got your story straight," Gwendolyn said. "And it's the truth. Mainly."

First thing that morning, Kathryn had gone to an out-of-the-way Western Union to send a telegram to Wilkerson's Paris hotel:

BEN ON WARPATH STOP LEAVE PARIS IMMEDIATELY STOP

Gwendolyn gently pushed the flask into her hand.

It seared Kathryn's throat like a brushfire. "Thank you both for being here. This is above and beyond the call of duty."

"The least we can do is get you there." Marcus twisted in his seat and took her left hand in his. "You're the one who has to walk inside."

"I shouldn't be leading you into danger like this. I should've let Nelson drive me." Kathryn took a second sip. This time, the burn was comforting.

Marcus restarted his car and pulled into the sparse traffic along Sunset. "But you went to his place and left that note," he pointed out. "And he never called you back."

"I should've tried the FBI offices downtown." She handed back the flask.

"You never did tell us how you found Hoyt at the Radio Room."

Because I avoided telling you. "After Bette laid out a strong case for Siegel planting that bug, I went to his father's store."

"So it was dear ol' dad who told you where to find him?" Marcus' carefully worded query oozed with suspicion. "That's some professional-grade sleuthing, Dick Tracy."

She stared at the back of his head some more and pressed her hands together. "Marcus, honey, pull over again."

"It's twenty to midnight."

"I have something I want—*need* to say."

"It can't wait?"

Her breathless "No!" was enough to convince him to draw alongside the curb out front of the Beverly Hills Hotel, where palm trees swayed in the evening breeze, backlit by artfully placed spotlights.

"I might not come out of that house alive," Kathryn said.

"Don't say that!" Gwendolyn cried out. "Don't even think it."

Kathryn grabbed both her friends by the hands. "Siegel and his goons, they play for keeps. And they play it with guns. I don't have the answers he wants, so he won't be too happy. Things could escalate, and if they do, I don't want outright lies to be the last thing I say to you two."

"Outright lies?" Marcus looked at Gwendolyn, then back to Kathryn. "What's that supposed to mean?"

Kathryn squeezed Marcus' hand. He didn't squeeze it in return. "Nelson Hoyt is one of the good guys."

"A good guy G-man is a contradiction in terms." Marcus tried to withdraw his hand, but she didn't let him.

She had been hoping that the revelation about the Mandeville Canyon raid would have encouraged Marcus to at least give Nelson the benefit of the doubt, especially seeing as how the bug in her villa had nothing to do with the FBI. But she couldn't blame him for being suspicious.

"He joined the Bureau because he wanted to do his part to keep America a beacon of freedom," she continued, "but all this anti-Commie Red and Pinko business has disillusioned him. He wants to leave."

"I thought the only way to leave the Bureau was in a pine box."

Now that Nelson had Gwendolyn's 38–38–38 dress, he was setting up his plan to entangle Hoover. He wouldn't tell Kathryn any of the details, but he promised to share them when the time came. What niggled at her, though, was why he didn't call her back after she left that note. Where was he? "He has an added extra incentive to leave." Kathryn was glad she'd downed those two shots.

"What incentive?" Marcus asked.

Kathryn drew in a silent breath. "I told him that I consider the Bureau to be as much an enemy to American freedom as the Communist Party, and that he'd have to be free of the FBI before I'd consider any sort of romantic attachment."

He jerked his hand from hers. "Hoyt wants to *date* you? The bastard who forced you into spying on your friends? And you feel the same?"

She couldn't bear to watch the betrayal fill his eyes. She tried to touch his shoulder, but he pulled away.

"It's a quarter of," he said. "You picked a hell of a time to share this." He started the DeSoto and pulled onto the road, heading for Linden Drive.

"Marcus," Kathryn pleaded, "it's been building for a while, but we haven't—done anything."

"You'll be walking into Ben Siegel's house in a couple of minutes." Marcus sounded almost ghostly. "I suggest you focus on how you're going to handle that."

"I didn't want our potentially last words—"

"I heard what you said." He ground to a stop in front of a small park at Sunset and Whittier Drive. Virginia Hill's place was just out of sight around the bend, a dozen houses down.

"Just go in there and tell him the truth." Gwendolyn pressed her cheek against Kathryn's. It was wet with tears. "We love her, don't we, Marcus?" she said more loudly.

Marcus continued facing forward. "Of course we do." His voice was low and breathy. "Just try to stay calm. Keep your wits about you."

Kathryn opened the door. "If I'm not back in half an hour . . ." *Then do what? Call the police? The FBI? Superman?*

"We're not budging," Gwendolyn said.

"I'll turn the car around," Marcus said, "in case we need a fast getaway."

"MARCUS!" Gwendolyn cuffed him across the head.

"I meant all three of us."

When Kathryn stepped out into the June night, the reality of the scene she had to face hit her. *In . . . out . . . in . . . out . . .* One breath for every step.

"The last time I saw my boss," she rehearsed out loud, "he was holding a ticket for the *Ile de France*. So my guess is that he's in Paris." *In . . . out . . . in . . . out . . .* "He's a man of habit, so try the Ritz or the Meurice."

She shook her hands to free them of the excess adrenaline pumping through her body. She realized she'd left her pocketbook back in Marcus' car. If she went back for it, she might not summon the courage to return, so she plowed on.

By the time she arrived at the Y-shaped fork, her knees felt like loose balls of cold linguine. She grabbed at the picket fence in front of her and breathed deeply. *Three, two, one . . . GO.*

When she rounded the corner, she saw the glow of lights flashing red-blue-red-blue in the branches of the Raywood Ash tree overhanging the sidewalk. It took her a moment to make sense of the black-and-whites that looked like fat hippos wallowing in the moonlight. It was the LAPD. Half a dozen cars. At least twenty officers. Ambulance. Fire truck. A sprinkling of nosey neighbors lingering behind fences.

She kept walking until a young officer stopped her. The silver shield on his cap glowed in the headlights. "Sorry ma'am, but I'll have to ask you to come no further."

"What's happened?" Kathryn asked.

"This is an active crime scene. We're still investigating."

She pointed behind her. "I have my press pass, but I left it in the car."

The officer looked her up and down. "Ain't you Kathryn Massey? I listen to you all the time."

Kathryn threw her shoulders back and lifted her chin to steady her voice. "Can you tell me what happened here, Officer?"

"There's been a shooting. Bugsy Siegel." He pronounced the name with an almost hushed reverence.

"Dead?" She felt like she might pass out.

"Right between the eyes."

Kathryn felt the tension ebb from her body, leaving her weak and shaky. "Thank you, Officer."

"You're the first press on the scene," he said. "I could have a word with the sarge. You know, get the scoop and all."

She struggled to offer him a smile. "I appreciate that, but crime isn't my beat." The guy looked disappointed.

She headed back up the sidewalk. For some reason, it seemed important not to step on the cracks. She set one foot carefully in front of the other on the way back to the car.

He's gone. He's dead. He's gone. He's dead. He's gone. He's dead.

She looked up when she was ten feet away. Marcus and Gwendolyn were leaning against the hood. They hadn't even moved the car yet.

"That didn't take long," Gwendolyn said. "Wasn't he home?"

Her own voice sounded distant and foreign when she said, "Someone shot him."

"Siegel?"

"Right between the eyes."

Gwendolyn and Marcus surrounded her, their arms a cocoon, asking questions she had no answers to. They hustled her into the back of the DeSoto and slammed the door. She squeezed her eyes shut and felt the engine rumble to life as Marcus swung into a U-turn. By the time they hit Sunset, her whole body was numb.

CHAPTER 41

The way Hollywood reacted to the news of Bugsy Siegel's death reminded Marcus of that scene in *The Wizard of Oz* when word of the Wicked Witch of the East's demise started to spread and the munchkins emerged from their thatched cottages. It was like the whole city breathed a sigh of relief and called for a round of drinks.

Lucius Beebe dubbed the Garden's revelry the "Bye-Bye Bugs Bash." It lasted until six the next morning — and even then only because both the Sahara Room and Schwab's had run out of ice, scotch, tonic water, and lemons.

Marcus spent most of that night watching Kathryn romp around like she'd shrugged an entire flock of dead albatrosses off her shoulders.

She Charlestoned on the diving board, drank champagne from anybody's glass, and flirted with every male in sight, regardless of marital status or sexual proclivity. Marcus sensed a measure of forced hysteria, but given how close she'd come to a sticky end, he hardly begrudged it.

But the more he thought of their conversation in the car, the more it ate at him. A romantic attachment to that FBI agent? Wasn't he the root of all her misery?

In the two weeks that followed, he struggled to put it out of his mind. Kathryn was the most levelheaded woman he knew, so he tried to rationalize her behavior. Pursuing a relationship with an FBI agent was so out of character that he decided she must have her reasons.

The thing about the Mandeville raid was to Nelson's credit, but the fact that he hadn't bugged her apartment hardly merited a cheering squad. Marcus needed to know why she was doing what she was doing, but since Wilkerson returned from Paris, she never seemed to be home. She was always out at one of his restaurants, or covering some swanky soirée or other.

When a letter from Marcus' sister arrived over the Fourth of July weekend, he really started to worry. Doris had visited him in LA during the war and kept in touch afterwards, writing to catch him up on life back home in McKeesport, and to ask for insider Hollywood gossip to impress her friends. She was always chipper, and her small-town news was refreshing and sweet. He'd forgotten what it was like to live where everybody was content to play the part they'd been given at birth.

But this letter was different. After three pages of news about the high school football team's last victory and the town hall's new paint job, she closed with uncharacteristic ambiguity.

I suspect Mom is suffering from her old trouble, but you'd never know it. That old Pennsylvania Dutch thing about keeping your trap shut and just getting on with life kicks in and nobody's the wiser. But I know her pretty good. She turns sixty this year, so her best years are behind her, as far as that sort of thing is concerned. I'm worried about her but bringing it up will cause no end of squabbling.

Marcus slipped the letter into his inside pocket as he dressed for a *Kraft Music Hall* broadcast. The producers had signed a new host: Al Jolson. His debut sparked new interest in the show and its ratings were stronger than ever, which was good news for Kathryn, considering the fact that Hedda Hopper's radio show, *This is Hollywood*, aired its final episode the last week of June.

After the show, Marcus met Kathryn at the stage door and they walked up Vine Street to the Brown Derby. It was as busy as ever, with all four rows of booths packed with a late crowd of chattering diners.

After they sat and ordered drinks, Kathryn said, "I'm glad you suggested this. I haven't seen you since —" She finished her sentence with a light sigh.

Marcus pulled out Doris' letter and tugged it free of the envelope. He unfolded the three sheets and handed her the final one, pointing to the last paragraph.

When she'd finished reading it, she looked up. "What sort of old trouble?"

Marcus took the letter back. "I thought you might be able to tell me, being a woman and all."

"You mean 'the change'? That'd be a new problem, not an old one, like from your childhood, maybe? What was she like when you were a kid?"

Marcus hadn't seen his mother in twenty years. He remembered that her hair was light brown, easily bleached by the sun, and tied up in a loose knot, Ma Kettle style. But other than that, the specifics had grown hazy.

"She was always cooking, mending, shopping, cleaning," he said. "If she had a health problem, she hid it well."

Kathryn shrugged. "Doris is pretty vague. It could be anything."

He tucked the letter back into his pocket. "And speaking of cleaning, we have some of our own to do." She raised her eyebrows expectantly. "We need to talk about what happened that night in the car. About you and — him."

She looked relieved. "We should have addressed it before now."

"It's been hard to pin you down."

She slid a finger around the rim of her highball. "Trouble is, I don't quite know what to say."

"Of all people, you had to choose him?"

"I didn't *choose* him. I didn't even like him. At first. But things change, Marcus. I didn't go looking for it, it just —" She broke off, her eyes darting around the room.

They both took long sips from their drinks. There was so much Marcus wanted to say, but he was no longer sure he could say it without coming across like some judgmental old fogey. Before he could begin, Kathryn grabbed his arm.

"We need to go," she said very softly. "Right now."

She slid out of the booth, leaving him to pay the check.

Vine was starting to empty of traffic and pedestrians. Streetlamps punctuated the night with pools of light every hundred feet.

Kathryn looked wildly around. "Where did you park?"

"Oliver needed my car tonight. I walked here. Why? What did—?"

"Of all nights!" She jaywalked him across Vine, peering over her shoulder again as they passed ABC's studios. They didn't stop until the Sunset-Vine corner outside Wallichs Music City.

"Not a taxi in sight!"

She grabbed his hand and started heading along Sunset. They'd scurried a whole block before Marcus could ask what they were running from.

"Last week, I was at a press conference at Columbia for their new Rita Hayworth picture, *Down to Earth*. Larry Parks was there, pleasant as can be, answering every inane question put to him. Then, just as things were winding up, some guy popped up out of nowhere and served Larry with a subpoena. And you know what *that* means."

After the death of Bugsy Siegel became yesterday's news, the next subject to consume Angelenos was the subpoenas being served around town. Hollywood was on official notice: the HUAC was serious in its campaign to investigate the Communistic influence in motion pictures.

As the subpoenas proliferated, accusations started flying. The victims weren't just screenwriters like MGM's Dalton Trumbo and Ring Lardner Jr. over at Fox, but also directors. Lewis Milestone at Paramount and Edward Dmytryk at RKO were collared, as well as producer Adrian Scott.

The question now asked at every cocktail bar and dinner party was, "Were you there when so-and-so got served?"

Hollywood was aflame with outrage at this bald infringement on its First Amendment rights, but not unanimously. Some people welcomed the HUAC with hosannas and palm fronds, especially members of the Motion Picture Alliance for the Preservation of American Ideals, not the least of whom was Billy Wilkerson. It took him less than a week to return from Paris, and instead of recognizing his narrow escape, he seemed to think he was invincible. He applauded the HUAC in his "TradeView" column.

"The guy who subpoenaed Larry Parks was eyeballing us from the bar," Kathryn explained. "Or more specifically, *you*. The guy in the gray suit with the porkpie."

Marcus snuck a look. The process server was a block and a half away. "Aren't we just delaying the inevitable? If he's got something to serve me, he's not going to stop."

"Maybe," Kathryn conceded, "but I heard that if you're served at work, the company has to foot the legal bill."

"Maybe it's not me he wants."

Kathryn suddenly stumbled over her own feet. "You really think they're after *me?*"

"I signed MGM's loyalty oath so I wouldn't be called."

As they reached the Crossroads of the World, Kathryn sped up. "Do you think Wilkerson knows about this? He's been a tiger in the press, but with me personally, he's been a teddy bear."

Suddenly, she hissed, "IN HERE!" and pulled open the door to a lamp store. She herded Marcus inside, slammed it shut, then spun the *OPEN* sign around.

"What the hell are you doing?" Marcus said. "You can't just—"

"Kathryn? Is that you?"

A kindly gent in his sixties emerged from the rear of the store. His face was a little crinkly around the edges, but Marcus could see he had been handsome in his day—strong jaw line, cheeks that hinted at dimples, lively gray-blue eyes.

Kathryn pulled her hand away from the sign. "Sorry to intrude, but we're in the biggest rush." The old guy looked at Marcus expectedly. "Oh, yes, sorry. This is Marcus Adler. Marcus, this is Wesley." She went to say the man's last name, but stopped, as though it slipped her mind. "Someone's following us. I was hoping we might cut through your store to the back alley. It'll take us through to Highland, right?"

This Wesley guy had an apprehensive look on his face that Kathryn wasn't seeing. Marcus caught her elbow and jutted his chin toward him.

"Is something wrong?" Kathryn asked. When Wesley flickered an unsure eye over Marcus, she added, "It's okay. This is my ex-husband."

"Have you heard from Nelson lately?"

"Not in a few weeks. Why?"

"You won't be," he said darkly.

"Won't be what? Hearing from—?" Kathryn sucked in a gasp of air. "W-why not?"

"He's been"—Wesley jammed his hands into his pockets in what struck Marcus as an obvious attempt to camouflage his emotions—"transferred."

Kathryn sighed. "I thought you were going to tell me . . ."

Wesley started playing with the little brass pull-chain on a desk lamp sitting just to his right. "I know what my son does for a living, but he shares little in the way of details."

"The less you know, the better?" Marcus offered.

"Precisely. He came to me a few nights ago. Two o'clock in the morning, it was. Damned near scared the next ten years out of me."

"He got himself into trouble?"

Wesley looked at Kathryn coolly. "Nelson was drunk, and therefore somewhat more voluble than usual. I learned that he and Mr. Hoover had a serious difference of opinion over something he was ordered to do."

"Did he tell you what it was?"

—

306

"It seems Hoover wanted Nelson to pull you out of hiding and hand you over to Bugsy Siegel 'like a prized spit-roast pig,' to quote Hoover's words."

Kathryn gave a stifled yelp. "And he refused?"

"He did more than that, Miss Massey. He told Hoover where to go and what to do when he got there."

"I can't imagine Hoover took that very well."

"To say the least." He gave the pull-chain one final flick. "My son fell on his sword for you. And as a result, he's been transferred."

"Where to? Did he tell you?"

"In a roundabout sort of way. Hoover has a history of punishing wayward agents. If he decides they're guilty of serious misconduct, they're liable to be relocated to one of the Bureau's far-flung outposts. Some one-mule dead-end back-of-beyond where nothing happens. The graver the crime, the more desolate the station. Our little joke was that the worst of the lot was a place we called Zanzibar."

"Isn't that off the coast of Africa?" Marcus asked.

"That's right. Of course, the Bureau doesn't have an office there, but I'd say wherever he's gone, life is about as much fun as it is on the real Zanzibar."

"So when you say 'transferred,' you really mean 'banished,' don't you?" Kathryn asked. "And we have no way of tracking him down?"

"That's about the size of it."

"Because of *me?*"

"I said pretty much the same thing to him, and he told me, 'No, Dad, I'm being punished because of a severe disagreement in philosophy. Miss Massey is the reason I grew a backbone and stood up for what I believe. She gave me the courage to speak my convictions, and I'd do it again.'"

"He actually said that?"

"His exact words."

Marcus pulled a handkerchief from his breast pocket and pressed it into Kathryn's trembling fingers. Wrapping an arm around her shoulders, he said to Mr. Hoyt, "Thank you. I think we ought to be going. The alley is through that door?"

"It is, but the city's repaving it. It's a god-awful mess back there."

"Come on," Marcus whispered into Kathryn's ear as he guided her through the store. "The walk home will do you good, and there's a stiff drink at the end of it for you. Maybe several."

The little bell above the front door tinkled as he opened it. The sun hung low over Sunset. *If this were a movie, a taxi would appear right now.* But the taxi failed to make its cue. They'd barely taken three or four paces when someone stepped in their path.

"Marcus Adler?"

The porkpie hat held out a folded piece of paper. Without thinking, Marcus took it, realizing too late what he'd done.

CHAPTER 42

As Gwendolyn waited for Cary Grant's butler to open the door, she eyed the check in her hand and felt her resolve start to wane. She wished she'd given herself a moment before knocking, just to be sure.

The door swung open and Gwendolyn was taken aback to find Grant stand there—and he was even more attractive in person. It made her think of that scene from *Notorious* when he and Ingrid Bergman got around the Breen Office's "No screen kiss shall last longer than three seconds" edict by kissing and nibbling and hesitating and succumbing again for the three-minute scene that had everyone talking.

"Oh," she said, momentarily lost for words, "I was expecting the butler."

"He's upstairs dealing with a recalcitrant window, so for this morning's performance, the part of the butler will be played by yours truly." Grant opened the door wider to reveal that he was dressed in exactly the sort of thing every girl in America would expect: a black velvet smoking jacket with wide, quilted lapels and matching cuffs the color of dark cranberries. "You must be—Guinevere, is it?"

"Gwendolyn."

"My mistake. Howard does tend to mumble. You'll find him out in the guesthouse."

He led her to a spacious sunroom that looked out over the pool and the guesthouse. Just as he was about to open the door for her, he stopped. "Can you do me a favor?"

She wondered if any woman in the past fifteen years had said no to that question, then noticed him fidgeting with the buttons of his smoking jacket. *Oh my goodness, does Cary Grant actually get nervous?* "Surely."

"Howard and I are very good friends, but he has three other places in LA he can go to. Enough is enough."

She winked at him. "I'll see what I can do."

When she stepped onto the tiled patio, the front door of the guesthouse slid open and Hughes emerged into the late-summer sun. His face had filled out and he'd managed to develop something resembling a tan. He offered her a seat.

"I came to return this." She pushed the check across the glass tabletop between them.

He pushed it back toward her. "I have a strict no-refund policy."

"Listen," Gwendolyn said, "I'm bowled over by your generosity, but I can't—"

"Of course you can. Shall I call for tea? Or are you more of a coffee girl? Something stronger, perhaps? Cary's wet bar is stocked better than the Biltmore Bowl."

"I appreciate the gesture, but I don't feel comfortable accepting this money."

He seemed genuinely confused. "You want to open your own store, don't you?"

"Yes."

His smile was charming, but dangerously rakish.

"Does it really matter where the funds come from?" His voice was Don Juan smooth now.

"It matters a great deal."

"Why?"

"I've been around long enough to know that money like this never comes without strings."

"Strings, huh?" A gold square box engraved with an intertwined pair of H's sat on the patio table. Hughes flipped it open and offered her one of the cigarettes inside. She shook her head, but he took one and lit it. "Precisely what sort of strings do you think they are?"

"I can rattle off half a dozen without even thinking."

"I'm listening."

"Lana Turner, Yvonne de Carlo, Linda Darnell, Ava Gardner, Rita Hayworth, Cyd Charisse."

"Ah! *Those* sorts of strings." The scars slicing his face distorted his smile, but it was still remarkably disarming.

Gwendolyn could feel the heat of a blush flaring out from under her. "I'm just trying to avoid unnecessary entanglements."

His smile became a giggle, which he tried to suppress—halfheartedly, it seemed. She was on the verge of standing when he said,

"I'm sorry. I don't mean to laugh." He tilted toward her. "If I could convince you that my motivations were not about tempting you into the sack, would you accept it then?"

This'll be worth the cab fare. "Give it your best shot."

"I have to warn you, it's not what girls like you want to hear."

Girls like me? She gestured for him to continue.

"The thing is . . . you're just too . . . old."

Gwendolyn fought to regain her composure. *Howard Hughes will bed anything in a skirt, but not me? Because I'm too old? At thirty-seven?*

Howard chuckled nervously. "You look like you want to stab me in the throat."

"Do you blame me?"

"I didn't tell you that lightly, but I wanted you to know my intentions are honorable." He paused for a moment. "There's another reason I want you to have that money."

She withdrew a cigarette from his golden box and held it out for him. "Should I brace myself?"

He lit it for her with a matching lighter. "You could easily have handed Linc Tattler over to Bugsy Siegel to save your own skin, but you didn't, and I wanted to show my appreciation."

"What's any of that got to do with you?"

"Before your boyfriend left town, he came to see me. He told me about a file box belonging to Leilah and Clem that had come into his possession. He said it had dozens of index cards detailing all her clients. He said my name was in the box, and he rattled off enough dates and girls to convince me. He said he was planning on taking it out of the country with him, and then he was going to burn it." Howard raised an eyebrow. "I don't suppose you know if he did?"

Gwendolyn wondered why Linc would go to the trouble of taking that box with him if he was only going to burn it later. Was it insurance in case someone had arranged to have him stopped at the border? She decided it was impossible to know at this point, and with Siegel gone, what did it matter? She shook her head.

He grimaced. "Pity. As far as I can tell, he paid a visit to every chump in the box and alerted them to how the O'Roarkes had been keeping records."

"Bugsy Siegel was real keen to track Linc down," Gwendolyn said.

Howard nodded soberly. "I suspect Siegel somehow knew Linc had all that information and wanted it to blackmail every mover and shaker in town."

Gwendolyn fell back into her chair and started to fan herself with her gloves. *Why didn't Linc tell me all this?*

"The point is," Howard continued, "Linc kept his trap shut, Siegel never tracked him down, and you didn't lead him to Linc. So this here five grand was my clumsy way of saying thank you without having to bring up all this sordidness."

He was looking at her so intensely that Gwendolyn had to turn away. Her eyes fell on the check. Five grand. *Together with my Licketysplitter money, Chez Gwendolyn could actually become real. All I have to do is say thank you.* And yet somehow she couldn't convince herself to reach across the table. Providence usually came with consequences.

He slid the check across the glass until it lay in front of her. "Tell you what, how about you take it with you today, stick it someplace safe, then tell me your decision on November second."

"What's happening then?"

"It's when I'll be conducting the test flight of my *Hercules* down in Long Beach. I want you to be my guest. Come down, watch the flight, and give me your answer then. How does that sound?"

Gwendolyn was no longer sure she could return the money. "That sounds fair." She popped open her purse and slid the check inside. "I'll see you there."

He fell back into his chair, smiling.

Gwendolyn leaned forward. "And seeing as how you were kind enough to be as blunt as a hammer with me, I must now repay the favor."

His hand held the gold cigarette lighter halfway to his mouth. It stopped, shaking slightly. "Shoot."

"It's Cary."

"What about him?"

"He wants you to get the hell out."

* * *

It was a long, steep walk down Benedict Canyon Drive to Sunset, where Gwendolyn would have any hope of flagging down a cab. By the first curve in the road, she wished she had selected more sensible shoes that morning, but how was she to know that she'd be leaving Cary Grant's house on foot? She wondered, too, if perhaps she shouldn't have declined Howard's offer to have Cary's driver take her back to the Garden. But she needed time to think about what had just happened back there.

It's not what girls like you want to hear.

She realized this was the first time she'd been rejected because of her age. She didn't think she looked thirty, let alone thirty-seven, and she certainly didn't feel any different than she had at twenty-one.

"Gwendolyn Brick," she declared out loud, "when Howard Hughes thinks you're too old, you really are past it."

She dropped her handbag on the sidewalk and plunked her rear end on the edge of the curb, held her face in her hands, and laughed and cried and laughed and cried.

CHAPTER 43

Kathryn knocked on Marcus' door. When he opened it, she pressed her finger to his lips. Given the recent tension between them, she knew it was a bold move, but desperate times called for audacity. He'd been the Rock of Gibraltar the night they learned of Nelson's banishment, but she couldn't shake the feeling that he was relieved Nelson was out of the picture. Knowing that Nelson sacrificed his career for her shook her to the core, and suddenly she missed him dreadfully.

"I want you to come with me," she told Marcus. "Now. Are you free?"

He nodded, with unblinking eyes, wary but hopeful.

It was October now, two months since that night at Wesley Hoyt's store. The following day, she presented him with a special bottle of Four Roses she'd tracked down. The guy at the liquor store on Wilshire assured her it was from the final batch they produced before Prohibition officially kicked in. This brought about a tacit détente, and since then they'd danced around each other like ballerinas in barbed wire tutus, but it wasn't enough. She missed their intimacy as desperately as she missed Nelson.

When he grabbed his hat and coat and asked if he'd need his car keys, she told him yes. They were driving past the Elizabeth Arden salon on the Sunset Strip before he asked where they were going.

"To a meeting of the Committee for the First Amendment."

He let out a terse "hm."

"When you testify to the HUAC, the people at this meeting will be the ones cheering you on."

After suffering through a summer of the HUAC's rabid headline-hogging, screenwriter Philip Dunne and directors John Huston and William Wyler decided they'd had enough and formed the Committee for the First Amendment. Word reached Kathryn that the next meeting was at Ira Gershwin's home in Beverly Hills that night. She wasn't sure if it was invitation only, but it was worth a shot.

Boisterous conversation poured through the open windows of 1021 Roxbury Drive as they walked up the flagstone path. Kathryn's heavy-handed tap on the silver knocker brought Paulette Goddard to the door. Her "Oh!" suggested she was surprised to see them standing there, but she stepped back and let them in. She pointed to a pair of white louvered doors on the far side of the marble and chandelier foyer. "Bar's on the left."

They walked into a living room that was easily four times the size of Kathryn's entire apartment. A Chagall dominated the room from above an ornate mantle and a picturesque pumpkin display filled the fireplace below.

Someone had artfully arranged a maze of sofas, love seats, and occasional chairs, all upholstered in autumnal colors, from the red of Japanese maples to the dark greens of a Pacific Northwest fir. Congregating around the furniture in bunches were some of the most prominent people in Hollywood. The huddle to Kathryn's right included Danny Kaye and Edward G. Robinson, deep in conversation with Frederic March and Rita Hayworth.

Past them, by Gershwin's floor-to-ceiling teak bookcase, stood Judy Garland and Groucho Marx. Kathryn nudged Marcus. "Let's break some ice with Judy and Groucho. I haven't seen him since the *Go West* premiere."

But they were still picking their way through the crowd when William Wyler pinged his martini glass with a spoon. "I think it's about time we started," he announced. "We do have an agenda, so unless somebody has a particularly urgent concern they want addressed, we can—"

"YEAH!" a voice pitched over the crowd, stopping all conversation cold. "I've got an issue, and I think it ought to be dealt with first."

All eyes turned to Edward G. Robinson. At a diminutive five foot seven, he was hardly the shortest star in Hollywood, but his magnetism ballooned to occupy a space twice his size.

The actor used his fat cigar to point at Kathryn. The bodies closest to her inched away silently. Marcus stayed put, but she sensed him stiffen.

"The whole point of this meeting is that we get to express our frustrations over what's been going on," Robinson said, his eyes unforgiving. "But now I see we've got Billy Wilkerson's handmaiden in our midst, and suddenly I'm not so sure I can speak my mind as freely as I'd like."

"Eddie," Wyler said, "I've never met Miss Massey myself, but she's got a reputation that hardly—"

"I want to hear what she has to say," Philip Dunne announced.

Kathryn considered his recent *The Ghost and Mrs. Muir* screenplay was about as close to perfection as one could get, and she was disappointed to hear his wary tone match Robinson's. She felt the heat of forty pairs of eyeballs on her, and decided to play offence.

"More than half the people here know me personally," she said, rotating slowly to survey the crowd. "Either from interviews, or on my radio show, or from some party or other. So I must say I'm disappointed that my motives have come into question here."

The room was graveyard silent. She glanced at Marcus to gauge how she was doing, but his face remained inert.

"Believe me," she persevered, "I am as horrified as any of you with my boss' views. If you've read my column, you'll know my stance in this situation, but for those who haven't, allow me to state it as clearly as I can. As far to the right as Billy Wilkerson sits on the political spectrum, I sit on the left."

Kathryn's stomach dropped a hundred feet when she realized what she'd said. The far-left equivalent of Wilkerson's right-wing stance wasn't bleeding-heart liberalism, but the extremity that encompassed anarchists, subversives — and Communists.

The only sound was the sonorous ticking of a grandfather clock in some other room.

Please, dear God, will somebody say something? Anything!

Gershwin's front door slammed. Humphrey Bogart appeared through the louvered doors with Lauren Bacall trailing him. He stopped when he realized he'd walked into a packed room where nobody was talking.

"What's going on?" he asked.

"I'm defending my right to be here," Kathryn said, "to a bunch of people who seem keen to pronounce me guilty by association to Wilkerson."

Bogie raised his eyebrows, slow and wary, as he looked around the room. Bacall stepped to one side to let Gene Kelly hobble into view on the crutches he needed after recently spraining his ankle in rehearsal.

Bogie said, "Maybe what they're really wondering is, Are you here as a concerned citizen, or as a responsible member of the press?"

Bless you, Humphrey Bogart, for inserting "responsible" in that question.

"Both," Kathryn said, 'but I'm starting to feel like this is Salem, and I'm Abigail Williams."

"She's right about one thing," Dunne said, "this whole stinkpile shows every indication of deteriorating into a witch hunt. Billy Wilkerson has been fanning the flames of this fire —"

"He's the one who started it in the first place!" someone interjected.

"The things he's said in his column have been malicious and incendiary," Dunne continued, "and will end up costing people their livelihoods if we don't fight back." A murmur of approval swelled across the room. "What troubles me is that it's Wilkerson who pays Miss Massey's salary, so at the end of the day, she owes her allegiance to—"

"May I say something?"

It was Marcus. Kathryn looked at him. *Please don't let me hang out to dry.*

"My name is Marcus Adler. I head up the writers' department at MGM. I am here because I've been subpoenaed to testify at the HUAC hearings in Washington next month."

The morning after the subpoena, Marcus had reported what happened to Mayer and Mannix, who told him it was no big deal. All he had to do was parrot the company line—and tell nobody about his summons. They wanted the drama of the HUAC's first surprise witness to be an MGM'er. He promised he would, so this announcement was a major transgression, but Kathryn could see it gave her instant credibility.

"I didn't know about tonight's meeting," Marcus continued, "until Kathryn knocked on my door an hour ago. She insisted we come here, and when I asked her why, she said, 'Because when you testify, those people will be the ones cheering you on.' Those HUAC pigs *want* us to suspect each other. They'd love nothing better than to see accusations of disloyalty and sabotage flying around town. If this committee is going to achieve anything, then everybody needs to start rowing in the same direction, because we have everything to lose."

Bogie started to clap—slow and rhythmic, like a metronome. Lauren joined him, then Gene Kelly. On the other side of the room, Frank Sinatra was the next to add his support, picking up the pace. One by one, each member of the Committee for the First Amendment added to the applause until Ira Gershwin's living room was filled with approval.

* * *

Marcus switched on his headlights and waited for Judy Garland to pass before pointing his car toward Sunset.

Kathryn settled back in her seat, still buzzing. She felt like she had the energy to run all the way home. "That sure was a hell of an evening, huh? So many articulate and savvy people, and so passionate and united over an issue. Did you read in the *Examiner* last month when it quoted that freshman congressman who just joined the HUAC?"

"Richard Nixon?"

"Yeah, him. What a weed. He said the HUAC will uncover the 'Red network' and names will be named, and the whole thing will be 'sensational.' Somehow, I don't think he quite reckoned on the Committee for the First Amendment. Did I tell you Wilkerson and I have been fighting over my pro-freedom-of-speech columns? Oh boy, but my boss sure can swear a blue streak. When I told him I want to be in Washington for the hearings, he said there's no value in a trip like that. I nearly threw his telephone at him."

"Do you miss him?"

The unexpected turn left Kathryn confused. "Wilkerson? I did when he was in Paris, but now I sometimes wish he hadn't hurried back so fast."

"I meant Hoyt."

Marcus' voice was low and measured. She briefly considered downplaying how she felt, but decided that would be disrespectful to both men. There'd been enough lying in Hollywood over the past year. "Yes," she told him, "I miss him terribly."

Marcus let a block or two slip past. "Have you been sleeping with him?"

She kept her eyes fixed on the deserted boulevard stretching before them. "I'm not going to answer that."

"On the grounds it may incriminate you?"

"On the grounds that it's none of your business."

Without warning, Marcus veered the car to the curb and pounded the brakes, his hands clenched around the steering wheel. "Since when is your life none of my business? I thought there were no fences between us."

"And I thought I had your unconditional support," she shot back.

"You do."

"I *did* . . . until I found myself in a situation that you didn't approve of. It's not ideal, I know that. But when love comes along—"

"So it's love, is it?"

The scorn in his voice felt like a slap.

"Heading that way." She chose her words prudently. "I don't dispute for a minute that you had every right to be suspicious of a guy like that, but after hearing what happened between him and Hoover, I'd have thought you'd give him some credit, if only for getting you out of the Mandeville raid."

"I still say he did it to further his own aims."

"What he did was save your career!" Suddenly it felt stuffy inside Marcus' car. She cracked open her window and let the cool October air breeze in. "And now he's probably saved mine—and, may I add, at the expense of his own. Jesus, Marcus, you make him sound like he's Goering or Himmler or somebody."

Marcus looked at her like a wounded dog. "He works for Hoover."

"Who deported him to Zanzibar. Look, Marcus, I'm thirty-nine and this is only the second time love has come along for me. The first one was married, so it's not like my track record is anything to write home about."

"You talk about it as though he's your last chance."

A part of Kathryn realized maybe Marcus was right. After all, everyone knew that turning forty led to a long, steep slide into middle age. But that was something to think about at another time. For right now, she felt like Marcus was slipping from her grip and she needed to change tack.

"If you stop and think about it, you can see everything that's been going on — the Pinkos, the Commies, *Reds in the Beds*, the Committee for the First Amendment, the HUAC — it's all about trust, isn't it? Me trusting you and you trusting me, Hollywood people trusting each other, and even Americans trusting their government, or rather knowing when not to. The point being, if we don't have people in our lives who we can trust, it all comes down."

"It *is* all coming down!" Marcus snarled.

"Exactly my point!" Kathryn wanted to reach out and grab Marcus by the hand, or maybe the arm. She wanted to feel connected to him, but couldn't be sure that it was the right strategy, so she just angled her body toward him.

"These are all just circumstances," she said soothingly. "We've both been around long enough to know this whole Pinko scare will blow over sooner or later. Hollywood's not going anywhere — there's too much money to be made. And when this whole Red thing crumbles away, we'll still be here. You, me, Gwennie, Oliver . . . maybe Nelson, if I can track him down. And if I do, all I want is for you to be happy for me, Marcus, as I was for you when Oliver came along."

"Oliver and I is a whole different situation," Marcus said.

Kathryn felt like her back foot was teetering on the edge of a cliff. She didn't want her friendship with the most precious person in her life to tumble over the brink, but she couldn't let him get away with a statement like that.

"It's not, you know," she said. "It's exactly the same."

"The hell it is."

She took a deep breath. "For you screenwriters, the Breen Office and its antiquated rules are the enemy. I may have kissed my enemy once or twice, but you've been sleeping with yours for how long now?"

"That's unfair and you know it."

"No, Marcus, I don't. We're both guilty of falling for the enemy, so you'd think we'd both understand how the other feels. But we can't if one of us is being a hypocrite."

"What did you just call me?" Marcus exploded.

She gripped the hand rest. "You heard right."

"Our circumstances are *completely* different!"

"How?"

"Because Oliver intentionally went to work for the Breen Office to change it from the inside. Your Nelson Hoyt joined the FBI through some misguided attempt to uphold patriotic ideals—"

"*MISGUIDED?* Oh, come on, you're assuming an awful lot."

"—to uphold patriotic ideals that Hoover regards as a temporary obstacle between him and his ambitions. When Oliver does his job, a couple of sex scenes and a joke about the clergy get taken out of some crummy movie nobody will remember a month later. When Hoyt does his job, lives are destroyed, careers are threatened, and reputations are ruined. It's hardly the same thing at all."

"It *is* the same thing," Kathryn insisted. "It just comes down to a matter of degrees."

"I'm about to get on a train and go to Washington, where I'll have to sit before the HUAC with the whole country listening. Meanwhile, you're tracking down some G-man because you think he's your last stop before Spinsterville. How is that the same thing?"

It took all the willpower Kathryn could summon not to take his bait.

"You need to trust me on this, Marcus. Nelson might be FBI, but he's a hell of a decent guy."

"That's a laugh and a half. You know, with everything that's been going on, I thought I could at least trust *you!*"

She felt as though the edge of that cliff was collapsing under her heel. "Of course you can!"

"Apparently not."

"Don't say that, Marcus, honey. Please, let's not fight—"

"Get out."

"What?"

"Get out of my car."

But you stood up in front of that crowd tonight, she wanted to say. *You came to my defense with such loyalty that I nearly cried. We've been there for each other for twenty years. Please tell me this just a hiccup along the way and not where it all ends.*

"GET THE HELL OUT OF MY CAR BEFORE I PUSH YOU OUT!"

Half-blinded by panic and trembling with fear of the unknown, Kathryn opened the passenger door and stepped onto the deserted sidewalk, and watched through tears as Marcus roared off without so much as a sideways glance.

CHAPTER 44

When they called his name, Marcus ran his hand down the
purple necktie knotted at his throat. Touching it felt like
stroking a rabbit's foot. He'd always considered it his lucky
tie, and if he'd ever needed luck on his side, it was today.
The uniformed page opened the door into the main chamber
where the HUAC hearings were taking place. A barrage of
noise engulfed him: clicking cameras, murmuring
politicians, chattering audience.

He had given no thought to the heat accumulated by
hundreds of bodies crammed into a room designed to take
half that number. As he squeezed through the labyrinth of
desks, microphones, wires, and newsreel cameras, he
wished he'd worn a lighter suit. Washington's October
weather was chilly and damp, so his wool jacket had been
an obvious choice. But this room was a sauna, and sweating
men look like liars.

He followed a succession of pages directing him toward
the witness stand until he arrived at a wooden desk in front
of the panel. He recognized all six of them from the
newspapers: Mundt from South Dakota, Wood from
Georgia, McDowell from Pennsylvania, Nixon from
California, Rankin from Mississippi, and the HUAC
chairman. J. Parnell Thomas — a man with a bowling-ball
head, lipless mouth, deer-in-headlight eyes, and a chin that
pleated when he looked down at his notes.

As Marcus took his seat, Thomas threaded his fingers
together and waited for the press photographers to get their
shots. When they were done, he said, "Please state your full
name and current occupation."

Blinded by the flash bulbs, Marcus leaned into the five microphones lining the edge of the desk. "My name is Marcus James Adler, and I am currently employed by Metro-Goldwyn-Mayer."

"In what capacity?"

A cruel case of cottonmouth left Marcus dry. The nearest person was a serious young man with stacks of filled notebooks piled in front of him. "Is there any way I could get some water?" The guy nodded. Marcus faced the panel again. "I head up the writing department at MGM, overseeing the screenplays for all MGM motion pictures."

"Mr. Adler," the man's tone had turned a shade brusque, "I'm now going to ask you the same question we are asking every witness, and I remind you that you are currently under oath. Are you now or have you ever been a member of the Communist Party?"

Where is that water? "No, I am not, nor have I ever been a member of the Communist Party."

His statement stirred a restless wave through the press corps.

"I'd like to ask you about a specific film," the chairman continued. "I'm referring to *Free Leningrad!*"

Before he left for Washington, a panel of MGM's lawyers had prepared Marcus for the types of questions he was likely to encounter. "Uniformity of response is crucial," they said. "To wit: You have never knowingly encountered Communists in MGM's writing department, nor have you identified the infiltration of the Communist message into any MGM screenplay under your jurisdiction. You have never knowingly worked with Communists at MGM in any capacity. You neither support nor endorse the guiding principle of the Communist Party. You're being called as a friendly witness," they told him. "You're simply there to support and reinforce Mayer's statement. Nothing more."

Mayer had been one of the first witnesses called to the stand on the first day of hearings. He read out a prepared statement condemning all things Communist, then sat through a lengthy session of questions from the panel. The same thing happened with the next three witnesses: Jack Warner, Ayn Rand, and Ronald Reagan, head of the Screen Actors Guild.

None of the MGM lawyers had warned him the committee might veer off into particulars. Marcus pressed his eyes closed to regain his poise.

"Is it correct," Nixon pressed, "that you authored the screenplay of *Free Leningrad!*?"

"Yes."

"Can you tell us, please, how you came to write it?"

Already thrown off kilter by this line of question, Marcus' mind grew foggy. "That was a while ago."

Nixon shook his head. "I must caution you against developing selective amnesia." Laughter rippled through the huge room. "*Free Leningrad!* came out only a couple of years ago. Surely you can recall its genesis."

Where is that water?

Groping around the back blocks of his mind, Marcus stumbled on the memory of a conference in Mayer's office.

"I was called to a meeting with Mr. Mayer and Mr. Mannix. They said we needed a new pro-Allies story. *Song of Russia* had already been released, and *Thirty Seconds Over Tokyo* was about to come out, but they saw the need for something else."

"So *Free Leningrad!* was your idea?" Thomas asked.

"I guess you could say that, yes."

"You *could* say it, Mr. Adler, or you *do* say it?"

A middle-aged blonde in an unadorned gray suit approached the witness stand with a pitcher of water and a glass. She set them on the table but made no attempt to pour any for him. She withdrew from his peripheral vision, slinking backwards like a slave girl in some Maria Montez melodrama.

Marcus poured the water himself and took a long sip.

"I'd had an idea for a picture about neighbors living on the same street, and how they each dealt with the war. I conceived it taking place on Main Street, USA, but Mayer and Mannix said they needed something international, so I reset the story during the siege of Leningrad."

"So you changed an American story into one that depicted Russians sympathetically?" The slope-nosed Nixon looked at him with a snicker in his eyes.

"The siege had just ended, so I saw it as a story of triumph over oppression."

"You wrote a film about the triumph of the Russian people?"

Nixon's question sounded more like a statement. Restlessness rolled through the audience gallery. Marcus searched it for a familiar face, but found only strangers. *Where's the Committee for the First Amendment?*

Much had been made in the press about the arrival in Washington of the CFA, who'd come to protest what they saw as a travesty of the freedom of speech guaranteed by the First Amendment. Many of the people who'd been in Ira Gershwin's living room that night arrived on a TWA airplane chartered by Howard Hughes. Marcus could see none of them.

He eyed the panel. "Was that a question?"

"I have one." This declaration came from John Rankin, the gaunt-faced representative from Mississippi. "Have you ever boarded a Soviet ship?"

The full impact of what was going on hit Marcus like a Joe Louis left hook. In two and a half days of testimonials, nobody had named names or admitted affiliation with the Communist Party. *They need to start playing rough, otherwise the public will lose interest and all their grandstanding will blow up in their faces. I'm being thrown to the goddamned lions.* He raked the gallery again for a specific face: Kathryn's. It was a moment before the memory of that fight in his car jabbed his chest.

"Mr. Adler, do you need me to repeat the question?"

He felt a ring of sweat circling his neck. "Yes, I have. It was a Russian battleship."

Another swell of anticipation throbbed through the Romans, their eyes fixed on the luckless Christian.

"Can you recall this ship's name?"

"No, sir, I cannot."

"Would it refresh your memory if I were to remind you that also present were Charlie Chaplin, Lewis Milestone, John Garfield, and their wives?"

"I know the evening you are referring to, but I cannot recall the name of the ship."

"And the reason you were there?"

"I'm invited to many social gatherings," Marcus said. "This particular one came from Konstantin Simonov. In the course of the evening, it became apparent that I was invited so that he could pitch a movie idea, a biopic on the life of prima ballerina Anna Pavlova."

"Another Russian?" Nixon asked. Before Marcus could respond, he interjected, "Do you consider yourself a friend of Charlie Chaplin?"

At a New York press conference held the day after the premiere of his new movie, *Monsieur Verdoux*, Chaplin was asked if he was a Communist. Things did not go Chaplin's way, nor had they ever since.

"Not especially," Marcus said.

Rankin picked up a photograph, handed it to a bailiff, and pointed in Marcus' direction. Marcus knew what photograph it was — the one taken aboard ship that night.

But he was wrong.

It was definitely him and Chaplin, but Marcus couldn't place it.

"Please identify this photograph, Mr. Adler," Thomas said.

"I — er — need a moment . . ."

Something in the background jostled Marcus' memory. It was taken at the premiere of *William Tell*. Chaplin had come over to greet Alla Nazimova, and when Alla told Chaplin that Marcus wrote the movie, he insisted the photograph be taken in front of a huge painting of Napoleon Bonaparte on horseback in the foyer of the Carthay Circle Theatre.

Realizing he'd been painted into a corner, Marcus identified the time and place of the photograph in his hand.

"I'd like to circle back to this *Free Leningrad!* picture, if I may." This came from Mundt.

Big surprise. You're all in this together.

"The portrayal of the Russian family in that motion picture, how would you categorize it?"

Unusable words like "sympathetic" and "brave" and "relatable" Ping-Ponged around Marcus' mind. He was still trying to come up with one that didn't sink him even deeper into this cesspool when Mundt said,

"You portrayed Russians as good, honest, hardworking people. Isn't that accurate?"

DAMN YOU! SCREW YOU! FUCK YOU!

Marcus took in the deepest breath he could muster.

"With all due respect, I am staggered that this committee appears to be incapable of recognizing that the sands of international allegiances are ever shifting. We were united *with* the Russians *against* the Axis. Hollywood's hand in maintaining this country's morale was to paint sympathetic portraits of the Allies — including Russia. You cannot hold me responsible for something I did when Russia was on our side any more than you can hold me to account for the fact that the US and Russia now find themselves on opposing sides of the ideological divide."

A dozen people in the gallery's back row broke into fervent applause. Marcus could make out Bogie and Bacall, Paul Heinrich and Ira Gershwin. A flash of guilt over his assumption they'd deserted him transmuted into a surge of confidence.

Thomas grabbed up his gavel and banged it several times.

"Mr. Adler, we would ask you to confine yourself to our questions instead of playing to the press." Chairman Thomas shuffled the papers in front of him and fixed Marcus with an unyielding stare. "Are you the son of Roland Adler, the current mayor of McKeesport, Pennsylvania?"

The question sucked the breath from Marcus' lungs.

"Please answer the question."

"Yes, I am."

"Are you aware that in 1895, your father joined the Communist Party?"

While the details of his mother's face had started to fray with the passage of time, he could still call to mind the thick black hair pomaded severely back from a round face with an aquiline nose that gave it edges it shouldn't have, scowling, thick eyebrows, and a downward sloping mouth. But more than that, Marcus could recall the uncompromisingly strict standpoint from which his father approached everything he did, everything he believed, and everything he was. Marcus could think of nobody less likely to be a Communist.

"That's a lie!" he shouted into the microphones.

Thomas held up a document for Marcus — and the press — to see. "I am in possession of a photograph of a Communist Party membership card dated 1895. It is made out to a Roland Adler, whose stated profession is coal miner. Mr. Adler, are you aware that your family came from Russia?"

From . . . Russia??? Forming words was beyond him.

"Are you aware that your ancestors migrated to America from the resort town of Adler on the Black Sea?" Thomas held up a map of Eastern Europe, from the western coast of Greece to the far side of the Caspian Sea. He used a pencil to pinpoint a dot he'd circled in black.

It's not far from Yalta, where Alla was born. Marcus wondered if that was why the two of them had such a close connection. *We were both Russian and never knew it.*

"Would the witness please answer the question?"

Marcus cleared his throat. "My father never talked about his family background. I know nothing of where his ancestors came from."

"Given the revelations unearthed in this line of questioning," Thomas said, "I feel we need to ask you again, Mr. Adler: Are you currently now or have you ever been a member of the Communist Party?"

I'm screwed nine ways to Sunday. Leilah O'Roarke's most popular whore on her busiest day of the year has never come close to being as screwed as this. "You're being called as a friendly witness," they said. "Just reinforce Mayer's statement." Nobody mentioned anything about a sacrificial lamb being led to slaughter.

He pushed his chair backwards. The sound of its feet scraping on the marble floor shot through the chamber as Marcus stood.

Thomas banged his gavel. "Sit down, Mr. Adler, you haven't been dismissed yet."

Marcus planted his hands on the table and focused on the largest microphone, ready to tell the panel that he'd said everything he had to say. But a realization hit him.

It didn't matter. He didn't matter. Nothing mattered.

As he turned his back to the panel, the Committee for the First Amendment started to cheer while the press chattered like overwrought monkeys. Marcus fumbled his way through the warren of desks and cables. Flashbulbs exploded in his face, blinding him, blocking his path out of the room. Somehow, he managed to find the exit. He threw his shoulder against the door and fell into the witness holding room.

He looked at the pallid faces around him, Gary Cooper and Leo McCarey among them. "Good luck," he spat out, and staggered toward the opposite door. It led to a hallway; miraculously it was empty. He spied a sign—*TO THE STREET*—with an arrow pointing to another door at the end.

Marcus trailed his hand along the wall as though to guide him away from hell. He tried to open the door, but it was locked. He pressed his head against it, and closed his eyes. Instantly, he wished he hadn't. All he could see was his father's face.

CHAPTER 45

As streetcar 56 crossed the Monongahela River and rattled its way into McKeesport, Marcus thought about the day he arrived in Los Angeles and took the streetcar to the Garden of Allah. That was twenty years ago. Now Los Angeles was home, and McKeesport was foreign territory.

The whole town knew their mayor was a Commie. Did he really think he could sneak in as though he was the Invisible Man?

Maybe Thomas Wolfe was right. You can't go home again.

He fanned himself with the telegram he'd received the previous day.

WE STILL LOVE YOU SIGNED KOG

When he realized "KOG" stood for "Kathryn, Oliver, Gwendolyn," he sat on his hotel bed and cried. He knew he couldn't count on much back in LA, but at least he had three friendly faces waiting for him. He wasn't sure whose idea the telegram had been, but the letter "K" made him cry extra hard.

He couldn't get his bearings until he found himself on Walnut Street. It was busier than he remembered. There were traffic lights now. More stores, taller trees. When the streetcar conductor gave him directions to the West Penn Furniture Company, he failed to mention how far it was, but Marcus didn't mind. It gave him a chance to wander through the streets of a town he never thought he'd see again.

The factory was a block long and made of weathered red brick, with few windows. The closest door was marked *Retail Showroom — Public Welcome.*

On both sides of the center aisle stood a range of sofas, breakfronts, dining tables and occasional chairs. A girl with lopsided bangs the color of dried corn smiled as he approached the desk. When Marcus told her he wanted to see Doris Adler, she asked his name.

He debated the wisdom of saying it out loud. "I was kind of hoping to surprise her."

The receptionist buzzed Doris and told her she was needed in the showroom. As Marcus retreated into the furniture display, a wave of fatigue overtook him. A very public humiliation had been followed by a gloomy two-day whiskey binge that may or may not have included a sexual encounter with the room service waiter, then a four-hour steam bath followed by a sleepless ride on an overnight train. *No wonder I feel like I've been flattened by King Kong.*

A wild scream pierced the air.

Marcus' sister came running toward him, her arms outstretched. She slammed into him, wrapping her arms around him as she gurgled incomprehensibly into the nape of his neck. When she pulled her face away to look at him, his shoulder was wet with tears.

"How? When? Why?" she gurgled.

"Surprise!" he said weakly, and looked around for a quiet corner. "Is there somewhere we can talk?"

A frown flickered across her face, but only for a moment. She led him down a long corridor and into an office with a large desk, trio of telephones, and a wall of filing cabinets.

She sat him down on one of the armchairs facing her desk, and she took the other. She then grabbed up his hands and squeezed them with surprising strength. "So what gives? You couldn't send a telegram?"

"It was a spur of the moment thing," Marcus said.

"All the way from Los Angeles? That's a heck of a spur."

"I'm en route back from Washington."

"DC?"

"I was there for the HUAC." Doris looked at him blankly. "The House Un-American Activities Committee hearings?"

It took a moment before his promptings registered. "Oh yeah, I heard about that. Must have been something, huh? Or was it just boring government stuff?"

Christ almighty! Marcus' body slackened. *McKeesport's mayor is revealed to be a Communist and it doesn't even make the news. What sort of podunk town did I come from?*

"Marcus, you're scaring me. Has something happened?"

He lifted his head. "Can we clear out of here and go someplace? Preferably a bar. I've got something to tell you and when you hear it, you're going to need a drink in front of you."

* * *

Doris tossed back the last of her lime rickey. "I don't believe it," she said.

"You mean the news that my testimony didn't reach McKeesport, or that our father is a Commie?"

She fiddled with the dusty silk daisies sitting in a vase at the center of their table. "Do you think it's true? About Dad, I mean?"

"He was a member of the United Mine Workers back then, and Communists are all about unions. So . . . maybe? It doesn't mean he still is, though," Marcus added, "or that he ever attended meetings."

Doris grabbed up her handbag and fished out her change purse. "I have a friend at the *McKeesport Daily News*. We can trust June to be discreet."

She beckoned him to follow her to the line of telephone booths lined up against the far wall and insisted they squeeze in together so that he could listen in.

When Doris asked if June had heard anything about McKeesport getting mentioned during the HUAC hearings, she said she hadn't, but offered to check the wires again. After a few moments, they could hear the sound of the girl's shoes slapping against the linoleum.

"Holy moly!" she panted. "There was nothing on the teletype today so I pawed through the trash. You're right! Roland was mentioned. How did we miss that?"

"What does it say?" Doris asked.

"It says, 'In a startling series of revelations — wait, your brother who went to Hollywood to write for the movies, isn't his name Marcus?"

"What does it say, June?"

"It talks about his testimony on the twenty-third and how he denied being a member of the Communist Party but wrote some pro-Russia movie, and . . . blah blah blah . . . oh, and how — is he really a friend of Charlie Chaplin?"

"Go on."

"Okay, so then they go back to the bit about Russia. And then they ask him if he's the son of Roland Adler, because — " June gasped, then there was silence.

"June?" Doris whispered. "Are you still there?"

"Uh-huh."

"Can you keep this under your hat? At least for the time being?"

"It's my job to take news to the editor. If I put it off too long, he'll want to know why. In fact, he's coming toward me right now. Gotta go."

The line went dead.

Even in the murky light of the Tube City Bar and Grill, Marcus could see his sister going pale.

"What're you going to do, Marcus?"

"Jump on the next streetcar leaving town." He headed back to their table to gulp the last mouthful of whiskey and pick up his hat. "How often do they run these days? Can I catch — " He caught the stricken look on his sister's face.

"You're not even going to see Mom?"

It was now coming up to five o'clock. From what June had just said, it sounded like the news of Roland Adler's Commie past was about to break the surface. He hooked his arm through hers and made for the exit. "In your last letter, you mentioned Mom's old trouble. Is she okay?"

Twilight was starting to descend when they stepped into the parking lot.

"I was talking about the way she volunteers too much," Doris said. "Remember how she'd work so hard that ol' Doc Hawker would have to order a weeklong bed rest? It got real bad during the war, and I really don't want her to do it again. She has the drive, but not the constitution. She'll be crushed if she hears you were in town and didn't come see her."

"And Dad?"

She unlocked her car. "I'm driving you to see Mom, we'll spend as much time as we dare, then I'll take you into Pittsburgh. If you miss the train to Chicago, we'll find you a nice place to hang your hat for the night. Get in!"

* * *

As Doris hurled her Ford Tudor around the darkening streets of McKeesport, Marcus grew excited to see his mother. He nodded when Doris told him their father never got home before six thirty — "That gives us more than an hour" — but the truth was he didn't care much. *What could my father say to me that's any worse than what I've just been through?*

Doris swung onto Cleveland Street and suddenly the old Sullivan place on the corner came into view, and he was thrown back to the night his father ran him out of town.

"You know there'll be tears, right?" Doris said, patting his knee.

"Hers, yours, or mine?"

She pulled up to a familiar house set back from the street with a long concrete path, a wraparound balcony out front, and a steeply angled roof atop the second floor.

Marcus needed a moment to fight off his father's voice from twenty years before: *Get into the car. I don't want to hear from you until the train pulls out. You got that, boy? Not one goddamned syllable.*

"It's white," he said. The last time he'd seen this house, it was sky blue with navy trim.

"It's been white since Betsy moved out."

Don't ever come back here again. And don't even think of writing your mother. I'll tell her something.

338

They got out of the Ford and walked up the concrete path. Doris opened the door without knocking. "Mom? It's me. I bought a visitor. You decent?"

When he heard his mother's laugh—a wind-chime sort of tinkling—he grabbed the stair banister for support. The streetlight out back of the house streamed in through the leadlight window at the end of the hall. It silhouetted Jean Adler in a halo of green and yellow, but obscured her face. She took a step toward him, then stopped. Her right hand flew to her throat.

"Hi, Mom." His words came out a low croak.

She flew toward him, her hands outstretched. Before he could say anything more, their arms were wrapped around each other. Her blouse still smelled of Lux soap flakes. He drank in the scent that was the anchor of his childhood.

She was the first to pull away, grabbing him by the shoulders and holding him at arm's length. "Oh my, that California sun we hear so much about, it certainly does sit well on you."

He wanted to tell her how good it was to see her, how much he'd missed her, and how sorry he was that he never got to say goodbye, but he couldn't get the words out. Instead, he soaked up every detail. Her face was still narrow, but her hair was gray now, pulled into a neat bun. She drew him into the front parlor. It hadn't changed. The lace curtains. The straight-backed chair. Even the black mantel clock with the gold trim was still in its place, keeping exact time with its quiet tick-tick-tick.

She led him to sofa. Plain pink tufted muslin had replaced the floral damask, but otherwise it looked the same. "Doris and I always go see every MGM picture that plays at the Loew's," Jean said, wiping her eyes, "just in case your name pops up in the credits. Every now and then it does, and we get so excited. I'm terribly proud of you!" She tried to blink away her tears. "How about I fix some tea? There are fresh oatmeal cookies—"

"I can't stay long, Mom," Marcus said. "I'm really just passing through."

"Oh?" Her smile deflated. She then pressed his hand between hers. They felt soft, like the sand along Venice Beach. "Tell me about yourself!" she exclaimed. "How's your health? Are you good? You do look awfully well." He nodded. "Are you married? Do you have children?"

Marcus looked for signposts of the story his father told her to explain his sudden departure. But he saw only sincerity. "Nope, no wife and kids. Those studios, they pay a guy well, but they sure do exact their pound of flesh. It's a good life, Mom. I work hard, but have great friends and a terrific place on Sunset Boulevard, so life's good. Very good."

She nodded, then smiled at him a naughty do-I-dare? grin. "I know I probably shouldn't ask, but is Clark Gable every bit the gentleman we hear him to be?"

"Yes, Mom, he is."

"Oh, that's so nice to hear."

"The first time I met him was during a costume fitting for *Gone with the Wind*."

"Imagine!"

"I had a lunch date with George Cukor—"

A flash of light filled the vestibule as the front door swung open and the voice of Roland Adler filled the entire ground floor. "JEAN! WHERE ARE"—he spotted Doris lingering in the parlor doorway— "Oh, it's you. Have you seen your mo—?"

The man stopped cold when he spotted Marcus on the sofa.

The past twenty years had taken a heavy toll. Marcus' father's hair was now gray and wispy, and he was substantially thicker around the waist. His face had taken on the rubicund complexion of a heavy drinker. Not quite W.C. Fields, but getting there. He started breathing through his nose like an angry bull with several banderillas thrust into his neck.

Marcus let go of his mother's hands and stood up. "Hello, Father."

"You." The word came hissing out from between Roland's tense, pale lips. "You've got such walloping goddamned nerve showing up here, boy." Each terse word came out loaded with the effort it took for the man to keep his fury in check.

Jean's voice took on a matronly authority. "Roland, we've talked about cussing inside this house."

He stepped to one side so that he could address his wife without having to look at his son.

"I received a phone call from Victor at the *Daily News*. You know what he wanted? A statement about the allegations against me in those House Un-American hearings up in Washington. First I've heard of it, I told him. So I asked him what allegations he was talking about." He waved his left hand at Marcus as though swatting a fly. "Your son testified I was a member of the goddamned Communist Party."

"I was testifying —"

"I don't care what you were doing."

You don't get to talk over me, Marcus thought. *Not this time.* He raised his voice to match his father's pitch. "I was testifying about a movie I wrote set in Russia, and all of a sudden they were waving a photograph in front of me — it was of your Communist Party membership card."

Marcus braced himself for an onslaught of denial, but Roland was stunned into silence.

Jesus! Look at that gaping pie hole. It's true!

He used his father's momentary lapse to face Doris. "Here's a fun fact about our family history, sis. Apparently Adler is some little town on the Black Sea. Do you know where the Black Sea is?" Doris shook her head. Marcus faced his father. "It's in Russia. Where all the Communists are."

Roland's face, already boozehound red, deepened to a shade of claret. "I told you never to come back here."

"Since when do I have to do what you say?"

"Dad," Doris stepped forward, "you can't blame Marcus for questions that committee threw at him. They're the ones who dug into your past."

But Roland kept his eyes fixed on Marcus. "Get. Out. NOW!"

"No, Dad," Doris persisted, "not this time. You ran Marcus out of town once—"

Jean was on her feet now. "What does she mean, ran him out of town?"

Roland clenched his fists and raised one above his head. "I will not stand for this in my own house!"

"Try doing it in Washington," Marcus retorted, "in front of microphones, and journalists, and committee members, and dozens of people you've worked with for *years*."

"You've ruined my life for a second time!" The spittle in the corners of Roland's mouth flew in several directions.

As Marcus stepped closer, he could see a film of sweat break out along the top of his father's mouth. "Tell me father, did you join the Communist Party?"

"You're like a plague!" Roland thundered. "You blow into town spreading your lies and your perversions!"

Doris stepped between her father and her brother. "For heaven's sake, Dad, will you just calm down?"

"You stay out of it, you silly girl!"

He grabbed Doris by her shoulder and shoved her aside.

Marcus caught her before she stumbled into a potted fern. By the time he'd spun around to face his father, he realized that if he'd never come back, Doris' friend wouldn't have pulled the old teletypes from the trash, and the news of his testimony could have passed the town by. In coming home, he'd caused the exact thing he was hoping to avoid.

The idea struck him as funny, partly because he knew the screenwriter inside him was filing it away as a possible movie plot. Then he realized he was most likely no longer employed by MGM—nor probably was he employable by *any* movie studio. The irony of the whole situation made him snicker.

"Look at him!" Roland pointed a pudgy finger at Marcus. "He wants nothing but to wreak havoc and destroy everything I've spent my life building up, and then laughs in our faces."

"I'm not laughing at you," Marcus said. "I'm laughing at myself because I've spent the last twenty years slogging my guts out to show you I am capable, and smart, and that there was a whole lot more to me than what you walked in on that night. And now, here we are, all these years later and what do I find? That I don't give two hoots about what you think. You're just a small-town bully with a small-town mind. But the laugh's on me because I've wasted two decades proving myself to someone whose approval I never needed in the first place. So thank you, Father, for being exactly the same as you were when I left. You can't begin to know the gift of freedom you've handed me."

Marcus turned to his mother. She pressed her hands to her cheeks, pale as the moon, her eyes darting between her son, her husband, and her daughter. "I love you, Mom." He fought the tears burning his eyes. "But I have a life in California that I must go back to."

He kissed her on the cheek, then pulled Doris into a hug. "Take care of yourself, sis," he whispered into her ear. He heard her sob, but couldn't bring himself to look at her. Instead, he walked out the front door and down the concrete steps.

When he heard the door slam behind him, he knew it was Doris without looking over his shoulder.

"There's a train leaving for Chicago in fifty minutes," she told him breathlessly.

"Will I make it?"

"The station's not far from here, but we have to stop by my place."

"What for?"

"I need ten minutes to pack." Doris looked like she was about to explode. "Iwanttocomewithyou!"

"Don't you need to clear that with your boss first?"

"I don't mean for a vacation. I want to move there." She opened the car door. "But I never had the courage. To up and leave like that, I mean. But you did it, and look at the life you made!"

Six months ago, Marcus would have cheered Doris' bold move, but now he was going back to a life that was probably in tatters. "Maybe you need to think this through."

A slightly hysterical laugh burst out of her. "Since the day I got back from my trip during the war, it's *all* I've thought about."

"But Mom—"

Doris jacked a thumb toward the house. "You should hear the way she laid into Dad just now. She's going to be just fine. It's time I lived the life I want."

"In LA?"

"The Garden of Allah, if there's room."

A firecracker of excitement shot through Marcus. "If there's not, we'll make room."

"So I can come?"

"Lord help the man who tries to stop you."

CHAPTER 46

When the limo Howard Hughes had provided turned into the Cabrillo Beach parking lot, Gwendolyn pinned her straw sun hat into place. "I don't know if we'll even get the chance to talk to him," she told Kathryn, "but if we do, remember— it's called the *Hercules*. For the sake of everything holy, don't call it the *Spruce Goose*. Cary Grant told me he hates that nickname. So remember, ixnay on the oosegay."

"It *is* made of spruce, isn't it?" Kathryn countered.

"That's not the point."

Hughes' chauffeur opened Gwendolyn's door. "Are you *sure* about that dress?" she asked Kathryn. "This is one man you don't want to be trifling with."

"I know what I'm doing."

It was windier down in Long Beach than Gwendolyn expected, so she was glad she'd grabbed her tangerine silk scarf at the last minute. It didn't quite match her olive-green outfit, but the breeze had a kick to it. A quick glance told Gwendolyn that this was the Hollywood-heavy crowd she'd been expecting.

As Kathryn beelined for Walter Pidgeon and Randolph Scott, Gwendolyn meandered through the sprinkling of famous faces until she spotted Edith Head enmeshed in conversation with Hedda Hopper. When Edith spotted Gwendolyn, she raised an arm to cut short Hedda's monologue. "Come, join us. You've met Hedda, haven't you?" In fact, Gwendolyn had never met the woman, but they nodded in that vague I'm-sure-we-have-at-some-point way that Hollywoodites always did because it was often true.

"Good grief!" Edith tried to hold her jet-black hair in place against the sea breezes, but it was a losing battle. "I should have brought a scarf. I have an appointment later with Joan Fontaine. She's starting *The Emperor's Waltz* with Bing next month, and I hate looking like I just crawled out of a wind tunnel."

Gwendolyn pulled the scarf from around her neck. "You're welcome to borrow mine." Edith took it gratefully and tied it over her hair. "I don't suppose you've seen the man of the hour," Gwendolyn said, looking around the growing mass of viewers. "I have something for him."

"It's an hour before takeoff," Hedda said. "He's probably in the cockpit. You see that humorless gaggle of suits?" She pointed out a dozen men in gunmetal-gray Brooks Brothers. "They're observers from the Senate committee that's been drilling him all month about financial irregularities. If this baby doesn't fly, poor Howard's *Spruce Goose* is cooked!"

* * *

It didn't take Kathryn long to spot Hoover. Clad in a white linen suit and a panama hat, he was standing next to his right-hand man, Clyde Tolson, who was dressed identically but for a lighter pocket square and a thinner hat band. The two were grown-up versions of the Bobbsey Twins, planted in a thicket of dark-suited gents with indistinguishable faces.

In the end, it had been a bootblack who brought everything to a head for Kathryn.

Jefferson Jones was one of her tipsters — her loose collection of hotel doormen, waiters, and cigarette girls who passed on useful snippets of information for a buck apiece.

When Marcus returned to the Garden from his eventful journey back East, he and Kathryn drowned each other in tears, apologies, and regrets. To celebrate, Kathryn treated him and his adorable sister to a night at the Cocoanut Grove, where she bumped into Jones, who worked the shoeshine stand opposite the Ambassador Hotel check-in desk.

He told her about a conversation he'd heard while shining the shoes of a pair of swaggering smart alecks who talked as though he had no ears or brains. They jawed about how someone called "The Hoov" was coming to Los Angeles to watch the *Hercules* test flight. And while he was out here, The Hoov intended to look into a missing dress that he was all upset over.

Kathryn pulled two one-dollar bills from her wallet and handed them to him. He tried to give one of them back, but she insisted that he'd been more help than he could possibly know.

She called out, "YOO-HOO! HEY FELLAS!"

She marched past the G-Men and approached Walter Pidgeon and Randolph Scott, who had their heads together comparing wristwatches.

"Fine day for a test flight!" she proclaimed. "What's with the watches?"

As Randolph explained that they'd both just bought the same timepiece at Desmond's, Kathryn snuck a quick glance at Hoover. Her subterfuge worked: he was staring at her, or more specifically at her outfit.

Gwennie had been understandably horrified when Kathryn asked her to duplicate the Hoover dress, but she needed a lure. Although Kathryn didn't care much for the rainbow overlay, the dark green foundation was very becoming, especially once Gwennie adjusted it to fit her measurements.

Hoover broke away from his hangers-on and strolled toward the end of the grass. The breeze picked up as he reached the sand, and he pushed his panama down more firmly on his squarish head.

Asking Walter and Randolph to excuse her, Kathryn joined Hoover at the periphery of the observation lawn, where he was surveying Hughes' silver aircraft out on the water. "I know he's Howard Hughes and all," Kathryn said, "but surely something that enormous can't fly."

Hoover kept his eyes on the aircraft. "Some people think they can do anything."

"Your suit is very spiffy, I must say. I do admire the pocket square. The whole black-and-white look is very Great Gatsby."

Hoover angled his head to take in her dress. "Did your roommate make that?"

"She hasn't been my roommate for a while now." Kathryn grabbed a fistful of material and let the skirt flutter in the breeze. "What do you think?"

"I think you've got bigger balls than I imagined."

The surprisingly humorous lilt to the man's declaration boosted Kathryn's courage. "You know I'm making a point, don't you?"

"I'm no fool."

"I had Bette Davis over for dinner before she gave birth and I commented on her dress. She told me that she was visiting with Orry-Kelly at Warners when a mysterious package arrived. It contained a dress that nobody knew anything about, so she had him turn it into a maternity smock. That's when she found the telltale "G" stitched into the cuff. When I asked Gwendolyn about it, she told me about the anonymous request. As far as she's concerned, I simply liked it and asked her to make one for me, too."

Hoover pulled a Montecristo from his inside breast pocket and slipped off the foil ring.

"You're going to have a terrible time trying to light that thing in this wind." She pulled her cigarette lighter out of her handbag. "Here, let me help you with that."

He jammed the fat cigar in his mouth and cupped his hands around the other end while she lit it. "What do you want?" he asked.

"I want you to bring Nelson Hoyt back from the dead."

* * *

Gwendolyn was relieved when Hedda took off to dig for gossip, leaving her and Edith to talk freely. Edith was hoping to finally get an Oscar nomination for her work on the Joan Fontaine picture — "The Academy just loves those frilly fancies from yesteryear" — but RKO was doing *Joan of Arc*, so she sensed she had some competition. They were still talking about it when three long blasts of a bullhorn indicated that Hughes was ready to attempt a flight.

The crowd gathered at the edge of the grass where massive boulders formed a breakwater; a flotilla of small pleasure crafts dotted the beach in front of them. Far off to the left, the hulking aircraft shone in the November sun like a bloated suit of armor. Eight propellers, four on each wing, whirred to life, and the *Hercules* began to move.

Its progress was slow at first, but it gathered momentum, leaving thick sprays in its wake as it skimmed across the surface. For the longest while, it looked like a meager handspan was about all the height it could manage. Gwendolyn heard someone mutter, "Don't tell me after all this, he can't even get it up."

The throng held its breath as the plane passed in front of them. The drone of the propellers vibrated the air as the behemoth bounced and strained to hurl itself into the air.

"Come on," Gwendolyn murmured. "Up you go, up you go!"

The churning white water dissipated. Someone from the senatorial committee yelled, "It's cleared!" and the crowd broke into applause.

Five feet. Twelve feet. Suddenly it was climbing twenty, thirty, sixty. The crowd cheered and waved and whistled. A mile later, it skidded along the water again and drew to a slow stop.

"Well, that's that," Edith said. "I must go." She headed toward her car.

The crowd broke up into knots of twos and threes. As Gwendolyn looked around for Kathryn, she spotted a disconcerting sight—the black-and-white diamond dress she glimpsed at the Florentine Gardens. Leilah had waylaid her that night before she could investigate, but now Gwendolyn was free to lurk and observe.

Her quarry was well into her forties and, judging from the ostentatious diamond bracelet and triple strand of pearls, comfortably well off. Curiously, the dress seemed to fit the woman fairly well. Gwendolyn hazarded a few steps nearer.

The woman pressed a pair of opera glasses to her eyes, studying the *Spruce Goose*. Without warning, she yanked them away. "What *are* you gawking at?"

Gwendolyn blushed. "Nothing. I—"

"Is it my bracelet?"

The assumption made Gwendolyn laugh. "No. The dress."

An odd smile came over the woman's face as she ran a fingernail along the décolletage. Gwendolyn and her client had fought over that neckline. He wanted a deeper cut until she pointed out how hairy his chest was.

"I know I'm overdressed," the woman admitted, "but I'm going straight to the opera afterwards."

"You should know something," Gwendolyn said, *if only to wipe that superior smile off your face.* "I made that dress."

The smug attitude dropped from the woman's face. Gwendolyn expected fright, horror, and embarrassment, but found instead wide-eyed excitement.

"Are you 'G'?" She turned the cuff of her right sleeve inside out. Gwendolyn nodded. The woman clapped her hands together. "This dress! I *love* it!"

Gwendolyn pictured her client—one of those anxious, sweaty types, who lived on nervous energy and probably drank cheap whiskey on the sly. "I'm happy to hear that."

"It's a funny story, actually!" the wife declared. "I found it hanging at the back of the closet. Naturally I assumed it was for me—our tenth anniversary was coming up. I had just put it on when he walked in. He nearly passed out right then and there! So I sat him down and we had a frank discussion about what he likes."

"How very open-minded of you," Gwendolyn murmured.

"Could be worse," the woman said with surprising pragmatism. "He might be a dope fiend or a gambler, or any number of things. But he likes to play dress-up, so who am I to judge?" She pulled Gwendolyn closer into her orbit so nobody would overhear. "The way I figure it, we have virtually the same measurements, so I get to expand my wardrobe. In fact, perhaps we can talk about getting you to sew some outfits for me. Or I suppose I should say for 'us.' Marriage is all about share and share alike, isn't it?"

The whole time she'd been working with her Licketysplitters, it'd never occurred to Gwendolyn they might come with wives.

"You know what?" the woman continued, "I'm a member of the Native Daughters of the Golden West. A whole brigade of us is going to the opera tonight. I know they're going to ask me where I got this dress. Do you have a card?"

* * *

When Kathryn told Hoover that she wanted him to bring Nelson back, he contemplated her with those callous eyes of his, then walked away. She thought she'd blown it, and kicked herself for overplaying her hand.

Back on shore, Hughes led the crowd to a huge white marquee where he'd arranged a celebratory spread for the press, investors, and senatorial committee.

Over glasses of champagne and handfuls of canapés, Kathryn watched Hoover and his phalanx of yes-men hover by the dessert table, but the FBI chief gave no indication he saw her there. She turned her back to them as Gwendolyn approached.

"I take it you didn't get the answer you wanted?"

Kathryn bit into a chicken liver on rye. "I thought I was playing my ace, but it was just the joker."

"What's the name of Hoover's assistant?"

"Clyde Tolson."

"Yeah, well, he's coming this way."

Gwendolyn's warning gave Kathryn just enough time to stuff the rest of the canapé into her mouth before Tolson appeared by her side. "The chief wants a word with you." He kept his voice to an even-keeled whisper. "Please follow me."

Kathryn shadowed Tolson to the parking lot where a black Cadillac sedan sat a little apart from the other cars. She could make out a silhouette in the back seat. Tolson opened the passenger door and motioned for her to join his boss inside.

"Are we going for a ride?" Kathryn asked lightly.

"I do not enjoy being taken for a ride, Miss Massey." He threw her a skeptical eye. "Nelson Hoyt. State your case."

"You must know I was not willingly recruited to be an informer." She waited for him to nod, but he didn't. "However, I did what I could." *Which was as little as possible to still make it seem like I was cooperating.* "But I think I came through for you in the end, with that information concerning the O'Roarkes and the money they laundered in order to finance Bugsy Siegel's casino." *Even though what I did was more motivated by my boss' welfare than anything else.* "You got your money's worth, Mr. Hoover, and considering what you did to my ex-husband, I think it's high time we all parted company. Nelson doesn't deserve—"

"What, exactly, did I do to your ex-so-called-husband?" Hoover sucked a shred of celery from between his teeth.

It was time to play a hunch she'd been harboring since Marcus returned from Washington. *What's the worst that could happen? He laughs at me? I've been laughed at before.* "You dug into his family background and shared it with the HUAC."

Hoover's silence was an admission of guilt.

"I assume you did it to teach me a lesson," she said. "As it happens, you did him a favor. So I guess I ought to thank you."

Sitting with Hoover in that hotel suite in Reno, Kathryn had sensed the power radiating from this bullfrog. She was impressed by it, but not awed. However, in the back seat of a motorcar with barely a foot of space between them, she could feel the weight of his authority.

"You're making a point with this outfit you're wearing," he stated.

Kathryn's dress felt suddenly sticky, like sitting on someone else's gum.

"Your secret's safe with me, Mr. Hoover."

"What makes you think I have a secret to keep safe?"

A sudden gust of wind blew along the shoreline, shaking the white marquee. The men held onto the tent poles and the ladies restrained their hats.

"Because the green in this dress brings out the brown in your eyes."

He smiled. It wasn't twisted with greed or rage, but instead held all the warmth of a fireside chat. "I admire you, Miss Massey."

Kathryn waited for the catch, but none came. "I find it hard to believe I'm anywhere near the list of people you admire."

"Oh, but you are."

He said it so simply, absent of all guile and duplicity, that all she could muster was a raise of the eyebrows.

"I consider loyalty to be one of the most important virtues." He ran a finger around his pinkie ring. "I have no time for mealy-mouthed jellyfish too afraid to say what they think. During that whole *Citizen Kane* ruckus, you stood up to Hearst. That takes guts, and I admire guts. The way you've faced off against your boss over this Communist issue takes a set of metal-plated *cojones*. I respect that."

"But that's all Nelson did—speak his mind. And yet you've banished him God knows where."

"Hoyt was disloyal," Hoover replied curtly.

Kathryn felt a sweat break out across her chest. She pictured Marcus sitting next to her, holding her hand. It was time for a judicious retreat. "So you admire the *cojones* it takes for me to speak my mind even though you don't like what I think?"

"I disagree with pretty much everything you've written in your column, but I admire the passion with which you say it."

What sort of backhanded — wait a minute. He's flattering me. Does he want something? She saw an opportunity and stuck her hand through it before it closed like an elevator door.

"You engaged Gwendolyn to make your dress," she said, "knowing she's one of my closest friends, didn't you?"

"My — ? What in tarnation — ?" Hoover dropped his supercilious tone. "You think I had that dress made *for me?* That I'm a — a — cross-dresser?" Hoover now seemed incredulous. Or amused? Or was he insulted? Kathryn could no longer read this brick wall beside her.

"See it from my point of view." She gave a fluttering laugh. "That dress Gwendolyn made would fit you, the color suits you, the payment was in cash, delivery address anonymous, and you've never been married." She saw a glint of surprise flare in his eyes. "I've seen loopier things, and you must have, too."

He stared at her intensely as though to say, *Go on. Think it through.*

"You wanted Gwendolyn to make the dress . . . because . . . you wanted me to see it. You want me to . . . recognize it? At some later date?"

Hoover exhaled as though he'd been holding his breath. "You're as astute as I hoped."

"So you intend using it as . . ." Kathryn's mind started racing. "As proof? Proof with which to . . . condemn someone as a cross-dresser? Character assassination. Am I close?"

"Remarkably."

"You want me to point a finger at someone and say 'I know that dress!'"

"Please credit me with some finesse, Miss Massey. I wanted you to see it, but you weren't supposed to trace it back to me. Losing the first one was unfortunate, and the heads are still rolling over that debacle. But I still need you to play your part."

"What's in it for me?" Kathryn regretted it as soon as the words had flown out of her. The man had more power than the president, with umpteen different ways to make her life a living hell. She'd wriggled free of his tax bill mousetrap, but doubted she could pull it off a second time.

He wagged a finger at her. "If Wilkerson ever cans your ass, I want you to know that I could always find a place for you with the Bureau."

I'd rather have my eyeballs tattooed.

"In return for recognizing the dress, I'll bring your Nelson Hoyt in from the cold."

Kathryn had to swallow her *YIPPEE!* so hard she nearly gagged on it. "*My* Nelson Hoyt?" she asked.

"You're screwing him, aren't you?"

"No, I'm not."

"Saving yourself?" he asked witheringly. "Is that why you want him back?"

Kathryn did her best to resist fidgeting with cuff of her jacket.

"So do we have a deal?" Hoover asked finally. "You get your Nelson Hoyt and all you have to do is point a finger when the time comes."

A sinking feeling told Kathryn she was getting the short end of the stick. The word *deal* perched on the tip of her tongue before she bit it back.

"Who will I be pointing my finger at?"

He watched the tide come in, nearly to the breakfront now. "Charlie Chaplin."

Kathryn burst out laughing, then wished she hadn't. "I'm sorry," she said, "but that's ludicrous. He's a lady-killer, and everyone knows it, especially after the paternity suit with that Joan Barry nutcase. And then he married Oona O'Neil."

"That damn limey is guilty of something, and probably a lot worse than his leftist politics. I want him out of the country. For good."

"May I say, Mr. Hoover, if that's your plan, it's very thin."

"Of course it's thin," he admitted. "It's supposed to be."

Kathryn had to turn away. Not far from the Cadillac, a flock of seagulls erupted into a squawking racket.

"You don't expect anyone will believe you," she said out loud, more to herself than to the schemer beside her. She watched the seagulls, who'd been distracted from the caviar and crabmeat by a slice of bread. "It's camouflage, isn't it? You're planning something else, but you want people distracted by this outrageous charge of yours."

Nobody's going to believe me, and he knows it, she realized. *That's even more insidious. I should have known he'd be three jumps ahead of everybody else. But all I'll have to do is point a finger at something everybody will dismiss, and then forget about. In return, Nelson will be back, and maybe we'll stand a chance.*

"All you need do is point to a dress," Hoover said.

She stuck out her hand to shake his, but he merely looked at it.

"That won't be necessary, Miss Massey. We have a deal."

* * *

After Kathryn had disappeared into Hoover's Cadillac, Gwendolyn did everything she could think of to attract Howard's attention. She swanned back and forth in front of him and his cluster of engineers, lingering at the buffet, waving at imaginary people in the crowd, laughing just a little too loudly at someone's joke. But the man was too preoccupied with congratulators and hand-shakers to notice. By the time she gave up, the wind had dropped, so she wandered out to the shoreline.

Soon, a long shadow cast across the grass in front of her.

"I'm glad you came."

Hughes' eyes were bleary and his body drooped like wet laundry.

"Only you could make an airplane the size of Catalina actually fly," she told him. "You must be very pleased."

He lifted his battered fedora to scratch his scalp. "You sure were trying hard to catch my eye."

Gwendolyn unhooked the clasp of her handbag and reached inside. "I wanted to congratulate you, of course, but also to return this."

She presented him with his five-thousand-dollar check.

He jutted his chin toward it. "To me, this doesn't even count as a drop in the ocean, but it could change your life."

"I know." Gwendolyn kept her hand outstretched. "And I appreciate the gesture. But I've decided to decline."

"Can I ask why?"

"I want Chez Gwendolyn to be all mine."

"I told you, it's a gift, not a loan."

"I've spent years watching people at the Cocoanut Grove and Bullocks Wilshire, and if there's one thing I've learned, it's that everybody's lives change, their luck sours, and their fortunes reverse. You may have millions now, but who's to say you always will?"

He chuckled, a mite condescendingly, Gwendolyn thought. "My money ain't going no place."

"I'm sure that's what Hearst said right up until the day Marion Davies sold a million bucks' worth of her jewelry to help him out of his hole. Nothing stays the same, Howard. The last thing I want is for someone to waltz in one day and say he's in some sort of scrape so half the store belongs to him because he put up half the money."

He went to say something but she cut him off by grabbing his hand and pressing the check into it.

"The war taught us women that we can do a lot more than we thought, and we don't need men to do it. I'd rather get that money together myself, secure in the knowledge that Chez Gwendolyn belongs solely to me."

"Is this because I made that crack about your age?"

She shook her head and was relieved to see him push the check into his pocket.

He doffed his hat and wished her the best of luck. "Let me know when you open your store." His eyes started to twinkle. "I might have a girl or two I can send you for a new wardrobe."

As she watched him saunter back to his cadre of hangers-on, she wondered for a gut-wrenching moment if she'd done the wrong thing. *That check meant no more to him than yesterday's banana peel.* She watched him pop open a magnum of champagne and pour a dozen glasses for his crew.

Kathryn appeared, looking as disheveled as Howard had.

"You could do with a drink." Gwendolyn followed Kathryn's eyes to the parking lot, where Hoover's car was pulling away in a spray of gravel. "That bad, huh?"

Kathryn shrugged. "Good and bad."

"Is Nelson the good part?"

"Yeah."

"Then why do you look like he just ran over your dog?"

Kathryn kept her eyes on the parking lot, so Gwendolyn wrapped her arm around her and started marching them toward the bar. "Let's make it a triple."

CHAPTER 47

Marcus sat in his office and tried to concentrate on the script in front of him. *Easter Parade* was supposed to star Gene Kelly and Judy Garland, but Kelly had busted his ankle, so Mayer cajoled and entreated (and probably dangled a huge check in front of) Fred Astaire to come out of self-imposed retirement. Astaire said yes, so now the script had to go through a process Marcus called Astairification — tailoring what was a very Gene Kelly role into a better fit for Fred.

When Marcus reported back to work, he'd expected a summons to the executive floor, but it never came. Then the House of Representatives voted 346 to 17 to cite ten Hollywood screenwriters — including Dalton Trumbo — for contempt of Congress. The Hollywood Ten, as the press dubbed them, were now facing jail time. Marcus felt like his career was hanging by a translucent silk filament, and that it was only a matter of time before he was pink-slipped. But until that happened, he would drive to the studio, sit at his desk, and do the work he was paid to do.

At first, he jumped every time his phone rang or a shadow filled his office doorway. But as each week bled into the next with no word from the higher-ups, he let himself relax. Oliver suggested it was because they didn't get him to admit he was a Commie. The evidence was circumstantial, and hadn't added up to much, so he was okay. Kathryn thought maybe Mayer had seen through Hoover's attempt to sabotage Marcus' family history, and life was simply going on as it had before that subpoena landed in his hand.

So he busied himself Astairificating *Easter Parade*. The movie was one of MGM's big hopes for 1948, and Marcus wanted to be sure it was in tip-top shape before he delivered it to Eddie Mannix's office.

But he'd only managed to battle through a page and a half before his attention meandered to his parents' front path and the look on Doris' face when she said, "To the Garden of Allah, if there's room." But there wasn't; the Garden was fully occupied. He worried that he'd led her to a rash decision, but Doris seemed happy enough on the sofa until something opened up.

His telephone rang. When he picked it up, he heard Mannix's secretary inform him that her boss was on his way. This was unprecedented — Mohammeds were always summoned to the mountain in this industry. "You are to assemble your staff in the conference room. He has an announcement to make." She hung up before he could dig any deeper.

He'd just managed to shepherd the last of them into the room when Mannix arrived, silencing all chatter.

"In a day or two, Eric Johnston from the Motion Picture Association of America will be making a statement that all the studio heads worked on for two days in the Waldorf-Astoria." He held up the stack of paper in his hand. "Henceforth known as the Waldorf Statement."

The Waldorf Statement? Marcus thought. *What is this, a government decree, like the Monroe Doctrine, or the Marshall Plan?* He could feel the strands of his translucent silk starting to fray.

"I'll save us all some time and paraphrase the content for you. The studios have banded together and agreed not to employ a Communist, or any member of any party which advocates the overthrow of the US government." He paused while a reaction unfurled across the room. "Furthermore, we will eliminate all subversives from the industry while safeguarding free speech wherever threatened."

"Paraphrasing" and "furthermore" were five-dollar words Marcus had never heard the ex-fairground bouncer use before. *He must have been practicing all morning.*

Tension thickened in the air. "Mr. Mannix," he said, "does your so-called Waldorf Statement affect anyone in this room? Personally, I mean?"

Mannix eyed him suspiciously, as though questioning whether Marcus had been given advance warning. "As a matter of fact, it does. While we've been in here, my secretary has been leaving envelopes on the desks of the people we're letting go."

Marcus shot to his feet. "You're *firing* us? Some of these people have worked here for years. They've produced some of the finest scripts in the industry. And the best you can do is an envelope on the desk?"

"Only those staff members who have shown cause to come under suspicion—"

He didn't get to finish his sentence, or gave up trying. People stampeded for the door.

Mannix dropped the pile of statements on the table. "Distribute these to your staff when you get a chance." He headed for the door.

"You mean whatever staff you've left me with?" Marcus called out after him. Sitting alone in the deserted conference room, it occurred to him that an envelope might be sitting on his own desk. He rushed down the corridor to his office. His desk was exactly as he left it. Behind him, he heard someone clear his throat. It was Donnie Stewart, an envelope in his hand, unopened.

Donnie held it up. "Marching orders!" He looked past Marcus. "Yes or no?"

Marcus shook his head.

"Listen, a bunch of us dirty low-down ratfink Pinko bastards are convening at the Retake Room. You'll join us, won't you?"

"Is your plan to get good and soaked?"

"Till there's not a drop left in the joint."

"I'll be there."

* * *

In less than half an hour, everyone deemed Waldorf-guilty
had left the studio. It felt like a bomb had wiped out a third
of Marcus' staff. Those still left were doing no work but
were, Marcus supposed, sitting at their desks staring blankly
at their sharpened pencils and balled-up pages. The only
sound Marcus could hear was the clack-clack of a sole
typewriter several offices down from him. *That's got to be
Anson Purvis. He could write through the London Blitz.*

Marcus was slingshotting a mound of rubber bands into
his trash can when his telephone rang. The caller was Ida
Koverman, Mayer's long-time secretary, telling him that his
immediate presence was commanded.

"Should I bring my copy of the Waldorf Statement?"

Miss Koverman hung up without dignifying his jab with
a reply.

Marcus was mildly surprised to find only Mayer waiting
for him behind the semicircular desk. Where was the usual
phalanx of lawyers and yes-men? He motioned for Marcus
to take one of the chairs in front of him.

"It's been a rough day," Mayer said cheerlessly.

Says the guy who still has his job.

Mayer's fingers strummed the desk. "We need to talk
about your future here."

Marcus glanced around Mayer's orderly desk in search
of an envelope with his name on it, but there wasn't one.

"I take it you've read the Waldorf Statement? You'll see
it's quite clear with respect to who we can and cannot have
working at the studio." Mayer took off his glasses and
rubbed the bridge of his nose. "We must acknowledge the
picture of you painted by the HUAC."

"That was all circumstantial!"

Marcus didn't mean to shout, but since he got back from
Washington—or more specifically, from McKeesport—he
found that the things he used to care so much about didn't
matter to him like they used to.

Mayer peered at him, unruffled. "Circumstantial or not, in the eyes of the outside world, it was not a rosy picture. However, we don't want to lose you, Adler, so we've come up with a way to get around all this Waldorf business."

The ink on your precious Waldorf Statement is barely dry and already you're looking at ways to get around it. "What have you got in mind?"

"You're one of the most skilled screenwriters I've ever encountered."

The praise caught Marcus off guard. He popped open his eyes, expecting to detect a hidden agenda. He found only candor.

"Here's what I propose," Mayer continued. "You can no longer head up the writing department. I suspect, though, that you'd prefer to just be writing our screenplays." He must have seen the *Yes!* in Marcus' eyes, because he smiled knowingly. "How about we reassign you to the screenwriter role, and allow you to do it from home?"

The chance to work away from the bean counters who seemed to think creating screenplays was like working on a Pontiac production line was every screenwriter's fantasy. *There must be a catch.*

"Is there something you're not telling me, Mr. Mayer?"

"Just one thing." *I'll be lucky if there's only one thing.* "We won't be able to offer you screen credit."

Marcus' eyes fell onto the copy of the Waldorf Statement that was pressed under Mayer's fingertips, onto the phrase "to safeguard free speech."

Of course they can't give you screen credit. That would undermine the whole arrangement.

But screen credit was currency. It was the screenwriter's calling card; his way up the ladder of financial compensation; his social standing in the pecking order; and his way of planting a flag in the soil and proclaiming, "I created this." It was his everything.

"But how would it work?" Marcus asked. "I'd still be on your payroll."

Mayer gave a self-satisfied leer. "We have more than one payroll, so don't worry about that. Think of it, Adler. You get to work from home! Get up when you want, write when you want, stop when you want, take Fridays off, sleep in Monday mornings. What a life!"

But something nagged at Marcus. "So I'd be sent my assignments from my replacement?" Mayer nodded. "Have you decided who that'll be? Because there are a couple of candidates I'd suggest you—"

"Won't be necessary, Adler. That's all been sorted out."

"You already know who the new department head is?" *Jesus Christ, the seat back at my desk is still warm.* "Who is it?"

DON'T SAY IT! DON'T SAY IT! DON'T SAY IT!

"Anson Purvis will be the new head."

Of course he is. And you've got nobody to blame but yourself. You brought Purvis on board even though you knew which slime pond he crawled out of.

"Have you read *Deadly Bedfellows*?" Marcus asked.

"Why would I bother with trash like that?"

He stood up and extended his hand. "Thank you for your offer, Mr. Mayer, but I won't be able to accept."

Mayer gaped up at him, thunderstruck. "At your current salary, of course."

"It doesn't always come down to the money, sir."

Mayer was now on his feet. "This is no time to be an idealist, Adler. After your fiasco in Washington—"

"I am not a Commie!"

"WHO FUCKING CARES?" Mayer picked up the Waldorf Statement and tossed it into the air. "This is all just for show. It's PR to keep Congress and the unwashed masses happy. Take the offer, get paid generously for doing what you do best, and keep your head down until it all blows over."

Marcus knew he might come to regret what he was about to do, but for now, he knew he'd loathe himself if he didn't. And if there was one thing he'd learned this year, it was that hating was a waste of time. He straightened his spine to give him a full three inches over the little man in front of him.

"Each of us must live with our conscience, Mr. Mayer. And if your shitty Waldorf Statement is what you have to do to sleep at night, then sweet dreams."

He walked the long white carpet to the walnut doors leading onto Mayer's outer office, and didn't break his stride until he hit the elevator button. To his right, a window overlooked the MGM lot. There was, as always, a throng of activity: racks of Victorian costumes, a line of hurrying chorus girls in Esther Williams bathing suits, a trio of clowns juggling in a side alley, violinists walking into the scoring stage.

They all have somewhere to go, he mused. *Surely I do, too.*

CHAPTER 48

Gwendolyn hoisted her pot. "Everyone having coffee?"

Marcus tried to stifle a yawn, but gave up halfway through. "Gwennie, honey, we've been up all night. I can't imagine anyone will be saying no."

Oliver caught Marcus' yawn. "If I'd known we were going to pull an all-nighter, I'd have had a nap beforehand." He slumped his head on Marcus' shoulder and pointed a wobbly finger at Doris. "And as for you. Doing the splits on the diving board."

"In heels," Kathryn added. "That was impressive as hell."

As Doris giggled, Gwendolyn counted off seven heads and walked into her kitchen. This crowd was going to need the strong stuff. She was wondering if she had the energy to duck over to Schwab's and pick up some donuts when she felt Marcus' hand on her shoulder.

"That was a hell of a party you put together," he told her.

"You're welcome, but it wasn't just me. Kay made the sign."

When Marcus arrived home from work that awful day last week, Gwendolyn decided he needed a better send-off than getting soused at the Retake Room with the other pink-slipped writers. With the help of Kathryn and Doris, she pulled together a party around the Garden pool and invited everyone they could think of.

The party itself didn't have an official name until Kay Thompson arrived with a cardboard banner she'd painted in a color she called "Irony Red."

THE MARCUS ADLER FREEDOM FROM
TYRANNY AND TREACHERY PARTY.

Oliver and Trevor took it upon themselves to hang it from a pair of tree branches. Though somewhat crooked, it looked pretty good when Arlene lit some tiki torches beneath the sign. The "Pinko Pink" cardboard stars Kay glued around the border twinkled in the flickering light, winking as though they were in on the joke.

Marcus nodded. "That sign was classic Kay. I hope someone took a picture."

"She didn't seem to mind when it ended up in the pool." Gwendolyn made a mental note to fish it out before she went to bed.

"At any rate," Marcus said, "thank you."

Gwendolyn couldn't tell if Marcus was tearing up or his eyes were just bloodshot from drinking. She pushed a stray lock of hair out of his eyes. "Are you really as okay as you seem?" She was relieved to see him smile.

"The day after it all happened, I went to Alla's grave to think things over. I got to wondering what she thought as she lay on her deathbed. I hope she was happy with the choices she'd made."

"Me too."

"I decided that I want to get to my own deathbed secure in the knowledge that I made more good choices than poor ones. Isn't that all any of us can do? You look at the pros and cons, go with your gut, make a decision, and hope it's the right one in the long run. That offer from MGM, it's not the way I want to live my life."

She kissed him on his cheek. "Good for you."

He gave a gentle shrug. *We'll see.* "Anything I can do to help?"

Gwendolyn was about to ask if he could jump over to Schwab's when she saw the way his whole body seemed to sway. She grabbed him by the shoulders and prodded him in the direction of her sofa. She scooped up her purse and told the crowd she'd be back before the coffee was ready.

She was halfway around the pool when she encountered a gentle-faced stranger in his sixties. "Are you lost?" she asked him.

"I'm looking for Miss Massey. She lives here, right?"

"She does, but we're coming down off an all-nighter. A big party, you see. None of us are in the best of shape—"

"Mr. Hoyt!"

Gwendolyn was surprised Kathryn had the wherewithal to rush along the gravel path toward them.

"What are you doing here?" she asked the stranger. Before he had a chance to respond, Kathryn threaded her arm through Gwendolyn's. "This is Wesley Hoyt. The father."

Kathryn had once described Nelson's dad as being the kind of guy Central Casting would send over if the director needed a sympathetic uncle or understanding judge. Gwendolyn could see what she meant.

"I'm here about my son," the old man said.

Gwendolyn felt Kathryn squeeze her arm as her whole body tensed. "He's not coming back, is he."

Hoyt pulled the scruffy old derby off his head. "No, ma'am, I wouldn't count on it."

"But we made a deal," Kathryn said weakly.

Yeah, Gwendolyn thought, *with J. Edgar Hoover. And he's about as trustworthy as an Everglades alligator.* "I don't suppose you can tell us anything," she said.

"As a matter of fact, yes."

Kathryn's head shot up. "You can?"

"A few years back, Nelson used to have a partner. They worked cases together. I only met him once, by chance at the Bimini Baths down on Third Street. He came to see me at my store last night."

Kathryn let out a groan so faint that Gwendolyn doubted Mr. Hoyt could have heard.

"Go on," Kathryn said.

"Two nights ago he and a bunch of guys were working back at the office—the Black Dahlia case, it's got 'em all working overtime like crazy. Hoover's right-hand man came in."

"Clyde Tolson."

"Yeah, him. They were surprised because he's always with Hoover, but he was by himself. And all agitated, which is mighty unusual, because he's normally so stitched up and buttoned down. Then they realized he was kinda tipsy."

He paused to smile. "Nelson's old partner sensed something was afoot, so he poured Tolson a drink and jiggered him for the lowdown. Turns out, Hoover's got the knives out for Charlie Chaplin but his efforts to have him branded a subversive have been stymied. Then he saw *Monsieur Verdoux*, and apparently he's got it all figured out."

"But Chaplin's picture was released months ago," Kathryn pointed out.

"Apparently Hoover only just got around to seeing it. He came out of that showing with notes written on every scrap of paper he could find, including his popcorn box. Tolson said he was just about frothing at the mouth with glee, giggling over the fact that they don't need to go ahead with some cockamamie cross-dressing scheme he'd cooked up, which meant he didn't need that—skuze my French—'smart alec Massey bitch' no more."

Gwendolyn felt Kathryn slump a little as she let loose a groan.

"I take it you tried to get Nelson back?" he ventured.

Kathryn nodded. "Nearly worked, too."

Mr. Hoyt stepped forward. "I'd like to thank you for trying." He reached out to shake her hand. She took it limply, and tried to make up for it with a feeble smile. "It's been a sincere pleasure." He released Kathryn's hand, gave Gwendolyn a polite nod, then retreated up the path and vanished into the main house.

"I gave it my best shot." Kathryn pressed the side of her head to Gwendolyn's. "But I've been outfoxed."

"At least you've been outfoxed by the master."

"Oh, Gwennie." A deep sigh followed. "I actually let myself think maybe Nelson was *my* turn at the swings. I should have known better. First a married man, and then an FBI agent. I seem to have a knack for choosing wildly inappropriate men. Why do you think that is?"

"Are you really turning to me for boyfriend advice?" Gwendolyn asked. "Me? With my history?"

"I really liked him, Gwennie."

"I know you did."

"I mean really, *really* liked him."

"But he came with a box of dynamite. And you know what your mama told you about playing with fire."

Kathryn closed her eyes. "Bette was right."

"About what?"

"About she and I not being the white-picket-fence type."

Gwendolyn giggled, hoping it would leaven her friend's spirits. "Oh, sugar-pie, ain't nobody at the Garden of Allah is the white picket fence type. It's how come we end up here and why most of us stay. And besides, I think white picket fences are overrated."

Kathryn lifted her head and swiped at her eyes. "Christ, Gwennie, I'm nearly forty!"

"So?"

"What if he really was my last chance?"

"Now you're being ridiculous." Gwendolyn pushed her away. "That's all the boo-hoo I'm going to listen to."

"Don't forget what Howard said, you're too old. That must have hurt."

"Sure it did," Gwendolyn admitted, "but then I went out and proved him wrong."

Kathryn did a double take. "What did you do?"

"After that incident at the store when Bugsy came in with a gun, Mr. Dewberry put on extra security. One of the guys—a tall, horsey type with big hands—he kept giving me the goo-goo eyes. So the day after Howard said I was too old for him, I wore a particularly low-cut dress. Worked like a charm."

"Oh, Gwennie!" Kathryn started to laugh. "How was he?"

"So enthusiastic he broke out into sweat. To hell with Howard Moneybags. I'm not about to let him or any man decide when I'm over the hill."

They heard a set of footsteps click against the path behind her. Kathryn braced herself. "Don't tell me he's come back?"

Even first thing on a Saturday morning, Edith Head looked like she was ready to step into a magazine photo shoot. She held a brown paper sack. "Did I come at a bad time?"

Gwendolyn shook her head. "You know Kathryn Massey, don't you?"

Edith nodded, and pulled Gwendolyn's tangerine scarf from her suit pocket. "It's been a month, and I feel wretched for having taken so long to get it back to you."

"That's quite all right—"

"No, it's not. I detest it when people take forever to return things. So, by way of an apology"—she lifted the paper bag— "I brought breakfast. There are some Danishes, muffins, biscuits—I didn't know what you like so I bought a whole bunch. And I finally found bagels on the West Coast!"

"Thank you," Gwendolyn said. "We've got a lot of hungry mouths to feed."

Arlene nearly had a conniption fit when she saw Edith walk into Gwendolyn's villa, and straightaway started to babble her adoration for Edith's work on a recent Betty Hutton movie, *The Stork Club*. Edith listened politely, then asked which studio she worked at. When Arlene meekly admitted that she was in MGM's legal department, Edith lost interest. By the time Gwendolyn entered her living room with Edith's contributions piled onto her biggest platter, she found her standing before the huge portrait.

"This is remarkable," Edith said, tapping a finger against her chin.

"A bit big for this place," Gwendolyn admitted."

"I could swear this is a—" She bent down to study the signature at the bottom, and let out a cry. "This *is* an Alistair Dunne!"

"You've heard of him?"

Edith kept her eyes on Alistair's portrait. "I presume you don't keep up with the New York art scene? Oh, my sweet girl, Alistair Dunne is one of *the* most important contributors to the postwar American art movement."

"He is?"

"And you've got a *pre*-war Dunne!" Edith slapped her thighs for emphasis. "Do you know how much this is worth?"

Marcus and Kathryn joined Gwendolyn. "Could you give us a rough idea?" he asked.

Edith stepped back from the painting. "I'm no expert, you understand, but a painting this size?" She shook her head and tsked.

Gwendolyn fumbled for Kathryn's hand. It was no longer cold, but damp with hope.

"This is from his California period," Edith said, "so I'd say fifteen on the conservative side." Gwendolyn felt lightheaded as Marcus grabbed her other hand. "Put it up at auction and you could see twenty. Those New Yorkers are simply mad for him!"

* * *

It was nearly noon before everybody had cleared out of Gwendolyn's apartment; only Marcus and Kathryn stayed behind. They stood shoulder to shoulder in front of Alistair's portrait, champagne in their hands.

Gwendolyn raised her glass. "Here's to the New York It Boy!"

"Here's to Edith Head," Marcus said, "without whom we might never have known."

They clinked glasses.

"Here's to Gwennie's scarf, without which Edith might never have come to the Garden."

Another clink. Another sip. In the last couple of hours, Alistair's portrait had taken on a hypnotic golden glow.

"If it comes to that," Gwendolyn added, "here's to Howard Hughes and his ridiculously overweening ego, without which there would have never been a *Spruce Goose* that he needed to prove at Long Beach, whose winds messed Edith's hair so badly she needed a scarf."

There was a pause.

"I'm sorry," Kathryn said, "what are we toasting now? Howard's ego?"

Marcus placed his coupe on the coffee table. "I'm too done in to figure that one out. It's been a long night so I'm off." He kissed the girls goodbye and reminded them of a dinner date they'd made with Lucius Beebe and his lover before the two men headed back East for Christmas.

His footsteps retreated down the path while Gwendolyn and Kathryn kept their eyes on the painting.

"I've walked past this thing I don't know how many times," Kathryn said, "but now I can't take my eyes off it."

"Isn't it amazing how one tidbit of information can change everything? It just goes to show, doesn't it?"

Kathryn threw her a baleful look. "It does?"

Gwendolyn could already see her store coming together in her mind. "I'm just saying that the direction of our lives can change at any time. Nothing stays the same for very long."

"Especially not in this wacky town." Kathryn nudged her, shoulder to shoulder. "Thanks," she said quietly.

"What for?"

"Showering me with little petals of hope, just when I need it."

Gwendolyn breathed deeply, taking in the stillness of the room as though to preserve it. She raised her glass. "One more toast."

"To what?"

"To white picket fences. May they never fence us in."

THE END

~oOo~

Did you enjoy this book? If you did, could I ask you to take the time to write a review on the website where you found it? Each review helps boost the book's profile so I'd really appreciate it. Just give it the number of stars you think it deserves and perhaps mention a few of the things you liked about it. That'd be great, thanks!

Martin Turnbull

~oOo~

ALSO BY MARTIN TURNBULL

Hollywood's Garden of Allah novels:

Book One: *The Garden on Sunset*

Book Two: *The Trouble with Scarlett*

Book Three: *Citizen Hollywood*

Book Four: *Searchlights and Shadows*

Book Five: *Reds in the Beds*

Book Six: *Twisted Boulevard*

Book Seven: *Tinseltown Confidential*

ACKNOWLEDGEMENTS

Heartfelt thanks to the following, who helped shaped this book:

My editor: Meghan Pinson, for her invaluable guidance, expert eye, and unfailing nitpickery.

My cover designer: Dan Yeager at Nu-Image Design

My beta readers: Vince Hans, Allen Crowe, Beth Riches, Bradley Brady, and especially Royce Sciortino and Gene Strange for their invaluable time, insight, feedback, and advice in shaping this novel.

My Proof Reader Extraordinaire: Bob Molinari

Connect with Martin Turnbull:

www.MartinTurnbull.com

Facebook.com/gardenofallahnovels

The Garden of Allah blog: martinturnbull.wordpress.com/

Goodreads: bit.ly/martingoodreads

If you'd like to keep current with the Garden of Allah novels related developments, feel free to sign up to my emailing list. I do NOT send out regular emails so I won't be clogging your inbox. I only do an email blast when I've got something relevant to say, like revealing the cover of the next book, or posting the first chapter. Go to http://bit.ly/goasignup

CPSIA information can be obtained
at www.ICGtesting.com
Printed in the USA
LVOW10s0125020817
543492LV00001B/81/P